CREATING K-PAX

CREATING K-PAX

or

Are You Sure You Want To Be A Writer?

Gene Brewer

author of *the K-PAX trilogy*

visit the author at www.genebrewer.com

To order additional copies of this book, contact:
Xlibris Corporation
1-888-795-4274
www.Xlibris.com
Orders@Xlibris.com
30138

CONTENTS

DEDICATION

IN MEMORY OF MY PARENTS

John Newton Brewer (1910-1987)
Osie Helen (Miller) Brewer (1911-1999)

"We come into the world, stare at everything for a while, and go out again."

—Knut Hamsun
The Women at the Pump

FOREWORD

In November, 2001, a man named Jason Laskay sued Universal Pictures and everyone connected with the film version of *K-PAX*: the producers, the director, the principal actors, the screenwriter, and me, the author of the novel on which the movie was based, as well as St. Martin's Press, which published it. The plaintiff, Laskay, alleged that he had obtained the rights to a remake of the Argentinian film, *Hombre Mirando al Sudeste* (*Man Facing Southeast*), that he had written an updated screenplay for the movie, and that *K-PAX* was virtually a carbon copy of that work.

Though somewhat surprised and even more chagrined, I wasn't totally shocked by this unwelcome development. I had seen *MFSE* (four and a half years after writing *K-PAX*), and had noted certain similarities between the two. Both featured a man of unknown history who appears at a mental institution claiming to be from another planet. Until then (late 1994), however, I had never even heard of that film. In fact, had I not written *K-PAX*, I would very likely *never* have known about *Man Facing Southeast*.

My attorney, Bob Harris, was unshaken by the news. Though he took the matter seriously, he considered it "a badge of honor." Whenever a major film appears in the theaters, he assured me, someone comes out of the woodwork claiming it was his idea. Bob's main concern was that hiring a litigator to defend myself in court might be expensive for me.

I wasn't apprehensive about a costly defense, however. I wasn't even concerned about being convicted of plagiarism, primarily because I wasn't guilty. My main concern was that potential publishers of my work might be suspicious of my integrity. That and the annoyance factor: I wondered whether this false accusation would stick in the back of my mind like a dull knife and make it more difficult to write. It's hard enough as it is, and there are already far too many daggers imbedded there.

About the time the suit was filed (only two weeks after the film was released) I started getting e-letters from people (mostly with Spanish-sounding names) accusing me of dastardly acts and advising me that, at best, I should be thoroughly ashamed of myself. There was a particularly nasty letter from someone claiming to be a critic named Cole Smithey, who tried McCarthy-type tactics ("I have a list of people who . . ." and then refused to name anyone on the list except himself) to get me to "confess."

The fact is, I *could* have seen *MFSE*. It was shown in Cleveland—we lived in a small town about an hour from the theater—on April 12, 1986 (one night only), but my diary indicates that my wife and I had dinner that evening in Kent. Had we wanted to see the film, we would undoubtedly have eaten in Cleveland before the showing, and I would certainly have mentioned the movie in any case. I could also have gone to Boston or New York or Toronto to see it. I did not. Nor did I know about these showings, not even the one in Cleveland. The entire premise of the lawsuit was based on a conjecture, and a spurious one at that.

But there's a silver lining in even the blackest of clouds. This whole mess got me to thinking where the ideas for *K-PAX* did, in fact, come from. Many sincerely curious correspondents had asked me essentially the same thing: where did I get my "inspiration" for the book; did I know someone like prot; is it a true story? I began to wonder, perhaps for the first time, where *I* was coming from, i.e., the sum total of my own experiences which compelled me to write a book like *K-PAX*.

I had long supposed that, if I had any success as a novelist, I would eventually write some sort of memoir, probably when I was on my last legs and hadn't any more ideas to develop. What follows, therefore, may be a bit premature—I'm only on my next-to-last legs—but it's something that would probably have happened anyway, albeit in somewhat different form or content. In any case I certainly have no plans for writing another autobiography, regardless of the volume of letters I get or how many people crawl out of the woodwork.

The following narrative is, in short, about the many factors that led to my becoming a writer, and what it's like to finally get a novel published after years of failure and disappointment and to find that book materialized, after several more frustrating years, on the big screen and the stage. It is also about the people I've encountered along the way who have helped, hindered, and changed the course of my life and my career(s). I hope it gives the reader, particularly the aspiring novelist or screenwriter, some insight into the worlds of publishing and filmmaking. Although it's not a tell-all, it is a tell-some, and I sincerely apologize to those whom I may have offended in these pages. Every word is true, regardless.

STAR DREAMS

I was born at 1022 Kirby Avenue in Muncie, Indiana, USA, at precisely four o'clock A.M. on Tuesday, July 4, 1937. No angels sang, but I understand that my mother uttered a shriek or two (she reminded me of the pain I caused her on numerous later occasions). That particular house, still standing, was my birthplace (as well as my parents' rented apartment) because my mother was afraid of hospitals. This fear came about, at least in part, because *her* mother, not long before, had checked into one for treatment of uterine cancer. As dread as this affliction was, it wasn't as bad, in Mom's surmise, as the radiation therapy. "They burnt her up," she told me later, and countless times thereafter, confusing, perhaps, the awful symptoms with the treatment rather than the disease.

Before my parents were married, Dad worked on a farm. With a new wife and prospective family he tried to get a job in town, but they were scarce—the country was still coming out of the depression. He applied for one at Warner Gear, a division of Borg-Warner Corporation (he had been laid off, after a few months, from Ball Brothers, Inc., makers of Ball dome jars and benefactors of Ball Memorial Hospital and Ball State University). When he made an appearance at the factory and spoke to the manager, his personal application was summarily rejected. He whirled and started running toward the door. The guy shouted, "Hey, where you going?" "I've got to find a job!" Dad yelled back. He got the job, and stood on the assembly line for 38 years grinding gears for General Motors cars and trucks. Except for a near-fatal eye injury, and a collapsed lung, I don't believe he ever missed a day of work. Nonetheless, even after all those years, he never rose to the level of foreman.

I nearly died very early on. My mother's milk was "no good" (as she put it), so I was given regular cows' milk at the outset. I couldn't digest it and was chronically constipated. Dad told me much later that one day my "stomach was hard as a rock," and the doctor didn't expect me to live through the night. When I embarrassed him by being alive the next morning he prescribed a very fat-rich milk, the kind produced by Jerseys or Guernseys, rather than Holsteins.

Other close calls include my mother's rocking me in her arms in the porch swing, which suddenly collapsed, and she flung me over her head against the wall of the house. And I still have a tiny scar on my forehead from being gouged by an unforgiving doorlatch. Fortunately I don't remember any of the above.

The rest of the house on Kirby Avenue was occupied by my 300+-pound Aunt Mag and her husband Mac (for McClellan), thirty years her senior, who were childless (they later adopted a boy, Joe, and girl, Henrietta). My first memory is of going somewhere in an old Model A Ford. I was in the back seat, Mag was driving, and Mom, who was almost nine months pregnant with my sister Nancy, was to my left. We had just pulled into the alley next to the tiny side yard when the car backfired. It didn't frighten me, but it did get my attention, and I can still see my surroundings, if vaguely, on that night. I was twenty months old.

After that memorable incident nothing happened until I was well into my threes. Sometime during that year I burned my finger on the kitchen stove. This would not be noteworthy except that it suggests an early curiosity about my environment, and for my discovery during supper (Hoosier for dinner) that if I held my burnt finger against the fat-rich-milk bottle, the pain went away. At the same time, I could see my father, his back to us, urinating in the tiny bathroom off the kitchen. Somehow, all of that together made a lasting impression.

In 1941, when I was four, we visited my paternal great-grandmother in Spencer, IN, where I was goaded into standing in a field with my little fingers wrapped around the enormous horn of a bull. I was terrified but did it anyway for fear, I suspect, of being sneered or laughed at, a trait which surfaced at an early age and continues to this day. But I also remember the wonderful aroma of Grandma Ashley's early-morning biscuits (we slept on the living room floor adjacent to the kitchen). I jumped up and hung around with her until breakfast was ready. Nothing has ever tasted better than those hot biscuits dripping with warm butter and homemade raspberry jam, though the pleasure may have been magnified by the relief I still felt on having escaped from being gored or trampled by a huge bovine the evening before.

Just before Pearl Harbor we moved into a home of our own at 3317 E. 15th Street, very near the southeast corner of town. An alley, ideal for playing and getting around the neighborhood, was in back. There was a heart-shaped tulip bed in the middle of the side yard (which ruined it for ball games), a blackberry bush, weeping willow tree, and sandbox in the back corner, and a few peonies (Mom called them "pineys") along the grassy unused driveway. My chief avocation was riding a tricycle around and around the two-bedroom house and yard.

The only heat came from a coal-burning stove with an isinglass window in the middle of the living room, where my sister and I used to huddle immediately after getting up on frigid winter mornings. Other memorable features were the big Philco radio, an attic stuffed with curtain stretchers, and a spider-webbed basement with a dirt floor and a coal bin, and a shelf of home-canned peaches.

Despite having two small children, Dad volunteered for the army, but was rejected because of flat feet. He seemed to walk normally, and I couldn't understand why this condition precluded military service. Another thing I didn't get: since he could write checks for whatever we needed, why did he have to make money?

Mom had eleven brothers and sisters, including two stillbirths (twins), and Dad nine. I never knew my maternal grandparents—my grandmother, a farm wife, died before I was born, and my grandfather, a farmer and miller, not long after. Sometime before that he became a one-armed milkman, having lost a limb while loading a muzzle shotgun. He also belonged to the Ku Klux Klan, though, to his credit, dropped out after witnessing a hanging.

My mother was the youngest of the family, most of whom, including her, had red hair. The only thing I know about Uncle Cliff is that he "dropped dead in the grocery store" at the age of forty-five. Uncle Oat was insane. Mom told me that once, on the farm, she had asked her mother what the screaming in the barn was about. "Oh, that's just Oatie beating the horses again." Many years later, his wife committed suicide. For months Oat and his son watched each other carefully, until the latter managed to run off and electrocute himself by jumping onto a high-tension power line. My uncle saw the whole thing but was unable to stop him, and shot himself to death immediately afterward.

The only things I remember about Uncle Frank are that his upper lip seemed to be a double one, and his nose was filled with red hair. He, too, was a farmer and we rarely saw him. Uncle Ab (Albert) appeared only once, when he came to visit very late in his life.

Uncle Pete, the youngest boy, was an inventor. He owned several patents, the most famous of which was probably "Pound Pup," a toy along which a kid pounded tight-fitting wooden dowels into holes and then turned the dachshund over and pounded them the other way. My favorite uncle, though, was Roy, who was quiet, gentle, and soft-spoken, perhaps because he had a defective heart valve, and couldn't exert himself. And a boisterous wife, Aunt Katherine, whose laugh sounded like a car trying to start on a winter morning.

There were four girls: Maggie, Angie, Mae, and my mother, Osie. I didn't get to know Angie until she was elderly. I liked her. But it was Aunt Mae who had the strongest influence on my life. She lived on a farm "way out in the country," and I loved to visit her and Uncle Lester. A World War I veteran—he enlisted at fourteen—Lester worked off and on for a vegetable canning company in Redkey (Mae peeled tomatoes there in the summers). He was a big fan of the St. Louis Cardinals, and he enjoyed listening to their radio broadcasts, an empty two-pound Folger's coffee can standing beside his squeaky rocker for his well-aimed tobacco spit. To get a fair image of Aunt Mae and Uncle Lester, think of Aunt Loweezy and Snuffy Smith. Or, perhaps, Ma and Pa Kettle.

Lester disliked my father, probably because of his incessant chatter, which sometimes drowned out his ball game. Dad was also a know-it-all (even when he knew nothing), which further annoyed my uncle. After I had gone off to college he finally ordered Dad to "get the hell out" of the living room. The visits became far fewer after that.

Aunt Mae was a wonderful cook of the old-fashioned, country kind, and whenever we visited there was always an enormous platter of fried chicken (killed the same day by wringing their necks by hand), huge bowls of mashed potatoes and gravy, wonderful-tasting green beans fresh from the garden (in summer), her own canned pickles and beets, and two or three different kinds of pie. This was all cooked on a wood-burning stove, an appliance I adore to this day. The most poignant memory of all this, however, is that she never sat down until everyone else was almost finished, but hovered around making sure everyone had what he or she wanted, filling milk glasses and coffee mugs. Her selflessness made an enormous impact on me at a young age and, while I have never been able to match it, she is still the model I try to emulate.

Almost as memorable was the old pump organ in the corner of the living room. It smelled musty and didn't sound quite right, but to my pre-adolescent and teenage sensibilities it was a complex and beautiful instrument. I would often play gibberish on it, dreaming of the day I would know how to do it right. To my great amazement Mom could sit down at the organ (or a piano) and play a hymn or a popular song "by ear." That, too, made a big impression on me: how did she do that?

Mae and Lester moved a lot, but it was always to somewhere out in the country. One of these places had a big "sugar pear" tree (the fruit was exquisitely sweet) out front. It was here that I sometimes discovered cousin Patty Ann and her boyfriend Walter necking in the kitchen (they've been married now for more than half a century). Pat's younger brother, cousin Dick, was a year older than I. When he talked or sang he sounded like Gene Pitney, still my favorite country singer.

There was also a field with a cow named Cherry, whose huge eyes, rough tongue, and sweet breath seemed like the essence of life itself. I used to offer her grass through the fence (I was afraid to climb over), until Dick traded her for a friendly pony called Roany.

Their favorite place, I think, before infirmity drove them into the nearby town of Portland, was a big brick house, surrounded by alfalfa and cornfields, near New Mount Pleasant. This was always referred to as "the brick" (as in: "When we lived in the brick . . ."). Besides the inevitable chickens, there was another cow or two and an outhouse well-supplied with Sears catalogues, as well as chamber pots in the upstairs bedrooms. It was there that Mom and Aunt Mae lanced the boils I was afflicted with during puberty. Though I couldn't see them (they were always on my tush), I still get the shivers when I remember their cheerfully reporting that when they pushed or pulled on one, "matter" would ooze from another several inches away.

Despite this minor trauma, I, too, loved the brick. You came in through the "laundry room" (with a sink, tub, and washboard), which somehow imparted a fresh, soapy fragrance to the rest of the house. On a kitchen counter stood a bucket of cold water, recently pumped from the well just outside, which tasted faintly of iron. A dipper hung nearby. A drink of water like that always takes me back to Aunt Mae's kitchen.

My mother was "just a housewife" (as she described herself), who claimed she was born at 11:00 A.M. on 11/11/11. In all the years I knew her she wore "print" dresses exclusively—except later in life to church on Sundays—never slacks and certainly never shorts, or even a skirt. She was a creature of unvarying routine: Monday was washday (on the stove bubbled a huge pot of Great Northern beans with a couple of hambones); sprinkling and ironing came on Tuesday; mending and darning on Wednesday or until everything was repaired; cooking and cleaning every day.

Despite her adeptness at the keyboard, Mom may have been retarded. When we went to a movie she would ask me to count the change and make sure it was right. We entered the theater whenever we got there. At some point she would ask us, "Is this where we came in?" and we would reluctantly shuffle through the Necco Wafers wrappers and Milk Duds boxes to the aisle and stagger uphill to the exit, looking over our shoulders at the screen. If she hadn't paid enough attention, we got to see whole stretches of the film twice.

She didn't drive because it was too complicated and she was too nervous. She could no more balance a checkbook than she could fly around the block, and didn't know the difference between a city and a state. She could never pronounce certain words. And she was uncommonly superstitious: we weren't allowed to rock an empty rocking chair, for example, as it signified that someone was about to die.

I attributed her mental insufficiency to brain damage incurred during a near-death experience resulting from her choking on an apple peel, a story she related countless times, beginning when I was five or six. She turned blue, she colorfully reminded me, while the world turned black. The only reason she was alive, she reckoned, was that her mother stuck her finger down her throat and forced her to "throw it up." In order to understand what that might have been like, I held my breath as long as I could. It felt terrible; I wanted no part of death or even near-death. I wasn't able to eat an apple, or tomato, or anything else with a "skin" on it, for years. (I would clandestinely peel these fruits with my teeth and deposit the skins in a comic book I was reading or hiding behind. When the fossils were discovered, sometimes much later, they would elicit outraged laughter.)

Once in particular I remember walking home from school for lunch (though I usually carried a little container with a lunchmeat sandwich, potato chips, milk, and Twinkies or a little packaged pie inside) and finding a plate of Great Northern beans waiting for me on the kitchen table. Because they were enclosed in chokeable skins, I couldn't eat them. Nor could I tell her why without broaching the subject of my phobia, and being sucked back into the same black hole I was trying to escape from. Of course she was worried about me, thinking I must be sick. For my part, I was both terrified and profoundly saddened by the whole episode because she had prepared what she thought was a nice lunch for me and I wouldn't touch it.

It was about this time that I suffered my first genuine panic attack. Everyone in the school was taken to the big room at the center of the building, a chairless auditorium with a stage at the end, where we were shown a film on tuberculosis. In those days TB was far more prevalent than it is now (though it's making a comeback), and the authorities thought we should know all about it in detail. I remember sitting on the floor staring wide-eyed at the germs, depicted as large, multi-legged creatures with eyes, as they were transferred from one person to another by a shared spoon or drinking glass. The crawly black bugs multiplied in the victim's lungs, which eventually resulted in blood being coughed up into the victim's handkerchief. That was more than I could take, and I dissociated myself from the terror, as well as everything else around me. I could barely hear the sound of the film, if at all. Not only was I certain that TB was my fate (I had eaten or drunk after my mother or sister many times), I could already feel the vile organisms wriggling around in my lungs. I hyperventilated, felt increasingly lightheaded, became totally withdrawn somewhere inside myself, and avoided passing out only by strength of will. It was an experience that was to repeat itself many times in those early years and well into adulthood.

I finally returned to reality when the lights came back on, but now, sixty years later, the memory of that ordeal remains crystal clear in my mind. Again, I was afraid to tell anyone about the experience, perhaps because I sensed that there was nothing anyone could do to help, least of all my seemingly ineffectual parents. I knew I would have to learn to deal with this underlying fear on my own, then and for the rest of my (horrifyingly short, I presumed) life.

Another phobia she managed to instill in me was that of German shepherds. Before my first professional haircut we passed one of the breed on the way to the barber shop. "If you cry, I'm going to let that dog get you," she threatened. I had no intention of crying—I thought of it as an adventure—but I was very much afraid to leave the shop afterward (fortunately, the dog was gone).

It was probably the latter incident that precipitated a persistent childhood dream. A pack of wolves, or similar toothy animals, was in pursuit. I tried to get to the steps leading up to the back porch, but my feet were treading something like molasses. I struggled hard but the beasts (German shepherds?) were catching up with me. Fortunately, I always woke up before their fangs sunk in.

Mom suffered all her days from an implacable fear of the elements. Terrified of thunderstorms, she would unplug every lamp and appliance in the house and refuse to answer the phone at the first rumble of distant thunder. She worried ceaselessly about the prospect of tornadoes. If we encountered a snowstorm or slippery road while driving, she became rigid, started to wail, and made Dad pull over until it stopped snowing, or slow to a crawl on the tiniest patch of ice.

As if that weren't enough, she also harbored a severe social anxiety. The curtains and drapes were usually kept closed. When a car came up the driveway she would peek through the blinds and, if it was a stranger, admonish us to be quiet and pretend nobody was home. If she was forced into a social situation she smiled and nodded, but was otherwise tongue-tied. She was comfortable only with her immediate family and among familiar objects.

But if Mom taught me fear and anxiety, she also exerted a profoundly positive influence on my life. One afternoon, when I stepped on a sidewalk ant, she informed me (with tongue in cheek, perhaps—she herself killed flies without mercy) that the dead insect "might have been somebody's mother." Whatever her motive, it was an epiphany for me, and led me to think about the other creatures inhabiting the Earth and whether they had lives and feelings, and perhaps to examine more carefully other preconceived notions I held about everyday existence. Not long after that we went to see *Bambi*, which reinforced and expanded my sense of empathy toward the fate of wild, as well as domestic, animals. Having no apparent alternative, I nevertheless continued to eat the meat provided at every meal, and stifled my concern about how the animals in the refrigerator had died and the families they left behind.

Another determinant was her tale (repeated many times) of a railroad worker who ate his lunch "way down the tracks" from everybody else. Someone sneaked up behind him once to see what was in his paper bag. It was orange peelings—that was all he had to eat. From that time on, the word "eat" itself made me sad—it conjured up images of people who didn't have anything—and I still dislike eating in front of anyone who isn't sharing the meal, at a sidewalk café, for instance, where hungry people might be walking by.

Although she would never admit or even understand it, Mom was firmly prejudiced (so was Dad, but more subtly). She was disgusted with "the Catholics," who "can do anything they want to on Saturday night as long as they confess the next day." Never mind that this strategy essentially applied to Protestants as well. She informed me once, with absolute conviction, that the "colored" high school players "stunk to high heaven" after a basketball game (how she obtained this information was a mystery to me). Probably her favorite story, reiterated at least twice a year, was about "a fat old colored woman" who came into a hardware store looking for a washtub because, according to Mom, "I splattuh so." And there was a well-known black policeman in Muncie who had, in fact, been a basketball star at Muncie Central, Jack Mann. Mom resented the way he directed traffic with confident authority. "Look at him. Ain't he briggy (cocky)?"

In addition to her word creations, there were many homilies of unknown origin. If one of us was crying about something, she would remind us that "The more you cry, the less you'll pee." "He don't buy me no peanuts," was reserved for those to whom she owed nothing, but who nevertheless wanted something from her. When she was annoyed by someone, she would advise him to "Go flip sand up a rathole." If we misbehaved, she was prepared to "jerk a knot in our tails." And she delighted in posing the following conundrum: "Would you rather climb a ladder of knives or swim a river of snot?"

My father's family was vastly different. Grandpa was a glassblower at Ball Brothers and elsewhere around the state. According to Dad, he once won a citation from the governor of Kansas (his family came from there) for figuring out how high the water in a bucket would rise when a ball of a certain size was tossed into it. I only knew him when he was old and, with his stiff white hair, looked even older. Worn out, I surmised. My paternal grandmother was one of those stern, no-nonsense matriarchs who raised her ten children without allowing any guff.

When I was growing up, Uncles Bob and Don, as well as Aunts Diana and Orpha, still lived at home, a crumbling yellow brick house in an old neighborhood not far from the center of town. I rarely saw the not-so-young women in anything other than a bathrobe.

A favorite family picture is of Bob and Don in their army uniforms, both smiling and handsome. Bob came out of the war an abusive alcoholic married to a French woman; Don a neurotic disaster. Aunt Mary's boyfriend never came back at all.

Other than Uncle Don, I never got to know my aunts and uncles very well (they almost never visited us), but most seemed a little nutty to me. Uncle Bill, for example, turned virtually his entire backyard into a get-rich scheme—a pit for growing fishing worms—that quickly failed. (His younger son, after being routinely dressed as a girl by his mother, actually ended up in a mental institution.) Much later, when Aunt Diana died, she left 26 dogs and cats behind. And I once watched my Aunt Orpha freak out because she thought she had swallowed a fly. Such is the nature of my paternal genes.

Dad was the most boring person I ever knew. On the street, whenever we met someone he knew, he would talk and talk and talk, primarily about himself, while both his "victim" (as I thought of him) and I shuffled our feet and desperately sought a chance to get away. He had no real friends, no one he would, or could, socialize with.

I vowed at an early age never to talk about myself except when someone asked me something specific, and then to answer succinctly. Instead, I made it a point to listen to what other people had to say and to encourage them to speak about their own lives, which, I discovered, most people very much like to do. I became popular ("well-liked," one teacher wrote) as a result of this program. Not because of any natural gregariousness or interest in other people, but because I tried hard to divert attention away from myself. I never sought popularity; I just didn't want to be thought of as dull, like my father. At home, on the other hand, I was a little shit, pushing my siblings around, making demands. I suppose I just couldn't maintain the "nice" façade twenty-four hours a day, needed a pressure relief valve.

As a bonus, listening to others probably forced me to notice facial expression, mannerism, body language, and all the rest, and equate these with feelings. On the downside, however, I found it difficult, with so little speaking experience, to organize and elaborate my thoughts in such a way as to present them in an orderly manner.

To his family Dad was cold and unsympathetic. I don't recall ever getting a kiss or a hug or even a pat on the back from him until he was old and sick, or even a simple expression of gratitude if we brought him something (except for a distorted "*Thank you, sir,*" or the like). It was as if it embarrassed him to engage in any kind of normal interaction.

Empathy was a foreign concept to him. If we were sick or hurt he would seem more angry than concerned. His view of accidents was that there weren't any. If we broke something, his response would be an angry or disbelieving, "Now *why* did you do that?" The verbal abuse led to a fear of committing an error and, eventually, I learned to hide mistakes and stifle my emotions, so as not to anger or upset him. He seemed almost a father manqué, as though he became a parent because he thought he was supposed to, or it came with the sex act, but he didn't know how to follow it up.

Praise from Dad was rare and precious. Even when I did something right, I could never please him *enough*. I felt a need to accomplish more than was possible in order to satisfy the desire for approval, but no matter how much I got I wanted more. It became almost impossible even to please myself.

He also displayed a number of hang-ups which I never understood and still don't (Dad might lecture you for an hour, but you didn't *discuss* anything with him). For example, he was violently opposed to the consumption of alcohol, invariably referring to taverns and bars as "beer joints." He *never* mentioned sex, and I never saw him undressed, or even his knees. Rightly or wrongly, the possibility occurred to me later in life that *his* father, the glassblowing math whiz (or someone else) might have been an alcoholic and/or abused him.

Dad had a terrible temper and sometimes kicked inanimate objects. When he was frustrated about some little job he was doing he would whine, "Why doesn't anything ever go right?" On the other hand he rarely swore, and even then his vocabulary was limited to two words: "Damnation!" and "damnable," as in "You damnable thing!" Never a "goddamn," or even a "damn," or anything else. (My mother, on the other hand, was particularly fond of the word "shit," or sometimes, in frustration, "Shitawiggle!" And she occasionally called us boys "Fuzznuts.")

And he could be incredibly stubborn. When he was going into the eighth grade, my grandparents moved to a different town and, for some reason, he was mistakenly put back into the seventh. Rather than explain the situation, he pouted in the back row and refused to speak. So, assuming he was an idiot, the teacher kept him there another year. He finally got promoted, but finally left school in the tenth grade to go to work on a farm (my mother didn't get past the eighth).

A blue-collar worker if there ever was one, and a strong believer in unions, Dad nevertheless remained a Republican until the day he died (Mom never voted at all). On election day in 1944, when I was in the second grade, the bigger kids roamed the playground demanding to know whether we small ones were Republicans or Democrats. After a couple of punches and arm twists, I changed my vote to Democrat. I didn't make the same mistake in 1948 (in neither case did I have a clue as to what the difference between the two parties might be).

But if my father was difficult, unloving, embarrassing, and maybe a little crazy, he was also endowed with certain redeeming features. I don't think he ever told a lie, and I simply never learned, from him or Mom, how to be devious or disingenuous. He once saved cousin Dick's foot from amputation by insisting that Lester take him to a doctor (on a Sunday) when it became gangrenous after a farm accident. And if I inherited a scientific bent from anyone, it was Dad. He knew things like the speeds of light and sound, and explained that the moon revolved around the Earth, and the planets around the sun, which was really just a star like all the millions in the firmament. Whenever I looked up into the night sky I was filled with wonder. *Where did all of this come from?* Had my parents been religious I might have turned to theology, as did some of my numerous cousins. But God was rarely mentioned in our house, and there was no praying at meals or at bedtime. Without that countervailing impetus, I was certain, from my earliest years, that I would become a scientist.

At the same time, his plodding interest in the nuts and bolts of mechanical objects turned me off entirely from that aspect of the sciences, perhaps because it made them into something mundane and—yes, boring—in his rough, oil-stained hands, whose nails were perpetually tattooed with little blue-black crescents where they had been hammered by tools and gears. To this day I wonder if current science "popularizers" are on the wrong track by focusing, as they tend to do, on "everyday objects," and "things you can do in your own backyard." That approach would have distanced me completely from the wonders of it all. When I actually became a scientist I loved to plan experiments, carry them out, and wait impatiently for the results, but was bored to the point of nausea by the mechanics of the instruments I had to use, undoubtedly to my detriment.

Saturday night was bath and Grand Ole Opry night. For years we listened to the big Philco as we paraded into the bathroom and then to bed, our hair reeking of vinegar. Later, on a cold and intensely exciting February evening, the whole family went to the Masonic Temple for a live stage show featuring Roy Acuff, Little Jimmy Dickens, and Minnie Pearl, among others. I was thrilled: it was the first time I had ever seen anyone famous. It was there that the enthusiastic audience may have planted the seeds which later germinated into a craving for wide attention and appreciation in order to obtain the approval from others that I didn't get from my father.

As far as I could see, the biggest difference between the war and post-war years was that after it was over we could get bubble gum. It meant standing in a long line, but for a penny a kid could get a sweet, rubbery ball (it was round then) of Fleers wrapped in colorful paper and a tiny cartoon. I'd never tasted it before—it was delicious. Since supplies were so limited Nan and I kept ours going for days or weeks, parking it on the bedpost at night. It was gray and tasteless and rock-hard in the morning, but we could still soften it up enough to blow bubbles with it.

There was a girl in the first grade, Nancy McDonald, whom I admired from a distance. She had pale, blonde, curly hair and blue-grey eyes, which, with her polka-dotted dresses, gave her quite a striking appearance. My infatuation ended abruptly when she threw up in class. Vomiting, closely associated with choking to death in my mind, was something I simply couldn't cope with.

A Popsicle machine stood outside the lunchroom. Sometimes, when I had a nickel knotted in my handkerchief, I would buy one. Despite my innate desire to share, I learned to get to a far corner of the auditorium or playground to eat it before one of the big boys would yell "Dibs," and chomp out a huge bite, if not consume the whole thing. Where eating was concerned, *taking* was somehow different from *not having*.

Most of the boys wore clodhoppers with metal plates nailed to the heels, which made hundreds of snappy clicks when we clomped out through the auditorium for recess. On the playground we could choose from baseball or basketball (boys), kickball (mostly girls), and marbles (boys). When you knocked another marble out of a circle drawn in the dirt, you could keep shooting until you missed. I had a beautiful sky-blue shooter, layered inside with white clouds, that I loved. I lost it one day and never found one that could begin to replace it. I'm still looking.

We rode the city bus everywhere (except to the west side—there was nothing there but rich people, the hospital, and Ball State Teachers College). My sister Nancy and I sometimes went shopping in town with Mom. I loved to pull the string to signal the driver we wanted to get off. Later on, I created an amazingly satisfying fantasy in which, using a pie pan as a steering wheel, I would walk around the empty field to the west of the neighbors' house, pretending to be a bus driver. Somehow this caught on, and other kids would wait for me to pick them up. I would stop and open the door ("psssst"), then close it ("psssst") and drive on. Sometimes there would be several "passengers" trailing along behind me. When I got to college I wrote an essay about it for English 101.

One day the manager of the Rivoli Theater announced that the first twenty people to buy tickets for the upcoming *The Yearling* would receive "a free phonograph." On the designated day I was first in line, and waited hours for the doors to open. The free gift turned out to be a *photograph*. I hid my dejection, of course, which was thoroughly exacerbated by the movie itself, surely one of the saddest in film history.

By the time I was eight I was allowed to ride the bus and go to movies by myself. On Saturdays I watched Frank Buck "Bring 'Em Back Alive" at the YMCA or Roy Rogers, Gene Autry, Lash LaRue or Hopalong Cassidy capture the bad guys at the Wysor Grande, which also featured serials like Superman and Buck Rogers.

On the way home one day I got off the bus at Aunt Mag's house (ten twenty-TWO, Kirby AveNUE). I vividly remember two images from the visit: one was watching her iron shirts with something called, appropriately, a "mangle." I dearly wanted to try this hellish machine. Fortunately I repressed the urge, or maybe I couldn't figure out how to turn it back on after she left the room. (A couple of years later I got my hand caught in the washer wringer and it pulled my arm clear up to the pit before Mom could rescue me.)

The other clear memory was of being put to bed that night, Aunt Mag kneeling at my bedside to pray for me. She trucked only with "colored" preachers, who "had the fire," and was the only white person in the congregation. Her humble supplication seemed strange and made me very uncomfortable (our family didn't pray), especially since it seemed to go on interminably.

My brother Bob was born (on Kirby Avenue, where Aunt Mag could again act as nurse/midwife) in 1942, and Larry (same place) in 1945. Mag died of a stroke, at age forty-five, not long after Larry's birth and my only solo visit. It was my first direct experience with the nightmare of death. During the funeral my intense curiosity overcame my anxiety, and I left the front pew for a closer look at the body. I stood next to the casket, hyperventilating and feeling faint, checking her over for signs of breathing. There weren't any. Her eyes seemed to be glued shut, and I knew they would *never* re-open. Though I well understood she was dead, her physical presence itself jolted me far more than the abstract concept of mortality. I tried to imagine the whole process from her point of view (what was it like to have died?). Unfortunately, I probably succeeded.

Grades 4 and 5 were combined in one room under Mrs. Armstrong. In 1946 (fourth grade), Uncle Bob and his wife Yvonne came to the school to tell us something about France. When they arrived I was asked, without warning, to introduce them. I had no idea how people were introduced, or even that they *were* introduced. Breathlessly, my stomach churning, I came up with the unmemorable: "This is my Uncle Bob. When he was in the war he married a French girl. That's her." This was followed by much laughter, which embarrassed me even more. Nevertheless, my lovely Aunt Yvonne redeemed my awkwardness and made a gracious presentation. She taught us some French words and songs, and was a big hit with everyone.

In the fifth grade Mrs. Armstrong decided that Cynthia McAllister and I would write a play about the Pilgrims. She asked us if we knew how to use a typewriter. Cynthia said she did. So we sat in the back of the room and wrote it (I learned to type with one finger), staged it, and performed in it as well. The other "actors" and I were dressed in choir robes and tall black cardboard hats, with white paper squares, representing buckles, rubber-banded to our shoes. The only line I remember was Miles Standish (me) uttering the historical: "I must drill my men. I will go with you." It was undoubtedly a flop, but Cynthia and I and the typewriter got our pictures in the Muncie paper.

Sometime later, the school choir was invited to sing on the radio. "We're going to be on the radiator??" I exclaimed, using my father's smart-ass word for the medium. I was elected to act as host, to introduce the two or three pieces we sung. Oddly, I had no nervousness whatever in the studio. It was thrilling to be there and see how radio productions happened—the unnatural quiet of the room, the glass wall with the engineer watching from behind it, a close-up view of the silvery microphone. When I got home that afternoon Mom confessed that she had "bawled" when she heard my voice coming out of the kitchen radio. In her moist eyes, at least, I was as famous as Little Jimmy Dickens.

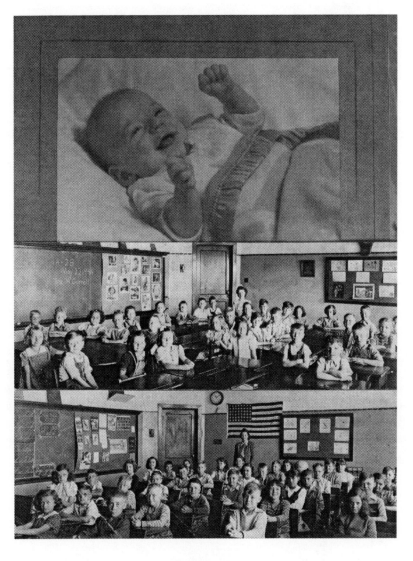

Top: Little Gene
Middle: First grade. That's me on left, in front of Nancy McDonald.
Bottom: Fourth grade. I'm in the center of the picture.

My first literary/acting endeavor. I'm the middle pilgrim.

An ever-appealing pastime in those grades (when Mrs. Armstrong stepped out) was to wham small chewed-up paper wads onto the ceiling, where they usually stuck. They fell off sporadically as they dried, which elicited delighted giggling among the students and deep frowns between our teacher's eyebrows. But I was generally obedient, as were most of us, and earned only one paddling in grade school. Iris Marsh, the girl at the desk in front of mine, had pigtails, and I sometimes couldn't resist the urge to pull them. When she shrieked once too often, Mrs. Armstrong escorted me out of the room and whacked me good three times. It might have been more had I not straightened up after the third painful insult and marched quickly back into the classroom. Of course I refused to cry, even when I gingerly sat down at my desk, though my eyes were stinging as much as my rear end.

It was during these years, too, that there were hints about what the sexual apparati were for, primarily through silly little playground jokes, like: "Daddy, what's that thing between your legs?" "That's my banana." "Mommy, what's that thing between your legs?" "That's my fruit basket." "Daddy, why don't you put your banana in Mommy's fruit basket?"

I got the general idea, but, like most kids, couldn't imagine my own parents doing such a thing, and to what purpose (I didn't know it was a pleasurable experience). It wasn't until later that I learned how the banana and the fruit basket came together to make babies. I could hardly believe that, either.

I spent much of my youthful summers "swimming" (floating around on an inner tube along with other neighborhood kids) or fishing in the nearby White

River, a muddy brown misnomer. Once, while sitting on the bank, I noticed a herd of cows coming toward me, animals that I had feared ever since the photo shoot with Ferdinand when I was four. I jumped onto my bike and pedaled hard for the bridge. Apparently thinking this was a great new game, they loped after me. I pedaled faster. When my pole got caught in the spokes of the front wheel, the bicycle stopped immediately and catapulted me over the handlebars. I tumbled a couple of times and got up running, leaving everything else behind. Mom had to walk over to the river and retrieve my bike and my fishing gear while I watched, humiliated, from the bridge.

Christmas and Easter were secular holidays at our house. To us, the former meant lots of gifts, as if to make up for everything else, even if it meant going into (further) debt. Rarely clothes, which were mundane things, but toys and games and, occasionally, something even better. It was impossible to stay in bed on Christmas morning. At dawn we tiptoed out to the cold living room and inspected the foot of the tree. Eyes glimmering, it was back to bed to whisper and wait until we heard the shuffling of tired feet on the hallway floor.

On various Christmases my sister and I were given *Black Beauty*, *The Swiss Family Robinson*, *Donald Duck Visits South America* (which contains the memorable line, "If you stop to look at anything, you won't see everything!"), and a compilation called *Big, Big Story Book*, which included abridged fables like *Heidi*, *Hans Brinker: or the Silver Skates*, and a few Grimm's fairy tales. The latter particularly delighted me because I learned that magical things can happen, that almost anything is possible, and, of course, that good always triumphs over evil.

On one magical morning I found a brand-new bicycle leaning against the wall. Until then I had ridden one with pint-size wheels, forcing me to pedal around the neighborhood twice as fast as my peers. I badly wanted an "adult" bike. But my heart sank when I spotted the new Roadmaster: it was full-size, but, unlike those of the other kids, the handlebars were circular. It was better than the old bike, but I hated it because it was different from everyone else's, somehow a reflection of my parents' oddness. I wanted desperately to be like the other kids, to be one of them.

Another year I found a new bat and glove under the Christmas tree. These were the real thing, just like everyone else had. When spring came and the bigger neighborhood boys discovered my toys, I was invited to join them for a game. I was jubilant. But when it was time to choose up sides, I was elected batboy. They had only wanted me for my new equipment.

Easter was a gorge of candy. There was no church, no coloring of eggs. But even in college and beyond, whenever I was home on that Sunday I got a big basket with fake green grass containing every confection to be found at Woolworth's: golf ball-sized candy eggs, hollow chocolate animals, yellow marshmallow chickens and white rabbits with little red eyes, Hershey's kisses, M & M's. The ritual never varied: after the usual Sunday breakfast of sausage and pancakes with homemade syrup (brown sugar dissolved in water and boiled), I would eat one each of the various tooth-decaying treats and fight off sleep and nausea the rest of the morning.

While down the street at a neighbor's house one Saturday afternoon, I accidentally swallowed a butterscotch candy. It hurt; I was sure it was stuck in my throat and I was going to choke to death. I ran home as fast as I could (I don't know what the other kids thought about my sudden departure). The only person there was Dad. When I squeaked to him what happened he laughed. Though stung by the absence of sympathy as much as the lack of help, his chuckles made me realize that the lethal treat was already in my stomach and I was, in fact, still breathing.

One of my neighborhood friends had a kindly, soft-spoken father much like Uncle Roy. On one occasion, when he was driving us somewhere, David asked Mr. Whitenack, "Daddy, what does it mean when your nose whistles?"

"It usually means it needs blowing. Why?"

"Yours is whistling."

That was an unforgettable experience for me. For one thing, I could never have asked my father something like that. It seemed too personal, too invasive. And if I had, there would have been a lengthy lecture on whistles, with many digressions and asides, and I still wouldn't have known what a whistling nose meant. I wished I could have been Dave Whitenack.

Religion manages to seep through every Hoosier's skin, and children are often asked by well-meaning adults, "What church do you go to?" Thus, it was no surprise that, when I was in the fifth grade, Mom and Dad decided to send Nancy and me to the nearby "United Brethren Church" (Southern Baptist, I believe) for Sunday School, where we sang songs like "Jesus Loves the Little Children," and I learned many, many verses from the Good Book, for which I received a gold star each. When my tally sheet was full of stars I was suitably rewarded with my own pint-sized copy of—the Bible.

One night in bed I decided to read it through, regardless of how long it took. I began at the Beginning. It went well, if slowly, until I came to the begats. Night after night I tried to get through them, but fell asleep every time. I never got any farther.

On a particularly adventurous Sunday I decided to stay for the later church service. I didn't get very far with that, either—maybe two or three weeks—I couldn't take the wailing. I did love to sing the hymns, however, often taking the baritone or bass part (an octave higher than written). I paid little attention to the words—it was the music I felt.

When I wasn't in school or church, or playing with the neighborhood kids, I had a running dialogue with God. Nothing theological; He was just someone (like a Father?) to talk to. We even played games: "God, I'm going to run to that telephone pole. If I don't make it there in ten steps, I'll kill myself." The experiments became progressively more daring. Once, when I didn't make it in time, I was sick with horror—I would have to kill myself (I had told *God* I would), something I profoundly didn't want to do. I escaped my fate only by exclaiming, "I didn't say it was the Final Test!"

By then I had learned of His terrible wrath, and because I had reneged on my promise I felt He was always watching me, waiting for me to screw up again. When I uttered my first swear word ("shit" or "damnation," I imagine) I waited with considerable trepidation for the sky to fall. It didn't. It was probably then that I began to wonder whether Anyone was listening.

And there were many questions for which there seemed to be no answers. If your wife dies and you re-marry, which one will be with you in heaven? If you're over a hundred, and blind, deaf and lame, do you end up like that for eternity? If you survive a natural disaster, and you thank God for being spared, should those who didn't make it curse Him? And why, if Heaven is so wonderful, do so many people try to defer the trip for as long as possible? Even though I continued to believe, I was becoming more dubious by the day. I began to wonder how many people were faking it, went to church because of upbringing or peer pressure and didn't really believe a Word they heard. Despite all the misgivings, however, religion seemed such an *important* part of life that I even considered chucking all the trivialities, like science, and becoming a minister.

Dad could play the guitar. I dearly wanted to learn it, too, but he was the kind of teacher who would say, "See this? This is a G7," and then strum it and move on to another chord or two and lapse into a song. I finally gave up asking.

Somehow he became Scoutmaster, and I a Cub. There were plenty of activities, games and school-wide contests. One of the latter involved building a birdhouse. I entered two, one of which came in first, the other third. I felt terrible. In allegedly showing me how to do it, my father had built both of them himself.

From the beginning I was afflicted with amblyopia, and have had to wear glasses since I was six (my eyes were crossed by then). To this day I can see very little with my left one, though, fortunately, both of them point in the same direction. Any action requiring a precise measurement of speed and distance—catching an outfield fly, for example—was difficult for me, and embarrassing as well. Nevertheless, despite the lack of depth perception, I was a pretty good athlete in elementary school, well-coordinated and quick. There was a summer touch football league, and between the fifth and sixth grades I ran for all of our touchdowns (three or four).

Even though Dad never took a vacation, and used the extra income to pay bills, the burden of raising four children was beginning to have a serious economic effect on our lives. In the late forties, the CIO (Congress of Industrial Organizations, the chief factory workers' union) went on strike regularly, and Dad was sometimes out of a job. Whenever he was on the picket lines we became significantly poorer. No more movies or comic books until he went back to work. We racked up a terrific bill at Gray's grocery store, ending at about $1800 in debt, a lot of money in those days. Many families were not so lucky as to have such an extraordinarily sympathetic and generous grocer as Clyde Gray. Despite these financial difficulties, Mom and Dad decided that the house on East Fifteenth Street had become too small, and it was time to move.

Just before the 1948 election I went with the Whitenacks to the train depot in Muncie to watch President Truman roll through. He was standing at the rear of the caboose, waving and smiling, in a crisp dark blue suit. I was jolted by the fact that he looked *exactly* the same as he did on *Movietone News*. He defeated Dewey that year, and I have wondered ever since if it was because of that cross-country train ride, during which he was seen by countless people as impressed by his presidential appearance as was I.

That year, when I was eleven, my family moved out of town to a little house "in the country" (though not "way" out). Football was the only sport Selma School didn't have, and my athletic career as star halfback came to an abrupt end.

THE DIFFICULT YEARS

We had moved ostensibly because our growing family (there were six of us) needed more room. We looked at some wonderful possibilities—a big old farmhouse north of town, for one. (I remember this place because Uncle Bob drove us to the site, and he let me sit between him and Dad and shift the gears). But the one my folks chose, primarily for its newness, had the same number (four) of rooms as the old one, and they were even smaller than those we were leaving. Dad planned to "add on" when he had the time and money; he never found either. Consequently, my sister and two brothers and I shared a tiny bedroom until Nan got a little older and moved out to the living-room sofa. This arrangement, accompanied by the music of Dad's rhythmic snoring and Mom's first noisy bathroom visit of the day, continued until I left home to go to college. My eventual absence didn't get Nan off the davenport, but at least Bob and Larry no longer had to sleep together in a twin bed.

The only heat in *this* house was generated by an oil-fired floor furnace with a single large grating on which we all fought for space on winter mornings. But there was an attached garage, connected to the house by a "breezeway," which was probably another factor in the move. Dad found an eleven-year-old Buick somewhere, borrowed the money, and bought it. We had it until it was seventeen.

Despite the impossibly crowded conditions, I will always be grateful for that move because something wonderful happened at Selma School: the sixth-grade teacher, Mrs. Heaton, *read* to us. Every day, right after lunch as I remember, she would read a chapter or two of a Hardy boys or Nancy Drew mystery. I became totally absorbed in these stories of adventure and mystery, can even remember where my desk was in the classroom. In addition to the fun and excitement, the books gave the reader (listener) some idea of how families were supposed to operate, which was not at all like my own. Reading, I suddenly understood, was a way to experience a better—or at least different—world.

Another pleasure was learning to play the tonette, a tiny plastic "woodwind" that looked like a miniature clarinet and sounded something like a recorder. There were about thirty kids in the class, and most of us were in the "tonette band." In later years, thanks primarily to Arthur Godfrey, the whole family (exept Mom) took up the ukulele (cheap little plastic ones), played with a felt pick. They sounded pretty tinny, but it was quite satisfying to sing and accompany oneself with an easy-to-play harmonious instrument.

Not long after the move I developed warts on the back of my hands. Mom was convinced I'd been peed on by a toad, the generally-agreed causative agent for this affliction. I tried hard to hide these embarrassing excrescences, which seemed as horrific as leprosy to me, and didn't raise my hand very much in class until they went away.

The house was situated on three-quarters of an acre adjacent to Reese's airport at the back. In the spring, Dad dug up most of the acreage by hand and planted it in vegetables. Long, long rows of corn and beans, hill after hill of cucumbers and melons. It was the kids' job to weed this garden and mow the smaller yard. I spent much of that first summer watching the planes take off and land right across our fence (I could see the pilot inside!) while pulling up butterprint, whipping milkweed, and desuckering corn. It never occurred to me that one of them could crash and burn, though Mom filled in this knowledge gap soon enough.

What inspired me most about amateur gardening, however, was the remarkable way the little vegetables started on the stalks or vines and slowly became the big ones found in the grocery stores. I don't know what I expected, but it amazed me to see them turn out exactly the way they should have (even the pygmy melons), like a half-acre of little Harry Trumans.

Mom and Dad liked their vegetables overripe, to the point of toughness, and some (especially the watermelons) didn't grow well. But it was quite wonderful to sit in the tomato patch with a saltshaker on a sunny August day and eat your fill. Even much of the good stuff was wasted: we rarely saw our relatives and had few neighbors to unload it on.

The front of the garden was bordered by a row of sunflowers. One night I dreamt that I pulled the yellow petals off one of them and found seeds beneath. The next morning I discovered this absurdity to be absolutely true! For a brief period I thought I might be a seer, or at least possessed of a remarkable prescience. To my great disappointment, however, such dreams never recurred. The only other boggling experience I ever had was during a drive-in movie with Dad (the other kids must have been sick, and Mom stayed home with them). Just before the film began we spotted a steady orange light in the northern sky. It moved across the windshield faster than a jet, but slower than a meteor, and the transit lasted for several minutes. We were both sure we had seen a flying saucer. The next morning a full report of the phenomenon appeared in the *Muncie Star*. The UFO seemed to have flown across Northern Indiana, too far from the theater and too fast to have been an airplane. Though I doubt it was an alien spacecraft, no better explanation has yet come forth.

Tommy and Lewie (Reese), the farmers who owned the airport, sometimes took the neighbor kids up for rides. I was awed by the experience, especially by the way the plane seemed to go nowhere when in flight. "You think we're not moving?" Tommy asked us one day. "Pick out something and look for it again in five minutes." I was further impressed by the quart-size ice cream container, which served as a vomit receptor. Unfamiliar with the concept of airsickness, I wondered why anyone would be out flying if he were that sick. Unable to stem my curiosity, I opened it one day and was aghast to discover that it had, in fact, been used at least once.

That summer of 1949 I became a lifelong Chicago Cubs fan, at least in part because of their wonderful broadcasters, starting with Bert Wilson ("There's a long drive! It's way back by the wall! It's gonna be outta here! It is! It's a home run for Hank Sauer!"), who was replaced after his unfortunate death by Jack Quinlan, the game losing little of the phraseology and excitement in the transition. But, despite their enthusiastic reporting, the Cubs were awful that year and for many more to come. Quinlan's radio backup, Charlie Grimm, once traded places with manager Lou Durocher. Didn't help. Nothing ever did, even when the great Ernie Banks took over at shortstop. It was all about hope.

Later, when we finally got television, I learned to hate the Yankees even though they were in the other league. I would turn on the set looking for a Cubs game, almost invariably to find the damn Yankees, whose "color commentator," Dizzy Dean, almost ruined the sport for me with his persistent guffawing and cute terminology (there were no "basemen" around the infield, only "sackers"). Not his fault, I suppose, but that of the powers who hired him and the Yankees to dominate the Saturday afternoons of my youth.

In the seventh grade I began reading on my own: Albert Payson Terhune's magnificent dog novels, the Howard Pease seafaring books (*The Black Tanker* and others) and, of course, all the rest of the Hardy boys and Nancy Drew mysteries in the school library. The Pease books eventually led me to *Mutiny on the Bounty* and *The Caine Mutiny,* both of which I loved. Another of my favorites was Owen Wister's *The Virginian.* Two of its scenes have stuck with me ever since. The first came early in the book, when the protagonist is watching a cowboy trying to rope a horse and failing; he imagines the horse and his brothers "roaring with laughter."

The second and more famous line came later, when the Virginian advises a card player who has labeled him a son-of-a—: "When you call me that, *smile!*" (i.e., only a friend can get by with an epithet like that).

Despite the laborious attempts to grow our own food, our financial difficulties steadily worsened. We had enough to eat, but little else. Our mother was busy mending and patching our clothes, and movies or ball gloves were things of the past. Still, we each got a new comic book every Friday (payday)—Superman, Captain Marvel, Donald Duck, Little Lulu—which we exchanged with the neighbor kids for those we didn't have. Mom was quite annoyed when I traded a new "funny book" for one without a cover. I didn't care—it was the stories that mattered to me—but she was more concerned with appearances and fair play. That's another trait I inherited from her: she hated to be taken advantage of.

Since we had so little money we usually took our own lunches, which was embarrassing—few of the other kids brought theirs. If we had fifty cents we went to the cafeteria for a hot meal, but it was still mortifying: the kids who were "in" went down the street for hamburgers or pizza.

Dad tried to start his own business installing furnaces and commodes in the evenings and on weekends, usually in various housing developments around Muncie. He called it General Home Service. Said it all. Not very exciting, but it was him all over.

The first thing he did was to hire his younger brother Don to help him. Uncle Don, the soldier, who had the best sense of humor of anyone I ever knew, suffered from a serious neurosis, at least when I was a boy. It took the form of a desultory retching which came without warning. It was said that this condition stemmed from his service in the Army's military police, when he had to participate in the hanging of a deserter, but I suspect the malady would have manifested itself in one form or another regardless of his war experience. When they went out on a job I had to sit between them in the Buick listening to Don gag, or worse: waiting, shaking and sweating, for him to erupt. On the other hand I learned how to "rough in" and install heating vents; cut, thread, and connect water pipes; and do some wiring without electrocuting myself, some of which became useful later on.

On the rare occasions when Mom and the kids got to an afternoon movie, we sometimes had to wait for hours for Dad to pick us up. Whatever his latest excuse—he lost track of time, he wanted to finish the job so he wouldn't have to go back, he just plain forgot—Mom was furious.

But one Saturday he came home after installing a furnace for a local farmer and tossed seven hundred-dollar bills on the kitchen table. We all stared at them for a while. Most of that went into expenses, of course—the furnace itself, for one thing—but, nevertheless, it was one of the memorable moments in our lives, and Mom forgave him his insensitivity for a while.

On the downside, he was once cheated out of a large sum of money, to Mom's further consternation, by a contractor for whom he had installed the plumbing and heating equipment for several new houses. He never got paid. Dad, too, was distraught over this for a long time—we could have settled the grocery bill with the lost income. Soon after that he gave up the business and went to work evenings for Nayco Distributors, a nearby plumbing/heating wholesaler.

Despite our financial difficulties Dad maintained his pathetic sense of humor. Not that the jokes were so bad (example: "Doorman, call me a taxi." "Okay—you're a taxi!"), but they were few and he repeated them endlessly. I often wondered whether he had no memory of past tellings or if he liked them so much that he saw no reason to expand his repertoire. He rarely came home with contemporary jokes he had heard from his fellow workers, most of which were probably off-color.

Whatever our resources we were well supplied with jigsaw puzzles and games, including Flinch, Touring, Monopoly, War (we called it "Battleships, Cruisers and Destroyers"), and card games like Canasta and Hearts and Crazy Eights. By then Bob and Larry were old enough to join in the "fun." Infected with the need to prevail in these contests, we sharpened our logic and debating skills arguing with one another about every point in every game. Perhaps the insufficiency of Dad's approval fueled this burning desire to win.

Stimulated by our proximity to the airport, and because Uncle Don did it (I liked him despite his fearsome affliction), I became a model airplane builder. At that time we made them from balsa sticks—infinitely more realistic and satisfying than the ubiquitous plastic toys available today. I also owned one of the great playthings of all time, an Erector Set, with which I could construct anything from a wagon to a Ferris wheel. It was enormously gratifying to build something recognizable, and that actually worked, from scratch.

In the seventh grade I rediscovered *The Swiss Family Robinson* and *Black Beauty*. Even in junior high school I was beginning to think that something wasn't quite right with the world, which seemed to me a violent and somehow oppressive place. The Robinson family was fortunate enough to be shipwrecked on an undiscovered island, and they took full advantage of the opportunity to build a simple, idyllic world of their own. I would have given almost anything to join them. (Years later, one of my favorite movies was *When Worlds Collide*, in which a few lucky people leave our doomed planet for an uninhabited world.)

The other book was about the abuse of animals, a custom I had abhorred ever since the ant episode. I sympathized with some of the neighborhood dogs, who lived their entire lives at the end of a rope next to an empty or frozen water bowl, and the various animals killed on the road that passed by the house. We always had stray dogs and cats hanging around waiting for food. The former never came inside, but Mom always gave them our leftover bones and gravy. *Black Beauty* was a maltreated horse, but it is a wonderful story about overcoming the odds, of hope for a better life for all animals.

As much as I enjoyed these and other books, however, I was an exceptionally slow reader. Part of this ineptness might have been due to my faulty eyesight, but mainly, I think, it resulted from my being distracted by other concerns—choking and dying, for example—while trying to focus on the page. I would often have to read a paragraph, or even a sentence, several times before moving on. It wasn't a matter of comprehension, but of concentration. Perhaps I was suffering from a form of Attention Deficit Disorder, which wasn't well understood at the time.

I was especially bad at reading out loud in class. I would stumble over words and emphasize the wrong ones, not really knowing what I was saying, and was probably thinking something like: *Why can't I read this right? I'm so embarrassed! Everybody's staring at me! God, please let this be over!* which only made things worse.

My father was quite disappointed that I never became the high-school athlete he wanted me to be (partly to fulfill his own failed ambitions and partly because my cousin Billy, the elder son of Uncle Bill, the worm entrepreneur, was a star football lineman for the Muncie Central Bearcats, and a state champion shot-putter as well). My lack of depth perception precluded basketball or baseball, and even if I could have made the track team, my increasingly intense fear of death/dying/choking/vomiting had, by now, made me terrified of doctors and examinations for fear of finding some dread disease. Oddly, you could run at full speed for an hour in gym class without ever encountering a stethoscope, but you had to have a checkup to qualify for a couple of minutes of activity in a school-sponsored sport.

I began to dread winter, the flu season, fearing I might come down with a stomach virus, and was delighted to see the crocuses and daffodils of spring. It meant I was safe from awful illness for the next eight or nine months. I was even afraid I would encounter *someone else* who was choking or vomiting, and avoided public restrooms for years. When my sister or brothers chewed gum while lying down, I vamoosed. I once came roaring through the breezeway and accidentally bashed the head of a kitten with the door, killing him. While he was dying his mouth opened and, like a beached fish, he seemed to be trying to breathe. Acutely feeling his anguish, I tore around the house several times, not knowing what else to do. My mother loved to recount this incident, even decades later: "Remember when you ran around the house after you killed that kitten? Ha ha ha ha ha ha ha." "Yeah, Mom, that was pretty funny."

But all of this paled in comparison to the nightmare I encountered one afternoon in the school hallway, where I discovered a teacher violently shaking a little girl. Curious, I crept closer. A foot-long drool hung from the girl's mouth—she couldn't breathe at all. It was my own greatest fear personified, the butterscotch candy that stuck. As ignorant as the teacher about what to do about the catastrophe, and not wanting to watch somebody die, I took off for the nearest exit, passing Mr. Hays, the basketball coach, running the other way (someone must have gone to find him). He immediately reached into the girl's throat and pulled out the jawbreaker she was choking on. Like a newborn baby, she began to cry. At that moment, Richard Hays became a genuine life-saving hero in my glittering eyes. And he was a very good coach, too.

Dad's only real avocation was horseshoes. He built an official court in the backyard, meticulously measured, with concrete walks and precisely the right percentage of clay in the pits. He desperately wanted to be good at the game, and we often went to Muncie's Heekin Park, where Wayne Nelson, a national-class pitcher, practiced his sport. To my knowledge Dad never got an opportunity to play him, but he went up against everyone else who would take up the challenge. I don't recall his winning a single game, but I still remember the names of the half-dozen regulars who frequented the courts.

He taught my two brothers and me to play, enticing us outside with "Feel like getting your tail beat?" All three of us became better than average pitchers, and we competed in local and regional tournaments. Larry did well as a teenager, once finishing second in the junior world's championships, held that year in Muncie—our father was one of the organizers.

Dad also tried roller skating (there was a rink in Selma). Though I secretly admired his getting out on the floor, with his long legs (he was 6'2") and general clumsiness he looked like a giraffe on rollers. I don't know where Dad got the money for the skates— he probably borrowed it. In my family, you didn't ask what something cost, but how much a month it was.

Though not much of a singer, either, he was determined to form a Brewer family quartet with my sister and two brothers and me singing barbershop harmonies, primarily for the entertainment of family members on the rare occasions (usually Christmas) we visited them, though perhaps with a grander vision in mind. Much to his disappointment and disgust, I loathed these command performances and refused to participate, partly from innate reticence and partly, I'm sure, to deflate what I thought was his oversized sense of self-importance. Bob and Larry went on to become excellent singers, however, performing at weddings and the like. Brother Bob eventually became a fixture with amateur theater groups in the Baltimore area. I sing, too, but never overcame my fear and insecurity enough to try it in public.

Like the birdhouses of my earlier youth, my first soap box derby car, with GENERAL HOME SERVICE painted on the side, was built by him (entrants were supposed to build their own racers). Ostensibly he was merely teaching me some carpentry skills ("See? This is how you pound a nail . . ."), but I never got to use the hammer. I was annoyed and ashamed, but couldn't figure out a way to deal with his interference. Fortunately, I never came close to winning.

My siblings and I rode the bus six and a half miles to school every day. A kid in my grade, Jack Bales, got on about halfway there. Many times he would give me a good punch on the shoulder when he sat down, or even in passing by. We didn't talk much otherwise.

When we got off the bus one day, I pulled him aside and threatened, "The next time you punch me on the shoulder I'm going to beat the shit out of you." I don't know what I actually would have done—I was afraid to get hurt, and he might have killed me for all I knew—but he never punched me again, and afterward we became the best of friends. We were inseparable, did everything together. We devised our own code and passed secret messages back and forth. We learned the statistics for all the major league players, played a thousand games of ping-pong in a church basement, shot each other in the ass with B-B guns and played chess on a pocket-sized card in class. We were so close that we were accused of being "homos," even though I had no idea at the time what the designation really entailed. Later, we played poker and golf, double-dated and bowled together. Jack taught me the meaning of true friendship, for which I will always be grateful. Even with him, however, I couldn't discuss my inner problems.

Puberty arrived almost simultaneously among my classmates sometime between the seventh and eighth grades. When the roll was called on the first day of class, it was funny, and somehow exciting, to hear a yodeling bass, where not long before there had been a soprano, answer the call. Girls sat up and took notice. We all smiled and laughed. It meant things were going to be different.

I ended up with what someone described as a "pleasant baritone," which probably helped later on in debate competitions. Along with it, however, came an unpleasant rash of pimples. At home, Clearasil became a staple, along with Brylcreem and safety razors. And I couldn't do my impression of Woody Woodpecker anymore.

It was in the eighth grade that Mrs. George taught us to diagram sentences. I loved it, and was surprised to discover that this wasn't easy for everyone (including Jack, who didn't care much about grades). For me it was a game, a puzzle, something that, like an algebra problem, was fun to solve. And it was useful, too, in writing themes and reports, to know the parts of a sentence, the relationships between nouns and adjectives, verbs and adverbs.

That year North Korea invaded the South, and the United Nations (read: United States) answered the summons. Every day there was a map of South Korea on the front page of the newspaper, with a gray area indicating the territory still held by UN and South Korean troops. This sector shrank daily. Though technically we weren't at war (it was merely a "police action," President Truman informed us), it seemed that, for the first time, the country was heading for a humiliating defeat. But General Douglas MacArthur's forces opened a second front on the opposite side of the country. Now there were two gray areas, and they grew and grew until the North Koreans were driven back to the 38th parallel. MacArthur wanted to pursue them, but diplomatic considerations precluded this offensive. When Chinese forces entered the South he formulated plans to invade China as well. Instead, he was fired. Later, after the Republican National Convention, where he was nominated for President, he went before a joint session of Congress and delivered his famous line, "Old soldiers never die—they just fade away . . . ." The general received a standing ovation. It was a critical time in American history, and a powerful civics lesson.

It's difficult to know what Korea and the Cold War did to the psyches of the children of that time. Although everyone at Selma High wanted to push back the North Koreans, we were also consciously or unconsciously afraid that the Soviet Union might become involved in any military conflict, and that could mean a nuclear war. While Senator McCarthy went after unnamed communists in the State Department and elsewhere, we practiced atomic bomb drills (i.e., we crawled under our desks). To one degree or another, we all knew that every day might be our last.

This horror, at least in my case, was superimposed on my already well-developed fear of death and dying. During the summer of 1951, in fact, I experienced my first probable psychosomatic illness, which manifested itself as a difficulty in swallowing. I suspected there was something wrong with my throat, but I couldn't look at it for fear of discovering a grotesque tumor (I couldn't imagine anything worse) staring back at me. I desperately hoped the symptoms would go away. But they persisted, and I began to take peeks in the bathroom mirror. Quick ones, then maybe a tenth of a second longer, until eventually I was able to give my throat a good scan. Even though I couldn't find anything ominous-looking there, the swallowing problem worsened, and there finally came a time when I couldn't eat at all for fear of choking on something. I watched other kids at play and wondered why they had been allowed to live carefree and happy when I had to die so cruelly—did they realize how lucky they were?

One hot August day when dinner (lunch) was ready, I refused to come to the table. It must have been a Sunday because Dad was home. I sat in the worn-out chair in the living room listening in agony as my parents discussed what might be wrong with me. Mom came to the conclusion that I was distressed because school was about to start again and I didn't have any new clothes to wear. I couldn't have cared less about anything so trivial, particularly since I was sure I would be dead by then.

In the dark recesses of my convoluted mind I imagined the worst possible scenario: I would go to a doctor, who wouldn't find anything wrong, but I would need to have something pushed down my gagging throat in order in order to examine my stomach. If I survived that terrible ordeal I would learn that I was suffering from the cancer residing there. I would then have to go to the hospital and be irradiated until I was burned up. But if I declined this fiery treatment, I would vomit blood until there was no more in my body, which, I presumed, would be even worse. (Chemotherapy hadn't been discovered yet, or I would have been terrified of the possible effects from *that*). As Mom had regularly pointed out, we'll die the way we are most afraid to die.

Had I done something to offend God? Maybe it was the promise to kill myself I had reneged on a few years earlier . . . . I thought about the United Brethren and considered begging Him for good health, but what good would that do if He had already decided to end my life? Eventually I gave in to reality, decided that neither the horrible disease nor the pitiless treatment could be any worse than the awful dread, and asked Mom to make an appointment with our "family doctor," whom I had never visited.

The next afternoon Dad came home early from work and took me to see Dr. Funk. He looked at my throat (a little red, he said), listened to my heart from front and back. "Can't you find it?" I panted. "You're too young to lose your heart," he replied with a sympathetic smile, and asked whether I was allergic to penicillin. "I don't know, I've never had it." "Then you're not allergic to it!" he pronounced, jabbing me in the shoulder with a needle and handing me a package of pills. It was over! I was going to live a while longer!

It might have been a minor infection—I never found out and didn't ask—but I doubt it. By the time we got home, the symptoms were completely gone. I walked around the back yard gazing poignantly at the sky and the grass, which I had been certain I would never see again. Everything was so wonderfully alive, including me! (Much later I discovered that this feeling could be recaptured with the aid of a few ounces of rye whiskey.) I didn't have cancer, I wasn't going to the hospital, I wasn't at death's gaping door. On top of that, I had been to see a *doctor*, so there couldn't be *anything* seriously wrong with me. In fact, Dr. Funk had been a very nice man, and it had been an almost pleasant experience, despite everything. I began to consider becoming a physician.

I picked up a horseshoe and threw a ringer. That night I ate like a starving boy, gulping down big bites with impunity, grinning like an idiot.

But I soon forgot about becoming a doctor. When school started I was again ready to pursue my dream—to become a scientist—unfettered by cancerous growths and concern about the lack of new clothes.

As a freshman I learned to overcome what might well have become another lifelong terror: the fear of public speaking. At first I hated standing in front of the class, but once I learned to breathe and was able to think beyond the embarrassment and discomfort, I began to enjoy it. The trick, I learned, was to be intimately familiar with the material—it was only when I tried to discuss something I knew little about that I got into trouble.

Once, after delivering a comic monologue, Mrs. (Edna) Gilmore asked me to give a dramatic reading to a large group—it was a charity fundraiser—from the stage of the same Masonic Temple where I had been thrilled by the stars of the Grand Ole Opry. The piece was called "From Whence Cometh My Help?" I remember nothing from the text except for the last line: "My help cometh from the Lord!" It went without a glitch (at least that's my recollection), and I wallowed for a minute or two in the warm applause, just like Roy Acuff!

Of course I was beginning to notice girls. Their tight sweaters begged for attention and generated considerable discussion among the boys as to which bosoms were real and which were not. Some had information allegedly obtained by first-hand experience. I wasn't a breast boy; my focus was on viewing as much leg as possible and wondering what it was like higher up. To my dismay, however, it was several more years before I found out.

Our jokes began to take on a decidedly raunchy character, e.g., "Confucius say: girl who fly upside-down have crack up," and "What's next to the best thing in the world?" "A girl's panties!" Little sex comics called, appropriately, "eight-pagers," were passed around. Someone had a deck of playing cards, supposedly obtained from France, with photos of naked women on the backs. Jack had found a manuscript copy of *Behind the Green Door* (later made into a film) in his parents' dresser. Good friend that he was, he loaned it to me. Unlike "From Whence . . . ," I still remember every scene.

The second semester I moved up to the debate team. The issue that year was: *Resolved: That All Citizens Be Subject to Conscription for Essential Service in Time of War.* My partner and I were on the negative side and, whenever the opponents made a point, I pulled out the appropriate response, in summary form, from a little green box of 3x5 cards. When it was my turn to speak I gathered up all the pulled cards and lambasted the other side. I still disliked reading aloud but, because of the debate experience, I learned to improvise from a key word or two. Unfortunately, the program was dropped from the curriculum after that year, for reasons I never learned.

Perhaps because of my newly-discovered facility for public speaking I began to notice that the announcers and newscasters on the radio talked differently from me or anyone I knew. There was none of the whiny twang, the casual dropping of "g's," the automatic lapses of grammar. I began to imitate their style in thought if not in deed: I didn't want to undermine my hard-won popularity by speaking "properly" with my schoolmates—that would have been considered "highfalutin." I simply took note of the differences for later. Even now I lapse, at least in part, into "Hoosier" the minute I cross the state line.

That summer, when I turned fifteen, Dad tried to teach me how to drive. I already knew the fundamentals, having studied him and other drivers carefully over the years. So I did okay until I came to a stop sign at the top of a hill. Every time I tried to start moving again I'd roll back or kill the engine (it's not easy with a stick shift). Dad was furious, and ended up driving home. I decided to wait for the upcoming driver's training course to complete the lessons.

Since he came home from Warner Gear at 4:00 P.M., smelling of oil and sweat, and went off to the plumbing and heating place at five, we always had a very early supper not long after we got off the school bus: meat, gravy, potatoes, a canned vegetable or two, dessert, milk for the kids, coffee for Mom and Dad. The latter beverage was made by adding water to a pile of grounds in the bottom of a pot and boiling for a while; it was muddy and must have been saturated with caffeine. The meat was fried (in recovered bacon grease, a pot of which always stood on the stove), until very well done. Even hamburgers and sausage were scorched in the deadly lubricant.

As a result of eating so early we were always starved by later in the evening, when Dad returned from his night job. Sandwiches, cookies, bowls of cereal and/or ice cream inevitably appeared. Sometimes popcorn was popped (on the stove in a skillet), or fudge made. One night I ate a whole package of cookies, the sandwich type with yellow filling. Whether it was a coincidence I can't say, but that night I was violently ill. At first I fought the nausea, morbidly fearing to vomit. In the middle of the night I involuntarily rose up, turned my head, and tossed the cookies all over the wall next to my bed. Mom was extremely dismayed the next morning: after I had gone to school (I felt better after the voluminous expulsion) she had to clean the wall and the floor under the bed. "'Bout made me puke, myself," she saw need to inform me later.

It was only the beginning. Though I never again ate one of those icing-filled cookies (I couldn't stand the sight or smell of them) or barfed on the wall, I was nonetheless nauseated every night. By trial and error I learned a couple of ways to minimize the unpleasant sensation. One was to go to sleep lying on my stomach (why that worked I haven't a clue). The other was not to consume anything for three hours or more before bedtime. Mom, of course, couldn't understand why I didn't want the cereal or the lunchmeat sandwiches or any of the other snacks, though she never failed to offer them ("Don't you want no ice cream?"). Even in the rare instances when we went into town for a movie I declined the popcorn, the Milk Duds, the Necco Wafers. I don't know how concerned she was by this peculiar behavior; perhaps she considered it part of my being a teenager, hoping, perhaps, that I would eventually return to normal.

It was a kind of stalemate. The nocturnal nausea never became worse, but it didn't get any better. After some months of this distressing tug-of-war I discovered a sizable cavity in a lower molar (we never saw a dentist until a persistent ache developed, and then the offending tooth was pulled). I was delighted with this find. It seemed obvious, to me at least, that the decaying molar was the root cause, so to speak, of my gastrointestinal discomfort.

For some reason I wasn't afraid of dentists: teeth were right there, not down deep inside. Furthermore, I had had teeth pulled before without incident, and needles didn't bother me. So I had the thing jerked out, and . . . no more nausea! Perhaps the decaying tooth had led to a form of "blood poisoning." Whatever the cause of the nighttime distress, it wouldn't have occurred to me that I might have been the victim of a diurnal anxiety triggered by a fear of repeating the cookie debacle.

As a sophomore I took Latin, the source of many English words, and the only language course available at SHS. That year Mrs. Gilmore drove Rachel Moody and me to the state Latin contest, where I won a bronze medal for the third highest score. But the most memorable event of the trip to Indianapolis was my first visit to a restaurant. I self-consciously asked our teacher to please tell me in case I did something wrong: "Aren't you hep to all the rules?"

"The first rule," she informed me with a gentle smile, "is to enjoy yourself."

Owing, perhaps, to the study of Latin, I was becoming much more aware of the derivation of words and how tenuous their meanings. For instance, I would read in the *Muncie Evening Press* that someone had gone into the hospital "complaining" of chest pains. It was a long time before I understood that the poor bastard wasn't griping to anyone about his discomfort, he just wanted help. People who "entertained" guests didn't have to perform a soft-shoe for them. When a film was held over at the Rivoli by popular "demand," it didn't mean there were crowds of people snarling and kicking at the box office. Most affecting of all was the term "serve," as in "dinner is served." I imagined the server humbly bowing as she set the plates in front of her masters. To this day I dislike being "served," by a waiter or anyone else, and I usually leave too large a tip as compensation for the inequality of it all.

Some words generated double images in my head. "Matter" conjured up not only atoms and molecules but also the pus that oozed from the boils on my rear end. A "bleeding heart" projected a sanguinary disaster as well as compassion. And I always got a chuckle whenever someone would shout, "I'm coming!"

Other times I read too much into them. I would have intensely disliked being named (as a fellow student was) Snodgrass. On the other hand, people named Legg or Hogg cracked me up. There was a baseball pitcher for the New York Giants named Hearn; I loathed reading or hearing his name—it sounded too much like "hernia," another medical nightmare I was sure I would never survive. If there was a Rice University, was there somewhere in this vast country a Corn College or University of Wheat? And surely it should be "Treat or trick!"

I rarely experienced a panic attack as intense as the one precipitated by the horrible black tuberculosis bugs, but occasionally some frightening experience would send me back "inside." One of these was an article in *Reader's Digest* about Red Barber, the Brooklyn Dodgers/NY Yankees sportscaster, who suffered from stomach ulcers. Though I read it well over half a century ago, I can still quote the salient phrases from memory. Barber was out on the golf course when he was "suddenly gripped by a fit of nausea." "A *geyser* (emphasis mine) of blood *poured* from his mouth." "The *horrible hemorrhage* continued all the way to the hospital . . . ." The worst conceivable nightmare! Threaten me with this in *1984* and I'd blab anything. I re-lived that story a million times over the next few decades, worrying constantly that I might develop an ulcer. Every morning I fearfully checked my pillow to ascertain whether it had any blood on it. Same with the toilet paper in the bowl. It was probably then that the nervous tics and the lip- and cheek-chewing began.

Sometimes an attack would come in a movie theater. One such time was during a showing of *The Prince and the Pauper*. (It must have been a re-release, because it originally came out the year I was born.) There's a scene in which the king suffers a heart attack. Gasping for breath, he staggers toward the camera and, in terrible distress, expires. I don't know whether anyone noticed that my eyes were as big as the moon, but I didn't care—I was someplace else. I didn't stop panting until I left the theater.

In films of the late 40's and early 50's, young native pearl divers were routinely caught in giant clams and held underwater until blood invariably streamed from their mouths (their lungs exploded?). In *The Wake of the Red Witch*, John Wayne's air hose gets ripped from his diving suit, his helmet fills with water, and he drowns. I did, too. (The Duke's co-star in that film, incidentally, was the most beautiful woman who ever lived, the fragile Gail Russell, who died much too soon of a heart ailment. I loved her then, and I love her still.)

On the other hand, the gunslingers and slashers and bombers never fazed me, unless the victim started drooling blood before he bit the dust. But it was usually a clean, quick demise, nothing to fear. I realized it wasn't death that terrified me, but the awful process of dying. The grotesque minutes, or even hours, between life and not life. I could think of nothing more felicitous than being here one minute and gone the next.

Besides driver's training and Latin, my favorite tenth-grade course was English, taught by Mr. (Bill) Langdon, another of Selma High's excellent teachers. We read some unforgettable stories and poems that year, as well as *Julius Caesar* and *Silas Marner*. Here are some of the lines I remember:

'oo's that black against the sun?
It's Danny fightin' 'ard for life . . . .

and

It was Din! Din! Din!
Where the mischief 'ave you been?

and

Poor burnt, blind 'Pache . . .
I love him—that's why.

and

Water, water everywhere
And all the boards did shrink . . .

and, most importantly,

Cowards die many times before their deaths;
The valiant never taste of death but once.

and

I took the road less traveled by—
And that has made all the difference.

Great stuff, and it opened my mind not only to the wider world of adventure and beauty and possibility, but also to the inner world of emotion and feeling.

That year, 1953, we finally got a television set, and our lives suddenly became centered around this sound- and light-box in the corner. It never went off (except when we went to bed), even during meals or the rare times when someone was visiting. There were only three channels to choose from, and everyone knew when everything was on.

One such program was the Friday Night Fights, Dad's favorite, sponsored, not surprisingly, by a beer company ("What'll you have? Pabst Blue Ribbon!"). A tall, cone-shaped glass would be poured, the foam inevitably running downs the outside, Dad sneering in his easy chair. Having no friends to go with, he took me to the local Golden Gloves tournaments so we could see the blood and saliva in person. I hated it. The spectacle of two people trying to kill each other in front of thousands of encouraging fans seemed revolting to me.

Dad eventually developed a cute trick: whenever there was something on the screen that he didn't want to see, he would get up and change the channel, or ask one of us to do it, claiming magnanimously that "Mom doesn't want to see that." (She was usually in the kitchen and couldn't care less.) He especially didn't like the sopranos who were regular visitors to the Ed Sullivan Show ("Mom doesn't want to hear all that caterwaulin'."). Fortunately, he wasn't often present weeknights until after Nayco, the wholesale plumbing/heating store, closed at nine.

In my junior year we got a new principal, a man who had played second base for the Muncie Reds, a farm club for the Cincinnati baseball organization. With the co-operation of the Green Hills Golf and Country Club, Mr. Locke started up a golf program at Selma High, and I joined in (no physical examination required). The pro at Green Hills showed us how to swing the various clubs, taught us some golf etiquette, and turned us loose. We could play for free anytime after school, and often did. Jack and I bought and divvied up a very cheap set of used clubs (two woods, three irons, and a putter each), some of which were so old that they had wooden shafts, and the irons were imprinted with designations like "mashie" and "niblick." I discovered an extraordinarily helpful book by Ben Hogan, *Power Golf*, and learned to drive the ball close to 250 yards, even with my ancient woods. Although we both became pretty good golfers and easily made the team, no one took the trouble to schedule any matches with other schools. Nevertheless I could finally claim to be a high school athlete, to the muted delight of my father.

Curious incident: one late afternoon the husband of Mrs. Denton, our math and civics teacher (and the best instructor I've ever had) drove Jack and me, and a couple of other guys, to the golf course. Oscar was a southerner, and fond of words like "horseshit." For some reason I had never heard that term, and I fell into a fit of uncontrollable laughter. I'm not sure why—I think it was a combination of what he said and the way he said it. And perhaps I suddenly understood that Marge Denton (and all the other teachers?) was a lot earthier than I had realized. I was embarrassed because no one else was laughing, and I chortled as silently as I could. A little later, while I was still quietly giggling, he asked those of us in the back seat if we knew what "TCP" (a gasoline additive) stood for. When no one responded he said, "Tom Cat Piss." I almost wet my pants.

I learned to type with all my fingers that year, up to 100 words/minute (ignoring mistakes). Our teacher, Mrs. (Sue) Reedy, asked me if I would compete in the county typing contest. "Sure," I said. Almost immediately thereafter I learned that the math contest was held at the same time on the same day. Mrs. Denton was irate, and let Mrs. Reedy know it. I would much rather have entered the latter, but I had already said I would type, and type I did. Errors were weighted heavily, however, and I finished far down the list. Another lesson: the road taken can sometimes be the wrong one.

There was a period of weeks or months when I couldn't seem to get enough air. This would be quite disconcerting for anyone, I suppose, but for me it was like standing on the edge of hell and peering into the fiery pit. I couldn't tell anyone for fear I'd have to go back to Dr. Funk, who would be stone-faced and unsmiling this time, and soberly inform me that I had lung cancer or tuberculosis. I couldn't feel the little black bugs crawling around inside, but I knew they were there. Fortunately, this distressing affliction gradually diminished, but it was still quite worrisome because, I thought, it might very well come back.

Other unpleasant experiences came and went during this period—a persistent nervous twitch in an abdominal muscle, for example, and sometimes a mysterious "funny" feeling in my chest—but these were overwhelmed by the problems most high school juniors and seniors have to face: how to deal with the opposite sex, what causes these stupid pimples, how to get into college or find a job.

Like a baby songbird raised in isolation is never taught to sing properly, I was ignorant of the most fundamental social graces and, living far away from town and school, had little opportunity to learn. This was compounded by my having no car, and a father who worked evenings and wasn't able to take me to school functions or social events.

I never realized that Dad's carnal modesty was somewhat unusual—I had no one to compare him with. All I knew about the subject came from my classmates and from self-experimentation. I bought a condom at the bus station (praying Mom wouldn't find it in my dresser drawer or billfold) "just in case," though I hadn't the least idea how I could convince a girl to let me try it out. And the situation was further complicated by other considerations. First, I most certainly didn't want to get anyone pregnant and ruin my chance to become a scientist; and second, there were only two or three girls in school who were all that appealing to me. (From the beginning, I think, I was looking for a prospective mate rather than "a good lay.") Finally, sex wasn't nearly so casual as it is now. A "score" was a big deal then. So, as with most adolescents of my generation, I had to settle for daydreams and masturbation.

Aside from riding the bus to a basketball game at another county school and occasionally holding hands with someone, my first serious date was probably the junior prom. I remember very little about it except that I spent weeks trying, with the help of my sympathetic sister Nancy, to learn how to dance the foxtrot and the waltz. I don't even recall asking anyone to go—maybe Nila asked me. I do remember that the gym was hot as hell and everyone was sweating heavily, especially me. But the evening wasn't a total disaster: we danced a little, talked a little, drank some punch, talked and danced a little more, admired the good dancers who seemed to have been born with the ability. Then it was time to go home and, at last, to deal with the problem of kissing a girl goodnight. But that didn't happen on this occasion because the other couple (Jack and his date) were watching us from the car, or so we imagined. In retrospect, I suspect he was busy making out while we were gone. In any case, we said our farewells, she went into the house, and it was over. The best thing about the whole affair was that I had gotten through my first real date, and it had turned out okay. It was a small, nearly unproductive, but necessary step toward better things.

One classmate who had interested me was a girl who, unfortunately, moved away when we were sophomores. Besides her good looks she was one of the most interesting of my peers. When the subject of dying came up in class, she volunteered that she, like Wendy in *Peter Pan*, was "curious to know what it's like." I thought that was not only very brave, but quite profound as well. Nothing may have come of this putative relationship—I don't think she knew I was alive—but, nevertheless, I often played the "what if" game: What if Barbara's father hadn't been transferred out-of-state? What if she had noticed and liked me? What if we had started having dates? What if—?

Another was the only girl *friend* I had. Carole, too, was interesting, but in a different way. She spent a lot of her spare time at the playhouse in Muncie, acting, painting sets, whatever needed to be done. Everyone thought she was going to become an actress, and perhaps she did. She had dark circles under her eyes, which I imagined came from staying up late every night at the theater.

There were a couple of times we studied together at her house (I stayed after school and Dad picked me up after work). That's where I had my first-ever cup of coffee. The reason I remember the event so well is that when I went to bed that night I couldn't go to sleep . . . but I felt terrific! I lay there listening to the cars rattling over the wooden-floored bridge a mile away and *The Tonight Show*, Dad in the nearby living room smoking and laughing by himself.

Despite getting only a few hours' sleep I wasn't tired the next day. Coffee was wonderful stuff! So I started to sip some on a regular basis, to the chagrin of my father and amusement of my mother, who figured it was a sign of approaching adulthood.

That summer, 1954, I often awoke to the sound of Mom swatting flies, which, she believed, carried the polio virus. I never knew anyone who contracted this awful disease, but there were many in Muncie who did, including a former primary schoolmate. The swimming pools were closed, and few people braved seeing a movie. We didn't know that clinical trials of the Salk vaccine were already underway. The results were good: 70% of the children who would've been afflicted (compared to the placebo group) were protected. The following year massive inoculations, with an even better vaccine, were carried out all over the country, and polio went the way of smallpox and many other diseases.

But for a stroke of incredible luck, my father would almost certainly have died that year. Warner Gear instituted a new policy requiring the wearing of safety glasses while on the job, and within a couple of weeks Dad was hit in the eye by sliver of steel shrapnel. The glasses didn't stop the projectile, but they slowed it down considerably and kept it from penetrating his brain. He was taken to Ball Hospital, and then to Indianapolis for surgery. The eye healed, but its acuity was never the same. As compensation, the corporation gave him $2500 and, at long last, he finally paid off Clyde Gray, the benevolent grocer.

During my senior year Mr. Cool, the chemistry teacher, loaned me his college physics text (there was no course at Selma High) so I might be better prepared for what lay ahead, and he later saw to it that I won the prestigious, if non-monetary, Bausch and Lomb award. Inasmuch as I was the only senior planning to become a scientist, the tribute was probably a bit hollow. Nevertheless, I greatly appreciated the gesture.

Sometimes, without warning, I would feel a strange sensation or two in my chest, and then nothing more for several days. Of course I worried (obsessively) about what this little disturbance might be until, standing on a ladder in the garage one afternoon, it suddenly occurred to me that it had to be a heart problem. The next time it happened I checked my pulse and there it was: a missed beat! I was certain once again that I was doomed.

Many people can't feel these palpitations, so they never even know they're occurring. Others, like me, wonder whether or not our hearts will start beating again, and breathlessly wait until we feel it pounding. But it wasn't until later that these little horrors persisted beyond a few skipped beats at a time.

And there were other curious problems as well. For example, I was preparing to represent Yemen on two successive weekends at a county-wide model United Nations conference. Oddly, I came down with a respiratory infection *both weekends*. I'm sure these illnesses, like the swallowing and the nausea problems, were psychosomatic, precipitated in this case by the fear of exposing my ignorance of world history and politics.

By then college was looming and I hadn't even applied. The truth is I didn't know I needed to or how to go about it. I was hoping for a Storer scholarship to get me into one, and figured I could worry about the details later.

This award was one of the greatest financial benefits possible for a student graduating from a small Midwestern high school. If memory serves, it paid tuition, fees, books, and half of one's living expenses for any college or university in the United States. I hadn't a clue where I should go; all I knew was that I didn't want to attend the local one, Ball State Teachers' College (now Ball State University), because I didn't want to be a teacher, I wanted to be a scientist. Nor did I want to live at home.

My grades were excellent: mostly A's, a few B's, and one C imposed by Mr. Colvin, the Industrial Arts teacher. The C was well-deserved—I was terrible in shop, ending up with a bumpy ashtray and a nightstand with about fifty nailheads showing on the top. Despite this manifestation of manual incompetence (I was the only kid in the state of Indiana, probably, who had no idea what dual carbs were for), I was sure I was going to get the Storer.

I didn't. When the last of the grades were figured, my Latin contest colleague, Rachel Moody, beat my average by 0.07 points. I realized then that I should have used glue rather than nails for the nightstand, but it was far too late for that. Devastated, I prepared to stay at home, where there wasn't even a desk, and the nearby TV was always on, and go to Ball State.

But for one of the best men I ever knew, that's where I would have ended up, and perhaps become a high school chemistry teacher and never left the state. (NB: there is nothing whatsoever wrong with this profession; it just wasn't what I wanted to do with my life if, in fact, I lived long enough to do anything at all.) Principal Claude B. ("Sport") Williams called me into his office not long before graduation and, without even asking me where I wanted to go to college, told me about an attorney in Muncie who had graduated from DePauw University in Greencastle. I probably wouldn't even have known about the place had another classmate not gone down on an earlier recruiting trip (I couldn't go because I hadn't a cent to make the journey). He mentioned a scholarship (the Rector) awarded to qualified students, and suggested I talk to the lawyer about it. Understanding that a good impression would make all the difference, and undoubtedly aware of my shyness and social ignorance, Mr. Williams advised me to give him a firm handshake, look him right in the eye, and explain why I wanted to go to DPU.

I crushed a few small bones, stared the guy down, and got the scholarship.

LITTLE MAN ON CAMPUS

The summer before college I worked at the wholesale plumbing and heating store—where my father moonlighted as a salesman—making deliveries in a beat-up truck, shelving plumbing fixtures and other hardware, and helping buyers find what they were looking for. Though I didn't mind the endless unloading, checking, and organizing, I hated dealing with the customers: I had no interest in plumbing fixtures, and had no idea what I was talking about. But I loved that old red truck with its protruding side mirrors and hydraulic lift. Several mornings a week I loaded it and headed out to various construction sites, where I would take my time delivering the septic tanks, toilets, and sink fixtures, enjoy a quiet lunch at an unfinished house, often with no one around, and get back to Nayco Distributors before Wilbur, the boss, began to wonder where I was. I made less than a dollar an hour that summer and much of that went for fuel and maintenance for an ancient brush-painted (by me) Chevy, which I sold before leaving home, probably to a junkyard. My only pre-college investments were a mailable laundry box and a pair of white bucks.

Dad drove me down to Greencastle and left me there with my cardboard suitcase and next to no money. After unpacking my minimal wardrobe, the first thing I did was to find a drugstore and buy a pack of cigarettes. They were awful, but it was something I had to do to prove (to myself, and later to him) my manhood. The salesperson graciously advised me that my glowing white bucks should be well-smeared with dirt before I reappeared in public. "Only Pat Boone wears clean bucks," he said. I took care of that necessity immediately and every September for the duration of my undergraduate career.

When I ventured forth again, cigarette between lips, I noticed that it was a pretty campus, with a mix of old and new buildings, acres of walks and grass, and a huge rock squatting at the center of it all. I soon learned that this landmark was used by everyone as a focal point for almost every student or faculty activity ("I'll meet you at the Boulder . . . ."), and that DePauw was a school "for rich girls and poor boys." I was at the very bottom of that heap, the poorest of them all.

I didn't "rush" to get into a fraternity. Even if I had been deemed acceptable I couldn't have afforded the extra expense. My registration, however, came too late to get me into the dormitory, so I ended up in an old house belonging to the Hudlins, an eighty-five-year-old couple—she an energetic banty hen, her rooster a retired accountant who sat in the living room after dinner gasping "Whew" every few minutes as he struggled to digest his meal. I studiously avoided the ground floor, afraid I would stumble in just as he took his last breath and keeled over.

David—another chemistry major—and I each had a room upstairs, and a shared bathroom, but no meals. He ate at the dining room in the dorm. I had already been told it was too late to get a table-waiting job, the only way I could have eaten regularly, and there weren't any student loans available. After paying the matriculation fees (the scholarship covered tuition only) and room rent, and buying a few used books, I had very little left for food.

But starvation would have to wait—my first problem was getting through the entrance physical. Terrified that the examiners would find something wrong with me (I hadn't been to a doctor since my swallowing difficulty four years earlier), I lingered at the end of the long line. By that time I had learned to deal with the frigid sweat and hyperventilation (hold my breath for a few seconds), but the unrelenting fear almost made me want to chuck the whole thing and head back to Nayco. Everyone ahead of me was joking and laughing; I was silent, trembling, alone.

Many readers may be wondering why the hell I didn't pull myself together and face up to my problems, or talk to a professional about them. I dearly wish I could have. While we wait at the end of this fast-moving line of carefree classmates, I'll try to explain:

First, I had no idea my medical concerns could be anxiety-related. When you have chest pain, for example, you immediately wonder if it's a heart problem, not a mind trick. But the dread of people in white coats with stethoscopes hanging from the pockets precludes the victim from finding out and getting the necessary treatment; this is part of the phobia. So he/she goes on worrying and agonizing, toughing it out until the pain is so severe that he has no options, or passes out and an ambulance hauls him to the emergency room. Seeing a doctor for your problems would be like someone with a fear of heights going bungee jumping.

But that's only the beginning. Aside from the acute sensations that often arise, there is a *constant, never-ending undercurrent of fear and discomfort* strong enough to disrupt, and sometimes preclude, normal thought and concentration. Your mind focuses on and magnifies the sensations, which lead to even greater anxiety. Imagine a bear loping toward you; you're in an open field and there's nowhere to hide. While this toothy giant canters closer and closer, try to solve a math problem. That's the kind of existence suffered by those with an anxiety disorder.

In order not to be found out, however, the victim becomes an excellent actor. He smiles inanely, responds to questions he only half hears, eats, plays golf—all the things normal people do. But his mind is on something else: himself and his imminent demise.

(Note: anxiety is *not* the same as hypochondria. Hypochondriacs run to the doctor at the first sign of a problem, anxiatics stay away even at the final indication of a terminal illness. When nothing is found to be wrong with the patient, the former, certain they have a medical problem, head immediately for another doctor. The latter are beside themselves with joy.)

On the other hand, it's conceivable that anxiety sufferers live more intensely than the rest of the human race. If that is true, however, I would trade this acute awareness of life in a nanosecond for a single moment of utter peace and complete relaxation. We're on our toes every second, monitoring our surroundings for danger, keeping tabs on the well-being of the smallest fiber in our bodies, counting every heartbeat.

At last the queue shrunk to only me, and I came to the devil himself, a stethoscope hanging menacingly from his neck. My heart was racing at 150 bpm. The guy listened hard, frowned, and demanded, "Ever had any heart problems?" "Not as far as I know," I squeaked, almost certain I did. He shrugged and passed me along to the next representative of Hades (an Indiana University medical student checking for hernias). I coughed. Naturally, I had one. "You might want to get that repaired some vacation," he advised with a huge grin (delighted that he had finally found someone with an affliction, I suppose). "I'll do that," I lied, returning his sparkling smile. Mine was genuine enough: the exam was over and, unless I busted a gut on the way to class, I probably wouldn't have to worry about another one for at least four years.

Amazingly, at a reception for incoming freshmen, Dean of Admissions Wittich greeted each of us by name. There were speeches informing us of how fortunate we were to be at DPU, mentions made of illustrious graduates, and analyses of who we were (with one or two exceptions, the cream of the white, middle-class crop). We were reminded that students weren't allowed to have automobiles or consume alcohol. I didn't have a car, and drinking wasn't a problem for me—I was afraid even to taste any such potion, fearing what it might do to my fragile constitution (trigger a fatal heart arrhythmia, for example).

The top officer of the Air Force Reserve Officers Training Corps was also there to convince us (men only) that we might as well join up now as wait to be drafted into the Army later (the catch was that ROTC graduates would be required to serve four years in the Air Force; draftees were in for three). Knowing I could never pass the flight physical, and not wanting to be a mechanic or clerk, I decided to take my chances with the Selective Service.

Finally, there were stacks of forms to complete and tests to take. I remember one question in particular: Would you rather be a) president of a large corporation, b) secretary to a great scientist, or c) a famous artist. I could see what they were after, and I fully satisfied their prurient interest by admitting that I would rather be a secretary than not be in the sciences at all.

I signed up for chemistry, calculus, freshman English (required), physical education (required), and German (two years of a language was also required), and dug in with relish. To my astonishment, however, I discovered that I didn't much like the chemistry class. Balancing equations was fun, as was the laboratory work (various colorful reactions and precipitations), but the course was slanted toward industrial applications, the textbook filled with pictures of enormous rooms crowded with huge vats and pipes. Factories (my father's main source of income) held no appeal for me, and I couldn't have cared less about resins and adhesives.

But I loved calculus. What a clever way to look at the world, I thought, as a series of closer and closer approximations. And the symbols were like those seen in science fiction movies featuring Albert Einstein's blackboard.

PE meant swimming (required), which I hated—I had left the sea millions of years earlier, and had no desire to go back. I tried to fake the preliminary test by hanging on to the side of the pool pretending I could stay afloat, fooling no one. I ended up sitting on benches with a couple dozen other naked guys, our dicks all pointing toward the instructor. I did learn to swim, however, though I found the piquant aroma of chlorine and the sensation of tons of water pressing on my chest, making it more difficult to breathe, quite unpleasant if not distressing.

German was fun, thanks primarily to the teacher, Hans Grueninger, a true gentleman with a wonderful sense of humor. The class was at eight o'clock in the morning, and everyone was bloodshot. "Herr Doktah Brewah," he once began. *"Nennen Sie mir ein Fruchtbar"* (name me a fruit juice). Remembering Dad's "call me a taxi" joke, I responded with, *"Sie sind ein Fruchtbar."* Even at that early hour the class howled. But no one enjoyed the joke more than Dr. Grueninger.

In freshman English I found myself reading Hemingway and Conrad and E.B. White for the first time. *The Secret Agent* seemed a bit slow and dry to my untrained eye until I came to the scene in which a person of unknown identity is obliterated by a bomb:

> The man, whoever he was, had died instantaneously, and yet it seemed impossible to believe that a human body could have reached that state of disintegration without passing through the pangs of inconceivable agony. No physiologist, and still less of a metaphysician, Chief Inspector Heat rose by the force of his sympathy, which is a form of fear, above the vulgar conception of time. Instantaneous! He remembered all he had ever read in popular publications of long and terrifying dreams dreamed in the instant of waking; of the whole past life lived with frightful intensity by a drowning man as his doomed head bobs up, screaming, for the last time. The inexplicable mysteries of conscious existence beset Chief Inspector Heat till he evolved a horrible notion that ages of atrocious pain and mental torture could be contained between two successive winks of an eye.

I had long assumed there were quick and painless ways to go, exploding into atoms and molecules being one of the best. Evidently I had been far too optimistic. Now I could fear a slow, miserable death by any means imaginable!

Prof. Galligan, who habitually wore brown from head to toe, including the corduroy jacket with obligatory elbow patches, spoke with a funny dialect that seemed to come from a distant shore—Massachusetts, perhaps. But he liked my essays (including the one about driving an invisible bus through neighborhood fields), and asked me to write something for the campus magazine, *The Hoot*. To my great regret I never found time for that project. It didn't occur to me then that his genuine encouragement, combined with my disillusionment with industrial chemistry, might have been telling me something I should have been listening to.

When I came back to DPU to give a lecture in 2002 I visited the registrar's office to find out what had happened to Prof. Galligan. Unfortunately there was no record of where he had gone. I wish I knew; I owe Ed Galligan a lot. He gave me the confidence that I might be able to write, something that stuck in the back of my mind, intertwined with the long threads of fear and anxiety, and became, much later, a brick in the foundation of my decision to try it.

By November of that first semester, what little cash I had started with was almost gone. Mom and Dad never asked about my circumstances, probably because they didn't want to hear the answer, or perhaps they simply assumed I was managing, somehow, to make my way. I couldn't ask them for money, of course—they didn't have any, either. Fortunately, "The Duck," a popular campus hangout, featured a Saturday night special: eight (small) hamburgers for a dollar. I didn't hang out, but I hustled the sandwiches, overflowing with ketchup, mustard, and pickles, back to my room, where I ate two of them that evening, stored the rest in an empty dresser drawer, and enjoyed two more on Sunday, Monday, and Tuesday. It was a long time until the following Saturday. I stopped buying cigarettes, but there were always manufacturers' representatives passing out little free packets at the Student Union, so I could still smoke while studying to alleviate the hunger.

Somehow I discovered that I could get a single ticket for the buffet breakfast at the men's dorm (for eighty cents, as I remember). The headwaiter at the time was Bill Clinton's latterly friend Vernon Jordan, who was a couple of years ahead of me and dealing with his own problems as one of the three or four token blacks on campus. He took my ticket, and the rest was up to me. I had three or four glasses of various juices, half-a-dozen hunks of coffee cake, eggs, bacon, pancakes, and all the coffee and milk I wanted. It was a wonderful personal preview of Sydney Poitier's coffee shop scene in *Lilies of the Field*.

In a few days I was back. Vern was nowhere in sight. I actually went into the kitchen to search for him, but he wasn't there, either. So I stuffed my stomach again and, when I was finally finished, spotted him and gave him my ticket. He looked at me as if I were bothering him. Whenever I came in after that he turned the other way. I carried the same ticket the rest of the semester. More often than not, breakfast was the only meal (except for Saturday through Tuesday) I had all day. I didn't want to overstay my welcome, however, and didn't show up at the dorm every morning, especially after having gorged on a pair of tiny hamburgers the night before. A good man, Vernon Jordan, even as a college junior.

Despite the occasional giant breakfast, however, I lost more than 30 pounds (to 126) by Thanksgiving. The day after that, at home in Muncie, I got a phone call from Mr. Timmons, the director of food services at DPU. He was blunt: "I don't think you're getting enough to eat. I'm putting you down for banquet service at the Student Union." How he learned about my situation is a mystery to me—perhaps Hans Grueninger or Vern Jordan told him. Embarrassed, especially with my mother hovering nearby, I denied the assertion. But I gratefully accepted the job.

Two or three evenings a week I helped serve dinners for meetings, conferences, and other food-oriented occasions. Again I gorged whenever possible. A good thing, too: the 8 for $1 hamburger deal had ended. Eating was still a desultory affair, but I was beginning to re-gain the weight I had lost. By the end of the semester I was "promoted" to regular hours at the soda fountain in "The Hub," where I became popular by overdoing the Coke flavorings and sundae toppings.

Whenever Dr. Grueninger came in for coffee he would chat (in English) with me as I stood behind the counter listening to "Heartbreak Hotel." He gave me an "A" that semester, not because I had learned German so well—I hadn't—but because he knew I would have done better if I hadn't had to work to make enough money for food. "Doc" Grueninger lived into his nineties, and I have no doubt that his warmth, generosity, and sense of humor never diminished during his lifetime. I wish that, later in life, I had told him what his kindness meant to me.

I was working about twenty hours a week, and when an opening for a room became available in the dorm for the second semester I happily accepted it, as did housemate David Uhrick. My new roommates were terrific, though neither appeared to study much. Jim Vandivier was a pre-med upperclassman, Chuck Smidl a six-five freshman economics major who seemed to sleep most of the time.

Early in the semester the budding physician came down with mononucleosis, "the kissing disease," and left school for a while. Before that, though, Chuck and I helped him create some smutty (though hilarious) takeoffs on various other students in the dorm, names changed only slightly, which was posted on the bulletin board in the lounge. I don't know who reported us, but soon thereafter we were called before the Dean of Students and his disciplinary council. "Don't say a word," Jim advised us. "Let me do the talking." No problem there. But when the offending material was passed around, the council members could barely refrain from chortling. We were let off with gentle slaps on the wrists, and admonished to refrain from creative humor for the duration.

With enough caloric intake to sustain myself, I managed to produce sufficient energy to take up intramural sports. From then on I played everything: basketball, volleyball, softball (pitcher), flag football (quarterback), ping-pong, golf, horseshoes, bowling. I won the annual horseshoe tournament a couple of times, and actually made the university bowling team one year. Intramural sports provided the fun and relaxation I needed to concentrate more fully on my often difficult courses, and I think they minimized the incidence of heart palpitations as well—I rarely experienced them while on the athletic fields. On the other hand, for stimulation I went back to cigarettes.

Dormitory life was socially important, too, and I enjoyed going to movies and basketball games with my dormmates, some of whom became great friends, as well as singing in the in-house chorus, watching *Victory at Sea* on the lounge TV, and eating most of my evening meals in the dining room. I learned to be "gung ho," to "hang loose," to appreciate "tough" girls, to tell "sick" jokes ("Mrs. Jones, can Johnny come out and play?" "Of course not. You know he doesn't have any arms or legs." "We know. We wanted to use him for second base."). For the first time I felt as if I belonged somewhere.

One of my biggest thrills that year was the night Count Basie and his orchestra (Joe Williams *et al.*) came to play for the spring dance at the Student Union. I was working downstairs in the Hub, but could hear the music coming from the ballroom. Sometime after midnight the whole band came down for food. Dozens of steak sandwiches and gallons of thick, eggy shakes. This was my first close-up encounter with fame. When the Count himself came to the soda fountain I shoved a pencil and a piece of paper toward him and asked for his autograph. He looked it over carefully, as if it might be a blank check, but finally signed it in the most beautiful flowing hand I had ever seen, or ever would again. His eyes were dark and clear, his smile beatific, his skin a lovely, smooth chocolate. He seemed to be a genuinely nice man. I kept that autograph in my billfold for decades, until it finally disintegrated.

The rest of my freshman year passed less eventfully except for the time I suddenly developed a persistent chest pain, which lasted for days. Certain that I was suffering a drawn-out heart attack or, at best, a chronic ailment brought about by all those missed heartbeats, I watched the minute hand creep around the wall clock and listened to Chuck's snoring over *The Lullaby of Birdland*. In case of imminent demise I sent my sister a birthday card several weeks early. Finally, unable to take the stress anymore, I called my former landlady, the spry eighty-five-year-old, and tremulously asked for the name of her doctor, with whom I made an appointment for the following afternoon. (I was afraid to go to Student Health, where, I figured, they had been sharpening their knives, expecting me to show up ever since my failed entrance exam.)

The local physician listened to my chest and announced that I had a heart murmur. He assured me, however, that it would probably be of no concern until I was in my forties . . . . I was ecstatic—I wouldn't be forty for more than twenty years! He gave me some pills and suggested I get plenty of sleep in the meantime.

That night, before a routine dorm meeting, I took one of the pills. During a break I got a bottle of Coke from the machine. I was soon alert, painless, and feeling great. It wasn't until later that I realized the medication had been aspirin, which, combined with the caffeine in the soda, had lifted me to a happy little high.

But I soon remembered his warning to "get plenty of sleep." From then on I became obsessed with the fear that my incipient heart disease would come sooner *if I didn't*. The palpitations did, in fact, occur more frequently when I stayed up late, but sometimes there were exams to prepare for. I chose to study, but my concentration undoubtedly suffered along with my grades.

Nevertheless, since I had been officially informed that I was safe from heart failure for a considerable length of time, I decided to ride in the first DePauw Little 500 bicycle race. I borrowed a bike and started pumping. Unfortunately, as the day of the event drew closer, our captain informed me that I would have to go in for a sports physical. When I didn't show up for it he asked the Health Service whether they would accept, instead, the results of my entrance examination of a few months earlier. His appeal was rejected, as I knew it would be, and I dropped out of the race before it even started.

I wasn't having any luck with the rich girls, either, partly because I had to work during campus-wide dances and other festivities, partly because I still had very little extra money, and mostly because I was too timid to ask. But there *was* a sorority girl who sometimes came into the Hub. She was exceptionally pretty, and friendly, too, once calling me "a good jerk." Palms perspiring, I stumbled around the dorm for a few days until I finally dredged up the courage to call her. Unfortunately she was booked until—I don't know—2009 or thereabouts. She eventually married a fellow student who became a well-known physician and medical researcher. Probably a good choice.

But owing, perhaps, to my nominal social life, I ended my first year of college with a "B" average, my weight back to normal, a couple of dollars in my pocket, and enormous anticipation for the next one.

* * *

When I got home for the summer I discovered that Mom knew I was a smoker: she had found strands of tobacco in the pockets of the shirts I had sent home for laundering (in my embarrassing cloth-covered cardboard box, not aluminum like everyone else's). She found the revelation amusing. Dad, a heavy smoker himself, was appalled. If we were watching television and I pulled out a cigarette, he would emit a guttural noise and scowl until I finally snuffed it out. I guess he still thought of me as being eleven. Whatever he thought, I stuck it out—I was a college man now. Mom even insisted he buy me a carton whenever he got one for himself, usually Camels. I asked her once why Dad smoked, pointing out how much it cost every year. She looked at me a little sadly and declared, "It's the only pleasure he has." After that I never begrudged him a cent for his habit.

That summer was a disaster for my precarious economic situation. I decided not to work for the plumbing/heating place at less than a dollar an hour. Instead, I looked through newspaper ads, found a job that promised easy sales and big money. I was interviewed by a guy with a crew cut in a cheap hotel room, signed up to sell Bibles door-to-door. They were huge purple ones (the exact color of Christ's robe when he went to the cross, he explained), crammed with colorful pictures. They sold for $34.95, or $5 down and $5 a month.

Since I didn't have a car, and Dad went to work at some ungodly hour, he left me at a downtown restaurant, where I drank coffee and waited for the rest of the Bible crew to show up for breakfast. The six of us always went somewhere on the road for lunch, too, usually beef Manhattan sandwiches and a clump of mashed potatoes, all buried under a gluepot of brown gravy, and ending with apple or cherry pie. These feasts ate up most of my pay.

The boss, the guy with the crew cut, drove up from Indianapolis every morning in a huge cream-colored Cadillac, hauled his crew to a neighborhood in Muncie or one of the surrounding towns, and dumped us off to scatter and sell. The victims were housewives hanging clothes on the line or vacuuming the rugs. The patter was: "We're calling on all the Protestants in this neighborhood, and I wonder if that might include you?" If the prospective customer admitted that it did, we would open the Bible we were carrying and demonstrate its nice big print and beautiful pictures, taking care to explain the reason for the purple jacket. If she said, "No, we're Catholic," usually with obvious relief, we were programmed to come back with, "Well, that's fine, we're calling on all the Catholics, too!" (there was another version of the book for adherents to that faith).

Rarely did I make a sale. The few that come to mind involved elderly ladies toothlessly sipping something or other on their porch swings, barely able to see or hear (I vociferated loudly on the subject of the nice big print). They would find the down payment somewhere on their persons, or toddle in to the cookie jar, and I would get out of there before someone of authority came home to nix the deal. Once, I was invited in by a very friendly housewife only to be discovered by the returning husband, who loudly and very physically evicted me. On one or two occasions the police rounded all of us up and threw us out of town.

I hated the job for a lot of reasons, not the least of which was being paid a commission later, much later, on sales that were putrid in the first place. Nevertheless, in the newsletter published by the company, I turned out to be one of their top salesmen! I never saw the names of my fellow hustlers on the lists, though they all claimed to have made more sales than I did. I finally realized that all had been too proud or embarrassed to admit they hadn't sold a single Bible. But even as a top salesman I hadn't made nearly enough money to get me through my sophomore year. It was back to the Hub for another go at jerking sodas, and three more summers of bathtubs and septic tanks.

*   *   *

I moved in with another Chuck (Boyer), a fellow chemistry major, and found a second job collecting laundry and dry cleaning to send out for my dormmates. This wasn't a high-paying enterprise, but it helped with the room and board.

It was Chuck #2 who introduced me to the wonderful worlds of classical and Broadway music. When I found it necessary to study in the library I discovered Risë

Stevens' *Carmen*, donned a pair of earphones, and played it over and over again as I attempted to solve chem and math problems. It is still my favorite opera.

Having had enough of factory chemistry I switched to a physics major. But this was even worse, perhaps the dullest course I had encountered since high school history. Dr. Correll (head of the department of two faculty members, including himself) almost never got a demonstration to come out right. He would carefully set it up, turn it on, and . . . nothing happened. It was embarrassing for him and for us. Moreover, the "lab" part of the course involved soporific experiments like measuring how fast a billiard ball rolled down a pine board. We were learning fundamental principles, I suppose, but I was sick with boredom. Even so, I almost wish I had stuck it out. I might now be working with the Cassini Saturn probe team or teaching astrophysics in a major university. Or, perhaps, rolling billiard balls down pine boards in a small college somewhere—DePauw University, possibly. Or maybe writing novels . . . .

At Thanksgiving my whole family was food-poisoned. As always I fought off the nausea for as long as possible, but at least I made it to the bathroom in time. Like performing for an audience, the anticipation was far worse than the event itself.

While at the depot in Indianapolis waiting for the bus back to Greencastle (it was weather-delayed), a thirtyish man invited me to spend the night at his house; he "had a spare bedroom," he assured me. Fearing to ruin my precarious health by staying up all night trying to get to DPU, I was tempted to accept. But why was he wandering around looking for stranded souls in the bus terminal? I decided to take my chances on cardiac arrest and declined the offer.

By the second semester it was back to chemistry. Still not the exciting prospect I had been looking forward to since grade school, but quantitative analysis was certainly more fun than beginning physics. Determining *precisely* how much of this or that was present in your crucible or beaker was almost like a puzzle or game.

Because of the workload, the stress, the lack of sleep, or a combination of all three, the irregular heartbeats increased in frequency and duration. I often lay in bed at night, whirling like a dervish, trying to find a position in which my heart would beat normally. I discovered that this fretful spinning was more likely to happen after chain-smoking to keep awake. It occurred to me that the problem might be exacerbated by nicotine, but I needed it. The resulting anxiety, of course, only made matters worse. I would drop off to sleep from sheer exhaustion only to be awakened seconds later (it seemed) by my clock radio. Sometimes I would go back to sleep and miss my first class, but I was just too damn tired to get up.

Sometime that winter I joined the Young Republicans. Not to discuss politics— I still didn't know one party from another—but for social reasons. Unfortunately, it didn't help. Not only was I preoccupied with matters of health and finding a science I liked, I had to deal with a return of the annoying nervous tics. None of the three or four girls who came to the meetings appealed to me anyway, I told myself.

Chuck was a great roomie—bright, interesting, and fun. A good athlete, a decent singer, and a respectable bass player, too. And he had a cute girlfriend, whom I admired from near and far. He finally moved on to another girl, leaving the tough Mary Jane up for grabs. I asked her out a couple of times, once to the spring dance (I managed to get off work), but the relationship was a disaster from the start. She was extremely gregarious, engaging herself in conversation with anyone in the vicinity, while paying little attention to me, or so it seemed to my blighted ego. Though this latest attempt to find a soulmate didn't work out, I well remember her pretty face, soft skin, and ample figure. However, there were a couple of other girls who weren't booked into the next century, so I kept at it . . . .

My biggest disappointment that year was mathematics. Differential equations was a quantum step more difficult than the parent calculus and, on top of that, Dr. Gass delighted in inserting false leads and little traps into his exams, which I usually fell for. I struggled to a C in the course, on a par with my high school shop success, and my interest in math fizzled out.

In sum, I limped through another year with a certain amount of disillusionment and disappointment. Chemistry was still not the great joy I had dreamed about, and I was beginning to realize that I wasn't as smart as I had thought, at least not in mathematics. My health was becoming more and more a concern, I still had difficulty making ends meet, and my love life was barely minimal. The future didn't seem nearly so bright as it once had.

*   *   *

That summer I went back to wholesale plumbing and heating. The money was still pathetic (now a whole dollar an hour), but it was more lucrative than Bible selling. There was a new secretary in the place, and one of the other guys suggested I "take her to a dance or something" (it turned out to be her idea). I liked her, and probably should have seized the opportunity to do something about my virginal status. But I procrastinated: though separated, she was still married. On the day I finally decided to take a chance, her husband tried to commit suicide by climbing into his truck and going mano a mano with a telephone pole. He survived, however, and they got back together, at least for a while. I still wonder what if—? She would have needed a lot of consoling.

I remember *her* lovely face and ample figure, too.

One night I saw *The Ten Commandments* at the Rivoli. By then my interest in religion was a charred ruin. If God were paying any attention to what was going on here, I reasoned, there was no sign of it. But watching that movie, after two years of disillusionment with chemistry, suddenly rekindled my apparently still-smoldering thoughts of the ministry. Perhaps it was an early-life crisis. In any case, this unscientific sentiment lasted only a few days and I soon returned to my usual agnostic philosophy.

Another nightmare: one night Dad started running around the house shouting, "I can't get my breath!" I was already in bed, but instead of getting up to help him in some way (though I had no idea how), I covered my ears so I wouldn't have to bear his anguish. Fortunately, Nan and her boyfriend had just returned from a date, and they took him to the emergency room at Ball Hospital. One of his lungs had collapsed— perhaps an inhaled cigarette ember had hit a wall and caused the air to hiss out like that from a deflating balloon.

I visited him on my lunch hours. Within a week his lung had refilled the empty cavity and he was soon back to work. I had hoped the experience would induce him to quit smoking (even though I was addicted myself), but he went on as if nothing had happened. By the time I went back to DPU in the fall, however, I had switched to a pipe.

*   *   *

Still unsure about a chemistry major, I decided to take bacteriology, as well as organic chemistry, my junior year. Much to my amazement and delight, I loved it! Had I switched to a life sciences major instead of physics the previous year, I might have ended up a microbiologist. But, as it turned out, organic chemistry was also a great deal of fun (the term "organic," in this context, means the chemistry of carbon compounds, the basis of all the forms of life we know about). My enjoyment of these courses, however, may have had as much to do with the professors in charge of them as their content. They were wonderful teachers in both classroom and laboratory.

But organic was still chemistry, while microbiology was entirely new to me. It's hard to describe the amazement one feels when he inoculates a test tube or Petri dish half-filled with a nutrient medium and, the next day, finds a culture growing there. Under the microscope the tiny organisms moved around, going about the business of finding whatever they needed. We weren't studying some dull mechanical process, but life itself; it was beautiful, mysterious, even *magical!*

Mr. Fletcher (who, like Prof. Galligan, was still working on his doctorate) truly loved his subject. One of the books he assigned was something that had a profound influence on me and, I suspect, many others, perhaps even today. It was Paul de Kruif's *Microbe Hunters*. There has never been a work that better conveys the excitement of scientific research—nor, probably, one that seems more hyperbolic to the non-dreamer. De Kruif leads you down the long, crooked road from the awe-inspiring beginning of microbiology (the invention of the microscope) to "present-day" (the 1920s) research. There isn't a dull moment in the entire book. Over the years I've probably read it twenty times.

This, for example, from Chapter V, "PASTEUR: And the Mad Dog":

> . . . But at last one day Pasteur told the laboratory servant: "Bring up some healthy birds, new chickens, and get them ready for inoculation."
>
> "But we only have a couple of unused chickens left, Mr. Pasteur—remember, you used the last ones before you went away—you injected the old cultures into them, and they got sick but didn't die?"

Pasteur made a few appropriate remarks about servants who neglected to keep a good supply of fresh chickens on hand. "Well, all right, bring up what new chickens you have left—and let's have a couple of those used ones too—the ones that had the cholera but got better . . . ."

The squawking birds were brought up. The assistant shot the soup with its myriads of germs into the breast muscles of the chickens—into the new ones, *and into the ones that had got better!* (emphasis de Kruif's). Roux and Chamberland came into the laboratory next morning—Pasteur was always there an hour or so ahead of them—they heard the muffled voice of their master shouting to them from the animal room below stairs:

"Roux, Chamberland, come down here—hurry!"

They found him pacing up and down before the chicken cages. "Look!" said Pasteur. "The new birds we shot yesterday—they're dead all right, as they ought to be . . . . But now see these chickens that recovered after we shot them with the old cultures last month . . . . They got the same murderous dose yesterday—but look at them—they have resisted the virulent dose perfectly . . . they are gay . . . they are eating!"

Roux and Chamberland were puzzled for a moment.

Then Pasteur raved: "But don't you see what this means? Everything is found! Now I have found out how to make a beast a little sick—just a little sick so that he will get better, from a disease . . . . All we have to do is to let our virulent microbes grow old in their bottles . . . instead of planting them into new ones every day . . . . When the microbes age, they get tame . . . they give the chickens the disease . . . but only a little of it . . . and when she gets better she can stand all the vicious virulent microbes in the world . . . . This is our chance—this is my most remarkable discovery—this is a *vaccine* I've discovered, much more sure, more scientific than the one for smallpox where no one has seen the germ . . . . We'll apply this to anthrax too . . . to all virulent diseases . . . . We will save lives . . . !"

I itched—I *ached*—to go into a laboratory and save lives. But first I had to get through college and into graduate school, then find a lab to save them in . . . .

On the downside, I learned from the course the myriad ways one can contract food poisoning, especially on summer picnics, with meat- and mayonnaise-filled sandwiches and various other creamy treats lolling in the sun. I avoided chicken salad for years afterward.

Dr. Burkett was friendly and open, and had a good sense of humor. He made the study of organic chemistry into a series of puzzles: starting with this compound, how do you make that one in the fewest possible steps? How do you separate and identify the constituents of an organic mixture?

It was a pleasure to be in the lab, too, with its beautiful crystals and crisp, sparkling liquids. The myriad aromas, some pungent and biting, others sweet and enticing, mingled to generate a pleasant olfactory milieu. And what could be more satisfying than gently heating a flask containing a mixture of volatile liquids, watching the vapors of the one with the lowest boiling point condense as they pass down a long, cold tube and drip, shimmering and pure, into a squeaky-clean receptacle?

I decided to combine chemistry with biology. I would be a biochemist.

A couple of other junior year courses also stick in my mind. Of great concern to my first-year philosophy professor was the question of what is "really real." Looking back, I find this a reasonable, even an important, question. At the time, though, it seemed silly to me (I hadn't yet encountered psychosis or quantum electrodynamics). I wrote a paper on the subject inviting Prof. Newton, or his designate, to try walking through a brick wall. The latter, I suggested, was *really real*. He declined to accept the challenge, and gave me not only an F for the insult (the whole paper, as I remember, was only a couple of sentences long), but a D in the course, both firsts. A sophomoric shenanigan, perhaps, but to this day I haven't found a better definition of reality.

It was Rev. Newton (at DPU, all the philosophy professors had to be Methodist ministers) who introduced us to Descartes and the dictum, "I think, therefore I am." That makes sense, of course, but he also came up with the rarely-cited corollary, "Animals don't think, therefore they aren't," i.e., they have no feelings, no thoughts, no souls. This pronouncement was to instill in the minds of many the idea that man can do anything he wants to non-human animals—they won't know the difference. Unfortunately, this cruel, obsolete belief persists among the majority of people even today.

Astronomy was an entirely different thing. I will never forget, and still get a tingle in the spine when I remember, my first look through the department's telescope. It was only a nine-inch refractor, I think, but through that lens I got my first live look at Saturn. If that beautiful image doesn't make you stand up and take notice of reality, I don't know what would. Merely seeing pictures of these heavenly objects is like looking at photographs of Paris. Other objects—the moon, Jupiter, the great star cluster in Hercules—were almost as striking. Astronomy/cosmology subsequently became a lifelong hobby of mine.

In October there came one of those rare events than inspire and change the world: the Russians launched a satellite called *Sputnik* (and soon thereafter, *Sputnik II*). The importance of this achievement was obvious to everyone, and the U.S. government suddenly became much more serious about space exploration. A few months later Explorer I was put in the sky. The race was on.

1957-58 was also the year of the Asian flu epidemic, probably the most virulent such variant since the 1918 pandemic. Almost everyone in the dorm got it, including me. My new roommate was one of the few who didn't. To comfort me, I suppose, Alan McDonald, a math major, would read a few poems aloud, including James Whitcomb Riley's *Out to Old Aunt Mary's* (at my request). Not a great poem, perhaps, but one that resonated strongly with me—it was like going to see Aunt Mae again. A non-smoker, he never complained about the second-hand nicotine (though I often found the window wide open when I got back from class).

That spring he and I and the two Chucks drove to Fort Lauderdale. An adventure to be sure—I, at least, had never been out-of-state—and fraught with sexual possibility. It was a week of fun in the sun—swimming, Frisbee, girl-watching, card-playing—but no alcohol. (We didn't dare—it was rumored that a student had been expelled for drinking a can of beer in his own home and with his parents' consent. Someone had seen him through the window and reported him.) Whether coincidental or not, the sex part, unfortunately, never materialized.

The sun felt *different*, somehow, from the Hoosier version: bigger, warmer. The ocean, the huge beach, the palm trees, birds and flowers I'd never seen, were an entirely different world from the sycamores and Queen Anne's lace of home. I had my first lobster there, with drawn butter. It tasted better than I could have dreamed. But I remember feeling, as we left the restaurant, that I had gained several pounds.

Roommate Al was a terrific baseball player, a left-handed relief pitcher on the varsity squad, and he decided to practice on the beach with me as battery mate. He had a sweeping curve, and a fastball that was like catching a rock. I can still hear his giggle when I took off my glove and blew on my hand after a few of the latter. I was clowning to cover up the pain, and stalling as well; with my poor depth perception, I dreaded each pitch, fearing a smashed nose and loosened teeth.

Also that spring our organic chemistry class visited the laboratories of the Eli Lilly pharmaceutical company in Indianapolis. I particularly remember two scenes from that trip: 1) millions of pills sliding down sloping walls and funneling into endless rows of bottles, and 2) dozens of laboratories with dogs strapped to stainless steel tables, their legs splayed, making the ultimate sacrifice for the benefit of their human friends. The latter experience was revelatory—I had known many strays in my life, some of which looked very much like the mutts tied down to the cold tables in the experimental labs. I felt sorry for them but I accepted their fate and, indeed, was prepared to make use of whatever animals were necessary in my own research, whose day was rapidly approaching.

A few more dates—one whose breath was bad, another whom I had to drop off at a sorority house under a very bright and unromantic spotlight—but no one I wanted to spend the rest of my life with. On the other hand I never won the "beastpool." However, aside from the endless disappointments and palpitations, my junior year was the best ever.

*   *   *

Another summer, a few dozen more deliveries of cast-iron bathtubs and galvanized pipe, a few hundred more dollars, but, alas, no semi-divorced secretaries. The only pursuit that made this "vacation" different was taking a biology book to work with me and reading a little at lunch or on breaks. I had planned to memorize all the phyla and classes, but there were far more than I realized. As with the "begats" of my youth, I didn't get very far.

The hot summer days oozed by, but, like flying, you're soon somewhere else, in this case the fall of 1958. I was already a college senior.

* * *

Having decided to get more serious about my career, I roomed that final year with two other serious-minded chemistry majors. No goofing off here; it was a room of bug-eyed studiers looking to get into graduate school. The first semester I took physiology, qualitative (organic) analysis, physical chemistry, a chemistry seminar, determinative bacteriology, and a "slough" course, Russian.

Though reticent of having anyone, even a disinterested fellow student, check my heart rate, blood pressure, urine sugar and all the rest, I nonetheless loved the physiology course. It confirmed the suspicion that I was more interested in the life, than the physical, sciences. We cut open a frog, for example, and watched its heart beat. I could feel my own pulse rate climb as I realized how beautiful, and how tenuous, life really is. I even contemplated the possibility (again) of going to medical school. The fear factor aside, however, it seemed to me that doctors were really more like auto mechanics than scientists. They examine and fix, but don't (I presumed) do much research. It didn't occur to me until years later that medical research per se could be as scientific, exciting, and rewarding (possibly even more so) as any other kind.

Physical chemistry could have been a disaster—I didn't care much more about gas volumes and pressures than in balls rolling down boards—but, thanks to Dr. Ricketts, another very fine teacher, I more or less enjoyed it and did well enough to get B's in the course.

Qual organic and determinative bactee were pure delight. There are set procedures to separate bacterial colonies, as well as organic compounds, and it was exhilarating to resolve mixtures into their individual components and then to identify them. If I could return to the past, two of my first stops would be these marvelous laboratories.

Though I learned the Russian alphabet and a few phrases, memorizing foreign words, especially those containing Cyrillic letters, was not a talent I possessed in abundance, despite my success with high school Latin. Nevertheless, it seemed exotic and faintly evil, and I enjoyed this course, too.

Regardless of health considerations and the possibility of another physical exam requirement, I badly wanted to get into post-graduate school. Thus, at some point, I had to take the graduate record exam. I still remember sitting in the rear of that classroom, hands shaking, intensely checking and rechecking to be sure I had properly filled in the right circles with #2 pencil lead. My overall scores weren't fabulous, but apparently they didn't hurt my chances: 98 percentile nationwide (99 among men) in the "comprehensive" part of the test (solving conceptual problems); 84 in chemistry; 68 for verbal skills (primarily vocabulary). Burkett and Ricketts were quite pleased and forecast a successful, if not brilliant, career. I was pleased, too, until I learned that one of my classmates (not a chemistry major) had scored 99/99/99 among graduating seniors of all genders. I don't know what happened to that guy, but I presume he has enjoyed a successful, and probably brilliant, career.

But my senior year wasn't all sweat and midnight oil. Some of us (including the two Chucks) went up to Indianapolis for the film version of *South Pacific* in Todd-AO. I, at least, was completely swept away, and it's been my favorite Broadway musical ever since (there's an even better version produced by Disney in 2001). We went back in May for the Indy 500 time trials. It was everything I had imagined, and we got to see the some of the world's greatest drivers close-up. I would have given an organ to be in their fireproof shoes, at least for a day.

I applied to three Big Ten schools, and thanks to excellent letters of recommendation and a cum laude (though not magna) record, was accepted by all three: Indiana University, the University of Wisconsin, and the University of Illinois. Harry Day at IU sent a very cordial letter inviting me to study with him, as did Frank Strong at UW. I read and re-read those invitations, finally decided on Wisconsin because the Biochemistry Department was a separate entity. At Indiana it was part of the Chemistry Dept., and I really wanted to get more into bio- than chemistry. And Dr. Burkett couldn't say enough good things about Madison. Perhaps a third reason was that Bloomington was too close to home. I accepted Dr. Strong, declined Dr. Day. I soon got a congratulatory note from the latter that was so flattering, encouraging, and just plain nice, that I almost wished I had gone with him. Had I done that, of course, I never would have met my wife, probably wouldn't have become a writer, and you wouldn't be reading this book. On a personal level there are many possible universes. I chose the road to UW not because it was the one less traveled, but because it was Howard Burkett's alma mater.

Like many male students (though a couple of my former dates might have accomplished it) I grew a beard during finals week. I shaved it off again when exams were over, but I had made an important discovery: a man can hide his true identity behind a mask of facial hair. Somehow I felt bolder and more confident with a wiry red beard. Still do, though now it's streaked with white.

The entire family drove down for my graduation. In previous years DPU had enticed several distinguished speakers for graduations and other ceremonial occasions: Vice-President Richard Nixon, British Prime Minister Heath (whose mother was a Hoosier—"Hoo-zi-er," he called it), and other, lesser, lights. Our class attracted the CEO of Montgomery Ward. A bit of a letdown given my profound lack of interest in retail sales and business in general. It was a pretty good speech, though, and all commencement speakers say the same thing anyway: *the opportunities for you lucky graduates are enormous; go out there and seize them!* What one is supposed to seize, exactly, is left to the individuals concerned.

The fond memories of that day, however, were overwhelmed by our departure. We loaded the car with all my clothes and books and, in honor of the occasion (maybe he figured, at last, that I was approaching manhood), Dad let me drive home. Mom fretted in the back seat with brother Bob and sister Nancy, brother Larry up front between my father and me. As luck would have it, several of my friends were hanging around the sidewalk waiting for one thing and another. The driveway ended in a sharp decline where it met the street and, while I was waving to them, our overloaded old Buick banged its undercarriage against the pavement. Since it was a warm day all the windows were open and my grinning classmates heard my mother shout, "Gene! Don't wreck the car!" and my father snarl, "Now *why* did you do that?"

But the nightmare wasn't over yet. I had squashed the exhaust pipe, and the old Buick sputtered and died before we had gotten half a block. Dad had to get out and angrily pry it open again. I finally chugged on down the street, red-faced as a stop light, while the tirade went on, my embarrassment assuaged only by the knowledge that I had, at last, made it through college and would soon be even farther away from my oppressively dysfunctional parents.

*   *   *

For the first time I was earning a little money that I didn't have to save for college (my assistantship at UW would take care of my graduate school expenses). I decided to fulfill an eleven-year dream and learn to fly.

Tommy Reese was a calm, soft-spoken farmer (he grew corn and other grains in the fields surrounding the airport). Nothing excited him—perfect for teaching people how to handle an airplane. The trainer was a Cessna 140 equipped with a tail wheel. This meant that, when taxiing, the nose pointed toward the sky and you couldn't see where you were going; you had to tack toward your destination. Once you got up some speed you could lift the tail and finally see over the instrument panel. Occasionally (though rarely) we would begin our takeoff roll only to discover someone else taxiing down the grass runway toward us. Regardless of that little design flaw, I never saw an accident at Reese's airport.

After a few hours of takeoffs and landings ("Point the nose at the first part of the runway; if you feel nervous, wiggle your toes."), stalls, and orientation ("You can always find your way back to the airport from that little pond over there."), I was ready to solo. Before I could do that, however, I had to pass another goddamn physical. This, indeed, was one of the reasons I had taken flight lessons: I was hoping I could combine it with the entrance requirement (I had already received the medical form) at UW, and maybe not have to stand at the end of a long line, my heart pounding and skipping beats until it stopped altogether and I keeled over and died an excruciatingly slow and painful death.

The examining physician was a well-known ophthalmologist who did all the flight physicals in Muncie, or at least for the Reeses. I reasoned (and my psyche hoped) that an eye doctor might not know much about the rest of the body and would miss anything seriously wrong. Furthermore, if I just walked in without an appointment he might squeeze me in between patients for an even less careful look. By the time I arrived I was vibrating with fear and my pulse rate had surged to its absolute maximum.

It was a Wednesday afternoon. His office was closed. I had forgotten about doctors' golf days.

Oddly, on my second try, I was hardly nervous at all. Perhaps I half-expected him to be out on the links again, or maybe it was simply familiarity with the approach to his office. Happily, my assessment turned out to be essentially correct: although he examined my eyes, he barely put a stethoscope on my chest and the rest was just a question. "Anything wrong with you?" "*Nothing that I know of.*" Watching him scribe neat little marks alongside all the things he was supposed to check for the UW Health Service was one of the most joyful moments of my life. (I can still see that office with its dark wood paneling, the worn green leather chair I sat in, his little stool, the eye chart off in the distance.) I was free! I could literally fly! I probably wouldn't have to have another physical for years!

I bought a carton of cigarettes.

The solo went perfectly, as the first one usually does (the student is too utterly focused to screw it up), and was quite unforgettable, like remembering where you were when President Kennedy was shot. I did a couple more that afternoon. By the third I was already experimenting: how close can I get to the very beginning of the runway on landing? What's the bare minimum distance I need to take off? Amazingly, there was no apprehension in this faintly reckless study. It never occurred to me that I might make a silly mistake and nose down into the corn, or if my heart stopped beating in mid-flight I would be utterly doomed.

I climbed the back fence for a few more solo flights late that summer, once when Dad was in the back yard, watching. I waved as I climbed away, but I don't think he saw the gesture—at least he didn't return it. I wondered then, and still do, what he thought about my adventure. Was he pleased, proud, amazed? (Dad himself was terrified of flying.) That may have been another reason I had taken the lessons, to try to prove something to him, to obtain some kind of accolade. It never came.

Another dream was born: to fly into Reese's from a distant locale and climb over the fence to visit the folks. But that would have to wait for later . . . .

On the day before I was due to arrive in Madison I slid into my recently-acquired turquoise-and-white '54 Ford Fairlane, left Mom weeping in the driveway, and turned north. It was the end of August, 1959. I was twenty-two.

DAVID CLARK VAN MATRE
"The high and the mighty"
Selma H.S. 1,2,3,4; Class Pres. 2,3,4; Baseball 2; Track 2,3,4; Math Club 1,2,3,4; Latin Club 2,4; The Atomic Blonde 3; "Mountain House Mystery" 4; Pep Bloc 2,3; Math Contest 1,2; Reflector Staff 3,4; Retro Staff 4; Boys' State Alt. 3; Model U.N. Meeting 3,4; Purdue Legisl. Assembly 4; Essay Contest 1; Commercial Contest 3; Stunt Night 2; Quill and Scroll 4.

SHELVA JEANN MURRELL
"I laugh and the world laughs with me."
Selma H.S. 1,2,3,4; Class Treas. 3,4; F.H.A. 1,2,3,4; Math Club 1; Speech Club 1; 4-H Club 1,2; 4-H Jr. Leader 1,2; "The Atomic Blonde" 3; "Mountain House Mystery" 4; Pep Bloc 1,2,3,4; Chorus 1,2,3; Reflector Staff 3,4; Retro Staff 4; Library Staff 2; Girls' State 3; Model U.N. Meeting 3; Commercial Contest 3; Stunt Night 1,2; Quill and Scroll 3.

HARRIETT FRANCES MOORE
"A face like a doll"
Selma H.S. 1,2,3,4; Class Hist. and Reporter 1; Treas. 2; Sec. 3,4; F.H.A. 1,2,3,4; Pres. 3; Parl. 4; Math Club 1; "The Atomic Blonde" 3; "Mountain House Mystery" 4; Pep Bloc 1,2,3,4; Chorus 1,2,3; Reflector Staff 3,4; Retro Staff 4; Library Staff 1,2,3,4; Girls' State 4; Stunt Night 1,2,3; Operetta 3.

EUGENE NEWTON BREWER
"All great men are dead, and I'm not feeling well."
Selma H.S. 1,2,3,4; Class V.-Pres. 2,3,4; Stud. Council 3; Math Club 1,2,3,4; Latin Club 2,4; Speech Club 1,2; "The Atomic Blonde" 3; Pep Bloc 1,2,3,4; Latin Contest 2; Model U.N. 1,2; Purdue Legisl. Assembly 4; Commercial Contest 3; Debate 1; Stunt Night 2.

DONALD RAMON WRIGHT
"Destined to be great"
Selma H.S. 1,2,3,4; Class Treas. 1; Business Mgr. 3,4; Math Club 1,2,3,4; Latin Club 2,4; Speech Club 1,2; 4-H Club 1,2,3,4; 4-H Jr. Leader 2,3,4; "The Atomic Blonde" 3; "Mountain House Mystery" 4; Pep Bloc 1,2,3,4; Math Contest 2; Reflector Staff 3,4; Retro Staff 4; Library Staff 2; Boys' State 4; Model U.N. Meeting 1,2,3,4; Purdue Legisl. Assembly 1,2,4; Band 1; Stud. Mgr. 1; Debate 1,2; Stunt Night 1,2; Quill and Scroll.

SYLVIA CAROL RUPE
"The look of angel"
Selma H.S. 1,2,3,4; Class Hist. 3,4; Reporter 4; F.H.A. 1,2,3,4; Math Club 1,2,3,4; Latin Club 2,4; Speech Club 1; "Mountain House Mystery" 4; Pep Bloc 1,2,3,4; Reflector Staff 4; Retro Staff 4; Library Staff 4; Stunt Night 2,3.

First Thought of Leaving

Don't get the wrong idea! The man is not measuring Duane Jump and Bob Shady for halos. He is measuring them for their graduation caps and gowns.

Selma High School, 1955 yearbook

Top: SHS, class of '55
Middle: Al McDonald and I, surrounded by the two Chucks, in Florida
Bottom left: college graduate
Bottom right: Al Ehrhart in the lab at UW

A HIGHER DEGREE

Except for a post-doctoral fellow from India, Laboratory 170 was dark and deserted when I showed up (it was a Sunday night). I introduced myself and was assured, in a lovely sing-songy way, that Dr. Strong would be in his office the next morning at eight o'clock. After taking in the layout (much like the organic chemistry lab at DPU), I went to look for a motel. Somewhere on the other side of town I found some pizza, and bedded down in a Holiday Inn. Didn't sleep much, though: it was a night to reflect, to anticipate.

My new mentor, Frank Strong, was quite a handsome man, trim, early sixties, black hair streaked with gray. He was already at his desk when I came into his office, just off the lab. He welcomed me with a big, white smile, got out a yellow pad, asked me some questions, e.g., what were my final semester's grades (5A's, 1B), and jotted down the information.

A natural-products chemist, Frank's forte was isolating and characterizing certain compounds, such as antibiotics, from a wide variety of plant and microbial sources. He suggested a couple of research avenues, but he obviously wanted me to work on a hoof disease in cattle (the Biochemistry Department at UW was in the School of Agriculture, which was heavily favored by the dairy industry and the state legislature).

"Fescue foot," brought about by the cows' consuming fescue hay, caused their hooves to rot, making it very difficult for the animals to walk. My master's project (required at UW to enter the Ph.D. program) would be to identify the causative agent (Frank thought it might be a boron-containing compound). Not exactly anthrax or cholera, but at least it was science!

After I agreed to take on the problem we talked a little about the courses I might, or was required, to take. Then he took me into the lab to introduce me to my fellow students. That was essentially the last I saw of him for the next half-decade.

Frank taught a couple of courses (which his graduate students assisted with, thereby earning our "assistantships"). Otherwise he spent the bulk of his time preparing lectures or writing reports or reviewing other scientists' papers for publication in one or another journal. Astonishingly self-disciplined, he arrived in the lab five days a week at precisely 8:00 A.M. and departed at 5:00 P.M. sharp. He left at noon for lunch, and reappeared exactly at one o'clock. He seemed to pay little attention to *our* work habits, however, figuring, I suppose, that we all had a college degree and the sense to do enough work to get out of there in the minimum possible time. Of course, if we had a problem or question about our research or courses, we could go in and talk to him. Because of my father's unwanted interference with my birdhouses and soapbox racers, however, I preferred to work out any such difficulties on my own. That seemed to be okay with Frank, too.

The laboratory housed eight graduate students, a couple of post-doctoral fellows, and one research associate who had been with him for years. I hit it off right away with most of them. They were a nice bunch of guys, especially the one whose desk faced mine (with a partition between us), and Al Ehrhart and I have been friends to this day. Unfortunately, he was so calm, gentle, and wise that everyone else in the lab spent considerable time hanging around his desk. Consequently he didn't get much work done during the day, nor, by association, did I.

One of the first requirements I needed to fulfill for a chemistry minor was the identification of the constituents of an unknown mixture, just as I had done in Howard Burkett's qualitative organic course. Though it wasn't an unusually difficult assignment, I came down with the equivalent of writer's block. After all those years of preparation for a scientific career, it must have occurred to me that now, finally, I had to defecate or get off the commode. It was an epiphany of sorts, one of those rare moments when you can see your whole life as a pine board, and you're a little ball accelerating down it. Regardless of the cause for my malaise, I fiddled with my unknown mix every morning, started reading the novels of James Michener and Irving Stone and Kyle Onstott in the afternoons while listening to *Scheherazade* and *Kismet*, and hardly ever appeared in Lab 170.

I roomed in an undergraduate dorm with a heavy-smoking freshman, and I awoke every morning to the guttural music of deep inhalations. A typical breakfast (I usually got up too late for the dining room) during those first weeks was a couple of crullers (called "long johns" in Wisconsin) and cereal with half milk and half half-and-half. When I made a rare appearance in the lab one day, Frank unexpectedly came out to ask me how things were going. I think he may have been concerned that something was wrong with me (one of my peers may have reported my weight gain and frequent absence). In any case I took it as a gentle kick in the ass, and from then on I was fine. I finished the unknown mixture in short order and got busy figuring out what might cause fescue foot.

I spent most of my time those first few months in the nearby College of Agriculture library reading whatever I could find about the disease, about hay, and about boron chemistry—getting organized, feeling my way. It was dusty in the stacks, and I sneezed a lot. But the not unpleasant odor soon became familiar, and I began to associate it with old books and warmth and quiet. Whenever I encounter a similar fragrance I find myself back in the Ag library among those old, moldy tomes.

I took notes on IBM cards, a system commonly used at the time. The cards had a string of holes punched all around the periphery. For each subject, one cut a channel to the appropriate hole, and by inserting a stiff wire through that opening in the entire stack of note cards, could retrieve his personal information on that topic. A primitive computer to be sure, but it worked quite well enough.

Thanks, perhaps, to Frank's laissez-faire policy, it was a laid-back group, with nearly perfect attendance at morning and afternoon coffee breaks. After lunch we played touch football on the little lawn in back of the building until the hard Wisconsin winter set in, and then it was bridge (I had never played before, and learned by doing it). We rarely discussed our various science projects—the talk was mostly about sports and politics.

Although I had gone to a conservative college and was a member of its "Young Republicans," I didn't much care, really, who was running the government as long as I could pursue my career unhindered. After a few weeks with my new mates, however, I discovered that even that selfish objective might depend on the whim of the government in power. I argued with Al and the others in the lab (I was in the minority) about my vision of democracy, asserting that if every citizen voted for his own needs, everything would work out best for the majority. Even though I was sympathetic to the plights of the underprivileged and downtrodden, I wasn't convinced that racial integration, social security, welfare, and other social programs could only have been implemented by people who voted for the well-being of the citizenry as a whole, rather than their own. But I was hearing, probably for the first time, that side of the issue. (I remembered my father's bemoaning the fact that colleges were infiltrated with communists. I don't know where he got that idea, but I was learning that the truth was just the opposite: smart people brought together discuss ideas, such as whether democracy works for the common good, and if not, is there something better? Some of these are bound to become communists.)

On the way back from Thanksgiving vacation that first year (there was train service to Muncie then) I spotted a lovely undergraduate studying a French book. I asked for permission to sit beside her and we struck up a conversation. By the time we got back to UW I liked her a lot, especially her sense of humor and the way she ended an amusing observation by forcing out the last few words as she segued into a laugh. I think the feeling was mutual; in any case, when I asked for her phone number she readily gave it to me.

Not long afterward there was a Christmas party at the apartment of one of my fellow biochem majors. My new girlfriend agreed to come with me. The central feature of this celebration was a huge punchbowl filled with a mixture of grapefruit juice and lab-made gin (one of the vacuum hoods had been occupied for weeks with the distillation apparatus), heavy on the latter. Although I had never tasted a genuine adult beverage for fear it would make me violently sick or pass out and choke to death on my own vomit, I didn't want my date to think I was a wimp. I swallowed the first slug incorrectly and coughed for several minutes, unable to breathe or get the tightness out of my throat. When I was finally able to speak again, I made a remark about grapefruit juice having that effect on some people. Betsy, who didn't drink either (probably not for the same reason), smiled sympathetically.

We had a couple of other fun times, but whenever I took her back to her dorm she ran inside with a quick "goodnight." I was both disappointed and mystified—I was almost certain she was "the one." On our last date (a UW basketball game—we were sitting alone, high up in the rafters), she decided to tell me that she was engaged to some guy in the army. Stunned and hurt, I managed to wish her a good life, or some such inanity. I didn't see much of the game.

On the way back to her dorm she bemoaned the fact that we couldn't just be friends. But for young men it doesn't usually work that way. She was the first girl I really *wanted*. Horniness aside, I was looking for a mate, and being with her would have been a frustrating experience (unfortunately, it didn't occur to me to ask her to fix me up with one or two of her dormmates). It took me a while to get over that almost-relationship, but the memory gradually faded. Like the background microwave radiation, though, it never entirely disappeared, and I still occasionally wonder what if—?

Back to fescue foot: it had been reported that fescue hay contained a significant amount of boron, and there was a suspicion that a boron-containing substance might have been the causative factor. My job was to isolate and characterize it. This meant, first, extracting the pleasant-smelling feed with something that dissolved the alleged compound. In this case, I discovered that hot water removed virtually all the boron from the hay. The only thing left to do, then, was to separate the boron compound from the thousands of other constituents in the "tea," and chemically identify the pure toxin.

The second requirement was to find a method for determining the amount of boron in various fractions of the extract. This turned out to be simple enough: evaporate down the sample and bake it or the insoluble residue in an oven until dry. The final step was to dissolve the test material (after adding a color-producing reagent) in ethyl alcohol. Any boron in the sample would turn orange when the ethanol was added, and the deeper the color, the more boron there was. This intensity was determined using a colorimeter, which measured the amount of light at a certain wavelength passing through the liquid in the tubes.

Once I had mastered this technique, the rest of the project became a matter of separating, from everything else, whatever boron-containing compounds were present in the aqueous extract. This is where the science began: What procedures, out of dozens that were available (distilling off some of the impurities; extracting with various water-immiscible solvents; precipitating with certain reagents; column, paper, or thin-layer chromatography; etc.), would best separate the active material from the rest of the compounds in the soup; what additional procedures, and in what order, would further enrich the boron-containing substance; and so on until the active compound finally came out perfectly pure, preferably as a crystalline solid. And, once it was purified, how to chemically identify it and determine whether it would cause fescue foot in cattle. It was a time-consuming process.

My first winter in Wisconsin was a miserable experience. It was always freezing cold. One night the mercury got down to -30F. I walked to the lab the following morning through a Bernoulli wind tunnel created by the peculiar alignment of two adjacent buildings. The wind chill temperature must have been fifty below. By the time I got to my desk I was lightheaded and dizzy. I was sure I had frozen my brain. After a few minutes I felt better, but I never took that route again, not in the middle of winter. By the following year, however, I had become acclimatized and could go outside without serious discomfort, despite the temperature. But I never really learned to enjoy the frigid weather.

That spring (1960) there came political awakening for many Americans, including me. Gary Francis Powers, flying a spy plane called a U-2, was shot down over the U.S.S.R. Eisenhower denied the flights until world pressure forced him to admit them. Avuncular Ike? Like most people I trusted the president; it was a shock to learn that he was a liar, regardless of how noble his motives might have been. What else had he lied about? And since he was at the top of the pyramid, what could anyone believe from anyone else in government?

In the summer I moved out of the dorm and into a house with two other guys, both chemistry majors. We took turns being "cook of the week." Our goal was to shop for and prepare dinners featuring cheap fried meat and canned vegetables for a total of $10.50/week for the three of us. To my knowledge, no one ever went over budget. Awful food, but none of us could afford better, and we had two weeks off out of every three. Whoever was around on Friday nights watched *Route 66* and *Rawhide*. The rest of the time, except for necessary chores (like visiting the laundromat), we were in our respective laboratories.

Still, I played softball (pitcher) on a pickup team, as well as the aforementioned bridge at nearly every lunch hour. One evening my partner and I entered a tournament. We didn't win, but neither did we finish last. The most vivid memory I have of that night, though, was of coming home from that small game room fogged with cigarette smoke (some of which was mine) and being kept up all night with heart palpitations. None of the usual tricks helped: deep breathing, coughing, etc. I was sure I would be dead by morning. When I wasn't, I vowed to cut down on the damn things, and I did for a while. But I still couldn't quit.

That fall I went to the Student Union for a beer and watched the first Kennedy-Nixon debate. The vice-president seemed almost baffled at times, and his sweaty upper lip made him look so pathetic that I decided to vote for him—otherwise I was afraid he wouldn't get a single one. (Nixon, it was reported later, was suffering from a painful, swollen, possibly infected, knee injury at the time.) I also went out to Truax

Field to see him fly in for a speech, which was forcefully delivered, but the most impressive part of the visit was watching his campaign plane use every inch of the short runway to take off after it was over. Kennedy won, but the election was a very close one.

For the next year I tried almost every procedure available for separating the putative toxic boron compound from all the others that might be present in the original extract, but the answer was always the same: the only boron-containing substance present in fescue hay was boric acid, the same thing you find in certain laundry detergents.

Although disappointed not to have found any new and interesting compounds (as was Frank Strong and the legislature, no doubt), they would have had nothing to do with fescue foot, which is now known to be caused by a mold toxin, ergovaline, a peptide containing lysergic acid and the amino acids alanine, valine, and proline. But I had accomplished my objective and the work earned me a master's degree, which was certainly of importance to me, if not to Wisconsin farmers, and it was on to the Ph.D. and another attempt to isolate and characterize a natural product, this time from the slime mold, *Physarum polycephalum*.

Physarum sometimes behaves like an ameba (an animal), other times like a plant, producing spores when conditions (e.g., weather) are harsh. These, like seeds, can survive almost anything. When conditions improve, they germinate back into the yellow-orange blobs that often grow on tree stumps and the like. Occasionally you will hear that someone has called the police because an "alien creature" has appeared in her yard. As often as not, this unearthly visitor will turn out to be a slime mold.

The unusual characteristic of these organisms that makes them useful for researching cellular division—all organisms are made of cells, which divide to produce growth—is that there are no walls separating their nuclei (the little spheres inside cells where most of the DNA resides). Unlike a culture of, say, liver cells, all the slime mold nuclei divide at the same time (like observing Saturn through a telescope lens, it's quite a striking phenomenon to behold). Thus, whatever factors might control the division process can be isolated, at any point in the cycle, from a large amount of material, as opposed to a tiny individual cell.

As a graduate student in a natural products laboratory, however, my job was not to study the division process—that would come later—but to isolate and characterize the pigments that made the organism yellow-orange (it was thought that these compounds, by reacting to light of certain wavelengths, might have something to do with sporulation). I was the third person in Frank's lab to tackle this project. The first, a student whose desk I now occupied, had gotten almost nowhere. The second was a Japanese post-doctoral fellow who isolated a red pigment from *Physarum* but was unable to completely purify or identify it.

Laboratory cultures of the organism are usually grown in 500-ml. Erlenmeyer "shake" flasks, each of which produced only a miniscule amount of pigment. I managed to scale this up to 15-liter stir jars, but only with the addition of an anti-foam agent—the organism was apparently sensitive to the agitation of the culture medium by the propeller blades used to stir oxygen into it, perhaps by becoming desiccated after being carried to the surface by the rising bubbles. Better, but still not enough material from which to extract enough pigment to work with.

I scaled the production up to 50-gallon tanks. After three such runs I had sufficient material for my Ph.D. project, as well as my first scientific paper (noteworthy only for the discovery that the anti-foam agent made such large-scale growth possible). Once I had separated the "mold" from the broth and extracted the organism with aqueous acetone, I had three or four carboys (5-gallon bottles) of a deep yellow-orange extract to work with. I stored them in the cold room and retrieved some of the liquid as needed.

During this work I assisted Frank in teaching his biochemistry laboratory course for non-majors, mostly home economics and nursing students. I managed to get a few dates out of that, but nothing much came of them. One of the farm girls, whose hands were like sandpaper, asked me after some fooling around, "Now do I get an 'A'?" The smartest and prettiest one, unfortunately, wouldn't go out with me at all (she got the "A"). Nor would a lovely fellow graduate student, who, I later discovered, already had a boyfriend (she later married him). This revelation was beginning to sound a bit too familiar; I was seriously beginning to wonder if I would ever find someone to share my life with, or whether all the best girls (women) were already taken.

One day I walked into the lab and announced that I had formulated "The Brewer Uncertainty Principle." It had occurred to me that it would never be possible to travel back in time. If it were, there would be future beings around, and where were they? (I was gratified to learn that, much later, Stephen Hawking had come up with the same idea, though it was probably not original with either of us). It was at about this time that I ground my first 6-inch telescope mirror. Unfortunately, I calculated the focal point incorrectly, became discouraged, and never finished it (it would have meant re-grinding it, for one thing, and I might as well have started over—which I did, but not for more than a decade).

But the highlight of that year (1961) was the departmental Christmas show, in which I volunteered to do a stand-up comedy monolog. There were several hundred faculty and students in the big lecture hall, more than can be accommodated by some New York theaters. The premise: I was a lab instructor in Prof. Strong's biochemistry course for non-majors, giving instructions to the students about how to prepare for the morning's work. I can remember virtually all of that routine, written by me and the other denizens of Lab 170. For example, instructor: "This experiment is to test the ability of saliva to digest a complex carbohydrate." (Repeating student's question): "Where do we get the saliva?" (laughter) "We order it in ten-gallon drums . . ." (pause for laughter to die down) "We have this little old lady in Madison who does nothing else all day but—" (interruption by uproarious laughter). All the giggling and guffawing was hugely rewarding, as was the loud applause at the end of the routine. Okay, so it was an easy audience and it wasn't exactly Bob Newhart. But when I got back to my seat, one of my neighbors shouted, over the noise, "You missed your calling, Gene!" Unfortunately, it didn't occur to me at the time that she might have been right.

In the summer of 1962 I met my wife.

I had begun to study for the "preliminary" exam (a last chance for the faculty to throw out any student who doesn't seem worthy of pursuing a doctoral degree). The test was oral and comprehensive: any topic—methodologies, current research in any number of related fields, various biological processes, historical facts— might be brought up. I didn't know much about the relatively new and exciting fields of cellular and molecular biology (Watson and Crick had deduced the structure of DNA less than a decade earlier), so I began to spend a fair amount of time in the Medical School (rather than the Agriculture) library to familiarize myself with these disciplines.

In the evenings there was often a pretty undergraduate behind the circulation desk—dark blonde, blue-eyed, a beautiful smile, and the best legs I've ever seen (they're still quite wonderful at sixty-plus). I didn't have enough nerve to ask her out right away, but I showed up every night requesting a certain reserved book (a reference tome kept behind the desk so it would always be available), which I opened and never read. Fortunately, there was another lab party, and I finally asked her to go with me. She turned around to see who I was talking to, apparently not believing I would be asking her for a date. I think I began to fall in love with her at that moment. (On the other hand, maybe she was *hoping* there was someone else behind her.)

We went to the party—by then I was able to drink the lab gin without choking— and on to Lake Monona for the Fourth of July (my birthday; I was twenty-five) fireworks. We had two or three more dates, usually movies like the powerful *Judgement at Nuremburg* and *The Miracle Worker*, a few nice kisses and caresses, and she invited me over to meet her family, who lived in Madison. When she introduced me to her father, a university plumber known to everyone as "Lefty," he laughed in my face, perhaps because he instinctively realized that I might be a suitable partner for his nineteen-year-old daughter. I loved her mother, a kind of citified Aunt Mae. Everything seemed to be falling into place.

Then she told me she had a boyfriend. She liked me, but had thought carefully about the situation and decided we shouldn't see each other any more . . . .

I was devastated. Living in a nightmare where the wolves were endless boyfriends peering around every corner. I couldn't get her out of my mind. This time I wasn't going to give up so easily. Amazed at my own temerity, I showed up at the library and asked her who he was and where he lived—I was going to settle the matter with him. To my greater amazement, she said that wouldn't be necessary, she would talk to him. In another three months we were engaged, and the wedding was set for the following June.

For a few horrible days in August, however, it seemed that 1963 might never come. I was in the grocery store with my $10.50 shopping for liver and canned purple plums when I heard that President Kennedy had set up a naval blockade to prevent the Soviet Union from bringing missile parts into Cuba. It was a dangerous, potentially catastrophic gamble, but in the end Secretary Krushchev kept a surprisingly (given his unpredictable antics at other times) cool head and Armageddon was postponed for a while.

We did everything together that fall and winter. Karen was enrolled in a liberal arts program with a major in Asian Studies. I sat in on two of her courses—classical music and renaissance art. Since I knew little about either, these were eye-opening adventures, visits to worlds I might not otherwise have known existed.

When the weather was warm we ate lunches from paper bags on a hill overlooking Lake Mendota. In the winter we sat on a bench in the Historical Society Museum gazing at the dioramas. We never seemed to run out of things to talk about. Like most of my laboratory colleagues she was a Democrat. It seemed to me that I had been asleep all my life and was just beginning to wake up.

On another front, this was the year that the devastating effects of Thalidomide on embryonic development was discovered. As a budding biochemist thinking about a career in medical research, I was bewildered and disturbed by this revelation. How could this happen? Hadn't the drug been thoroughly tested before it was approved for clinical use? I stored the information away for further contemplation at a later date.

In the spring of 1963 I took a few weeks off from my research to cram for the preliminary exam. Night after night I stayed in the lab, my feet on my desk, reading papers and texts while listening to my favorite soft pop/jazz music program hosted by "Papa Hambone," who always ended his show at some late hour with: "And that's how the world ends—not with a bang, but with a whimper . . . ."

I managed to pass the oral exam and went back to the *Physarum* extracts. When I returned to the cold room I discovered that some white crystals had formed in the bottom of the carboys. This had nothing to do with the pigments, but, curious, I spent some time filtering them out and identifying them. They turned out to be a steroid, much like cholesterol, but one which hadn't been reported before. It was the first (and last) time I had obtained, in pure form, a naturally-occurring substance. What the stuff did for the organism I hadn't a clue.

It was during this time also that Karen and I began to prepare for our upcoming wedding. One afternoon I accompanied her to her doctor's office for her regular physical (and a supply of birth-control pills). She wanted me to meet the family physician, but when she brought him out after the exam, I was long gone. Ostensibly I had decided to save time by looking at some shoes while she was in his office. The truth was that I didn't want to meet him, or anyone else wearing a stethoscope, for fear that he would ask me to come in for my own checkup.

Karen was quite upset by my erratic behavior. But the fear was so intense that it overcame even my love and trust for her (I gradually filled her in, of course, after we were married).

Fortunately, her confusion and anger were relieved somewhat by the return to the shoe store, where Nunnbush footwear filled every shelf, and no other brands were in evidence. When the salesman finally came over and opened with, "Something in a Nunnbush?" we both burst out laughing.

Karen and her family were Presbyterians who attended church regularly. Her mother, Charlotte, in fact, was church secretary, and Lefty, an elder. Her brother Gary was a theology student who later became a minister. Having little choice, I went to church with them. Though I was uncomfortable with that, the situation was eased by the wonderful Sunday dinners afterward, often followed by a Green Bay Packers game on the downstairs television set. The churchgoing ended after we were married (and living on the other side of town), but the dinners and football (and the week's laundry) continued until we left Madison almost four years later.

Her grandmother, incidentally, owned a rural tavern not far from the city. Whenever we came for a visit, she would greet us with a cheerful, "Can Grandma buy you a drink?" Some day I hope to use that line in a novel.

In April I invited Karen home to meet my folks (she stayed with my sister, who was married by then). Dad tried to impress her with his humor and endless chatter, with little success. My siblings liked her. Mom, who called her "Cairn," stayed out of the way. We visited Mae and Lester, too, and a couple of other aunts and uncles, as well as some of her mother's family, who, amazingly, lived just down the pike in Albany (Charlotte had been born there).

We were married on June 22, 1963. Mom and Dad came (by bus) for the ceremony, the first time either of them had been out of Indiana. We honeymooned for a week on Oxbow Lake in Northern Wisconsin, where we proceeded, stupidly enough, to become thoroughly sunburned the first day. For the first time, sex was uninhibited by fears of someone's stumbling upon us. However, as it later turned out to be on K-PAX, it was a very painful experience.

We settled in upstairs at 153 Ohio Avenue; the lower floor was occupied by the landlord's brother, who was endowed with a loud, chronic cough. Karen was a good cook (she learned from her mother), but if she or I needed to stay late—she was still working part-time at the Medical Library—we usually ate at Rennebohm's, the campus drugstore, where we could get a turkey dinner for ninety-nine cents each. Since the rent took most of our income, these ultra-cheap meals were a windfall, many times saving us from exhaustion or hunger, as they did, no doubt, for countless other UW students of the time.

That year also, a Buddhist-led military coup overthrew the South Vietnam government. The U.S., under President Kennedy, sent economic and military aid . . . .

Top left: Little Karen
Top right: the Schultz family at Christmas
Middle: Feeding the pigeons
Bottom: Karen the librarian

Engagement and wedding. Al is at far right.

Back in the laboratory, I discovered how frustrating a thesis project can be. Sometimes you're lucky, and good things happen (like the sterol that precipitated from the *Physarum* extracts), and other times you're not so fortunate. While grappling with the intractable pigment problem, I came back from the library one Friday afternoon in November to find everyone grouped around the only radio in the lab. President Kennedy had been shot in Dallas, and the outlook was grim. In case I hadn't heard,

Karen came over to tell me about it, and we left early for her parents' house, where we hovered around the TV set for three days. Gordon, especially, was openly moved by the caisson carrying the body of JFK, his little son saluting him, a riderless horse trailing behind the funeral procession.

By this time I had become a solid Democrat, if not yet a liberal. On the other hand, it seemed to me that neither party was even nominally concerned about one of the most catastrophic problems facing all of us: the seemingly never-ending increase in the Earth's human population. Not long after we were married, the government of Japan (which was already stuffed with people) encouraged a population *increase* in order for that country to maintain its rapidly-growing economy. I don't believe any decision handed down by any public official anywhere in the world has been more short-sighted (although a couple of more recent actions by the U.S. government are strong competitors). I began to wonder if anyone was concerned about the well-being of our planet as a whole, rather than merely his own country, or even his family. In any case, this is one of the reasons Karen and I never had any children: we didn't want to add to an already serious problem. Though we've undoubtedly missed many joys (and heartaches) over the years, we still think it was the right decision.

To summarize the two and a half years of Ph.D. research: 1) The red pigment found by Dr. Kuraishi turned out to be an artifact which only appeared when the extracts were dried, probably by exposure to the air; 2) There were two naturally-occurring (unoxidized) pigments, neither of which I could completely purify (they were oily substances, rather than crystallizable solids). But I was able to identify both as polyene compounds, long-chain carbon molecules connected by alternating single and double bonds; 3) One of these possessed some antibacterial activity, but not enough to warrant further study; 4) By subjecting the red artifact to hydrogenation I was able to produce a crystalline material that probably could have been identified, thereby providing a more detailed characterization of the two natural pigments. Perhaps I should have stayed in Frank's laboratory another few months to do that. But I had been a graduate student for five years, about average for a doctorate in biochemistry at UW, and was ready to move on. It was August, 1964, the same month that a U.S. Navy destroyer was allegedly attacked by North Vietnamese PT boats in the Gulf of Tonkin. President Johnson ordered immediate retaliation, and was granted nearly absolute authority by the Congress to wage war against that country.

I wasn't paying much attention. At long last, I was a scientist.

PAPA RUSCH

When I successfully defended my doctoral thesis, Karen, my wife of one year, was still an undergraduate student. Rather than apply to another university (I'd had an inquiry from Cal Tech), I sought out a post-doctoral position with Harold P. Rusch, director of the Department of Oncology (and friend of Secretary of Defense Melvin Laird), who had initiated the interest in slime mold research a few years earlier and whose lab supplied the *Physarum* I had used for my own studies. I spoke with him in his cramped little office in the Medical School, where we mutually agreed that my joining his group could be beneficial for both of us. The pay was low (around $7000 a year, as I remember), but much higher than I was getting as a graduate research assistant. I took the job.

But there were a couple of problems. Rusch didn't want me to start until October, when the new McArdle Laboratory for Cancer Research would be ready for occupation. I could live with that two-month postponement, but the other was far more significant: I had received a notice from the draft board advising that, unless I were able to continue my deferred status, I would have to come in for a physical. This shocking and unexpected development was quite alarming for me, as it undoubtedly was for thousands of other young men. I was terrified of going in for the exam, of course, but, beyond that horror, I wasn't eager to interrupt a lifelong dream for an indeterminate period of combat, or worse, even if I passed it.

After the notice came I started to pay more attention to the war itself and U.S. policy toward Vietnam and other Asian countries. I certainly didn't want to kill anyone or die in a swamp on the other side of the world to prop up an incompetent, and probably corrupt, dictator, even if my government assured me it was a good idea; after the U-2 incident I no longer believed the President and his advisors were necessarily telling the truth about the dangers of a putative communist overrun. On the other hand, if I could postpone military service a little longer, the goddamn war might be over by the time I was called up.

Fortunately, there was a dean who specialized in this sort of thing. I went to see him, hoping to get an extended deferment letter so I could continue my training as a scientist, which would be of greater benefit to the country, I presumed, than serving as a foot soldier in the war.

"Do you think your post-doctoral training should get you a deferment?" he inquired. "Or is it the work you'll be doing in the lab that qualifies you?"

Figuring that post-doctoral training was much like being an advanced student, I responded, "Oh, it's the training." I could see on his face immediately that this was the wrong answer; it was only the valuable *research* a man would be doing that would justify his escaping the swamps and jungles of Asia. Before he could respond, I added, "But it's really both. There are actually two reasons for my deferment." This feeble comeback generated a sad, knowing smile, a nod, and a piece of paper stating that, as a young scientist, I was too valuable to the country to end up as cannon fodder in Vietnam.

But would this assessment of my great worth hold water in Muncie, Indiana? For the next few weeks I passionately dreaded coming home at night and looking in the mailbox. When I found nothing from the draft board I could breathe again until the next evening. Saturdays were wonderful: no more mail for two whole days!

An envelope finally came. I stared at it for a long while before opening it and reading, "Please be advise [sic] that we are presently not calling up men who have reached their twenty-sixth birthday . . ." I was already twenty-seven! I hadn't even needed the damn deferment!

It's difficult to convey how good I felt about escaping the physical exam and, of course, the war itself, but my elation was tempered by continuing reports of men like me who had been shipped to Southeast Asia, only to return in pieces, for no legitimate or well-considered reason. If the war ultimately accomplished anything, it was to make many of my generation even more suspicious of government claims of danger abroad. Along with many others, I thought American involvement in a Vietnam-type war would never happen again, that no future President would be stupid enough to make the same mistake Lyndon Johnson did.

I puttered around in Frank's lab for a month or two, and read all the papers that had come out of Rusch's group, as well as books and reports describing the latest advances in DNA replication and cell division. I began to think of myself as a molecular biologist, rather than a biochemist. There was a certain cachet to the former title. Molecular biology was just beginning to assert itself and integrate the disciplines of biochemistry and medicine. It was an exciting time and I was thrilled to be coming on board. Finally, in October, I was able to get into the new building, a strange white cube with Egyptian markings around the top and excrescences everywhere else, which, I believe, represented the chaos of scientific research. To many in the community, however, it was simply the ugliest building on the campus, if not the world.

I spent the rest of the autumn in the library. Not because I was trying to avoid facing up to my responsibilities (possible failure?), as I was five years earlier, but because I realized I still knew so little about the intricacies of basic biological processes. I wasn't even fully conversant with the fundamentals and terminology. I remember asking once, in the group's weekly research meeting, something about bacterial mitochondria, only to be stared at with the retort: "Bacteria don't *have* mitochondria."

I may have been a molecular biologist, but it was a completely different world of macromolecules and their organization. Like any new language, however, it became more and more familiar with time and practice, and by the end of the year I was beginning to feel far more comfortable in my new surroundings.

Known as "Papa" Rusch by those toiling in his laboratory, Harold was an enigma. No one could figure out how he got to be head of a prestigious institution such as the McArdle Laboratory. He didn't appear to be particularly bright (perhaps even stupid sometimes), and seemed to understand only vaguely what our discussions were about. We figured he had been "kicked upstairs," where he did the dirty administrative work without wasting too much money in research. If so, that may have backfired. Since he controlled the available funds, he had one of the biggest groups in the building.

Yet, he comprehended the bigger picture of our endeavors, and occasionally came up with a penetrating question. On the other hand, he didn't care what you did with his pet organism as long as you got results and published them (his name went on all the papers). For me it was a perfect situation. For the first time, I could follow my interests wherever they might take me.

My work at McArdle was greatly enhanced by interaction with a number of other post-doctoral fellows and research associates, and with the permanent faculty itself, which included some of the brightest stars in the fields of molecular biology and cancer research: Howard Temin, Van Potter, Charlie Heidelberger, and many others, one of whom was Waclaw Szybalski, who seemed intimidating and unknowable. My father-in-law, who spent a fair amount of time among the pipes and fixtures of the medical facilities, fully agreed with that assessment. Whenever we discussed the people at McArdle he would advise me to "watch out for Szybalski!" Karen and I never learned what we were supposed to watch out *for*, but it became an inside joke between us (if we weren't sure of someone's motives, we would say, "Watch out for Szybalski!"). Nevertheless, I watched out for him, and was not a little chagrined to observe that Waclaw himself appeared to be completely indifferent to my calculated avoidance.

I hadn't been at McArdle long before I got a notice to come in for a staff physical, a horror I thought I had escaped by outliving the draft. This soon became my primary research project, i.e., trying to figure out some way to avoid it. I discovered that faculty members (and other employees) didn't have to take such exams if they were also enrolled as students, who had already fulfilled their own requirements. I signed up for a course in microscopy, which I badly needed to master anyway, and when the departmental secretary called to remind me that I hadn't yet come in for the exam, I was able to tell her truthfully that I was a student as well as a post-doc, and the obligation was already fulfilled (albeit five years earlier). It may have been the first and only time this situation had ever arisen at the University of Wisconsin, but, fortunately, she bought it.

Not long afterward I quit smoking and have never touched a cigarette since. The balance was tipped not by a particularly severe pulse irregularity but by a lecture in which slides of the lungs of smokers and non-smokers were flashed onto a big screen. Even though I was thoroughly addicted to nicotine, the pictures of the smokers' lungs, even the ones without cancerous growths, were so grotesque that I went home and threw out every shred of tobacco I had. I noticed right away that my occasional heart palpitations decreased in frequency and intensity. So, at the beginning of the New Year, free of nicotine addiction and with temporarily reduced medical concerns, I relaxed and settled into (I hoped) an exciting and promising post-doctoral career studying the control mechanisms for DNA replication and nuclear/cell division.

When a cell divides, there is a period of time (G1 period) in each of the "daughter" cells when they prepare to reproduce their DNA, followed by DNA replication itself (S period). After that process is completed there is a second "gap" (G2 period) when the cells prepare to divide again. In *Physarum*, Rusch's group had shown that DNA synthesis began immediately after mitosis (nuclear division)—i.e., there was no G1 period. My first project was to determine whether the same pattern would be found in isolated nuclei. If so, the study of DNA replication would be greatly simplified because it could be carried out without the complicating presence of all the substances present in the cell's cytoplasm. This turned out to be precisely the case, and I was able to get the results to the Federation of American Societies for Experimental Biology in time for presentation at its annual meeting in April, 1965 (my first paper from Rusch's lab, further describing the apparent authenticity of DNA synthesis *in vitro*, came out later that year).

Since there were several of Rusch's post-docs going to this meeting, we drove, stopping overnight in Cleveland, where I visited my graduate student friend Al Ehrhart (then at the Cleveland Clinic), and his family. At the time there was one other group actively engaged in DNA research using *Physarum*, several members of Oddvar Nygaard's Division of Radiation Biology at Case Western University. In addition to these colleagues, the UW group was privileged to meet one of the foremost researchers in the field of cell division, Ron Rustad, famous for his brilliant studies on a protozoan, *Tetrahymena pyriformis*. Surprisingly youngish, he was a chain-smoker, and his tiny (I thought) office and lab were dense with smoke. I listened intently and said nothing. Ron was one of only two geniuses I have met during my lifetime, the other being current friend Newton R. Bowles, still active with UNICEF at the age of eighty-nine.

Atlantic City was a thrilling experience for me. For one thing, it was only my second look (after the DPU spring trip to Daytona Beach) at the huge, restlessly noisy Atlantic Ocean. Secondly, I discovered that the Monopoly game board was based on the streets leading off the endless boardwalk along the beach. The exhibition hall itself (where book and instrument vendors hawked their wares) was the size of a blimp hangar. There were dozens of meetings and presentations taking place simultaneously there and in several hotels along the boardwalk. I went to as many as possible, trying to learn everything I could.

I returned to the laboratory with great enthusiasm and determination. Eager to become familiar with all aspects of molecular biology, I engaged in a variety of projects, some of which led to something, some not, though I continued to work on DNA replication *in vitro* for the duration of my stay at McArdle and, indeed, for the remainder of my career as a molecular biologist.

One such project was a study (with Joe Cummins) of the need for protein synthesis nearly up to the time of mitosis; i.e., those proteins required for the formation of the mitotic apparatus are made immediately before they are incorporated into the physical structures which allow nuclear division to proceed. Without these structures, this beautiful and necessary process can't happen. Others involved the effects of certain compounds (methylglyoxal, spermine) on DNA synthesis *in vitro*, and the demonstration that isolated mitochondria are also capable of DNA replication.

I followed these up with a study of RNA synthesis throughout the mitotic cycle in isolated nuclei. Again, the same pattern was obtained (a peak of RNA production in S-phase, another in G2) as had been found in the intact organism. I reported this the following spring (1966) at the annual FASEB meetings in Atlantic City. This time I was allowed to go by air. It was my first commercial flight and I was amazed to discover, once on the runway, that I was afraid to fly! When the wheels banged up into the wings I jumped in my seat, certain that something had broken. Every ding and rattle was frightening. Oddly, I had experienced no such terror when I was flying myself a few years earlier. I concluded that I trusted my own skills, but not those of the professional airline pilots! Perhaps it wasn't dying I was afraid of so much as being powerless to do anything about it. Was it the loss of control that terrified me? If I had needed hernia surgery, I might not have feared it as long as I could have done it myself.

The paper was titled, "Nucleic Acid Synthesis by Isolated Nuclei in the Mitotic Cycle of *Physarum polychephalum*," in which I showed that the requirements (Mg++ concentration, etc.) for maximum RNA synthesis in nuclei isolated during the S-phase were different from those isolated during G2. Since the newly-synthesized RNAs are of different types at the two phases of the cell cycle, this finding seemed to be of some importance, at least to me. On the other hand, I had no idea what its significance might be to the organism.

The return flight was another nightmare. It was bumpier, and I could see that the wings were flapping up and down, like those of a huge, metallic bird, as the plane rose and fell. I was certain they would snap off and I would arrive back in Madison in a Vietnam-type body bag.

Karen was also working hard, pursuing her own dream of obtaining a master's degree in library science (she had graduated with a B.A. the previous June). Even so, we enjoyed a number of plays, concerts and operas at UW, including recitals by the great Elizabeth Schwarzkopf and by Dietrich Fischer-Dieskau. We once attended a performance by the Philadelphia Orchestra conducted by Eugene Ormandy. I can still see the maestro windmilling his arms at the dramatic climax of Dvorak's 8th Symphony.

Mostly, though, it was movies. But imagine my dismay when, out of nowhere, there appeared on the big screen a violent, graphically-depicted rape and murder in

The Virgin Spring, followed by one of the characters vomiting not once, but *twice*, which disturbed me even more than the awful assault. The success of this film seemed to initiate a theme that continued throughout the 60s and 70s. *Elvira Madigan*, for example, coughed up a pint of poisonous mushrooms. Jill Clayburgh, in *An Unmarried Woman*, performed the most disgusting heave of all because it was so obviously staged. While she's gulping down a salad in a restaurant with her husband, he informs her without warning that he's leaving her. So she runs out and chucks it back up. But there wasn't a shred of lettuce, a floret of broccoli, in the spew; it was clearly a case of gratuitous puking. I came to think of such eruptions as "the obligatory vomit scene." If I knew a film had one, I'd refuse to go. If I didn't know, I'd cover my eyes if a hurl seemed imminent. These noxious scenes utterly ruined movies for me, and I despise their inclusion even now.

We even made a few trips to Chicago, invariably stopping at the magnificent Art Institute and at George Diamond's, a steakhouse, among other favorites. Once, we even got to "the friendly confines" of Wrigley Field, the world's most beautiful ball park, when Warren Spahn pitched one of his final games for the Braves. He gave up several runs and the Cubs easily won it, but he still displayed the magnificent form he was famous for.

All of this left little time for reading. But there was one wonderful book we loved so much that we read it aloud (I still wasn't very good at that) to each other, usually in bed at night. Decades later I would write an homage to *Platero and I*, by Juan Ramón Jiménez (Nobel prize, 1957). But I'm getting way ahead of myself.

The most rewarding discovery of my post-doctoral venture was that heat "shocks"— a brief period of time during which cultures are placed in an incubator set several degrees higher than their preferred temperature—caused little delay of the subsequent mitosis when applied during the S phase, but there were significant delays when cultures were shocked during G2, reaching a peak effect about two hours before the nuclei divided. After that time, heat treatment resulted in lesser delays. Now here comes the interesting part: *repeated* heat shocks during G2 delayed mitosis indefinitely (although the cultures continued to grow). Moreover, shocks applied very near the time of mitosis prevented nuclear division *without blocking DNA synthesis*. Because replication occurred without mitosis, the nuclei doubled in size, but, nonetheless *divided normally at the time of the next expected mitosis*. If nuclei were briefly heated again just prior to *that* division, the nuclei grew to four times their normal size during the next scheduled S-phase. This was the first report of a dissociation of DNA replication from mitosis.

That summer (1966), Karen earned her M.S. in Library Science. At last we were free to go anywhere. She opted for taking some time off to do some serious traveling. "Otherwise," she wisely suggested, "we might never do it." She was right about that— I didn't even want to go *then*. Not because it wouldn't have been interesting and fun, but I was terrified. Afraid that I would have to take some kind of medical exam to go, afraid to fly over the ocean, afraid of getting food poisoning in some cheap foreign restaurant, afraid of the unknown, afraid of *everything*.

I didn't tell her these things, though; I just dragged my feet. When she missed a period, she was extremely distraught, fearing a pregnancy would destroy our chance to go. I had mixed feelings about it. I didn't want a child, and certainly not then, but it might have been better than going to unfamiliar places fraught with great dangers. The apparent pregnancy turned out to be a false alarm, so we turned again to the study of travel books and maps. As it turned out, all we needed were some inoculations. No problem.

But first we had to find jobs to go to on our return.

There were only three places I wanted to work: The University of Colorado, The Oak Ridge National Laboratory, and St. Jude Children's Research Hospital, all of which seemed to be carrying out the kinds of research I wanted to be a part of. Of the three, I got two invitations to visit: Knoxville and Memphis. (I spoke to David Prescott of UC at a scientific meeting, but he wasn't very encouraging: the government was beginning to cut back on research funds so that the money could go to the war effort. After a long period of growth in funding, budgets were being trimmed everywhere.)

I went to Oak Ridge first. The facility was located in the beautiful Smoky Mountains, but I found its organization a complete mess. Although I was scheduled to talk to several people, some of them didn't show up and the others seemed disinterested or preoccupied. I felt invisible. I don't think I even got a rejection letter, or anything else, from them. The flight back was a bumpy nightmare. When they brought dinner to us in the plane, I told myself over and over that "I'm hungry and I'm gonna eat." Oddly, the mantra seemed to help a little.

St. Jude was better. The guy who interviewed me, Bruce Sells, seemed quite interested in my work and wanted me to start in his lab as soon as possible. But there were a couple of conditions. He asked me, for example, "Would you mind that your salary would come from our training grant?"

I informed him that I wasn't interested in another post-doctoral fellowship.

"You wouldn't be a post-doc. It's just that there is salary money in that fund. We'll try to get you appointed Assistant Professor at the University of Tennessee Medical School (with which the hospital was affiliated).

"Try?"

"Well, we can't guarantee the appointment, but no one has ever turned down our request." I thought no more about it, particularly since my salary would be considerably higher than what I earned at McArdle, one that, I presumed, a post-doc could never earn.

The other catch was that my office and research space would be in Sells' laboratory, and I would be expected to spend a quarter of my time working on a project involving his own interests, protein synthesis in rats.

He took me out to dinner at one of Memphis's popular restaurants, where, in order to sample the local cuisine, I had ham with "red-eye gravy." It wasn't until later that I learned what "red-eye" meant: the gravy was made with coffee. Combined with my anxiety about meeting the rest of the staff and giving a lecture the next day, not to mention the cup or two of coffee I had with dessert, it literally kept me awake all night. When it came time for me to present a seminar describing my heat shock experiments, I was so bleary that I could barely speak. Too tired, even, to worry about the flight home that evening. I figured I must have thoroughly blown the opportunity to work at a world-famous research institution, one with plenty of space, money, and equipment, and one, moreover, whose focus was on childhood cancer! It would have been a dream come true. . . .

The interviews and lecture must have gone all right, though, because soon after the visit I received an invitation to join the staff at St. Jude. Of course I was thrilled. But I was also suspicious of the offer, which didn't mention a faculty appointment. Even though time, and federal funding, were running out and I had nowhere else to go, I wrote to Sells, reminded him that I wasn't interested in anything less than an assistant professorship, certainly not another post-doctoral appointment, and turned his offer down. Then, unfortunately, I made a costly mistake: owing to time pressures (we were late for a dinner invitation, as I remember), I got the letter out to Sells without making a copy of it.

Rusch advised me not to worry—he was planning an article for *Scientific American*, and if I didn't have a position by the fall, I could return to his lab for a few months and co-write it while looking for a permanent position.

Another letter from St. Jude: they would definitely recommend me for an assistant professorship at the University of Tennessee. This time I accepted the offer. Karen, a lifelong Madisonian, wasn't eager to move to the mid-South, but I assured her it was only temporary, a necessary stepping stone to something better.

That Thanksgiving we visited my folks in Muncie, where I read an article by D.J. Hamblin (*Life* magazine, March 18, 1966, pp. 106-8) called "They Are 'Idiot Savants'— Wizards of the Calendar." It was one of the most fascinating stories I had ever read, and it stuck. It was nearly a quarter-century later that I rediscovered it while researching for *K-PAX*.

The old Ford Falcon was a wreck, so we traded it in for a Volkswagen squareback to be picked up in Luxembourg. We couldn't have done this but for the "nothing down, no payments until September" deal they offered; we had spent most of the money we had on plane tickets. Fortunately, we found a book called *Europe on $5 a Day* ($10 for the two of us), by Arthur Frommer. Amazingly, it turned out to be just about right.

There were still a lot of loose ends to tie up—a few experiments to repeat, papers to write. One cold January evening, while I was finishing up some work in the lab, Papa Hambone's miscellaneous music program was interrupted by the news that astronauts Grissom, White, and Chaffee had been killed by a fire on the Apollo launch pad. Chaffee's last words, it was said, were: "Get us out of here—we're burning up!" It wasn't difficult to place myself in his situation. I could feel the invisible flames, sense what must have been in his mind, live his final agonizing moments. It was a terrible situation, and a very sad one, but I was also angry—I couldn't believe NASA had built a capsule with no escape hatch. Was it an attempt to save money, to speed up the process in order to beat the Soviets to the moon, or just plain stupidity? In any case, I hoped they would learn something from this tragedy so that such a disaster would never happen again.

EUROPE

We had booked tickets on Icelandic Airlines from New York to Luxembourg. I was marginally comforted by the fact that this particular company had never experienced a fatal accident. However, we had to take another carrier from Madison to New York, one that no doubt had sustained thousands of deadly crashes. When we got on the plane I was rigid with fear. Karen noticed that my hands were cold, and wondered whether I was feeling well. During the endless wait for takeoff, I began to think about how helpless I'd be if my heart started to skip beats in the middle of the ocean. I consoled myself with the thought that if St. Jude had a physical exam requirement, we would, by then, have survived this trip. If we died, on the other hand, I wouldn't have to take the exam. Regardless of what happened, I sardonically reasoned, I couldn't lose.

The flight to the East Coast was uneventful. In New York, however, there was a sixteen-hour delay because of a broken propeller on our Icelandic plane. What, I wondered, would have happened had the damn thing fallen apart in flight? But they put us up for the night, and the next morning we were on our way to Iceland as if nothing out of the ordinary had happened.

Soon after we departed and were already high over the vast ocean, both the engines quit. While my stomach was dropping, the pilot came on to kindly inform us that we should not be alarmed—this was standard procedure. A few minutes of horror on top of the underlying terror. The engines started up again and it was a tolerable flight to Iceland despite the icy blackness lurking far below.

In Reykjavik there was something wrong (I knew it!) with the plane that was supposed to take us to Luxembourg. (What if they hadn't discovered *this* problem until after we had taken off??) They had to call in another carrier—the unheard-of Martin's Air Service—which would arrive from Amsterdam in a few hours. In the meantime, they fed us a Salisbury steak dinner. It was after midnight in Iceland.

By the time we left for Europe it was four o'clock in the morning, we were cramped into a smaller plane, and I didn't give a damn whether we crashed into the sea or not; I just wanted to sleep, and did. When the drizzly morning came we awoke to find ourselves flying low over bright green fields. Though still February, it was already spring in Europe! My frozen muscles began to thaw a little.

We picked up our new VW squareback in Luxembourg and drove it all over the continent. We ate crayfish in Paris, horse in Belgium (we didn't know what it was), doves in Cairo. We saw Michelangelo's *David* in Florence and his *Pieta* at the Vatican (where the Pope unexpectedly made an appearance to loud applause), *The Mona Lisa* in Paris, *Nefertiti* in London, van Goch's *Sunflowers* in Amsterdam, El Greco in Madrid, Bechmann in Munich, Moore and Renoir in Nice. We dissolved suppositories in tea because we couldn't read the instructions (Italy); dealt with government red tape and barely missed a coup (Greece) and a six-day war (Egypt); experienced the tragedy of the bull ring (Spain); paid an eighty-cent fine for speeding (Yugoslavia); ate at five (Norway) or ten (Spain) P.M. depending on the local custom; had a run-in with a border guard who wanted to confiscate our camera (East Berlin—Karen refused to give it up and he backed off); experienced the serenity of mighty cathedrals and beautiful vistas (everywhere); hiked in lush mountain valleys among placid sheep and cows (Switzerland); mastered the art of driving in congested cities (Rome, Paris) and on the "wrong" side of the road (Great Britain); stood where the bravest and most brilliant of historical figures had once spoken; learned the value of a dollar and what bidets were for. We gave rides to hitchhikers in Yugoslavia who insisted, to the man, on paying us (eight cents) for the privilege, and were insulted if we didn't accept; wept at a spontaneous cornet-accompanied dance outside a church in Barcelona; exchanged money on the Czechoslovakian black market; were verbally abused by a British landlady when we declined to stay in one of her rooms; enjoyed the generous hospitality of a Swedish family, friends of a relative, whom we had never met; rode donkeys in Egypt and cablecars in Switzerland; gorged on Danish pastry and French croissants with café au lait, and potatoes fried in olive oil (we sent some Greek pastry and goat cheese back to Mom and Dad—"It 'bout made us puke."). In Naples I accidentally ate two dinners (the bouillabaisse "appetizer" turned out to be a full meal) the night before we went to Capri, was nauseated on the ferry and deposited a great mound of fecal matter in an island cave.

The people of every country were uniquely themselves. Some of the cliché's we had heard were accurate, some not. But if we learned anything important from these travels, it was that people are fundamentally the same everywhere, a mixture of kindness and meanness and playfulness, courage and officiousness and cowardice. I wondered, as have many other travelers, no doubt, why the world hasn't yet developed an acceptable universal language, a simple basis for communication. It almost seems that people don't *want* to communicate on common ground, that no one wants to give up an iota of his own nationality for the good of everyone. I am convinced that when we have evolved a little further, this will happen. Until then, however, chauvinism will cling to us like a leech to a leg.

While we were in Spain a letter came (via American Express) from Donald Pinkel, M.D., the director of St. Jude Hospital, confirming my appointment as a "special trainee." I assumed this designation (which I had never heard of) meant a kind of probationary period to which I was assigned until the faculty thing could be worked out. Even so, this worried me a little. Something still didn't seem right about the whole deal. But there was no easy way to communicate this concern; it would have to wait until I got to Memphis.

The trip was finally over and we found ourselves flying back to the States. This time, when they cut the motors shortly after takeoff, I was ready for them. The flight was still horrible, with the far-from-pacific ocean waiting to swallow us down below, and an almost certain employment physical being planned for the end of the journey still to come. But when we landed in New York we felt we were already home. Not back in Madison yet, but it seemed, after struggling with foreign languages, food, money, and customs for half a year, that anywhere in America was home.

The feeling was short-lived. New Yorkers, paying no attention whatever to us, buzzed around like so many insects. Food was expensive. We stayed in a cheap hotel near Columbia University (in Harlem) while we waited for our Volkswagen to arrive in Newark. We were exhausted, and the heart palpitations had begun again in earnest, exacerbated, probably, by a shortage of rest, the stress of the present, and a profound fear of the future.

Karen knew nothing of these internal pressures, and, after four years of marriage, I still couldn't discuss them with her, with a doctor, with anyone. If I had, she would have insisted I seek help, which was precisely what I was most afraid to do. Although I was no longer smoking, I continued to drink coffee. I didn't know then that caffeine would also increase the frequency and duration of the frightening episodes. Thus, drinking it to relax had just the opposite effect.

By coincidence, Karen's cousin Carol, and her husband Mark, were in the city for a couple of days, waiting to take a freighter to Italy. We drove them and their luggage to the boat and, having no apparent alternative, left the squareback on the huge, empty dock just long enough to help carry their baggage aboard. From the deck we could see that a tow truck had already begun to hook up our VW. I ran for it, yelling at the guy in the truck, but was too late. The car was gone. It cost us $137, and the last of our traveler's checks, to get it out of the city garage. I vowed never to return to this heartless place, the city that never sleeps, but waits, like a giant predator, for innocent travelers to stumble into its trap.

Back in Madison (via Muncie), my trepidation about going to St. Jude began to expand like a Hoberman sphere. Hoping I might be able to delay the venture for a few weeks, I stopped in to see Papa Rusch about writing that article for *Scientific American*, but my former colleague, Joe Cummins, was already doing it. After boring everyone we knew with our 700 slides and a dozen or so Super 8 films, we loaded a U-Haul trailer with all our belongings and a potted plant, and headed for Memphis. It was September, 1967. I was already thirty, Karen twenty-four.

ST. JUDE

Within days we knew we had made a mistake. In order to help us find a place to live, a representative of Planters, the biggest bank in town, volunteered to drive us around the city to look at potential rental houses/apartments. Whenever we came to a black or mixed neighborhood, we learned that "The area is 'rundown.'" In one of the "better" locations, we got out to look at a house for rent and overheard two of the neighbor "ladies" discussing the merits of their respective "colored men," who did yard work and odd jobs for them. There was even a suburb called Whitehaven. We wondered whether this ad hoc real estate service had been offered to the lone African-American member of the faculty, or to any of the kitchen or janitorial staff. Ignoring the bank's advice, we opted for something in-between, a duplex with a nice wooded front yard within a couple blocks of a "rundown" neighborhood.

The laboratory situation wasn't much better. Although I had a large office and ample lab space, there seemed to be a problem with my faculty appointment at the university. I asked Bruce about this. "We're working on it," he assured me. Since it was early in the fall term, this seemed a reasonable answer.

I knew I was in further difficulty when I had my first meeting with the newly-arrived director of the Biochemistry Department, Martin Morrison, whose research effort had something to do with the proteins found in saliva (I never learned what this had to do with leukemia or any other form of childhood cancer). When he asked me what I planned to work on, I said, only half-jokingly, "The secrets of life." He laughed mirthlessly and repeated the question. I described what I planned to do with *Physarum*: to determine what biochemical factors were responsible for the control of DNA synthesis and cell division. He seemed only mildly interested at best. That incident alone told me something about what working at St. Jude was going to be like. A year or so later, when I proposed to him that we set up a Division of Molecular Biology (a reasonable proposition for a cancer research hospital, I thought) within the department, he angrily accused me of harboring "grandiose ideas." Large thoughts were apparently unwelcome at St. Jude Children's Research Hospital.

On the credit side, winters were mild—no more frigid gales, frozen brains. In the spring came azaleas, rhododendrons, dogwood blossoms. In contrast to Indiana or Wisconsin, golfers and tennis players could enjoy their sports almost throughout the year.

There were no openings for a librarian at the University of Tennessee Medical School. Instead, Karen found a job in the main public library on Front Street, where she spent much of her time helping elderly women, most of whom hoped to discover a relative who had floated over on the Mayflower, trace their family lineage. Knowing she wouldn't be there long, she accepted the position with equanimity.

The notice for the dread physical examination requirement soon came. This time there seemed no escaping it. I wasn't a student at UT, nor did I want to be. I ignored the summons for a few weeks, desperately hoping it would get lost in the paper shuffle. But one early afternoon, when Lowell Foster (Sells's new post-doc) and I were on our way to the cafeteria for lunch, the head nurse encountered us in the corridor and asked us when we were coming in for our exams. I said nothing. Lowell asked whether we were required to do this. "Only if you want to get paid," came the terrible response. "Then I guess I won't get paid," he replied. She shrugged and went on her way. It turned out that he was afraid of needles! We got paid anyway, and I realized with amazement, and enormous relief, that I had once again escaped the horrors of the stethoscope and the tongue depressor, one or both of which would surely have led to the diagnosis of a grotesquely fatal illness.

Since I had a three-year initial appointment and had agreed to devote a quarter of my time to one of Bruce's projects, I decided to get that nine-month period behind me so I could concentrate full-time on my own research with *Physarum*. That turned out to be another huge mistake.

Except for putting a few mice to "sleep" with ether (a painless death, I assumed), this was my first experience at animal "sacrifice," to use the then-common vernacular. To my horror and disgust, the project involved the barbaric practice of hitting the rats on the head with a hammer, followed by cutting their throats and letting them bleed to death, semi-conscious and quivering, in the sink.

Rats are gentle animals. When caged, they will often let you pick them up and play with them. But when they saw what had happened to one of their brothers, they became frantic—they knew they were next and tried desperately to avoid our outstretched fingers. Worse, they sometimes screamed when the hammer came down, a squeal much like that of hurt children. I had to force myself to believe that this torture might have some worthwhile benefits.

The work took a little longer than I had anticipated, almost a year. Lowell and I wrote up the results, which were published in the *Journal of Biological Chemistry*. I revived my slime mold cultures and went to work on what I really wanted to study, the control mechanisms for DNA replication and mitosis. (*Physarum polycephalum*, incidentally, has no brain or nervous system, and is therefore no more sensate than a carrot.)

One of the technicians in the lab had acquired a ten-week-old Dalmatian puppy. For Valentine's Day (1968), I gave Karen one of Tag's sisters. We called her Daisy the Dog. She was extremely intelligent, far smarter than the two canines who became part of our family in later years. She quickly learned dozens of words, and we had to spell them out when we didn't want her to know what we were up to. She soon learned that symbology, too, and we were forced to spell them incorrectly to keep anything secret from her.

Her sense of humor spanned the scatological repertoire. When she detected an unpleasant odor in the vicinity, she would smell her own behind to determine whether she was the guilty party. This could be embarrassing, especially when a visitor took off his shoes (or even just appeared in the room) and she would give her rear end a good sniff.

Daisy thoroughly disliked being left alone. As soon as the door clicked shut she would roar around the house upending the wastebaskets. She knew that we knew that she knew we weren't pleased with this reactionary behavior, but it was quite harmless and we didn't scold her much; perhaps it made her feel better about the forced solitude.

Since we lived on a quiet side street, on the other hand, we decided early on that it was worth the risk to let Daisy run free on occasion (can you imagine being a dog and never getting to run?). Under other circumstances, that might have been a disastrous decision. But, in this case, she took up with a few neighborhood dogs and had a wonderful time. Although she was hit by a car twice during her long life, the injuries in both cases were minor, and the experiences made her ever more cautious about getting on the road. We were fortunate to have known her for almost fifteen years.

Once I got my cultures going, I discovered that there was something present in aqueous extracts of the organism that stimulated mitosis (i.e., it occurred significantly earlier than in controls) when mixed with Petri dish cultures, and made some progress in characterizing it. The "mitosis-promoting factor" was a relatively low molecular weight, tenacious substance—resistant, for example, to high temperatures and strong acids. And a perfect project for me because of my background in natural products chemistry.

I reported this discovery to Papa Rusch (and later presented it at the 1969 FASEB meeting). Not long thereafter I received a letter from one of his worried post-docs. After seeing my results, Rusch had put her to work isolating and characterizing the active substance. This was clearly unethical, and I was thoroughly dismayed (as was the post-doc). He explained his action by reminding me that he had initiated the research on *Physarum*, and his group had been working on mitosis for years, which gave him, he insisted, a proprietary claim on virtually anything done with this particular organism. This was vastly untrue, even silly. However, not having the forces to compete with his large group in Madison, I dropped that study and proceeded with other projects, of which there was certainly no shortage. But I decided not to inform my previous "mentor" about any of my results until they were in print.

In one of these investigations I discovered that polysomes (the cell's protein-making apparatus) are equally well organized in homogenates obtained at any time during the mitotic cycle. This was surprising because, *in vivo*, there were two distinct peaks of protein synthesis, one in S and the other in G2, with little activity occurring between these two waves. (The pattern for DNA and RNA synthesis *in vitro*, on the other hand, mirrored that found in the intact organism.) This suggested that the control mechanism(s) for protein synthesis was rendered inactive in homogenates, and that something other than the structure of the polysomes themselves was responsible for the regulation of this process within the living organism.

In some ways this period was the happiest of my scientific career. The excitement of carrying out a big experiment and watching the results come in was much like that described by Paul de Kruif. It was a thrill just to enter the building every morning.

On the other hand, I sometimes had to stay up late to finish a procedure, which meant risking an onset of heart palpitations. The fear that they *might* be coming was almost as bad as the attacks themselves, and it began to carry over into other situations. For example, if I were asked to make a presentation or give a report, I often went home to take a nap a couple of hours before the event in order to make sure they didn't occur during the discussion. I had lost my confidence at the podium.

Owing to my increasingly longish hair and beard, no doubt, I was once asked by a small St. Jude patient: "Are you Jesus?" I assured him I was not, though he might have felt better if I had said "yes." On the other hand, I remember being stopped at a traffic light when a young man in a pickup truck pulled up alongside the VW and shouted, "You look like shit!" before peeling rubber all over the road. (Ironically, that same guy probably has hair down to his belly button now, and whatever beard he can muster.) Thanks, in part, to our experiences at a repressive institution in a bigoted city (in 1967-69, anyway), Karen and I were both becoming more and more liberal. It was a natural defense mechanism.

In a place almost devoid of art (even the famous Beale Street was a ghost of its former self), an avant-garde film theater magically appeared. We spent many an evening there losing ourselves for a couple of hours in the flickering light of the outside world. (Two films I particularly remember seeing were the powerful *The Andalusian Dog*, and perhaps the first "music video," *Monterey Pop*.) Whenever we went, however, I was constantly on edge because many small, independent filmmakers of the time had begun to adopt the "obligatory vomit scene" policy. Sometimes it came as an unpleasant surprise. On the other hand, I was always more relaxed afterward because I knew there wouldn't be any more puking for the rest of the movie.

One of our fondest Memphis memories, though, is of watching *Finian's Rainbow*, which contains the funniest scene, in our opinion, in film history. Imagine Keenan Wynn, an old Southern boy and U.S. Congressman, suffering a bout of dyspepsia on a porch swing. Prior to this, the wonderful Al Freeman, Jr. has just been trained (shuffle slowly, use "Massa" a lot) in the art of being a Negro servant. Wynn is suffering, wailing and pounding, in the swing while, in the background, we see Freeman shuffling toward him at a turtle's pace, keening, "I'se comin', Massa!" and "You gonna feel jes' fine!" Karen and I were unable to stop laughing, or even to sit up straight. None of our (white) neighbors, however, seemed the slightest bit amused, which only added to our uncontrollable glee.

We started subscribing to *The Christian Science Monitor* and *I.F. Stone's Weekly*. An article in the former, titled "How Should Cities Grow?" annoyed me a great deal. I wrote a letter to the editor expounding on the negative assumption inherent in the piece—that human population was destined to increase and increase and there was nothing that could be done about it—and concluding with: "How should cities grow? Not at all!" To my surprise they published it.

1968 was also a memorable year for many other reasons. Peace activists were everywhere, even in Memphis. There was a feeling in the country that, perhaps for the first time, people were better than their government, and would no longer go halfway around the world to fight its battles without a very good reason. At anti-war gatherings the atmosphere was warm, electric. The protests (and Gene McCarthy) forced President Johnson to abandon his plans to run for another term. The Democratic candidate in November would be either McCarthy, Bobby Kennedy, or Vice-President Hubert Humphrey. Despite the "LOVE IT OR LEAVE IT" bumper stickers that sprang up all over town, it was an exciting time to be an American citizen.

But . . . one late afternoon in April, as I was returning to St. Jude from some inconsequential errand, I noticed that the next-door Baptist Hospital emergency entrance was filled with police cars, lights blazing. Of course I knew that some disaster had happened, but I had no idea what it had been. When I got to the lab, someone said that Martin Luther King had been shot. No one knew whether he was still alive. I packed up my briefcase and started for home. On the way, the squareback was pelted by rocks thrown by a number of black kids. I understood the reason, and passed by them with sadness, rather than anger. No serious damage had been done to the car, but the country as a whole had suffered a virtually irreplaceable loss.

Dr. King had come to Memphis in support of the nearly all-black garbage workers, who were striking for a decent wage and benefits. Following his death there was a huge rally downtown. Tens of thousands of people came; Karen and I were among the very few (half-a-dozen?) whites who showed up. We marched past truckloads of National Guardsmen (white) who stared at us coldly as we passed by.

Many prominent Americans spoke at the rally, including a very strong Coretta Scott King; heir-apparent Ralph Abernathy; Jerry Furth, president of the American Federation of State, County, and Municipal Employees; and the courageous Rosa Parks, who had, in effect, started the civil rights movement a few years earlier by refusing to move to the back of the bus. Another highlight was the appearance of Bill Cosby and Robert Culp, stars of the popular television series, *I Spy*. Except for a brief moment when dozens of police officers rushed to intercept a car that had backfired, it was a peaceful demonstration that drew national attention, and the garbage workers eventually received a new, and much fairer, contract than they had ever known.

But the killing wasn't over. On June 4, Robert Kennedy was shot immediately following his victorious campaign in California's presidential primary. The Democrats were in chaos, and it looked as if underdog McCarthy, the anti-war candidate, might be able to win the nomination from Hubert Humphrey, the choice of the party regulars. It promised to be an interesting convention.

The impossible dream wasn't to be. In one of the great fiascos of American history, the Chicago Police Department, on orders from Mayor Daley (the elder), violently shut down the protests occurring outside the convention hall. Only the great Senator Abraham Ribicoff stood before the delegates to denounce the Gestapo tactics and was shouted down, most notably (and loudly) by the mayor himself. Humphrey went on to win the nomination and, in his acceptance speech, stood aloof from the controversy, apparently trying to please both sides. Although he campaigned hard, his weak stand on the war and electoral fairness resulted in the election of Richard M. Nixon to the presidency.

In September a position opened in the UT Medical School Library, and Karen accepted it. At about the same time I was invited by one of the hospital's bacteriologists to join the American Civil Liberties Union, southwest Tennessee branch. I was familiar with what they did (defend the constitution in court and elsewhere), and I was happy to do so. It turned out that the first meeting I attended was for the election of officers. My bacteriologist friend nominated me for secretary and, to my amazement, I was elected.

At the time, the primary concern for that organization in Tennessee was prayer in school. Other issues were raised and discussed, but this one was judged to be of prime importance because of the clear constitutional separation of church and state. In order to bring the matter into a courtroom, however, there had to be a plaintiff, someone with the courage to file a lawsuit against a school where prayer was condoned and encouraged (nearly every school in Tennessee). Unfortunately, during my tenure with that organization, no such individual could be found. Still, enough good things were happening to keep us occupied during our monthly meetings. Moreover, Karen and I acquired a lot of new friends, some of the best people in the city, both black and white.

Besides Daisy the Dog, we acquired two other valuables in Memphis. The first was a Harley-Davidson, obtained from a co-worker. Not a little putt-putt, but a real hog. I kept it for several months but it never ran right, or even started half the time (which is probably why the previous owner dumped it).

One day I borrowed a trailer and hauled the cycle to the license bureau, expecting to steer it around a few pylons and get a license for it, as well as one to drive the Volkswagen. But I never got on the bike or into the squareback. Instead, the examiner handed me a form to take to an eye doctor—this had to be done before the driving test could be administered. Dejected, I hauled the hog back home.

As luck would have it, I had begun to see little smoky wisps when I moved my eyes. Commonly known as "flies," these are tiny, harmless specks floating in the humors. But I was certain I had developed some horrible eye disease (cancer?), and that, at best, I would soon lose my sight, at worst my life (after a horrible struggle with some dread malignancy). There was no way I was going to see an optometrist and be pronounced one of the walking dead. I finally sold the Harley to an eager sixteen-year-old accompanied by his proud father.

The second acquisition was a complete set of *The Great Books*, bookcase included, obtained from a co-worker who never found time even to peruse them. Neither did I, though I gazed wistfully at the shelves from time to time.

In 1968, in fact, I was sure I'd never have a chance to read anything ever again. Besides the manifestly chronic heart condition and the insidious eye tumors, I was certain that one of my lungs had collapsed one night at a party hosted by a fellow ACLU stalwart. I had taken up pipe smoking again, not only to settle my jittery nerves but probably to enhance my image, and I occasionally inhaled the sweet smoke. That evening I felt a sudden and very sharp pain under my left ribs. From that point on, and for the next several weeks, I felt that I wasn't getting enough air. Based on Dad's similar experience I was pretty sure what had happened, and I should have headed directly to the hospital. Although I constantly felt the need to take deep breaths, which added significantly to my general pool of underlying anxiety, I reasoned that the lung would probably refill its cavity on its own, as my father's had done, and, in any case, I could live with only one (I quit the pipe, however). The recovery was gradual, but eventually I was able to suck in enough air so that I didn't feel a continuous hypoxia.

But the year ended well. On Christmas Eve we watched Borman & Co. fly around the moon while reading passages from the Bible. Everything seemed to be on schedule for a landing the following year, President Kennedy's announced deadline for this magnificent accomplishment.

I finally got my assistant professorship at UT, a year and a half late, in the spring of 1969. But something still wasn't right. I remember walking to the cafeteria one day (unless I was invited for lunch by another faculty member I usually ate with the technical and support staff, rather than in the doctors' dining room—I hated this kind of segregation based on presumed importance (most of the faculty disagreed with me). As I passed by that elite room I saw through the open door that Danny Thomas (the comic founder of the hospital) was speaking to the group. I backed up and looked again. I might have liked to hear what he had to say, but I hadn't even been told about the visit. An oversight, perhaps, but Bruce seemed a little embarrassed (or, as Lowell, a Southerner, would put it, he was wearing his "shit-eatin' grin") when I saw him later on.

In an attempt to get away from the mid-South for a while, Karen and I procured a stack of brochures distributed by local Chambers of Commerce describing inns, motels, and bed-and-breakfasts all over New England and maritime Canada. One of these, situated "high on a hill overlooking the Bay of Fundy" and boasting several two-hundred-year-old fishermen's cottages, each with fireplace and library, and hiking trails and myriad songbirds just out the door, sounded particularly appealing. There also happened to be a scientific meeting in June, a "Gordon Conference," in New Hampshire, along the way to our newly-discovered coastal New Brunswick retreat.

Since she had been employed at the UT Medical School library for less than a year, and wasn't entitled to a vacation for a few more weeks, Karen requested a special dispensation to accompany me to New England and Canada. It was refused—not because her services were desperately needed, but because the library director felt the need to assert her authority, a characteristic common among those in positions of power in late 60's Memphis. Choosing the lesser of the two evils (going with me and losing her job, or my going alone), she quit the library. We left Daisy with brother Larry *et fam.* in Muncie, and headed east.

The week-long conference, held in an austere private school, was interesting and fun. Although I didn't present a paper at this meeting, I participated fully in the discussions and came up with some ideas for later research.

Arriving at the dock early at Blacks Harbour, NB, on a Sunday afternoon, we were dismayed to find that the last boat for Grand Manan Island had just left. We called our hostess, who found our dilemma quite amusing (on an island, we discovered, one assumes everyone already knows anything of importance) and suggested we try again in the morning. Still vaguely annoyed, we stayed overnight in St. George and took the 9:30 A.M. ferry the next day.

As we approached Grand Manan, with the village of North Head placidly embracing the piers, we knew we were going to like this place. The Whale Cove Cottages were everything the brochure had promised, and more. We stayed in "Cooper Shop," a former barrel maker's cottage with a huge fireplace, several excellent watercolors, and shelves of well-read books. The early summer flowers, the song- and shorebirds, the rugged hiking trails, the foghorns, especially one called "The Whistle," crying out like lost souls, the electric-coil "shaving mugs" for heating water, the outdoor shower, the exquisite smell of the spruce forests in the strong sunlight, the gourmet meals in the rustic dining room, the spectacular views of the Bay of Fundy and its thirty-foot tides, our literate hosts (Jim and Kathleen Buckley, both Toronto schoolteachers in the winter months), the sophisticated guests and the friendly local people, primarily fishermen and dulse (a seaweed) gatherers—we found everything about the island to be magnificent. In short, we fell in love with the place.

Grand Manan

We had taken our eleven-inch portable TV (the only set we had) with us to watch Armstrong and Aldrin land on the moon. None of the other guests expressed any interest in this event. On the night of the great adventure, however, they came knocking, one by one, on the Cooper Shop door, and we all watched the incredible journey come to an end. (Armstrong, incidentally, meant to say "That's one small step for *a* man, one giant leap for mankind," but he forgot the "a," or the communicator didn't pick it up, and it went down in history as "That's one small step for man . . ." which makes no sense.)

Sunday dinner invariably included baked chicken with rice, tomatoes with a delicious sour cream, and hot fudge sundaes. It wasn't until years later that I learned Kathleen made the tomato dressing herself by simply placing some cream in a dish on a windowsill, i.e., it was basically a process of rotting by whatever organisms happened to be present. As far as I know no one ever developed food poisoning from it, but had I known how it was done I never would have ingested the stuff.

Regretfully, we put a borrowed car in line (that was the standard procedure) for the next morning's ferry, enjoyed one last wonderful dinner, and fell asleep to the sounds of nature. Assuming I would still be alive the following summer, we vowed we would be back, this time with Daisy the Dog, who, we discovered, would have been quite welcome at Whale Cove Cottages.

On returning to Memphis, Karen started to look for another job and I, thoroughly refreshed, buried myself deep in my research. As it happened, Sells had just begun a year's sabbatical leave. A few days later, on a Thursday afternoon at 4:00, after I had set up the next day's experiment involving dozens of cultures, I got a call from the departmental secretary: "Dr. Morrison would like you to give a report on the Gordon Conference at noon tomorrow."

"Sorry, I've got a big experiment already set up for tomorrow, but I'd be happy to discuss the conference at the next regular meeting" (there was one every Friday at noon).

"He wants you to do it tomorrow."

"I can't."

"I'll tell him."

On Monday there were two more calls. The first was from Morrison: "Come to my office." I did, and was promptly fired. He didn't want to hear any excuses. The second was from the hospital director's secretary. Dr. Pinkel wanted me to come to his office. I went right up.

Pinkel asked me why I hadn't obeyed Morrison's request to give the report: "After all, he didn't ask you to kill a Jew." I told him about the previous Friday's experiment, already in progress. He wasn't impressed, and suggested that perhaps I could get a job teaching at UT (the last place in the world I wanted to work). We discussed the situation for a few more minutes. I explained that a great deal of time and effort (not to mention valuable research funds) would have been wasted had I dropped everything and given the report, which I'd said I'd be happy to do the following week. With more notice I wouldn't plan a big experiment for the day of the meeting. He thought this sounded reasonable and suggested I go back to Morrison and work it out.

When I got to the latter's office, however, he had apparently already spoken to Pinkel. Before I said a word he declared: "It's too late—you're fired!"

"But Don said—"

A wave of the hand. I was beginning to smell a head-bashed rat. Had Sells and Morrison pre-planned an ignominious departure for me?

There was one final meeting between the parties concerned: Pinkel; the assistant director, a retired army officer; Morrison; and me. It appeared to be a formality. At the end, perhaps hoping they'd at least give me the year I still had coming, I mentioned that I planned to take the matter to court.

Only Pinkel seemed disturbed by this announcement (there was already a lawsuit pending against St. Jude, for sex discrimination, I believe). "You don't want to do that," he quickly asserted.

"Why not? This is unfair and unjust, and I think I can win." (For one thing, I knew some prominent ACLU attorneys.) The army shot back: "You a lawyer?" "No," I countered, "are *you*?"

I was given exactly two weeks to finish my tenure at St. Jude and clean out my office.

None of this made any sense—there was no reason I couldn't have made the report a week later—unless it was Bruce who had set this up. I had, after all, completed my obligation to him and he had nothing more to gain by my presence in his laboratory. From Sells' point of view, I was taking up valuable space.

From that moment I was a pariah, roundly avoided by almost everyone. I became invisible, even to my professional colleagues. At St. Jude, the last thing anyone wanted was a "troublemaker." I had hoped that some of the other faculty members would exhibit a little courage and speak out in my defense, or at least indicate some regret. Except for condolences from John Smith, the only African-American faculty member, it never happened.

On a quick trip to the cafeteria one afternoon I noticed a small sign stuck to a wall: "Dr. Eugene Brewer has resigned to take a position elsewhere." Why the powers that be felt the need to promulgate this lie was another mystery; everyone in the place knew what had actually transpired.

The project I especially wanted to finish that month involved the effect of heat shocks on the integrity of polysomes throughout the mitotic cycle in *Physarum*. I worked practically non-stop, missed heartbeats be damned, finishing late on a Friday night, too tired to gather up all my books and papers and load the squareback. But I accomplished what I had set out to do: the results indicated that polysomes disaggregated by heat shocks in G2 readily reformed when the cultures were returned to their normal incubation temperature; those shocked during the S-phase did not. The explanation for this finding (there were several possibilities), however, would have to await further experimentation.

When I came in on Saturday morning to haul everything away, I found that it had already been dumped into boxes which were sitting in the corridor. I hurriedly loaded them into the squareback before someone threw them in the trash. On my last trip into the building Morrison appeared, offered me a handshake and wished me good luck. I took the hand, but reminded him that, "This is wrong, Marty, and you know it."

I consulted an ACLU attorney, Ron Borod, whose father was a partner in one of Memphis's biggest law firms.

"You want to sue St. Jude Hospital??"

I explained that what happened to me was totally unprecedented in the scientific community and that if I did nothing, they, or any other institution, would feel free to fire anyone they chose for not showing up at a relatively trivial meeting called by an authoritarian department chairman.

"Okay, but your chances of winning are almost nil."

"I'll take that chance."

"We can't do it on a percentage basis. You'll have to pay the hourly fee." I agreed, but only in terms of a regular monthly payment—we had very little money in the bank and were both (temporarily we hoped) unemployed.

The next question was that of compensation for damage to reputation and future earnings. A scientist's being fired was nearly unheard-of, and such a smudge could easily have a profound effect on both. I wrote to three colleagues, got two rough estimates of $1,000,000 and one of $500,000. I decided to ask for $750,000.

The case would be argued by William Fones, one of the senior partners in the firm of Rosenfield, Borod (Ron's father), Fones, Bogatin & Kremer.

Before filing the lawsuit I wrote to Danny Thomas himself, naively thinking he might want to know what sort of people were running St. Jude for him. Several weeks later I received a letter from one of his minions suggesting that someone with my talents could undoubtedly find work elsewhere (no suggestions were made as to where), and urging me not to "rock the boat."

I began to look for such a position, an endeavor I had planned to pursue that final year at St. Jude anyway. But the Vietnam war was now at its apex, and research funding was becoming progressively more difficult to obtain. Even so, I was invited to give seminars at the University of Kansas and the Kettering Institute in Yellow Springs, Ohio. Either would have been fine with me: office and lab space at UK was more than adequate, though it would come with a heavy teaching load. Kettering, on the other hand, would have fewer teaching requirements to interfere with research time. Moreover, Yellow Springs was within easy driving distance of Muncie and Madison, and our parents were aging rapidly.

I also wrote to the head of the "other" *Physarum* group (at Case Western Reserve University), Oddvar Nygaard, who invited me to come to his lab, but only as a post-doctoral fellow (a faculty position wasn't available). I decided to hold his offer in reserve.

While all this was underway I continued to keep up with the literature in the library at UT. By this time, however, my Wisconsin driver's license had expired, and I sweated whenever I came near a squad car. Renewing my license would have required an eye exam, which would have exposed my fatal ophthalmologic disease. I began to look forward to the cocktail hour each evening.

During those seven months in limbo I even began a novel (I had plenty of free time). The plot revolved around a mysterious, deadly illness that was afflicting people all over the world at an increasing rate. The protagonist manages to trace the disease back to the time of the first space flights and the return of the (contaminated) vessels to Earth. Perhaps it would have turned out to be an earlier, though surely inferior, version of Michael Crichton's *The Andromeda Strain* (one of my favorite novels), but working on it was probably good therapy.

The first two job opportunities didn't pan out. I suspect my being fired didn't help much—not only for the obvious reason, but because it seriously interfered with my plans to spend my final year at St. Jude writing up all my experimental results for publication. I was working on these papers, but it wasn't possible to get them on my c.v. soon enough. The sacking was a double whammy.

Having no other option, I accepted the post-doctoral appointment at CWRU (a recent merger between The Case Institute of Technology and Western Reserve University). Suspicious by now of all academic appointments, I wrote, in my acceptance letter, that "I assume there will be a four-week vacation period (standard academic practice) and that there are no further requirements associated with the position." This probably sounded arrogant under the circumstances, but I figured that if I got an affirmative response I might be able to argue that I didn't have to submit to a required entrance physical because I had been assured there were "no other requirements" associated with the position. Furthermore, the phrase might have made it more difficult to fire me, if I missed a meeting, for example, without sufficient grounds. I learned later that this line angered Oddvar and he almost withdrew the offer. Another faculty member and fellow DPU alumnus Tom Evans apparently talked him out of it. I don't know what we would have done if he hadn't and the offer had been retracted.

After the movers took the furniture we loaded the VW with everything else we owned, including The Great Books, and pointed it north, toward Cleveland. Somewhere in Ohio we turned off the interstate to look for a restaurant to have lunch. The local squad car officer, perhaps thinking we were a couple of hippies looking for a place to settle down, literally stayed on our bumper until we circled through the town and were on our way back to the highway. I was terrified, of course, not of being arrested or beaten up, but of being found to have no driver's license and subjected to an eye exam or even a complete physical (I had read somewhere that one of the states—Pennsylvania, I think—was toying with the idea of requiring the latter for a license).

Soon after we got back on the interstate, the rear end of the VW suddenly fell. I thought all the weight had broken the axle. By now I was so distraught that I didn't even consider other possibilities. While we were standing around worrying and wondering what to do, a man from South Carolina stopped, peered underneath the car, and discovered that it was only a flat tire. He didn't say much else, simply got to work with a big jack that he had retrieved from his own vehicle, and we were soon back on the road, no charge. It almost seemed to be a reminder that, despite our experiences in Memphis, some very good people lived in the South.

It was March, 1970. I was thirty-two, Karen twenty-seven. We were flat broke and our prospects uncertain.

CWRU

We stored our chattel in graduate-school friend Al Ehrhart's garage, and spent a few days visiting our families in Indiana and Wisconsin. "Lefty" seemed a little colder, more distant than he had in the past. A child of the Great Depression, he couldn't understand how anyone would do *anything* that could get him fired from a salaried job.

I proceeded to devote much of these visits to worrying about a possible physical examination in the Department of Radiology at Case Western Reserve. For months afterward I dreaded checking my mailbox, but, amazingly, the notice never came and I settled down to work on DNA replication and the effect of gamma-radiation on that process (I had little interest in radiation biology; it was the price I had to pay for the opportunity to work as a new post-doc). Based in large part on Oddvar's recommendation, Karen was immediately offered a faculty appointment in the Medical School Library, which she gratefully accepted.

At that time there were half a million soldiers in Vietnam and the death toll (faithfully reported on the evening news programs) continued to climb. The anti-war protests were becoming more massive, more frequent, and more violent. All of that was crushed when Ohio Governor Rhodes ordered the National Guard to quell a May 4th demonstration at Kent State. By the time it was over they had quelled four students to death. Nixon and his henchmen had almost single-handedly repealed the First Amendment, which provided for the right of the American people "to peaceably assemble" to protest unpopular (or even popular) governmental policies. After Kent State, people became afraid to peaceably assemble for fear of their lives.

Not long after that we attended our first Cleveland Orchestra concert. George Szell, wearing a black armband, as were most of the players, directed his forces with energy and precision. It was a uniquely rich, sweet, almost indescribable sound, especially from the violins. We subscribed immediately. A few weeks later, unfortunately, Maestro Szell was dead from cancer.

My "office" was a narrow anteroom adjacent to the cobalt-60 irradiator used by everyone in the department for their research. Not only did I have another mortal threat to worry about (being continually zapped by Jabba the Hutt humming menacingly behind a thin, lead-lined door a few feet away), but everyone used the tiny room to set up their experiments and hang around to wait for the irradiator to do its job, making it difficult for me to read or plan experiments. Furthermore, I had to beg a little bench space in my colleagues' labs and borrow their equipment in order to do my work.

Nevertheless I was very grateful for the opportunity, and gave it all I had. Oddvar and I began a study of the repair of radiation-induced DNA strand breaks *in vivo* throughout the mitotic cycle of *Physarum* (due to the multiplicity of nuclei, perhaps, the intact organism is quite radiation-resistant), and I, on my own, began to investigate the repair of such breaks in isolated nuclei. These findings were of some interest to the U.S. Department of Energy, and I was able to contribute my part to the renewal of the DOE contract that supported the department's research program. I was soon offered the services of a part-time technician, a dental student, who promptly informed me of the death of a patient whose lower gum had been injected (the dentist had nicked a vein or artery) with xylocaine, thereby instilling another phobia, a fear of local anesthetics invading the vessels of my gums.

The weekly meeting of the staff of the Division of Radiation Biology took place, as at St. Jude, on Fridays at noon (I suspect this is true in many institutions—it helps ensure that the faculty will show up that day). I made sure I didn't have any big experiments planned for the end of the week or, if I did, that they didn't follow a conference or other event that I was expected to report on.

I was astonished, though, to discover that *almost nothing happened* at these meetings. A discussion of research was rare, only when there was an upcoming Department of Energy site visit or we were hosting a visiting colleague. The meetings were chaired by Hymer Friedell, M.D., who had been among the first Americans to arrive at Hiroshima after the blast to assess the damage done to the Japanese people. The conversation usually involved newly-discovered restaurants, the latest in golf-ball technology, upcoming parties or picnics, etc. It was a politically conservative group, some wearing ties and closely-cropped hair, generally unsupportive of the anti-war movement. It seemed more like a corporate board meeting than a gathering of dedicated researchers.

It is often said that 90% of all the scientists who ever lived are alive and working today. Nothing could be further from the truth. Most of the people running around in white coats got into the business simply because it was a job like any other, and are no more scientists than was Grandma Moses. Many, in fact, are quite ordinary human beings. I didn't dislike any of these guys (or the one or two women); I was just bored and didn't say much.

Another disaster: I broke one of the lenses of my glasses. Fortunately, it was the left one, which was virtually useless anyway. Somewhere I found a piece of ordinary glass about the same size and glued it in. Since it was flat, it reflected all the light in the room like those of a character in a cheap movie. I wore that until I discovered I could get a new pair using my old prescription. Moreover, the license bureau didn't require a professional eye examination. Suddenly I had new glasses, could legally drive again, and had one less burden squatting on my sagging shoulders.

In the meantime, the lawsuit against St. Jude (financed by regular $50-$100 monthly payments to Rosenfield *et al.*) went forward, and in November of that year (1970) I had to return to Memphis for a deposition. It was here I discovered the hospital's position: since I had been paid from an NIH training grant I was, by definition, a post-doctoral trainee. The letter (the *only* one I had failed to make a copy of) written to Sells informing him that I was not willing to come to work at St. Jude as a post-doc, but only as a faculty member at the assistant professor level, had been "lost or misplaced" (though he admitted that there had been a letter "of some kind" written at the time). I particularly remember his shit-eatin' grin when he glanced at me during the proceedings. At least we knew now what we were up against.

I was urged to find three well-placed scientists to serve as expert witnesses to back up my claim that one does not fire a faculty member, or even a post-doctoral fellow (if it came to that), without just cause (sleeping with the chairman's wife, or committing a federal crime, for example). Since what had happened to me was unheard of, I could probably have found hundreds. The first three I asked—Oddvar Nygaard and the research directors at the Kettering Laboratories and the Cleveland Clinic, all of whom were as shocked as I was about what had happened at St. Jude, agreed to go to Memphis to testify.

My attorneys had made it clear: in their opinion, no jury would come down on the side of an "outside agitator" against their own well-known, life-saving children's hospital, so we opted to put it in the hands of the federal (because my salary had come from a U.S. government grant) judge, the Hon. Bailey Brown.

The one-day trial took place in December. The cheapest shot came early, when I was on the stand. Defense attorney Heiskell asked me (on cross-examination) what I had published based on my "slime mold work" at the hospital. I had to confess that I hadn't yet had time to write up this work (several papers did eventually come out of that research). His obvious intention was to show that I hadn't accomplished anything at the hospital, presumably to convince the judge that I wasn't worthy of a faculty appointment at St. Jude and the University of Tennessee. I tried to point out the unfairness of that line of interrogation, that I was preoccupied with establishing a new research program at CWRU, but was cut off by the familiar Perry Mason line: "No further questions."

Otherwise I described the original interview with Bruce Sells, during which he told me that, even though my salary would come from a training grant, I could expect the rank of assistant professor, a faculty status not commensurate with a post-doctoral fellowship, as well as the details of my being precipitously fired by Morrison and Pinkel. I thought my testimony went well, and that any reasonable person could only conclude that I had obviously been screwed, railroaded, or both.

My litigating attorney, Mr. Fones, called only one of the three expert witnesses who came for the trial, Oddvar Nygaard. (Ron Borod later explained that his testimony would be sufficient to make the point—anything further would be "overkill.") In fact,

Oddvar testified that what happened to me was totally unprecedented *regardless of my status at the hospital,* and, furthermore, that the damages to a scientist's career by such a capricious action could be catastrophic. The plaintiff rested and we went to lunch.

In the afternoon the defense had its turn. The witnesses were Pinkel; Allan Granoff, "research director" at St. Jude; Morrison; and Sells, who again admitted to "not having found" the damning evidence that I had agreed to come to Memphis only as a member of the faculty, not as a post-doc. How well I remember his eyelids fluttering like butterflies when he made that assertion. When asked why, if I were only a "special trainee," he had requested a faculty appointment for me at the University of Tennessee, he replied, "It seemed to bother him."

Later, the judge asked Morrison what he thought I was going to do instead of appearing at meetings or doing research—"go out and drink beer?" His response was that he thought I could have done "anything."

I had spoken briefly to Granoff during my interview trip. Heiskell asked him to relate what had been discussed during that conversation. He said, "I asked him why he changed his mind." Not only was this untrue, it was startling because, all during the afternoon, no one had admitted that I had been negotiating anything *other than* a post-doctoral position. I quickly whispered this contradiction to Ron Borod, but the issue wasn't pursued by Mr. Fones (who, incidentally, was suffering from an intestinal infection).

Pinkel went on the stand to testify that the meeting between him, Morrison, the army guy, and me was "merely to give Dr. Brewer an opportunity to vent some steam." (If it had been to hear my appeal, it would have suggested I was a bona fide faculty member rather than a mere post-doctoral fellow, who, he asserted, would not be entitled to due process.) He absurdly stated further that the correspondence between Sells and me *"was for information only"* (i.e., the letters and discussions had no legal standing and were not part of my contract with the hospital, which was spelled out in Pinkel's "special trainee" letter to Spain).

Though there were some loose ends that hadn't been tied up, I was certain we had won the case. Karen and I stopped for the night somewhere on the way back to Cleveland (we drove, while paying for the flights of the three expert witnesses). I was on a kind of elation high, I suppose, and didn't close my eyes for a moment that night. I went over and over the testimony and invariably came down on the side of the plaintiff. I remember asking myself how someone like defense attorney Heiskell, who seemed a pleasant enough sort, could make straight-faced assertions based on false premises when it seemed so obvious that his clients weren't telling the truth.

Back at CWRU I again threw myself into my research. By the following February, 1971, I had worked almost a year virtually without a break. I decided to take a week off, and catch up on some sleep and a stack of unread books and magazines. A day or two into this hiatus a letter arrived from Rosenfield, Borod, Fones, Bogatin and Kremer: Judge Brown had come down on the side of St. Jude Children's Research

Hospital. In fact, his written *Opinion and Judgment* was virtually a photocopy of the defense brief, fully accepting the "facts" of the case to be exactly as stated by St. Jude. One of the false assertions accepted by the court was a quote from a letter I had written to Morrison in February, 1969, in support of a proposal I had made to apply for my own research grant, in which I opined that "It would benefit Bruce, and I'm sure he would agree with this, if he could hire *another post-doctoral fellow* to carry out his research programs, use his space, and his funds" (emphasis supplied by the judge). Since Sells already had a post-doctoral fellow, Francis Davis (Lowell was gone by then), I was suggesting that the money he was paying me from the training grant could be used as a stipend for a post-doc *in addition to Francis* (emphasis supplied by me). The court, in accepting St. Jude's interpretation, averred that I was admitting by this statement that *I* was the "other" trainee in question, a misconception based on an error in logic, if not a justification to rationalize a preconceived decision.

I couldn't believe that justice could be so badly served, even if the defendant was a famous hospital. I decided to appeal.

* * *

Though a gradual withdrawal of American troops from Vietnam was finally underway in the spring of 1971, the hostilities were expanded to Cambodia with President Nixon's order to bomb Viet Cong supply routes there. Shortly thereafter, the "Pentagon papers," exposing many of the government lies that had led to U.S. involvement in the war, were released by Daniel Ellsberg. I was beginning to wonder whether *anyone* in a position of authority was capable of telling the truth.

By summer, Karen had earned some time off and we spent a week or two on Grand Manan, where we met Andy Silber and Rea Wilmshurst, from Toronto, who became lifelong friends. Andy, an American, was a professor of English at the University of Toronto, and Rea a consummate copyeditor.

Daisy the Dog loved the beaches, where she could splash in the surf and fruitlessly chase flocks of gulls and other seabirds, who disdainfully watched her race toward them for a quarter-mile or more before bothering to fly away.

Since we passed along the tops of cliffs during our hikes, we worried about Daisy's joining us on the trails. I asked host Jim Buckley about it. "In all the years we've been coming here," he assured me, "there has only been one dog fall off the cliffs."

I said, "That's the one I'm worried about!"

Once, in fact, she disappeared right over of the edge, and we were sure we would find her lying three hundred feet below on the rocky shore. In a few seconds she hopped back up—there had been a little protrusion, just below the top, big enough for her to turn around on. It was Barbara, Andy's mother, who reminded us that dogs are quadripeds, and it's easier for them to maintain their footing than for us. But I still fretted about that poor mutt who, years before, had tumbled down the sheer face of the cliff to his death.

On August 16th, while we were away, our appeal brief was filed in the U.S. Court of Appeals, Sixth Circuit, in Cincinnati.

*   *   *

On our return to Cleveland I was surprised and pleased to learn that an unused laboratory belonging to another department had been found for me in the sub-basement of the Wearn Building (Radiation Biology was on the basement level). There were two lab benches, vacuum, air, and gas lines, and a spacious office. After more than a year in a passageway with no equipment, I had a real laboratory of my own and a full-time research assistant as well (by then I had been quietly promoted to the rank of Assistant Professor).

I brought in a fish tank.

The only drawback to the new quarters was that they were next door to something with the ominous-sounding designation, "Pain Research." I never found out what that involved (like a movie set, the door was always closed when an "experiment" was in progress), but I sometimes heard cats screaming in the huge, nearly-empty laboratory. An obviously successful program: some of my new neighbors had been able to figure out how to cause considerable pain, at least in cats.

That autumn (1971) we moved to Shaker Heights, a suburb of Cleveland. Discovering that one of my DPU roommates, Alan McDonald, the relief pitcher and lover of poetry, had ended up teaching math at the high school there, I gave him a call. There was no answer. I tried again in a day or two. Still no answer. In the mail a few weeks later was a copy of the *DePauw Alumnus*. While crossing a street, my old friend had been killed, not long before we had moved to the neighborhood, by a hit-and-run driver. I had hoped to renew our friendship; Al was one of the nicest guys I have ever known.

In the same magazine I learned that another alumnus had died from an allergic reaction to anesthesia during surgery. Death seemed to be lurking around every corner. I began to worry anew about a possible hernia operation, not to mention crossing a street.

The duplex we rented (we had the top two floors) was a beautiful old house on a quiet street, Winslow Road. It was carpeted wall-to-wall and came with a fireplace, a big dining room (with black walls!) and an open space at the top of a spiral staircase, overlooking the living room, which we used for a library. Daisy loved to run around the small front yard (and the adjacent ones) three times a day without a leash, but hated being left in the basement when we went to work. I developed the habit of coming home for lunch on occasion, sometimes staying for the rest of the afternoon if I had reading and writing to do and could leave the experiment in the hands of my assistant. On weekends we would sometimes drive into the country so she could run as much as she wanted, often on the grounds of the Buckminster Fuller geodesic dome not far from Cleveland. She slept well those nights.

After a lifetime of chasing pigeons, she finally caught one there (perhaps it was sick or injured). She hadn't a clue what to do with it, though, and immediately let it go, watching bemusedly as it waddled away.

In December (1971) the appeals court upheld Judge Brown, finding no compelling evidence to overturn his decision. The lawsuit had apparently been doomed from the start. I felt particularly bad about the precedent set by the case. It seemed that anyone could be fired from either a faculty or training position at any government-supported research institution on the flimsiest of grounds, and I considered appealing to the Supreme Court. My long-suffering wife advised against this, as did my attorneys. The consensus was that I had done the right thing, but it was over.

On a happier note, we learned that Don Pinkel, director of St. Jude Children's Research Hospital, had resigned to take a position elsewhere.

By the spring of 1972 I had done enough work to submit two papers to major research journals, and two others describing some of the studies I had initiated at St. Jude. Based on the former results, I proposed a unique model for DNA replication in *Physarum*. And with Oddvar Nygaard I reported the results of experiments which showed that the duration of the delay of mitosis by radiation during the S-period corresponded to the degree of unrepaired damage (strand breaks) incurred by the replicating DNA at the time of the exposure.

I was amazed to discover that my tropical fish had personalities. When I came into my borrowed laboratory every morning they would swim around excitedly, as if glad to see me (they were undoubtedly hungry, too). For this and other reasons, I made my first venture into vegetarianism that summer. Though I had scarfed down as many burgers in my lifetime as the next guy, all the while trying to ignore the nagging realization of where they came from, the time had come to say I wasn't going to step on the ant anymore.

Unfortunately, it turned out to be the wrong time. I had cut my hand on a piece of broken glass and, for some reason, it wasn't healing well. This went on for the couple of weeks I maintained my new diet regimen. I quite unscientifically concluded that there must be something in meat that promoted healing, so, in the name of science, I had a couple of burgers. The wound soon closed. Of course this had nothing to do with a "healing factor" (as I called it). Perhaps I wasn't getting all the proper vitamins, minerals, and amino acids with my poorly-devised vegetarian diet. Regretfully (and regrettably) I became an omnivore again. It was another decade before I experimented once more with animal-free food.

The American people bought into Nixon's "secret plan" to end the Vietnam War, as well as Kissinger's last-minute assurance that "peace is at hand," and the President was easily re-elected. But the ship of state was already leaking. Earlier in the year a few

Republican henchmen had broken into Democratic party headquarters at the Watergate apartment complex in Washington looking for useful or damaging information. No one paid much attention to this except for a couple of *Washington Post* reporters. Perhaps because I had been a personal victim of lies by those in positions of authority, I gleefully followed the Senate Hearings, the impeachment, and the rest of this historic effort to disrobe government untruths. It was both sad and gratifying to watch Richard M. Nixon resign the presidency nearly two years later, a fate brought on by his own duplicity.

In December I received a check from St. Jude in the amount of $2500. On the back it warned, "Endorsement of this check constitutes payment in full of any and all demands, claims, and/or benefits of any nature due payee and his attorney as of the date (Dec. 19, 1972) of this check." But why *then*—were they worried about another appeal? This wouldn't even have begun to cover my expenses for the fiasco, never mind any damages to my career. I still have the damn thing.

During the winter of 1972-73 I decided to take cello lessons. As it happened, Oddvar's daughter had an (temporarily) unused instrument which she was generous, and courageous, enough to loan me. I studied it for six months—until she needed it back—at the Cleveland Institute of Music, which was closely associated with the Cleveland Orchestra. I had a good teacher, and I learned to play it passably well. Technically it wasn't difficult, but I discovered that bowing is much more than hitting the right notes. There are certain subtleties in reading the music, in timing and emphasis, that don't appear on the printed page. Great art, I discovered, is much more than it appears to be.

Two new lines of evidence had come up suggesting I had been a faculty member at St. Jude, rather than a post-doctoral fellow. First, the Internal Revenue Service declared, as the result of a 1971 audit, that I had to pay taxes on my salary at St. Jude, i.e., that I was an employee, not a student or trainee. More importantly, I discovered that there were many other bona fide faculty members around the country whose salaries, like mine, came from training grants (a fact that was not known to my attorneys at the time of the original trial). Ron Borod wrote to the National Institutes of Health to confirm this, and requested that a representative testify to this important detail in court. The point was conceded, in writing, but the request for an appearance was denied. Nevertheless, my case, already strong, I thought, was further strengthened by these two new findings, and had a better chance of being reversed by the Sixth Circuit Court of Appeals in Cincinnati. My attorneys agreed.

That autumn, Dad retired at the age of sixty-three. He didn't want to, fearing he would wither and die with nothing to do, but my siblings and I convinced him that the difference between his salary and his retirement pay was so small that he would be working for almost nothing.

He took up golf.

I played with him a few times. He was no better at it than he was at horseshoes or roller skating, though he considered himself an aging Jack Nicklaus. It took him forever to line up a putt, regardless of how many players were chafing behind us. Embarrassingly, if we were paired with other players, he would introduce me as "my son, Dr. Gene."

His fear of boredom proved to be unfounded. He went back to serious gardening and added a roof to the little front porch. He worked a million crossword puzzles. The next decade was probably the best of his life. Mom was happy, too: she had long dreaded seeing him go to work in icy weather and early-morning darkness, or when she was sure that tornadoes were on the way.

But he was getting older and more overweight (he claimed he needed the extra poundage "to fall back on" in case of illness). I became increasingly worried about visiting them, fearing that Dad would suffer a massive heart attack over his plate of sausage and eggs.

He and Mom began to go out to eat on occasion. One evening as we were leaving the house I heard her remind him to "get that change off the dresser, Dad." They had never heard of a percentage tip, and left whatever they happened to have, even if it was only a few pennies.

Brother Larry, a born-again Christian, brought them into the Church of the Nazarene, where they became active choir members and nursing-home visitors. They sometimes sent us tapes of their performances in such facilities, singing hymns and reading the Scriptures, or played them when we visited. Suddenly they were praying at every meal (and before taking the car on the road) and faithfully attending evening prayer meetings.

Larry had turned into a fine musician, a trumpet virtuoso and terrific singer (he sounds much like Sammy Davis, Jr.). He could act, too (we saw him in a couple of church cantatas). I once suggested to him that, under different circumstances, he could have become a Broadway star. "I don't care anything about that," he scoffed. Instead, he became music director at several churches and, eventually, a Nazarene minister.

In November, 1973, I again appealed the federal court's decision. This time, in January, 1974, the appeals court unanimously agreed that I had grounds for seeking relief from the lower court's verdict, and referred the case back to Judge Brown in Memphis for reconsideration. The amended lawsuit was filed in the Federal District Court in March.

In July, the judge upheld his earlier decision.

Back to the Appellate Court, which decided once more, this time by a vote of 2-1, not to overturn. Again I queried attorney Borod about the possibility of taking the case on to the Supreme Court. He didn't recommend it—such appeals are rarely heard by the high court, he said. Despite the close decision, I decided not to waste any more time and money. Don Quixote had run up against his last windmill.

It was about this time that a grape-size cyst on the back of my neck became infected, and I had to go to Kaiser Permanente (our chosen health care provider) to have it lanced. Fortunately the guy wasn't wearing a stethoscope, but he recommended I have the thing removed "sometime soon." I told him I would do that, but I didn't say how soon (it was the spring of 1995).

During our fifth summer vacation on Grand Manan, we decided to build our own summer cabin. There was a beautiful 100 acres not far from Whale Cove Cottages that was rumored to be for sale. It was owned by a native Grand Mananer, Bev Parker, who lived in Toronto, and he happened to be on the island at the time. We tracked him down and asked him about the property. He told us he wasn't prepared to sell just yet (he was asking $5000), but we would have "first refusal." We gave him our address and waited for him to notify us when he was ready.

Before leaving, we scouted the property looking for a place to build our "dream" cottage. We stumbled around for a couple of days until Karen, up a hill fifty yards away, shouted, "Gene! I can see the water!" I made my way through the underbrush and fallen trees, and found she was right: it was the perfect spot. It even had an old logging trail running almost to the site from Whistle Road. We looked forward to 1975 with eager anticipation.

Not long after Nixon had resigned and was pardoned by President Ford, I was informed that "my" laboratory had been reclaimed, after three years, and I would be moving (again temporarily) to a vacant space on the third floor. By this time I had obtained a National Science Foundation grant covering my salary and that of my technical assistant, and was contributing my share to the department's large contract with the Department of Defense. Despite not having a permanent "home" after more than four years of hard work (my fish died at about this time, too), I felt that my situation had improved considerably, and I fully expected to have a long career in molecular biology.

I teamed up with Tom and Helen Evans for studies on the effect of the inhibition of protein synthesis by cycloheximide on DNA replication in the intact organism, and with Ron Rustad and Nancy Oleinick on the delay of mitosis late in the cell cycle by the same drug along with ionizing radiation. Ron was a hopeless alcoholic by then, though he still exhibited some lucid moments. The latter study was particularly interesting because it showed that within thirty minutes of mitosis there was no need for protein synthesis to occur in order for the nuclei to divide. Within twenty minutes of division, mitosis could not be stopped by radiation, either. But if cultures were irradiated between these two markers, mitosis was again delayed by preventing protein synthesis—i.e., when the cycloheximide would not otherwise cause the delay. The results suggested that radiation-induced mitotic delay is caused by damage to pre-existing mitotic structures which require protein synthesis for replacement or repair.

On a rainy Saturday morning in the spring of 1975, while taking Daisy to see the vet, I suddenly saw a ragged, zig-zaggy apparition in my field of vision. Within thirty minutes it moved to the side and disappeared, but the long-dreaded manifestation of my incipient eye disease had finally come to pass. I anxiously awaited another appearance of the "zig-zag thing," and in a few weeks it recurred, again lasting about half an hour. Although doomed, I did nothing about it except to anticipate the violent headaches and propulsive vomiting that would accompany the cancer after it had spread to my brain.

Karen and I knew what we wanted for our cabin on Grand Manan. It was an original design based on two of the Whale Cove Cottages: open space inside, everything made of wood, including huge beams supporting the plank ceiling. But when we arrived on the island that summer, we found someone building a house on "our" land. Extremely disappointed, we stopped to inquire about it. The builder's name was Walter Sydiaha (you don't pronounce the "ha"). He was from Toronto and a friend of Bev Parker's (both were Jehovah's Witnesses). Bev Parker had sold him the property the previous winter. He knew nothing about our "first refusal" arrangement, and we were left with another tattered dream and wondering whether there was anyone of any persuasion in this wide world who was capable of telling the truth.

However, Walter had subdivided the land and was willing to sell us some of it. We agreed to buy the two parcels at the ends of the tract, each about 30 acres, for $5000 each (the total size of the original property turned out to be about 130 acres).

An electrician by trade, Walter was also an excellent carpenter. We hired him to build our own cottage on the northernmost property, on the spot Karen had stumbled across the previous summer. We gave him our plans and sketches, marked the building site, and went back to Cleveland, where I discovered I had been moved again, this time to another "laboratory" with no gas, vacuum, or air pressure, and which was, ironically, directly across the corridor from the nice sub-basement facility (as well as the Pain Research Laboratory) I had vacated the year before. Once again I had to carry cultures and equipment back and forth, as I had done my first year at CWRU, but this time it involved stairs or elevators. It's not easy to move an ultracentrifuge rotor from floor to floor without disturbing the delicate distribution of density gradients, but I had no other option.

However, after six years at CWRU, five as assistant professor, someone noticed that the research space within the department could be rearranged to allow me to have a lab of my own, a bona fide, legitimate home within the Division of Radiation Biology. It took my ensconced colleague a few more months to move into his newly-refurbished facility, leaving me his old office and laboratory (he also left some instruments that took several more weeks to dislodge). I shelved all my books and research notes and just sat at the desk or wandered around the lab the rest of the first afternoon in my own research space. At last, it seemed, I belonged.

Regardless of my improved situation, the palpitations worsened. Sometimes I would get up from a meeting, ostensibly to visit the bathroom, in reality just to move, to get a drink of water, to try somehow to restore a regular heartbeat. Concentration was more difficult than ever: even when my pulse was regular I knew that it soon wouldn't be.

At night, as I lay in bed listening to my pulse pounding in my ears, I made up a wishful rule: if I could get to fifty steady beats without skipping one, I was going to be okay and could go to sleep. One, two three, four, five, six, seven—oh, God—one, two, three, four . . . Eventually, after several minutes, or hours, I would score a fifty and drift off. But D (Doctor)-Day was rapidly approaching. In less than two years I would be forty and no longer immune to heart disease.

On one particularly bad Sunday night, when I couldn't manage to get even to fifty, I remembered having some strong coffee at a friend's house that afternoon. Now utterly desperate, I decided to give up caffeine altogether. After a day or two of headaches and drowsiness, the irregular beats did, in fact, decrease in number and severity, though they never completely disappeared. One afternoon, after vacating the lab for an hour or so in an attempt to calm my nervous heart, I returned to my office only to experience a "fluttering"—not just missed beats, more like an ineffectual vibration. This long-anticipated nightmare precipitated a full-blown panic attack. Seeing or hearing nothing, I trotted down the corridor toward the hospital's emergency room. In case this was the fatal attack I had been waiting for since I was sixteen, I wanted to be where someone could get my heart started again (at some point the desire to live finally overcomes the inaction of fear). Halfway there, my heartbeat became regular again.

What did this mean? Did my pulse return to "normal" because I was surging down the hallway? Was an increased heart rate the antidote to an irregular beat? I almost never exerted myself and was a little overweight. Perhaps my general lack of fitness was a factor? Despite the risk of a fatal heart attack, I decided to try getting some exercise. It was either that or find the courage to see a doctor.

In the spring of 1976 I started loping around a baseball field near our rented duplex. I never got very far because the palpitations would begin, sometimes accompanied by chest pain, and I would immediately stop jogging. Once again I was stymied: my new athletic program didn't seem to be working. In fact, it occurred to me that exercise itself might bring on a fibrillation or even an infarction. I began to wonder if there was *anything* I could do safely, and what might happen if I had an attack while speaking to a group or sitting in a dentist's chair. Extrapolating from that scenario: what if xylocaine exacerbated the problem—especially if the dentist accidentally hit a blood vessel—would I die a horrible death, clawing at the arms of the chair and gasping for air? I was becoming increasingly fearful of treading too close to the edge of the cliff and falling to the jagged rocks below.

Maybe, I thought, I was working too hard. I took a painting course and entered one of my acrylics, called "Bicentennial," in the Cleveland Art Museum's May Show. It wasn't accepted. I started grinding another telescope mirror. It languished in the basement. I was almost thirty-nine.

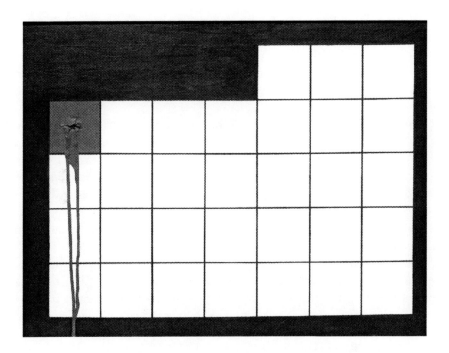

Bicentennial (the original is in red, white, and blue)

Summer came again. Gordon and Charlotte drove from Madison to Cleveland to accompany us to Grand Manan and see what all the fuss was about. We had bought some old furniture for the new cabin and transported it to Canada in a U-Haul trailer, the in-laws following along behind. Unfortunately, when we got to the island, we found that the cottage was being built on island time. Although the walls and windows and some of the cedar shingles were up, there was no fireplace, no water, and the new gravel driveway went only halfway to the house, so we had to hire someone with a tractor to take the furniture the rest of the way in (about 300 more yards). Nevertheless, it was a beautiful sight, and the view of the bay was spectacular. We ensconced the folks in one of the Whale Cove Cottages, made up a bed, and turned in. It was the first night of hundreds slept at Whistlewood.

That fall, Karen became director of the library in a brand-new medical school, the Northeast Ohio Universities College of Medicine (NEOUCOM), a consortium affiliated with three major universities: Kent State, Youngstown State, and the University of Akron. It was a big step up for her, but it required driving more than an hour twice a day. We decided to move somewhere between her job and mine. After a brief search, we ended up with a ranch-style house, the first we had ever owned, halfway between Aurora and Mantua. The house was only a few years old and set in a one-acre copse of young hardwoods. There were residences close by on either side, but only fields in front (across Pioneer Trail, a dirt road) and behind. We moved in on December 31st, 1976.

While waiting for the paperwork to be completed I voted for Jimmy Carter, primarily on his promise that "I'll never lie to you." And, although he wasn't a great president, he always told the truth (as far as I know), and I don't regret my vote in the slightest.

The bi-level house was attractive and comfortable, with fireplaces on both floors, and we looked out over forests and farmland. We had a small yard in front and back (which I enjoyed mowing), a little hand-dug garden, and eventually I bought a chainsaw to cut fallen trees for firewood. The only drawback was the sometimes icy drive to both universities, fifty minutes each way for me, a half hour for Karen. Though she was uncomfortable on the winter roads, I enjoyed the trip. It was a pleasure to drive home every afternoon or evening to the relative quiet and solitude of the country.

Like many strong-willed couples, however, Karen and I began to experience some marital difficulties. There had been minor differences before this, occasional arguments, etc.—perfectly normal relationship—but they were becoming nastier and more frequent. We knew there was a problem, but we thought we could work it out.

But then I made the mistake of falling in love with my technical assistant, who was in the process of getting a divorce (yes, *K-PAX* fans, I'm only human). Though she was beautiful, possessed a sparkling personality, and we liked each other a lot, I never gave her a romantic thought until she informed me of the separation from her husband. I took a closer look and was snared.

Unfortunately, Amanda had another boyfriend, an old and painfully familiar scenario. We discussed the options: there weren't any. I moved into an apartment in Cleveland, tried to convince her to change her mind, and failed. By now it was becoming difficult for me to work with her—I was too emotionally involved. Finally, we agreed that it would be mutually beneficial if she sought employment elsewhere. She moved up the street to the Cleveland Clinic, and later became a nurse. Despite my indiscretion, Karen took me back.

All of this was taking a toll on my nervous system, which was nearing its fortieth birthday and making unpleasant noises. It was time to take the bull by the horn. After an extended period of sleeplessly pondering the situation, I finally came up with a clever way to minimize the trauma: I would see a psychologist, who, I hoped, would help me overcome my apprehension and get me into a doctor's office. Not because I thought my health problems were mental—a psychological cause for the irregular heartbeats and other symptoms had still never occurred to me—but just to get me through the hell of picking up a phone and making an appointment for a physical examination.

I saw the analyst three or four times and, after diagnosing the problem as a kind of phobia (white coat syndrome), he generously agreed to set up an appointment for me with his own internist under terms I could accept. The physical would be broken down into parts: during the first visit we would discuss my history, on the second he would look into my ears, listen to my lungs, whatever I was comfortable with. And so on, regardless of how many encounters it required to get a stethoscope next to my chest.

It only took two tries. On the second, in a moment of unaccountable courage, or perhaps because my new physician seemed sympathetic to my plight, I allowed him to listen to my heart with his stethoscope. After doing so, he pronounced it "normal." Unbelievably elated, I asked him to proceed with the rest of the examination. There were no significant medical problems except that I had an incipient hernia, something I had known about since my college entrance exam more than twenty years earlier. As long as it didn't cause me any problems, he didn't even recommend surgery for that. As for the "heart murmur," also discovered while at DePauw, there was a "beta bundle blockage" which resulted in a little tick in the sound coming into his ears. It was a benign condition which precluded nothing. He instantly approved my desire to begin jogging, or any other exercise program I wanted. But what about the heart palpitations? I asked. They weren't, he informed me, "skipped beats," but premature contractions (an early beat followed by a rest period when the heart would normally have contracted, followed by another regular beat). Again, not dangerous. Chest pain? "Try running through it." The jagged lines I sometimes saw in front of my eyes were merely "pre-migraine" (though I never suffered the blinding headaches). I was okay! I was *healthy*! There was nothing really wrong with me!

How can I describe the feeling of ecstasy I experienced on skipping out of Dr. Cubberley's office? It was like crawling out from under a boulder that had been crushing me for thirty-five years. No, it was more like escaping from a cave filled with starving bears. No, it was a hundred times better than that. It was like crawling out from under a huge boulder in a cave full of starving bears and emerging into a glorious day filled with flowers and butterflies and bright sunlight, sweet smells and music. No. It was a hundred times better than that . . . . The fact is, it can't be described. And I had beaten the deadline by several weeks!

I went back to the lab the next day in an entirely different frame of mind. I could speak to a seminar group or at a meeting without fear of having a fatal run of premature beats. I wasn't going to drop dead in the grocery store like Uncle Cliff. I wasn't going to fall forward at my desk at lunchtime and choke to death on my pickle and pimiento sandwich.

I could do anything!

When we arrived on Grand Manan this time, our cottage was ready for us. We had a beautiful big fireplace, a dug well (I hauled the water in buckets up the hill), a gas refrigerator, but no phone or electricity, by choice. I borrowed a wheelbarrow from the Buckleys and carried dirt from the back to the front of the cabin to make a patio for chairs and a table, cut wood with my new chainsaw, installed bookshelves. We hiked all over the island with Andy and Rea, enjoyed lobster picnics and sunsets, cleared brush to improve the view of the Bay of Fundy, picked raspberries, worked puzzles, read in the evening. I don't think I ever felt so alive and happy!

Back at CWRU in September, though, I began to feel unhappier almost by the day. This was not only unfortunate but also untimely, especially after more than a decade of struggle to get to where I was. By now I was helping to bring in nearly a quarter of million dollars to the Division of Radiation Biology: my own $100,000 grant; another of about the same value with colleague Nancy Oleinick; and my share ($40,000) of the large Department of Energy contract, and I was enjoying the services of two or three assistants. I was becoming an "old boy" in an old-boy network.

Yet, I was beginning to enjoy research itself less and less. Part of this may have had to do with the endless striving for acceptance, the constant battle for every inch of forward movement, the internal political requirements from which there seemed to be no escape. A change of scene might have been salutary, but jobs were still scarce. I looked down the road and saw no forks, only the narrowing of the path as it receded farther and farther into the distance, and even that was becoming shorter by the minute.

I suppose there were a lot of factors contributing to the disillusionment I was feeling. Among these were my continuing concern and frustration over the way we human beings were overrunning the Earth and all the creatures inhabiting it, and the apparent lack of interest in the problem by almost everyone. With the planet disintegrating before our eyes, even research seemed unimportant in the comparison, at least to me.

In brief, I was experiencing, at forty, a full-blown mid-life crisis. I stuck it out for another couple of years, going through the motions, waiting for an opportunity that never came. Ironically, I was doing work that was more satisfying and potentially important than any I had ever done, but my heart was no longer in it.

For example, I found a substance in extracts of *Physarum* that stimulated the synthesis of DNA in isolated nuclei. The partially purified stimulatory substance had a molecular weight of about 30,000, and contained both protein and carbohydrate. Another study led to the first report of the repair of radiation-induced double-strand breaks in isolated nuclei. Finally, one of my research assistants, Peggy Busacca, and I found that extracts of isolated nuclei (i.e., they contained sub-nuclear entities) were capable of limited DNA synthesis which, again, appeared to be genuine replication (extracts of G2-phase nuclei were incapable of performing this feat). And in my spare time I was attempting to coax isolated nuclei to carry out mitosis *in vitro*.

The final blow came when Oddvar nominated me for promotion to associate professor with tenure. This step up the ladder usually comes when a faculty member has demonstrated excellence in research and teaching or service to the university. By this time I was obtaining nearly all of my funding from government grants and contracts. And, although I had done little teaching (I had been informed earlier that this was optional as long as my research was productive and I contributed to the university in other ways), I had served on a number of medical school committees, including those that reviewed theses and examined Ph.D. candidates, hosted several visiting scientists, and participated fully in intra- and inter-departmental symposia and other academic affairs and functions. I had been an assistant professor for seven years, the usual amount of time allowed for promotion. On the basis of publications and grants alone I should have been a shoo-in.

As it happened, Hymer Friedell, chair of the Department of Radiology, retired at just this time. His replacement was a well-known radiologist from the Cleveland Clinic, who immediately requested promotions (including mine) for three of his faculty members. When the decision finally came down, all of the applications had been denied. I went to see the head of the promotions and tenure committee, who had little to tell me except that "If you re-apply next year you'll get it—no problem." I learned later that the reason for the shutout was simply to demonstrate to the new department head that he couldn't have everything he wanted right away, couldn't throw his weight around the Medical School from the outset.

I knew then that, one way or other, I would soon be leaving Case Western Reserve University to the small-time politicians in charge. Indeed, I was beginning to seriously wonder whether there was *any* academic or research institution where fairness was the rule. I suppose such places exist; I was never lucky enough to find one.

With the full compliance of my doctor, in the meantime, I began to run. Sometimes I would feel a few early beats or a little chest (muscle) pain, and would slow down or walk for a while, but I kept at it. I increased the distance until I could run a mile, then two, then three. On my way home from the lab one Saturday afternoon I stumbled across a marathon that ended at Case Western Reserve. I stopped the car and watched for a while as the strung-out runners loped to the finish line. They looked tired but were still running. I thought: I can do that!

It was said that marathoners were immune to heart attacks. I subscribed to *Runner's World* and found a book called *The Complete Runner*, by Jim Fixx, which covered every aspect of distance running for the amateur. It was an invaluable guide and reference book, and is still quite relevant today. I began to run races, usually 4-milers or 10Ks. I didn't do very well, but I loved the challenge. As I got stronger and faster, the heart palpitations virtually disappeared. I attributed this bonus to my becoming fitter. It had still never occurred to me (though Dr. Cubberley might have known) that the premature heartbeats might be due to an anxiety disorder.

I applied, in the spring of 1978, for a position as a grants administrator at the National Institutes of Health, the agency that distributes most of the funding for research in the United States. The NIH offered a one-year internship for successful applicants. Upon completion of the training program, he or she would be ready to join the staff and begin judging research grant applications from all over the country.

I was invited to come for an interview. We drove to Washington, where I spoke with three of the resident administrators. The interviews went fine: mainly we discussed current events, surprisingly little about research topics. It all seemed routine, almost *pro forma*. All three, however, asked me what had happened at St. Jude Children's Research Hospital.

I got the peculiar feeling that this was more about the hospital than about me. It was as if they were weighing the pros and cons of a grant to St. Jude, and wanted an insider's look at what went on there. Most of the questions were about the way the hospital was run, and not what I did to get myself fired. Nevertheless, it's also possible that they were trying to determine whether I was still a boat rocker.

While waiting for the NIH decision I began to seriously consider what I would do if it were negative. In my early forties and still in the grip of uncertainty, I had reached the conclusion that I wanted to try to do something more significant than merely adding another drop or two to the ocean of data on DNA replication and cell division, or even the causes of various cancers, most of which were already known (smoking, sunlight, a meat-based diet, etc.). Moreover, I told myself, whatever you might discover in the laboratory, someone else would have found it eventually. And deep down I knew that, under the circumstances, I would never become the "great scientist" I had long aspired to be. On the other hand, I don't think I held any illusions of making an enormous impact on people's attitudes toward the Earth, either— on the order of a John Muir or Rachel Carson, for example—but my state of mind was forcing me to do *something*.

As I saw it, there were three possible options in my quixotic quest to wake people up to what we were doing to our planet: 1) become a politician; 2) become an activist; 3) become a writer.

The first of these I ruled out immediately. Had I been younger, I might have been willing to patiently work my way up from local councils, concerned with sewers and rights-of-way, to the state level, with its endless debates over taxes and budgets, and eventually try to get myself elected to Congress, where I might or might not have been able to shepherd a few environmental bills through the House. That is, if I could get elected to a local council to begin with.

The second option was a more attractive proposition. I could see myself liberating chickens or minks from their terrible fates, or driving spikes into redwood trees. If I were richer, or more courageous, or unmarried, I might have taken that route.

The third seemed the most promising. I was at least somewhat literate, I loved books, I could work at home in the country at my own pace and without dealing with petty internal politics. My college English professor had encouraged me to develop my writing talent and, later on, Karen had liked the partial novel I had written in Memphis after being fired. Besides, writing seemed easy: just make up a story and write it down. (As Mark Twain put it, all you have to do is cross out the wrong words.) I discussed this option with her, certain she would raise the obvious objections: my hard-won scientific career would probably be wasted; and, perhaps more compelling, our income would be cut in half. Instead, she said, "Go for it." Not because she was sure I had sufficient ability to be a successful writer, but because I wanted to try. At that time she thought I would either be published within three years or would give up and try some other line of work. She was wrong on both counts.

I ran my first marathon at age forty-one (May, 1979) in 3:29. No problems except for a blister on my left foot. But the next day I could barely walk.

The NIH informed me that they had no need for my services. Immediately after Labor Day I turned in my resignation effective Oct. 31. In the interim, Oddvar came into my office to request that I stay on until at least the end of the year, when my Dept. of Energy contract ended. No longer willing to drive two hours a day on slippery roads (I had experienced one or two close calls by then), and eager to get a fresh start on a new, and, I hoped, more worthwhile career, I declined. "You must really hate this place!" he shot back. I had no idea it was so obvious.

By early October I had phased out all my research projects. I spent a week or two going through and discarding or giving away every book, notebook, and journal article I had on my shelves. When I left my office and laboratory they were bare. Some of my colleagues lauded my "courage" in chucking it all and taking up what I really wanted to do. They were undoubtedly thinking in monetary terms. From my perspective, however, it would have taken far more courage to stay. I said good-bye to a life in science and took up my new career with the usual high hopes and expectations. I was forty-two, Karen thirty-six.

First race

STARTING OVER

I never looked back—not consciously, anyway—though I sometimes had dreams about the lab. As often as not I would discover that I had forgotten to transfer my cultures to fresh media, and they withered and died. At other times I hadn't the slightest idea what to do with them. I would even imagine I was about to give a lecture, and couldn't think of a thing to say. But, like old soldiers, these subconscious thrashings slowly faded away.

My parents accepted my decision with little comment. It was only Lefty, Karen's father, who had a problem with my career change. He couldn't begin to understand how anyone could give up a solid income for nothing, regardless of the slim prospect for even greater remuneration. He became even more distant. St. Jude redux.

The first year, when I wasn't at the Goodwill store buying old books for dimes and quarters, I was reading them. I wanted to learn how a novel was structured, how to write a story that would pull the reader along, how one goes about getting a book published. A few of those I read were:

Kurt Vonnegut: *Jailbird*
F. Scott Fitzgerald: *The Great Gatsby*
J.D. Salinger: *Franny and Zooey*
John Steinbeck: *East of Eden*
Erskine Caldwell: *God's Little Acre*
William Zinsser: *On Writing Well*
Agatha Christie: *And Then There Were None*
Pearl S. Buck: *The Good Earth*
William Styron: *Sophie's Choice*
Margaret Atwood: *Life Before Man*
Ursula K. LeGuin: *The Dispossessed*
Graham Greene: *Dr. Fischer of Geneva* or *The Bomb Party*
Ralph Daigh: *Maybe You Should Write a Book*

I don't know whether these and other books taught me how to structure a novel, but they did teach me one important lesson: what grabs the reader are a story's characters—the plot is of lesser importance. The wisdom I ignored is that any imbedded "messages" should be severely curtailed, if not omitted. (There are exceptions to the latter precept: *1984* and *Brave New World* come to mind.) It took me a long time to figure out how to convey something I wanted to say by disguising it as part of a story told by strong, believable, and likeable characters.

In the beginning, my head was putting out ideas at a prodigious rate no matter where I was or what I was doing. In order not to forget any of them I carried a pen and a three-times folded sheet of 8½ x 11 paper in my shirt pocket, and a pad on a bedside table, for the jotting of notes. I developed a picture system for use while jogging—for example a mental image of a giraffe waving a banana while chasing a truck—"g," "b," and "t" would be the first letters of the keywords I needed to remember. It usually worked for up to seven or eight letters.

At the same time I wasted a considerable number of hours in the Kent State Library reading through every issue of *Writer's Digest* and *The Writer*. Most of their advice was pretty useless, though there was the occasional seed of helpful information which, I hoped, would sprout into the beautiful flower of a published novel.

That first year out of the lab I also learned to cook a few things and to bake bread and rolls and muffins. To make jams and jellies (I glowed when Aunt Mae reported that my apple/cinnamon was the best she had ever tasted). To shop for groceries. To keep the house clean, and the furnace and water softener functioning. To scrape and paint the house. To maintain control of our meager income so we didn't have to go into unnecessary debt. The thousand things a househusband has to do.

Unfortunately for my supportive wife, a closet gourmet, I hated cooking. I had no feel for, or interest in, what it takes to make a dish look and taste good. I didn't have the necessary background, for one thing (Mom kept the boys out of the kitchen). But Karen suddenly developed some serious food sensitivities which forced her to adopt a very simple diet: a four-day rotation of foods she could eat and virtual elimination of others, like wheat, corn, sugar, yeast, and dairy products. With the limited options, I could cope.

I experimented with recipes, substituting other ingredients for the grains that were a problem for her. I kept a sourdough starter going for years. There are few things in the world more satisfying than kneading dough in a sunny kitchen, watching it rise, smelling it bake in the oven. And what tastes better than a freshly-made dinner roll? I even mastered the art of French baguettes and croissants.

Though I was having the time of my life (I thought), I began to have difficulty sleeping. I would wake up at 5:00 or 5:30 and not be able to doze off again. So I would have to take an afternoon nap and/or go to bed early the next night, and repeat the process. At about the same time I began to experience a persistent tingling sensation in my left arm and elbow. Of course I was certain I was on the verge of a heart attack, one of whose symptoms is often numbness in that arm.

During my annual checkup, Dr. Cubberley diagnosed the former problem as a mild depression, and advised me to eliminate the naps and stay up as late as I could. "The worst thing you can do for insomnia," he told me, "is to sleep." This may be true, but I'm one of those people who can't do a thing while drowsy—my mind is in a fog. I tried to follow his advice, however, and gradually learned to sleep better. The second problem, the tingly arm, was a case of "tennis elbow" (though I didn't play tennis). He predicted it would soon go away, and it did. In fact, both symptoms diminished when I finally began writing my first novel, perhaps because I unconsciously believed I was productively working again.

Daisy the Dog was a wonderful companion that first year, lying beside my reading chair in front of the downstairs fireplace while carefully studying the rabbits and squirrels outside the sliding glass doors; licking muffin bowls; accompanying me to haul in firewood or gather kindling; driving with me to the grocery store. She turned twelve that first Thanksgiving in the country, and was still frisky. After the day's work we would often go for a walk in the woods behind the house. In the big field behind that, she ran and ran.

So did I, slowly increasing my distance until I could run twenty miles easily, even in very cold weather. I never tired of running along country roads listening to the spring peepers and the Canada geese, admiring the beautiful horses and majestic great blue herons, gawking at huge patches of daffodils. Striving to fulfill the requirement for Boston (3:10 for runners over forty), I ran another couple of marathons that year. I came closer (3:22), but never quite made the cut.

In September, while still working full-time, Karen began writing her Ph.D. thesis (on the American Red Cross in China), for which she had been studying and taking notes for a couple of years, particularly on Grand Manan. It was wonderful when we were reading or writing together in the evening and on weekends. It took her almost three more years to finish it and earn her doctorate.

Many novelists begin a career by writing short stories, figuring, I suppose, that they can learn the craft and establish a track record that will impress editors. That plan has probably paid off for any number of writers. But it wasn't the way I wanted to go. I prefer to read (and write) novels for the same reason I prefer symphonies over songs, oil paintings over pencil drawings. It's their breadth and depth that resonate with me. Furthermore, Ernest Hemingway, one of the greatest writers of all time, had advised, "The only way to learn to write novels is to write novels." What was good enough for the master, I thought, was good enough for me.

RALPHY

On November 4, 1980, Ronald Reagan easily beat Jimmy Carter for the presidency, marking a significant turn to the right in American politics, though it was only a hint of the further leap, to the *far* right, that resulted in the election of George W. Bush twenty years later. It was in this climate that I began my second career, with the sketchy outline of a first novel and dozens of pages of notes on plot and character and how to write it.

I wrote with a ball-point pen in longhand on yellow pads, starting each day by typing what I had written the day before (unfortunately, computers were not in general use at the time—revising meant retyping the entire manuscript). Five hours of creative writing was about all I could manage in one twenty-four-hour period (this seems true of most writers). The rest of the day was devoted to household chores, during which I thought about the day's production and jotted down notes for the next day's work. It took me exactly one year to finish the novel, including two or three revisions.

Halfway through the manuscript, in the spring of 1981, Daisy began to have "spells," in which she would start to shake and almost lose consciousness. We thought it might be a form of epilepsy. The vet, however, diagnosed it as a reaction to pain, and prescribed Bufferin, which helped, but the episodes continued. It was on to phenobarbitol. By summer she was having difficulty walking, and was put on butazolidine. A myelogram in late August indicated that she was suffering from calcium deposits on her spine; these were removed in September. She improved briefly, but by the end of that month she could barely walk and had become incontinent. From then on she lay on a diaper, but she still enjoyed her limited life, especially her meals. This arrangement continued for more than a year.

While writing the novel I ran several more races, including two marathons. I was quite trim by then, my weight at about 140 lbs., and rarely experiencing palpitations. Once during this period I ran forty-eight miles in forty-eight hours—two twenties sandwiched around an eight-miler on three successive days. I was running so much, in fact, that I began to enjoy an afternoon snack of leftover pie or Little Debbies. I even started drinking coffee again until the Saturday, when Karen and I were shopping, I experienced one of those awful periods of heart "fluttering." It probably lasted only a few seconds, but it seemed like forever. I went back on the wagon again.

Ralphy is about a boy growing up in rural Indiana with his sister and two brothers. The twist comes in the form of a deformed younger brother. Here is the opening paragraph:

> Ralphy was born flat—his mother had tripped coming off the escalator at Sears and squashed her unborn baby. From the side he looked normal, more or less, but from the front he resembled a flounder. It was assumed that his brain had been flattened, too, and that its pancake-like configuration was what had made Ralphy "differnt." At the age of four he had not yet walked or said anything. He never cried, nor did he laugh, unless those peculiar sounds he made were little sobs and chuckles. By this time his body had rounded out, except for his head and a little hump on his back. The doctor said that Ralphy was physically healthy, but that he might be retarded. Although, he pointed out, Einstein had also appeared to be rather slow-witted early in life. He said they would have to wait and see. Ralphy was almost five now, and they were still waiting.

Thus, he is a fishlike creature, a throwback to an earlier time in evolution when we humans somehow made a wrong turn and began to focus on our own selfish desires at the expense of all the other creatures inhabiting the Earth. Another major character in the novel is the TV set in the corner, which is always on. It is through this instrument that we see what is happening in the outside world. The members of the household rarely hear it, however, focusing instead on their own individual problems.

Ralphy has little interest in his family, preferring instead the company of the animals inhabiting the surrounding fields and forests, who would often come into his yard at night. At the same time, his disdain for a plasticized and violent society suggests the only possible means by which mankind can save itself from self-destruction.

The complicity of religion in the family's indoctrination is personified by Reverend Turk. He is such a powerful force that Ralphy's brother Mark is contemplating becoming a minister. At first he has no doubts about the existence of God or his relationship to the Almighty:

> "And I say to you today that the devil is HERE!" boomed Reverend Turk. "He is right here in this sanctuary right NOW!"
>
> Ralphy's mother pondered what she was going to have for dinner with the roast beef. *well, boiled potatuhs n green beans would be good n*
>
> Mark wondered what the devil looked like. He glanced around him. *who would it be or did he mean the devil is in everybody*
>
> Becky looked over toward Gary Snider, who quickly turned away. *he's almost s cute s Doug I wonder why he's always so shy*
>
> "... of all marriages end up in divorce. Why? Is it because young people are getting married too soon? Is it because they don't try hard enough to make their marriages work? Well, I don't claim to be any highfalutin psyCHIatrist or ..."

oh Lord I didn forget to turn on the oven did I I wonder if

er what if Revern Turk's the devil wouldn that mean that everything he's sayin is

Doug ain't like that he looks right straight at you jist like Steve McQueen

". . . forces at work which will destroy family life in this great country. And I'm not talking now about the pornographers and the abortionists and the evolutionists and the environmentalists and the sex education people and the women's libbers and all the rest. I'm talking about . . ."

maybe Daddy or J.T. will notice that the oven ain't on doggone it I know they won't

or maybe the devil is in me an I don't even know it wouldn that be funny ah I'd know it if I was the devil wouldn I

I think you're so cute Dougy I love you Becky oh your breath smells so good and you taste so wonderful

"GOD!" thundered Reverend Turk. "We've let GOD go out of our hearts and minds and we've given in to our own selfish wishes and desires planted in us by the devil himself. But we can FIGHT the devil. We can . . ."

look at ol lady Turner over there asleep I wonder if she knows how people

wouldn it be jist weird if the devil really was here someplace an he jumped up on the stage n everything

oh Doug you taste so good you taste so good you taste so good

". . . what the BIBLE says. The Bible doesn't SAY for a man to covet his neighbor's wife. The Bible doesn't SAY for a woman to disobey her husband. The Bible doesn't SAY for a man to commit abomination. The Bible doesn't SAY . . ."

oh now I remember what I was gonna git at the store yesterdee oh how could I forgit bread . . . .

While Ralphy is communing with the surrounding animal life, his father, ignoring the pain and other symptoms, is quietly dying of cancer. His ordeal drastically alters Mark's view of God, Who now seems unfair and even capricious, and he decides to go into another line of work. Becky misses a period, spends a miserable couple of weeks thinking she's pregnant, and is overjoyed when she discovers she is not. J.T., on the other hand, tries for months to get lucky with Jennifer Bracken, concludes he will have to marry her to fulfill his desires. In the background the never-silent TV set personifies the relentless brainwashing of all of them by corporate America.

At the end, after his father dies of cancer, Ralphy leaves the house, never to return:

The yellow plastic bird popped from the clock in the living room and cuckooed twice. Ralphy stood looking out his window. Down the hall, someone was softly snoring. There was a nearly full moon, and he could see the shopping center looming behind the fence. Above it, a few stars twinkled.

He went to the door and gazed around his room—his bed, his pen, his kitchen chair. Finally he turned and padded down silently down the hallway to his mother's room. He watched her sleeping for a long time, then placed his hand gently on her head. His black eyes glistened.

In a moment he was at the front door. He unlocked it and stepped outside. It was cold, but there was no snow on the ground. He strode with quick little steps across the backyard and slipped through a hole in the fence into the SuperMart parking lot. An owl hooted in the distance. In his mind he saw two blinking yellow eyes, and he felt her soft feathers on his cheek. He smiled, turned toward Mercer's Woods, and was gone.

Okay, so it wasn't Hemingway. But it had a certain simplistic charm. Of course it was based, in part, on my own upbringing, as many first novels are. Perhaps, however, it was *too* personal, too autobiographical to be dispassionately universal.

On Grand Manan that summer Jim Buckley, our former host and Toronto English teacher, read and liked *Ralphy*, or at least thought it showed promise. Andy and Rea read it and did not. Based on their comments I made further revisions soon after we returned to Ohio.

I was further encouraged, however, by the responses of other friends and family, most of whom were pleasantly surprised that I could write something that even *resembled* a novel. My father, who had never read a book in his life, seemed to be as impressed as anyone, though he remarked that he "would have said it differently." (He soon started his own novel, though he never got to page two.) Brother Bob kindly called it "a minor American classic." A Kent State professor, from whom I was taking an evening course on twentieth-century American literature, thought the dialogue was "right on."

I decided to go to the publishers directly, rather than try to find an agent. This was partly because of something I'd read—that it was at least as difficult to find a good agent as it was an editor—and partly my distrust of putting my work into someone else's hands, losing control.

My sourcebook was *Writers' Market*. This is basically a list of editors and agents with a little useful information about them, such as the kinds of books they like to publish. I wrote letters describing my new novel to all those editors who professed a desire to see the work of "new authors," "writers with something to say," "originality," and the like, about twenty altogether. In the absence of a word processor, this again meant typing each letter one at a time. I limited the list to New York houses, thinking that all the action was there. I took the stack of queries—each containing a self-addressed, stamped envelope—to the post office, and went for a long run.

The next day and the next and the next I foolishly checked the mailbox, expecting to find twenty replies, at least some of which would be enthusiastic. In fact, the replies slowly dribbled in over a period of months, the first from a subsidy publisher, now defunct, which also published a certain percentage of its books in the usual manner, it claimed, with actual payment of royalties. Eventually there came half-a-dozen requests to see the manuscript, the other replies mainly flat rejections. Karen patiently hauled the original to work and made photocopies as needed (in those days there were no Kinkos or Mailboxes, Etc. on every corner). While waiting for the responses, I drew a rough sketch of what I thought would make a good cover illustration:

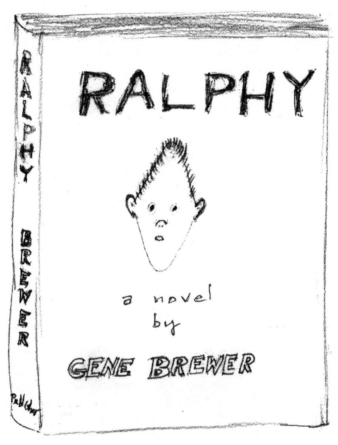

Ralphy

It took another six months for all the assessments to come back. One heartfelt reply from an editor at MacMillan, Rayanna Simons, informed me that the house wouldn't be interested in my "beautiful vision," as it had decided to focus on cookbooks. (When I tried to contact her later about my second novel, I learned she was no longer in the publishing business.) Only the subsidy publisher was enthusiastic: "If you were a well-known author, this would be a bestseller!" (Naturally—Patricia Cornwell could publish a dishrag and it would be an immediate success.) Nevertheless, I declined their gracious invitation to pay for the printing of *Ralphy* myself.

The novel (queries, samples, or the complete manuscript) was ultimately rejected by sixty-six editors. Religious diatribes aside, it may also have failed to find a home because there was little action or excitement; this is the challenge one faces in depicting the quotidian lives of ordinary people.

I considered sending the novel to the smaller, more obscure publishers, but by this time I was already well into the second one, and my printed sources all advised me to "put my best foot forward." Hoping opus #2 would be an improvement over #1, I scribbled on, and the typed pages piled up once more.

That summer (1982) we were fortunate enough to meet Rowell and Pres Bowles, who spent most of their summers on Grand Manan, their winters in Manhattan. Rowell had traveled all over the world with UNICEF; Pres was a retired editor at Golden Books. Like Andy and Rea, they became good friends. We didn't know at the time, of course, that we would be moving to New York City six years later.

That same year we met the Cronks, two brothers and their families. All of them are remarkable, especially Ron, who seemed to have read every novel ever written in the English language. Every summer thereafter he loaded me up with books to read over the winter, introducing me in particular to a number of fine Canadian writers— Timothy Findley, Lesley Choyce, and many others. The Cronk families are one of the many reasons we love to return to the island as often as possible.

Not long after our return to Mantua, Daisy suddenly started turning in circles when I helped her to urinate. It was probably only an ear infection, but it led to another trip to a surgeon, this time at the Ohio State University Veterinary School in Columbus. The spinal procedure was repeated, and she did well until I came to bring her home. I knew something was wrong when she refused one of the French fries I had bought for lunch. By the time we got back to Mantua she was vomiting. I called the surgeon, who recommended continuing the antibiotics she was on and seeing how she was the next day.

She was worse. The local vet told (and showed) us that moving her front legs caused her intense pain, and advised taking her back to OSU. When we arrived, most of the faculty were at a football game. One of the students placed her on a cart and wheeled her away. Knowing she was failing, probably, he allowed us to stay with her for as long as we wanted before we returned home. She went into kidney failure and died the next day of a massive infection at the site of the surgery, two months short of her fifteenth birthday. We had lost not only a dog but a cherished member of the family.

BREAKTHROUGH

My second opus was an undisguised attempt to capitalize on my scientific background. Surely, I thought, I had an advantage here. I knew how science worked, had experienced the joys and frustrations of research, the politics and infighting, the kinds of people it was populated with. *Breakthrough* was the story of an iconoclastic scientist, one who just wants to be left alone to do his work, but who slowly learns what it really takes to be a successful researcher.

The opening sentence gives the reader a clue about what's coming: "Arthur M. Raintree, Ph.D., stepped out of his yellow Volkswagen into a pile of dog shit." Amateurish, perhaps, but it's still one of my favorite lines of all those I've written.

Halfway through the novel I decided to attend a one-day local writer's conference. I listened attentively, took some notes, learned a few things (don't use dialect, as I had in *Ralphy*). I submitted a chapter of my work-in-progress, but I knew I was in trouble when the winning entry, "Grandfather's Shoes," was announced. Heartwarming little essays about family life just weren't what I wanted to write.

Breakthrough may not have been any good, and some of the scientists little more than caricatures, but at least the science was authentic. Tissue cells grown *in vitro* have a finite lifetime which depends on the animals they are derived from. Human cells, for example, live far longer than mouse cells, and this is true for virtually the entire spectrum of animal species. Moreover, cancer cells live indefinitely in culture dishes. Raintree's premise was that there might be a "longevity factor" present in cells that determines how long they live, whether *in vitro* or *in vivo*. He hopes to extract this substance from cancer cells and find out whether it will prolong the lives of normal cells. When he finally gets enough of the equipment and supplies he's been promised, he begins his adventure by preparing extracts of two different malignant cell types, and tests them for the presence of a "Ponce de Leon" factor:

> On Christmas Day, Raintree, alone in the department, began the Big Experiment. He set up several flasks of mouse cells, each of which would be treated with a different concentration of tumor cell extract, or with no extract at all. The protocol was exactly like that for the earlier hydrocortisone experiment except that

the extracts would be substituted for the hormone, and there were cross-combinations of lung tumor extract/normal mammary cell, and mammary tumor extract/normal lung cell, as well as a *rat* lung cell line tested with the mouse lung tumor extract.

Hour after hour he worked, forgetting lunch, forgetting time, until all the various combinations had been realized. It had been another very long day, a day that lasted only a moment. He enjoyed a great wave of satisfaction as he stepped back to admire the neat rows of culture flasks standing on the shelves of the 37C incubator room. To the bottom shelf he taped a large sign: DO NOT DISCARD THESE FLASKS. He would take a look at the cells, check them for contamination, and re-feed them every day or two for the duration of the experiment. In a few weeks he would be in the future, and he would know whether there was a Ponce de Leon factor present in tumor cell extracts.

Several days later Raintree, nursing a cold, brings the cultures out of the incubator and places them next to the microscope. He sits down in his rusty lab chair.

Squeak . . . whooooosh! Under the lens went a culture of untreated mouse lung cells. Up, down, back, forth . . . They were beginning to look old and sick, just like they should. He wiped his nose, coughed, and shakily picked up a flask of identical cells which had been treated with a 1:10 diluted extract of lung tumor cells. Back, forth, up, down . . . Oh. They, too, were dying of old age.

Ah, he should have known it wouldn't work; it was just too simple. What a dumbbell. Under the lens went another flask of lung cells, the one that had been exposed to the most concentrated tumor extract. Back, up, forth, down . . . Oh God, they were healthy! Down, forth, up, back . . . They were healthy! Suddenly it was difficult to breathe. A major breakthrough! For a moment he sat with his head bowed, trying not to explode. Then he emitted a kind of howl, and it was over. Back to the Big Experiment.

The lung cells treated with the mammary tumor extract . . . Still going strong. And the mammary cells treated with the lung tumor extract—lovely. Now the rat cells treated with the mouse tumor extract. No good! Raintree ran back to his office and quickly scribbled the results on a yellow pad, as though he might forget them: Highest concentration only! Species specific!! Tissue non-specific!!! Yes, Virginia, there *is* a Ponce de Leon factor. The only question left for the Big Experiment to answer was how long the treated cells would continue to grow and divide in the presence of the PDF.

Raintree scurried back to the little room with the microscope and returned all the flasks to the incubator. There was still a great deal of work to do: cell counts, transfers . . . But right now he just wanted to sit quietly in his office and contemplate what he might do next. He wished he could tell someone. But nobody was around except Watanabe, and he barely understood English.

For the next experiment he might try to prepare an even more concentrated extract, but he was pushing that limit already. Or treat the cells less often. Or begin to purify the PDF! Get some idea of what kind of substance it was. Wait. He would make a list:

1. PDF concentration
2. Age of cells at beginning of experiment (what happens if you *start* with old cells?!)
3. What happens if you take the stuff away?
4. Purify and characterize!!!
5. Try human cells!!!!!!
6. What if—

Wait a minute. What would Pasteur do next? What was the *ultimate* goal? To find out whether the PDF would prolong life, right? So why not try it? It would take a few years, of course; mice already lived a couple of years without the PDF. All the more reason to get started right away. While he waited for the mice to get old he could be doing all the other things on the list, and more. Suddenly it was fun again. Callison or no Callison. No matter what happened from now on, they could never take this moment away from him . . . .

As soon as he has enough fresh tumor extract, Raintree embarks on the Big, Big Experiment. He begins injecting six mice daily with the extract, and six controls with a placebo. Soon afterward, he learns that his beloved Uncle Mentor has suffered a heart attack. He explains to Callison that he must return temporarily to his hometown to help with the farm work, and won't be able to finish the NIH grant application. Callison insists he stay. It is the last straw. Raintree packs all his notebooks in his briefcase, steals a dog meant for a sequence of pain research experiments, gets into his yellow VW and, leaving the petty self-interests of the science world behind, heads west to join his ex-girlfriend, the mother of his unacknowledged daughter, and return to a simpler and more meaningful life.

Again semi-autobiographical, and satisfyingly cathartic, but with all the intrinsic problems associated with that self-serving exercise. I finished *Breakthrough* in March, 1983, and began the laborious process of typing out the query letters. This time they went to a half-dozen prospective agents as well as fifty publishing houses, some of which had already considered *Ralphy*. I showed it to only one colleague back in the lab, my former research collaborator, Nancy Oleinick. When she returned it she informed me that Ron Rustad had died of a heart attack. He was barely fifty and living in a nursing home, his mind and a brilliant career destroyed by alcohol.

Nancy said she liked the novel, but none of the professional judges did (I think Paul de Kruif would have). Looking back on it from another century, I find that I don't much like *Breakthrough*, either. I had violated a cardinal rule: though more complex than the characters in *Ralphy*, my protagonist was not sympathetic enough. He meant well, and was working to benefit humanity, but he was also something of a jerk to most of the people he interacted with, an overt expression of my own bitterness and disappointment, I suppose. In any case, I would know how to write a better, more likeable Raintree now. Maybe I will.

In February, just before I finished the novel, we adopted another Dalmatian, Shasta Daisy. When we picked her up and she ran out into the snow and immediately sat down, watching us expectantly, we were hooked. She wasn't as smart, or as human, as Daisy the Dog, but we came to love her just as much. She, too, was with us for almost fifteen years.

That spring, Karen successfully defended her thesis and was awarded the Ph.D. in American history. Now there were two doctorates in the family, neither of which was of much practical importance. I had become a writer, and Karen decided to stick with her job as head librarian at NEOUCOM, at least for a while. Between the two of us, however, we knew something about almost everything.

In May, while driving her to Cleveland Hopkins Airport, my left hand suddenly felt numb. It only lasted a couple of hours, and I soon forgot about it. It was a few years before it happened again.

In July, Dad suffered an apparent heart attack. An arteriogram showed that at least four arteries supplying his heart were 80-90% clogged. He needed bypass surgery. His doctor recommended that he have it done in Indianapolis or elsewhere (the procedure wasn't as routine then as it is today). Thanks to my old friend Al Ehrhart at the Cleveland Clinic, we were able to get him into this world-renowned hospital.

I was terrified. What if he had a heart episode while he was staying with us, waiting for the surgery? In October, I took a CPR class and learned exactly what to do in case the worst happened.

After hiding all the liquor in the attic (I didn't want the jarring knowledge that we were drinkers be the last thing he thought about as he was being anesthetized), I drove to Muncie and brought him (and Mom) back for the procedure. The next day he went in for tests, and the day after that, the operation. It was an enormous relief to leave him in his room that gray November day. I had done everything I could. The rest was up to the Clinic.

He came through it very well. However, during the post-surgical conference with the surgeon, we learned that Dad's legs had very few veins left (they had been stripped away due to varicosities years before), so they had resorted to using a couple of arteries they had found somewhere in his chest (a reversed artery can be used as a vein). As I remember, they replaced only the two most severely-blocked vessels. Nonetheless, the prognosis was good.

One afternoon while he was still in the hospital, Mom asked me, "With all those books in the house, how's come you don't have no Bibles?" As it happened, I did have one, and I went downstairs to retrieve it from the "philosophy and religion" section of our library. It was a copy of *The Revised English Bible*. She didn't like the looks of it, but grunted her apparent satisfaction.

A few days later I drove them back to Muncie, where they went right back to fresh side, bacon grease, and all the rest. I stayed overnight and left them in good spirits. But I suspect I was even happier to have the ordeal over than were they.

That October I ran my last marathon, the ninth. During the training phase I tore a calf muscle, which required butazolidine (the same drug we had given Daisy for arthritis) for treatment. It took a month to recover from that, and I learned to stretch more thoroughly before the training runs. By autumn I was fully recovered and well-prepared for the race. But halfway through the 26.2 miles I developed a blister on the sole of my right foot and had to take the golf cart back to the finish line. Although certainly not wasted, all the training had come to nothing on that day. Even without injury, marathon day was often too hot, or too cold, or too rainy. It just didn't seem worth it anymore.

But I did keep running, and still do. Only now I call it jogging.

Brewer family. Back row, left to right: Larry, Bob, Nan, and me.

Mae and Lester in their later years

A PRETTY GOOD PILOT

Senator Edward Kennedy was a popular figure in 1983—Chappaquiddick hadn't happened yet. I decided to elect him President. I called my third novel *2020*, an all-too-obvious double entendre.

The setting was the U.S. at a time when right-wing Republicans had taken over the government (a backlash to Kennedy's liberal presidency and the cover-up of his death in office) and asserted their conservative agenda. The novel featured identical twin brothers, one of whom was a television news reporter afraid to say anything on the air that might get him into trouble with the authorities, the other a super-genius who understood how the present political climate came about (told in flashback), and was out to change things.

I had barely gotten started on the novel, however, when I decided to try to conquer my fear of flying. Perhaps my failure (to that point) as a writer had precipitated yet another mid-life crisis, and I wanted to find something, besides bread baking, I could accomplish. Or maybe, after facing up to my father's bypass surgery, I simply wanted to look at my terrors head-on and conquer the apprehension by seeing for myself how safe flying really is. Or perhaps because I remembered how much fun it was a quarter-century earlier.

Since Karen was an employee of the consortium of Northeast Ohio colleges, I was able to sign up for flight training with free tuition. The only expenses would be for books and some small devices like a cross-country flight calculator.

Kent State was no rural airport with little traffic, as Reese's in Muncie had been. It was the number two non-military flight school in the country, second only to Florida's Embry-Riddle University. Ground school was not easy, and piloting was even more challenging, especially for someone in his late forties. I discovered it was much more than takeoffs and landings. It involved navigation, control tower communication, stalls and spins, emergency procedures, night and cross-country flying, and a thorough knowledge of meteorology and flight rules. It was wonderful!

Oddly, there was no fear with my instructor in the cockpit (which, incidentally, means just what it says—male pilots sometimes take girlfriends up for more than just the view. And vice versa, I suspect). For one thing, he was born to fly (and went on to become a captain at USAir) and his supreme knowledge of, and *feel* for, how an airplane works was extremely reassuring. As was his calmness, even when I was unsure of the situation. I must have understood implicitly that if I made a mistake he would get me out of trouble.

Since I had flown before, none of the procedures really surprised me. Except spins. It's quite a different sensation from watching them from the ground. Nothing can prepare you for the shock of seeing the Earth whirl rapidly in front of your eyes as you fall toward it. Though it's not difficult to recover from them, I never got used to their weirdness.

It was only when flying solo that I had any problem with anxiety. Like the morning I became disoriented and didn't know where I was, which precipitated the dread palpitations in the sky, forcing me to face the terror of sudden death by heart failure as well the horror of being lost. However, I managed to calm myself down and find my way back to the airport. Or when I practiced stall recovery and the plane would yaw and threaten to spin (recovery from which might have been more difficult without my instructor's balancing weight in the right seat). But most of the time I was quite comfortable flying around, navigating, and doing maneuvers—slow flying, steep turns, takeoffs and landings.

My closest call was when I was simulating an emergency landing in the big field behind our house on Pioneer Trail. I was climbing back up to altitude when I almost ran into another plane (the Cessna 152 is a high-wing aircraft, the other was a low-wing Piper: since I was coming up underneath him, neither of us could see the other). My propeller came within 20 or 30 feet of his tail. I don't think he ever saw me.

While flying to the Ohio State University airport on one leg of a solo cross-country expedition, I was instructed by the control tower to land on 27L (the left runway heading 270 on the compass—due west). Unbeknownst to me, the left and right parallel runways at OSU were nearly a mile apart. What I saw, coming down, were two parallel strips a few dozen yards apart, and I headed for the left one. Into my ears came the weary drawl, "543 Quebec, you're lined up with the taxiway." I did a little S-turn and landed without further incident. I suspect a lot of Kent State students had done the same, and that we were a standing joke at OSU.

My barely functional left eye turned out to be only a minor problem. Although my peripheral vision (necessary to sense the location of the airplane in relationship to the runway on takeoffs and landings) was excellent in both eyes, the FAA insisted I go up to Cleveland and fly around with an examiner to determine whether I could, in fact, spot features on the ground below, as well as judge distances and identify colors. Everything went fine—I could actually see smokestacks and tell red from green—until we came in for a landing. On the final approach he shrieked, "DON'T GET BELOW 50 KNOTS!" I wondered how many other student pilots he had examined and why he hadn't applied for a different kind of work.

The resident KSU examiner, Dick Schwabe, was a near-legend at the Kent State airport. There was a story, for example, that during World War II he had climbed out on the wing support strut of his aircraft and re-started the stopped engine by hand. Whatever his history, he was one of those rugged, steely guys who, when he looked you in the eye and said something, you listened. He reminded me of "Sport" Williams, the principal back at Selma High School. So when he assured me, after my final flight exam, that I was "a pretty good pilot," I was elated.

More importantly, while developing the confidence to fly my own plane, I lost my fear of riding in commercial airliners. Based on the men (and a couple of women) I had met in flight school, many of whom went on to air transport or military careers, it's clear that they are the best possible pilots, much better than I am, so why should I be afraid to fly with them any more than with myself? They know what to do in any conceivable situation. I had finally learned to relinquish control of the airplane and let them fly it.

For her part, however, Mom never failed to point out all the air disasters she had seen on the evening news.

I got my private pilot's license in May, 1984, and went back to *2020* full-time. Shortly thereafter, we bought a computer. I continued to write the first draft by hand, but it saved an enormous amount of time anyway because I no longer had to re-type the entire manuscript every time I finished a revision. Sending query letters was also far easier: all I had to do was substitute the name, address, and salutation of the agent or editor, and print again. I moved my study upstairs, where the computer was, and where I could look out the window and watch the birds and the rabbits and the squirrels playing in the neighbors' backyard and the woods beyond.

As the novel opens, Christopher, the genius twin, sits on top of the tallest building in downtown Atlanta a few hours before the New Year begins, when a million or more people will be cheering in the square below. It has become popular in 2020 for people to jump to their deaths from tall buildings, and the crowd is anticipating a good show. But my protagonist has a message to deliver.

Government agents try to come up with a way to stop Christopher, already wanted by the law for "mindpoisoning" (his followers call him "Teacher"), from saying his piece. But they are stymied because they can't kill him outright with thousands of witnesses watching from below. His brother Charles, a television reporter and narrator of the story, is also frustrated because the G-men have prohibited the station from broadcasting the event. It's a standoff until, without warning, Christopher begins to speak:

> The singing stopped and, despite the bright glare of the fireworks bursting on the big screen, most of the people were looking up at Christopher. He was still holding the mike in his right hand. Then he raised his left and said something I couldn't make out, with all the noise. I glanced at Ted, who was wearing an earcom. People, said Ted. He said People. Even the cops and vendors were looking up now. Somebody yelled, Jump, Teacher! A woman screamed Do it! When it was quiet again, except for the fireworks, Christopher lowered his hand. Then he began to speak. Softly, but very clearly, like a cold northern stream. As always he wasted no time, there were no preliminaries:
>
> MANKIND, LIKE INTELLIGENT SPECIES ELSEWHERE, EVOLVED FROM SIMPLER CREATURES. HOMO SAPIENS LEARNED TO SURVIVE BY COMPETING WITH HIS OWN AND OTHER SPECIES. THUS THERE

WAS INGRAINED IN THE MIND OF MAN A SYSTEM OF PRIORITIES. FIRST CAME THE WELFARE OF THE INDIVIDUAL, THEN THAT OF THE FAMILY, THEN THE COMMUNITY, AND FINALLY, THE STATE OR NATION. THIS ARRANGEMENT IS UNDOUBTEDLY A UNIVERSAL ONE. BUT WITH IT, WHEN CIVILIZATIONS HAVE ACQUIRED SUFFICIENT POWER, COMES INEVITABLE SELF-DESTRUCTION. NEITHER NUCLEAR BUILDUP OR DISARMAMENT IS THE ANSWER, NOR ANY OTHER POLITICAL SOLUTION. FOR ALL PEOPLE, CAPITALIST OR SOCIALIST OR COMMUNIST, ARE EQUALLY HUMAN. CIVILIZATION, IN ITS PRESENT FORM, CANNOT SOLVE THE PROBLEM BECAUSE CIVILIZATION *IS* THE PROBLEM. SURVIVAL WILL REQUIRE NOTHING SHORT OF A FUNDAMENTAL CHANGE IN THE CONSCIOUSNESS OF THE HUMAN MIND.

They turned up the fireworks and the band started to play again. But Christophers words rang out. IF THE HUMAN RACE IS TO SURVIVE, THE INDIVIDUAL WILL HAVE TO LEARN TO PUT HUMANITY FIRST IN HIS SYSTEM OF PRIORITIES. WITHOUT HUMANITY THERE CAN BE NO NATIONS, NO COMMUNITIES, NO FAMILIES, NO INDIVIDUALS. THIS IS HOW MUCH YOU MUST LOVE HUMANITY: IF YOU ARE ATTACKED BY ANOTHER NATIONS NUCLEAR WEAPONS YOU MUST NOT RETALIATE! ONLY WHEN YOU CAN LOVE LIFE TO THIS DEGREE WILL THERE BE ANY POSSIBILITY OF ITS CONTINUATION. There was scattered booing and shouts of Communist! and Criminal! Christopher ignored them.

BUT THERE IS SOMETHING EVEN MORE BASIC WHICH MUST BE DONE BEFORE THIS TRANSFORMATION IN HUMAN OUTLOOK CAN TAKE PLACE. Christopher paused for a mome. The people were looking up at him, absolutely silent once more, oblivious to all the whistling and banging. YOU WILL NEVER BE ABLE TO PUT HUMANITY FIRST, he said, AND THEREFORE THE SURVIVAL OF THE HUMAN SPECIES WILL NOT BE POSSIBLE, UNLESS—At that point Christopher suddenly doubled over and, without another sound, plunged off the roof. If there were shots, it was impossible to tell where they came from. He fell the entire eighteen floors from the top of the DuPont Building to the pavement below. Paul got the whole thing. He landed right next to one of the waiting ambulances, missing the nets altogether. From then on we couldn't see anything, and I couldn't tell whether he had landed on anyone. The crowd was screaming and sort of moving without moving, if you know what I mean. There was no place *to* move. It was like a giant amoeba.

This was much like something prot might have said a half-decade later. The most significant change in the five or six years between *2020* and *K-PAX* was the inclusion of non-human animal life into the equation. This was no small difference, either for my characters or myself. During that interim I came to the conclusion that the worldwide murder of both animals and humans is merely a variation on the same theme. Nevertheless, readers of *K-PAX* will immediately see a similarity to *2020*. Though I didn't know it at the time, the latter was, in fact, an early version of *the K-PAX trilogy*.

After Christopher falls to his death, the plot becomes a race between Chuck's deciphering the rest of Christopher's unfinished sentence, and the intrigue of trying to determine who in the newsroom is a government spy and who is not. And underlying everything is a warning about the election of an ultraconservative government, the nation's becoming an official Christian state, and the warmongering attempts to bring the rest of the world into the fold:

> President Falmouth took the oath that January, and he made one of the greatest inauguration speeches of all time. Without mentioning the Super Bomb or the Countries of Evil by name, he warned all Goliaths that our slingshots were ready and said we had an awful lot of rocks. We must not fear nuclear war, he said, only he pronounced it Nucular. He ended by saying The future will be bright if we face it with courage and a strong determination to preserve our God-given freedoms . . . .

And four years later:

> Just before the 04 elections an American energy company executive and his valet were kidnapped by Arab terrorists in Syria. The President wasted no time in sending troops to protect American lives. The mutilated bodies of the hostages, who turned out to be counter-counterspies, were recovered at the cost of hundreds of U.S. troops and God knows how many Syrians.
>
> Millions of viewers watched the bodies of the soldiers come home and The President pray with the grief-stricken families of the hostages. That did it as far as the election was concerned. Everybody tied yellow ribbons around their flagpoles, their houses, their arms and legs, and the next week President Falmouth won all fifty states and the District of Columbia, the first time in history that had happened, and a huge American Party majority took over both houses of Congress. The day after the election Rev Falmouth proclaimed a New Democracy in the United States, and made another call for a constitutional convention, declaring that God had instructed him to do so. This time he was supported by the newly-elected Congress and the vast majority of the American people.

Based on this mandate, President Falmouth continues to run roughshod over the Constitution. For example:

> The sanctity of life was encoded early in the twenty-first century by the Right to Life Declaration, which proclaimed that human life was sacred and made it a

crime to let anyone die, regardless of age or condition, if there were means available to keep him or her alive. This did not apply, of course, to capital punishment cases. Life was declared to begin at the mome of fertilization. Some of the more conservative members of Congress wanted to proclaim sperm and egg cells potential human beings as well, and to require the preservation of such entities, but the majority felt that such a provision would be too difficult to enforce. Nevertheless, millions of people across the country began to store their unfertilized entities, and the demand for freezers stimulated the economy for quite a period.

The twins' father dies shortly before Chuck marries his fiancée:

> We visited Father once in a while. He had been transferred to the chronic care ward by then, and was in an enormous room filled with hundreds of the living dead, packed together like fish in a crate, all hooked up to a gigantic computer named Mother by what they called Umbilicals. The oldest one there was 132 years old, had been a veggie for a decade, even before the ratification of the Right to Life Declaration. The youngest had just been born. Her mother had been injured in a train disaster several months earlier. The baby was born right on schedule, but unfortunately she turned out to be a veggie too, the first adult to be kept alive artificially for her entire lifetime. Shes in her thirties now. Some clown down at the station said they ought to inseminate her with sperm from another veggie, maybe the geezer, to see what would come of it, a cabbage or a tomato maybe . . . .

At the climax of the novel, Chuck races to get Christopher's words out to the television audience during The President's annual Message of Hope. He is intercepted by the Feds, some of whom turn out to be working for Christopher. Terrified of going to prison, and losing his job and his family, Chuck grabs the disc and runs back to his office to powder it. He no longer has the courage to get his brother's message out to the people: YOU WILL NEVER BE ABLE TO PUT HUMANITY FIRST, AND THEREFORE THE SURVIVAL OF THE HUMAN SPECIES WILL NOT BE POSSIBLE, UNLESS YOU GIVE UP GOD. Before he can turn on the powdermaker, however, Christopher appears to remind him that "It's not too late . . ." At that moment Minister Strehler barges in with a bunch of Feds. When Christopher raises an arm in self-defense, one of them kills him. They carry his body away, leaving Chuck to ponder what has happened and what to do with the message. One of Christopher's People, a station employee, enters to inform him that his brother is not dead: he has cloned himself and, no matter what the government does, they can't kill him. Still unable to telecast Christopher's message, Chuck makes his way to the hospital to wrap himself in the embrace of his senile mother.

By this time I had learned a few more submission tricks. Having heard that many editors are willing to look at a partial manuscript, even one that comes "over the transom," I sent out the first thirty pages with the query letters. From this came seven requests for the whole thing, followed in due course by seven rejections. In desperation, I sent samples also to the two agents who had actually *signed* a rejection letter for *Breakthrough*. I got a *call* from one of them; she liked it, but what did I think about changing the ending? "Nobody will publish a novel asking the reader to give up God," she informed me. I told her that was the whole point of the novel. "Think about it," she added, and hung up. I thought about it and declined her suggestion.

The final tally was seventy-one rejections by editors and two by agents. It was 1985. In a couple more years I would turn fifty. I had been a "writer" for six years already, with nothing to show for it. This did nothing to improve my self-image.

I had always hated parties. Because of my upbringing and the corresponding social anxiety, I never knew what to say or do at them. To make matters far worse, I worried for weeks when one I couldn't avoid was coming up. Having written three unpublished novels, I hated them even more:

"What kind of work do you do?"

"I'm a writer."

A hint of interest, even excitement. "Really? What have you written that I might have heard about?"

"Nothing."

"Oh."

I began to reply that I was a defrocked priest. Or a shepherd. Anything but "writer." Those of you who have written an unpublished novel or two know what I'm talking about.

Social anxiety in my case manifests itself as fatigue. I can get through a party, or a business lunch or the like, but I need a nap beforehand. Even if I come in well-rested, I'm exhausted afterward, a tightly-coiled spring.

One evening in December, 1984, a few months before finishing *2020*, I experienced some sharp chest pain while eating a filet of fish. It was snowing hard at the time and we had tickets for a concert (George Winston) that night. I told Karen I didn't think we should brave the storm, maybe get stuck somewhere on the road coming back. She was quite annoyed—she loves Winston. I couldn't tell her, of course, that the real reason was that I was afraid I had swallowed a fishbone and would have to have surgery to dig it out of my esophagus. Or that I might be having a heart attack and thought I might die if I had to shovel snow or walk a long way on a frigid night.

The pain recurred. Sometimes it came while running, other times it didn't. It might come after eating, but not always. I experimented with exercise, trying to determine exactly how long I could run before the pain came (a mile or less). Then it began to happen with little provocation. Though I was terrified, I decided not to call Peter Cubberley, and waited glumly for my regular exam in February. As he does with upcoming parties, the anxiatic dies a thousand deaths before his physical.

A month before I saw him, however, there was another storm and Karen's car got stuck in a snowbank. She walked back home and, despite the threat of an infarction, we returned to try to dig it out. We couldn't. It was about zero Fahrenheit, and we sat in the cold car waiting for the snowplow, which finally extricated it.

In the middle of that night I woke up and turned over, right side to left. The world began spinning as if I were spiraling down in a stalled airplane. I rotated back. The spinning stopped. I went to the bathroom. No problem. I got back in bed. No problem. Had I been dreaming? I turned over again and the world spun around and around. It had to be a stroke. Karen had an out-of-town meeting that day, but she drove me to a local doctor, whose office was much closer than were those at Kaiser Permanente. It wasn't a heart or brain problem, but a viral infection of the inner ear. He prescribed Antivert; the vertigo stopped immediately and didn't return. The chest pains, however, persisted.

The morning of my physical they came as I was washing the breakfast dishes, and seemed particularly severe. I was almost happy to get into the car and head for the Kaiser Foundation, knowing that if I made it I would at least have a chance to live.

Peter asked me what sort of activity caused the pain. I reported my experience a couple of hours earlier washing dishes. "Don't wash dishes!" he advised me, and did an EKG. Not a heart problem, he said. Instead it was probably esophagitis resulting from gastric reflux. He prescribed Maalox and made an appointment for an upper GI series.

When I arrived at the Gastroenterology Laboratory a few days later, there were eight large Styrofoam cups of a chalky white fluid standing on a shelf. I panicked, afraid I would have to drink all of them and undoubtedly throw up. The assistant handed me one of the cups. I asked meekly whether I would have to down all eight of them. "Just drink that one," the radiologist soberly ordered. I did so while he stared at the fluoroscope. I lay down on my side and drank another. That was it, I was done. I got right out of there.

No fish bones, no heart problems, no hiatal hernia, no cancerous growths, just gastric reflux disease. Peter put me on two tablespoons of Maalox every two hours. It wasn't enough, but it did allow me to continue running and carry out other activities. If I forgot the stuff, however, I knew it. The problem made sleeping particularly difficult. Even with the head of the bed elevated four inches above the foot, I would almost always wake up in the middle of the night and have to go to the kitchen and take more Maalox. I finally learned to keep a couple of extra-strength tablets at my bedside so I wouldn't have to get up. Nevertheless, it was sometimes difficult to get back to sleep.

One night in late 1985, while waiting to drift off, I thought about a plot for a short story: a young boy goes to a baseball game, where God appears high above the outfield grass. He tells the boy that He will return in exactly one year and, at that time, he may ask Him one question. The remainder of the story describes what happens when the rest of the world hears about the incident. The climax, centering on what question the boy (with the help of the President and various governmental committees) will ask, comes right on schedule.

It went out to almost every magazine publisher in the United States. No one wanted "The Boy Who Spoke with God." I finally incorporated it into my next novel, *Watson's God*.

FLYING BLIND

In January, 1986, the space shuttle Challenger exploded above Cape Canaveral and the pieces fell into the Atlantic. NASA had done it again: in order to save time and money, they had used defective rings connecting the various stages of the launch rockets, material that disintegrated in cool weather. Surely this was the last tragedy.

Returning to my Hoosier roots I began a fourth novel about a young man trying to make sense of his disastrous life. This time I decided to bypass the handwritten first drafts and type the novel directly into the computer. It didn't work. The fingers were flying, but they were producing drivel, unending chronicles of minutiae and trivia. By the time I got to page 87 the protagonist was still a small child and there were forty years to go. I threw it into the nearest wastebasket and decided to go for an instrument rating.

In order to get into the course I had to build up the necessary base—fifty hours of cross-country. I flew Karen to a few out-of-town library directors' meetings, two of which required landing at Columbus International, a major airport. Probably my biggest thrill as a pilot was when I found myself taxiing between two Boeing 727s. I was instructed to take off immediately after the first one, and turn left heading 060 (ENE) "without delay" after leaving the runway. I did, but my jubilation quickly turned to dread. The guy in front of me had turned 180 degrees around and was crossing right over my path several hundred feet above. I had been thoroughly instructed about the dangers of wake turbulence, which can upend a small aircraft, and quickly informed the control tower about my concern. The tower relayed the message to the commercial pilot, who responded with a laconic: "I've only got three engines," i.e., he was climbing out of range as fast as he could. To minimize the danger I slowed my climb and, fortunately, didn't get blown away.

On another occasion I flew fifty miles solo to find the destination runway covered with patches of ice, the airport closed. After flying low over it, I decided to land anyway (it wouldn't have counted as a cross-country flight otherwise), and made it without using the brakes or sliding off the icy asphalt. I departed with the "soft-field takeoff" procedure (holding the nose up and getting off the runway as soon as the 172 attained flight speed). This is the sort of thing that, if it doesn't kill you, makes you a more confident pilot.

Having heard that it was a serenely quiet and beautiful experience, I took my first glider ride that spring. Though I enjoyed the idea of flying without power, it was anything but peaceful. The wind whipping past the aircraft sounded like the roar of ocean waves during a winter storm. I went back to the relative quiet of a motorized aircraft.

On a long-anticipated flight to Muncie to visit the folks, I experienced an engine problem. As it happened, I was passing right over the Mansfield, Ohio, airport. After a moment or two of trepidation I explained the situation to the tower and requested permission for an emergency landing, and airport traffic was held until I was safely down. When the plane was inspected, it was found that the spark plugs were gummed up with deposits. A KSU student was there with his instructor, and we traded airplanes: they would wait for the plug replacements so I could be on my way.

When I got to Reese's I called home (a hundred yards away) to tell Mom I was coming over the fence, something I had wanted to do since I was eleven. When she picked up the phone I said, "Hi, Mom, it's Gene. I'm at the airport."

"Uh-huh," she replied. "What do you want?" I didn't want anything. Just to tell someone that I was a pilot who had fulfilled a lifelong dream.

With the encouragement of a couple of friends, I began to subscribe to animal rights magazines, read the few books on the subject (it was only a decade earlier, in 1975, that widespread interest in the welfare of animals began to catch on, thanks largely to Peter Singer's groundbreaking book, *Animal Liberation*). I started writing letters to Gillette and the other big companies that still insisted on testing endless new bleaches and shaving products on the skin and eyes of rabbits. I wrote hundreds of them. I don't know whether they had any effect, but the combined efforts of thousands of like-minded individuals eventually convinced most of the manufacturers of "health" and "beauty" products to eliminate animal testing of their merchandise. All except Procter and Gamble, the last major corporation to evolve. As far as I am aware, they still don't get it.

But animal testing is only the beginning. Though they think, feel, and suffer (Descartes notwithstanding), animals are still universally treated as if they are mindless "objects" or "property," and therefore it's acceptable to slaughter and eat them, experiment on them, hunt them, work them, and force them to entertain us. We condone all these things because of our superior intelligence. And how do we define "intelligence"? It's the kind human beings possess. But if we interpret intelligence to mean the ability to survive in a given environment, then we're far inferior to most other creatures, which have been around for millions of years. Homo sapiens, on the other hand, has already begun to destroy our common biosphere only a few tens of millennia. Which of us is stupider?

In May of that year (1986), having run across a list of impeccable vegetarians (and many of the smartest people who ever lived—Einstein, da Vinci, Voltaire, Socrates, Aristotle, Plato, Schweitzer, Shaw, Darwin, Newton, Tolstoy, Gandhi, and numerous others), I finally decided to try it again. This was not a welcome decision for Karen, who likes good food and is allergic to soy, the foundation of a meatless diet. It meant that she would have to join me or we would have to eat separate meals. It was especially difficult for her on Grand Manan, where the seafood is as fresh as can be. So we compromised: while on the island I would eat no animal flesh except for that from the ocean, but would eliminate one additional sea creature from my diet every summer thereafter—none the first year, fish the next, then clams, then scallops, and finally lobster. Neither of us was entirely happy with this arrangement, but that's the nature of compromise (and marriage). I stuck with that plan, and have been a total vegetarian ever since quitting lobster in 1990. As yet, no wounds have failed to heal properly.

By July I had written the first few chapters of my new novel, *Watson's God*. In order to improve my writing skills, if any (and perchance to find a publisher), I attended a national writer's conference in Boston. The instructor in the fiction category was impressed with the pages I sent, and read several to the group. In a private discussion with him afterward, however, he admitted he hadn't the slightest idea where to submit the manuscript. About all I learned from the experience was that becoming a published author depends on talent, luck, and perseverance, with the emphasis on the final element (there's really not much you can do about the other two). I went home and persevered.

At the end of 1986, having flown my fifty hours cross-country, I took another break from writing and signed up for instrument flying. I had no intention of routinely setting off in bad weather for distant runways, I just wanted to be able to get somewhere safely in case the ground unexpectedly disappeared in fog or snow during a long cross-country flight.

Instrument flying was the hardest course I had ever taken, far more difficult than any science or mathematics course. For one thing, flying in clouds (or through heavy rain or snow) means constant attention to several cockpit instruments: flight, navigation, communication. If a pilot's concentration lapses, he/she can stray off course or, worse, segue into an aptly-named "death spiral" (which he/she can't sense because the increased gravity brought about by turning is balanced by the loss of Gs in falling). For another, the intense instrument monitoring, some of it in a simulator, is tougher for a fifty-year-old than for a collegian (which may explain why it's not easy for us old farts to do well with computer games). Ground school—learning how all the instruments worked and what to do when one or more failed, as well as complex navigation and approach procedures (there are several)—was almost as difficult.

But I finished the training on schedule and did the test flights with Schwabie reasonably competently, managing to stay on the proper headings at the correct altitudes, while simultaneously navigating and communicating on the right frequencies, and greasing a couple of landings as well. I was pleased and so was he. "Not many people your age get through this course," he confided.

Had I taken the relatively easy maneuvers course, and a couple of hours of multi-engine training, I could have become a commercial flier (though not an airline pilot because of my bad eye), carrying packages or cancelled checks around the country in the dead of night. But I had other things to do, including finishing my fourth novel. It was back to my latest attempt to write something an editor might want, *Watson's God.*

WATSON'S GOD

Dad's health was beginning to deteriorate. He had come down with the flu in October (1986) and, despite having plenty of weight to fall back on, his kidneys were invaded by the virus. He was on dialysis for several weeks, until the doctors found a steroid that would get him off the machine. At about the same time, unfortunately, they discovered a malignancy in his prostate. In January he underwent surgery (implantation of cobalt-60 pellets), after which he was very weak and confused.

Here is his last letter to us in shaky handwriting, which became more tremulous as it progressed. It is undated, but probably from February, 1987:

> Dear Gene & Karen, I feel rather far from being able to write and to make sense, but here I go anyway—I guess it's been a long time since we have written, or is it wroten or is it just wrotten writin. I'll try to get it straight next time. I haven't done any writing for a long time, so please excuse how bad I am at this time. It always seems to take a long time to get started. If we don't write often and long, we can't do much. We will try to carry on a conversement and a little oftener and if I slow down to much, maybe I could stand a little prodding. There isn't much to record here, but we will try to make a showing as regular as we can. These last few months have been full of blanks and hard to fill in, but I guess we will have to just keep at it till something makes sense or we learn to write all over again. We hope for better days and a lot of great. So for now, we will still be able to keep a [unintelligible] I can't find any place for. I guess there is not much more to write, so we will quit for now. You all write whenever you all can and we will try to answer. So keep in touch. We will see if we can give an answer once in a while. I don't expect to hear from youse guys. Write when you feel like it You have always kept up with us on letters and such. end of communication. Will write again soon. I hope things are good with you. (unsigned)

His bewilderment progressed to a form of senility (his mother and one of his sisters had suffered the same fate). We visited Mom and Dad that spring, and again in July. Although he recognized us, he was no longer the father I knew. Sometimes he couldn't find his way to the bathroom. He had little to say. On the other hand, he was in no pain or distress and, indeed, was cheerful and apparently accepting of his situation. It was the last time I saw him alive.

I called him in early August, just before leaving for Grand Manan. He sounded quite lucid. I asked him how he was doing. "I feel good," he said.

I told him I was working on another novel, and ended with: "I'm going to make it, you know."

He replied, "I know you are."

I was on the second draft of *Watson's God* and wanted to do as much revising as possible before Karen joined Shasta and me on the island. On the afternoon of August 23rd (1987), Kathleen Buckley strolled up the long driveway with a neighbor, the hospital's head nurse Bessy Bass, to inform me that I had a telephone call at Whale Cove Cottages (we still had no phone or electricity in ours). I asked her if it was urgent. In her fabulously deliberate voice: "Yeeeeees, I think it iiiiis!" I raced back to the Main House to return Karen's call. Dad had suffered a heart attack.

"How is he?"

"Oh, honey, he never regained consciousness."

I called my sister Nancy, who was with Mom. Nan didn't think I needed to drive all the way (2 ½ days) to Muncie for the funeral, but my mother wanted me there.

The wonderful George Bass, Bessy's husband, had already placed his car in line, without my asking, for the morning boat. I said good-bye to Andy and Rea and a few other friends, packed quickly, and closed up the cabin. I would have the whole trip back to contemplate the meaning of losing a father. Oddly, there was no grief, just a kind of numbness. In my mind, I think, he had already died months earlier. I tried not to picture how he must have felt in the ambulance on the way to the hospital that Sunday morning; they had to strap down his arms to keep him from thrashing, or possibly to try to run from the pain and anguish, as if he had just bashed a kitten. He died an hour or two later, his eggs and sausage and pancakes lying cold on the kitchen table.

At the funeral were a great many relatives, most of whom I hadn't seen since I was a boy. My uncle Bob, as always, was the most interesting person in attendance, dressed as he was in a bright red T-shirt and suspenders. Long divorced from the French girl he had married during World War II, he congratulated me on my work at CWRU (which had made the local papers at the time), introduced me to his new wife, and insisted that I give him a call "the next time you're in town." I promised I would. (And I did. Unfortunately, there was no answer. I learned later that he was in the hospital, dying of liver cancer. He lived only a few months after Dad's burial.)

Finally we all went into the sanctuary—I escorted Mom and sat on her left—and listened to a long sermon about how happy Dad was to be in heaven. The preacher was especially pleased to note that John was all paid up in his tithing. I stared at the casket, half-expecting him to rise up and start talking (he was wearing his thick glasses, as if he'd just dropped off to sleep). I wasn't surprised by Dad's death, but I couldn't help thinking *he* must have been. Dying had never been a part of his agenda.

It was probably then that I realized both Dad and my grandfather died at exactly the same age, seventy-six. Now I had a fresh worry to add to my already bulging backpack. Was I destined to expire at that particular time in my life?

There was no overt grief on anyone's part except for that of Uncle Don, who broke down as we passed by the casket for the last time. Dad had been good to him, giving him a job at a bad time in his life. Even my mother maintained control as she reached out to touch Dad's cold face. She recoiled, but touched it again and remained strong. My own jaws were clamped shut to ward off incipient blubbering. Not for him, but for her.

We buried him in the Gardens of Memory, where an enterprising salesman had sold them a plot years before, undoubtedly for a small down payment and so much a month.

There was a nice buffet supper prepared by the women of the church. We ate the food, reminisced a little, and it was all over. The next day we drove back to Ohio, leaving Mom on her own (she seemed okay with this), with a little help from Nancy and her two daughters, Teresa and Sherri. From then until she became ill with Alzheimer's Disease, I called her every Saturday and visited three or four times a year. Although she knew I was a "writer," she never failed to ask me what I did to "pass away the time." When she couldn't live alone any more (she sometimes fell and couldn't get up), she moved in with Nan, and when my sister couldn't take care of her any longer she went into a nursing home, and then another and another. She hated them all.

I continued to practice instrument flying in hopes of taking my wife to a library meeting, or making the trip halfway across the country to Grand Manan, in inclement weather. But Karen had other plans. In September she applied for the directorship of the library at the New York University Medical School. In January, 1988, when the candidates were narrowed down to two, she visited again.

Though I had vowed twenty years earlier never to return to this heartless, car-grabbing city, I was now in favor of living in New York, the home of all the major publishers in the country, not to mention the Broadway stages, some of the finest museums in the country, and all the rest. While she was presenting her case to the Dean (though seriously ill from food poisoning the night before), I walked around mid-town looking for the publishing houses, some of whose addresses were carved into memory, a little disappointed to discover that they occupied unspectacular buildings little different from those housing other, less romantic, enterprises.

She was offered the job in February and accepted it in March. The appointment was to begin on September 1.

As *2020* was a precursor to the upcoming *K-PAX*, *Watson's God* had become a revised and expanded combination of *Ralphy* and *Breakthrough*, though spanning several decades. I did a substantial amount of research on the events of this period (the forties through the seventies and into the eighties), developed the characters better than in my previous novels, and tried to make the story more complex and, I hoped, more writerly.

Watson's God opens in a tiny Chicago apartment where Alan Watson is looking over his extensive used-book collection and the trophies he has won as an amateur runner. Except for two pet flies, he is alone. At last he sits down with a vial of amphetamines, a bottle of cheap wine and a .38, and begins to read his unpublished semi-autobiographical novel, *Watson's God*, planning to commit suicide as soon as he has finished it.

As he reads he relives all the events of his past—the death of his first girlfriend after a botched abortion (he blames himself, thinking he must have offended God by giving in to his sexual desires), his college and graduate school years, his life on a commune near Memphis, and finally his failed attempt to become a novelist. Fearing another pregnancy, he drives his college sweetheart away when she indicates a desire to conceive a child.

While reading his novel, Watson has come to realize that life is difficult and unfair for everyone. He accepts a call from his former lover, who is coming to visit him. After deciding to chuck his writing career and become a bus driver, he heads out to see the hapless Cubs play a ball game.

I finished *Watson's God* in April, and sent partials to twenty-two agents and no editors. It was the longest novel I had written, 550 double-spaced pages, 140,000 words, and was, by far, the most ambitious of the four, a novel within a novel. It had taken me two years to research and write it, except for the hiatus to learn to fly on instruments.

For the month or so that I was inputting the final revisions, I was experiencing moderate abdominal pain just below my navel. This time it was colon cancer for sure, but Peter diagnosed it as a "spastic colon" (a.k.a. "irritable bowel") and advised doing nothing. In fact, as soon as I finished the novel and got it into the mail, the pain began to dissipate.

Karen finished her work at NEOUCOM at the end of June and we headed for Grand Manan for a wonderful, relaxing five weeks. The local reviews for *Watson's God* were good. Andy and Rea in particular thought I had finally made the leap to publishable author. Coming from an English professor and a superb copyeditor, this was very high praise (Rea's first book in her series of collected stories of Lucy Maud Montgomery was in press). Others liked it also, or at least indicated that I had made significant progress since writing *2020*. Of course their reactions were encouraging, but I had yet to receive an equally positive letter from one of the queried agents.

While we were on Grand Manan, a realtor sold our house. Among a wad of rejection letters waiting in Mantua on our return there was one from George Ziegler (the last agent listed in *Writer's Market*), who wanted to see the rest of *Watson's God*:

July 25, 1988

Mr. Gene Brewer
3363 Pioneer Trail
Mantua, OH 44255

Dear Mr. Brewer:

I have now read the material you sent from your novel, [WATSON'S GOD] and while I like your writing (with the exception of two correctable bad habits), I get the feeling from the combination of the synopsis and the sample that the entire book will be too inclusive and short on plotted action for the demands of today's marketplace. I know that sounds crass, but it is a reality I am forced to recognize.

Specifically, I think the canvas is too broad in WATSON'S GOD. The nostalgic portrait of the 40s in these opening pages is very appealing but it's a long stretch from there to 1979 and what is pulling us forward? I think if you were to take a section of WATSON'S GOD that is strongly plotted and makes a complete literary whole, while the outercasing of [Watson] reading it before committing suicide would also benefit by some ongoing action, e.g., phone calls, including the one from [Melanie], could come earlier; or perhaps she could drop in on him so that there can be a dramatized scene in the present. Well, I can't tell you what to write and here I've just been doing it.

Obviously you seem to be of more than passing talent. Have you written anything else? What are your plans along these lines? I know you want publication, now, but I ask these questions because I am interested.

The two bad habits are on the reverse side. If you're not interested, don't read them. Thanks for letting me see this, and good luck!

BAD HABITS (quite common ones, actually):

1)   Using "then" as a conjunction (examples p. 24, par. 2, line 2; par. 3, line 3, line 6)

2)   Using weak participial phrases (example p. 42, par. 2, line 4); Note that when they are inaccurate, they're also weak: he can't take a slug of it at the same time as reaching for it, can he?

Sincerely,
George Ziegler

Of course I was thrilled, and the letter couldn't have come at a more opportune time. My response:

Mr. George Ziegler   Aug. 20, 1988
xxxxxxxxxxxxxxxx
New York, NY xxxxx

Dear Mr. Ziegler:

Please forgive my delay in responding to your kind letter of July 25: I have been vacationing in Canada.

Your comments are well taken, and I would seriously consider rewriting [WATSON'S GOD] along the lines you suggested. Before taking that drastic step, however, I wonder if you would be willing to take a look at the complete manuscript. Perhaps you would then get a better idea of whether the narrative "pulls us forward." Several quite literate friends have told me that it does just that, and builds to a powerful climax. If, after reading the rest of the novel, you disagree with this assessment, but are still interested, I will have a go at revising it.

[WATSON'S GOD] is my fourth novel. The first three were not successful, but I would of course be happy to send samples of any or all at your request.

Thanks for your encouragement, and for pointing out the two bad habits.

Sincerely,
Gene Brewer

P.S. My wife and I will be moving to New York City the week of August 29. Our new address will be: 3 Wash. Sq. Village #17L, 10012.

In his response dated Aug. 26, George declined to read the unrevised manuscript. However, he ended with:

. . . I don't mean to be difficult. I'm just trying to conserve my eyesight. If you decide to revise, I'll be happy to read it when it's finished . . . .

I decided to revise.

On Aug. 29, 1988, we moved to the Big Apple. I was 51, Karen 45, and life seemed once more to hold some promise for both of us.

NEW YORK

We helped the movers load a huge van, which also contained the belongings of two other families, packed the miscellaneous necessities and leftovers in our three-year-old Camry, and headed east. After a weekend visiting brother Bob and his wife Christina in Glen Burnie, MD, we arrived at the Holland tunnel just before noon on a Monday. It took more than an hour to get to the ticket booth, and I thought: we'll never be able to leave New York for a weekend without spending half of it waiting to be excreted from the bowels of the city.

The apartment we were assigned in #3 Washington Square Village seemed adequate, if not luxurious, with its two large rooms (we used bookcases to divide the living and dining rooms) and small terrace. We were on the top (seventeenth) floor, which afforded us a view of the Empire State Building to the north, and Hoboken, NJ, to the west. Washington Square Park was mostly hidden by one of the quadrangle's other apartment buildings, #1 WSV. We marveled at the total population of the four buildings, about 2500 people, equal to that of the entire island of Grand Manan (which is comparable in size to Manhattan). I set up my computer desk in the dining area; my writing place was on a wide windowsill in the living room overlooking the courtyard and LaGuardia Place. Not as relaxing as the birds and squirrels outside my study in Mantua, but never dull, at least, with its endless parade of trucks, taxis, pedestrians, dogs, and cops on horseback, all in Brownian motion sixteen stories below. There were few interruptions at first—little mail (e-mail hadn't been invented yet), no phone calls, no visitors or other distractions—except for the occasional horn or siren and the persistent tinkling of my life dripping down the drain and into the sewer.

Shasta didn't like the city much. It took her several days to get used to the idea of bare concrete as a toilet. Worried that she would explode on her first walk before she would relieve herself, we finally trespassed on the sacred lawn (the only grass anywhere around) at Silver Towers, the companion faculty apartment complex across Bleecker Street from Washington Square Village. After that we usually managed to find some bare dirt or pebbles to serve as a makeshift comfort station. This may seem like an inconsequential problem to some, but for me (and her) it encapsulated immediately the unnaturalness for both dog and man of living in multi-layered houses with concrete yards in a City That Never Sleeps. (I had always assumed the latter slogan meant that

New York bustled twenty-four hours a day; I soon discovered that the noise level made sleep impossible.)

City dwellers seem to have lost touch with nature, with *life*. The only non-canine or -equine animals most of the denizens ever see come in shrink-wrapped packages. Aside from Central Park and a few small facsimiles, there's hardly a blade of grass to be found, and even that is often fenced off. The ubiquitous, fast-growing ginkgo trees are mere manqués. The saddest radio commercial I've ever heard was one advertising a park of some kind far from the city, where one could actually experience some "nature." The last line, from a dubious client: "This natchuh—does it have pahking?" Even the sky is artificial. One sees very few stars in New York: the heavens are light-polluted, man-made. And I haven't even mentioned the ever-present garbage and dog shit strewn about. I suspect that most people who claim to like city life have always lived in one.

Karen, on the other hand, loved the whole experience from the beginning, especially the concerts at Avery Fisher and Carnegie Halls and opera at the Met, and we subscribed to all of them for several years, until we became too busy or too tired for scheduled attendance.

I had to give up flying: general aviation at LaGuardia or Kennedy or Newark was impossible. There were a couple of smaller airports outside the city (Teterboro, Islip), but using these would have required enormous amounts of time and money. I figured I could always go back to the hobby when we eventually moved (I devoutly hoped) out of the metropolitan area.

We had lived in the city for less than two weeks when I became ill with "flu-like" symptoms. After a week with no improvement, I finally went to see a physician recommended to Karen by colleagues at NYU. Surprisingly, I found Dr. Hoffman to be a good mix of professionalism and caring, and refreshingly liberal as well (she had been a secretary before going to medical school, and was especially concerned about women's rights). Until then my conception of a New York practitioner would have been that of a cold, unfeeling automaton.

When she learned that we had recently returned from Canada, where we had been drinking water from our ten-foot-deep dug well, she suspected a giardia infection and sent me to a laboratory for parasite testing. At the lab I was given a little cup of salty liquid to drink and then instructed to go out somewhere for breakfast. I barely made it back in time to completely fill a large cylindrical container, very much like an ice cream carton, with more than enough material for analysis. When I took it back to the technician, he peered at the contents, smiled broadly, and exclaimed, "Beautiful!"

Though the results were negative (the tests don't always identify the organism), Dr. Hoffman nevertheless prescribed a drug (Atabrine) to eradicate the putative giardia infection. I began to feel better immediately. She also put me on Zantac, a medication that inhibits the production of stomach acid. No more Maalox! Furthermore, she prescribed Bentyl for the recurring irritable bowel. I hadn't felt so good in a long time.

Eileen was our physician for several years, until the time she "fired" me to confine her practice to women only.

I began jogging again, this time around the nearby Washington Square Park, and generally felt fine afterward except for a persistent mild headache, which disappeared soon after I stopped. Was I jarring my brain? But it only happened while running, and didn't seem to get much worse as time went on, so I ignored it.

Even when I was sick I was working on *Watson's God*, trying to cut any extraneous material and generally shorten it. Except for a few "highlights," I essentially cut the first two hundred pages. The hatcheted manuscript went back to George Ziegler in October.

While waiting for his response I decided to try my hand at cartoons (I had been jotting down ideas, whenever something funny struck me about a given situation, ever since I left the lab; by this time I had upwards of a hundred). Here are a few examples:

— An elegant restaurant, snooty waiters in tuxedos, etc. Sign on wall: NO SPITTING.
— Two large women in coffee shop. One eating a very large sundae, the other a smaller one. Woman with smaller sundae: "I don't know . . . I don't think this new diet is working."
— Doctor to patient: "Well, the X-rays came out negative. Unfortunately, the X-rays themselves . . ."
— Highway sign: ROADWORK NEXT 3000 MILES.
— Home plate with batter, catcher and umpire. Next to ump: a seeing-eye dog.
— Cemetery: left half full, right half sparsely populated. Sign on left: SMOKING. On right: NO SMOKING
— Man walking past sidewalk produce stand. One of the hand-lettered signs: Soylent Green—$1.95/lb.

Unfortunately, the half-dozen I submitted were promptly rejected by *The New Yorker*, and eventually lost by *The National Lampoon*. My only copies, which I loaned to a friend, also disappeared.

C'est, I thought, *la vie*.

I also wrote letters petitioning various universities and corporations (as many as twenty at a time) to stop torturing animals, and spent a lot of time in the Strand Bookstore poring over the paperbacks, and in the Bobst (NYU) Library researching a novel about a mental patient. In between all these activities I took advantage of the opportunity to visit all the major museums of the city—the American Museum of Natural History, the Metropolitan Museum of Art, the Guggenheim, the Frick, the Whitney, and others—as well as an occasional Wednesday afternoon theater matinee. (I saw *A Chorus Line* two or three times: the story of artists of any kind trying to succeed against overwhelming odds resonated strongly with me, as well as with thousands of other New Yorkers.)

One November afternoon I decided to visit the Bronx Zoo. I managed to get on the right subway train, which came out into the bright sunlight after escaping the tunnels of Manhattan. I almost wished it hadn't. The lower Bronx was quite dismal at the time, much of it weedy lots strewn with rusting rubble. I stared at the view for a while until I noticed that the car I was in was empty except for three other guys. One was talking to himself, another was changing his clothes (I hoped) and the third, the one closest to me, was playing with a switchblade. I opted not to return their glances.

In early January (1989) I got a call from agent Ziegler. His first words were not "Hello," but, "It's good . . . . It's really good!" I didn't know who it was at first—we had never spoken—but I soon realized he was talking about *Watson's God*, and he wanted to try to sell it for me. Of course he had some suggestions and criticism, but he assured me they were minor.

His terms were outlined in the cover letter accompanying the manuscript, which he returned for my final editing. ". . . I maintain a handshake agreement with my clients. In this way, as long as we are happy with one another, we will remain faithful to one another; if not, we are free to go our separate ways amicably and without complication. My commission is 15% of all sales. If a sub-agent is used for foreign sales or the movies, the total commission is 20%." Of course this was perfectly agreeable to me.

It took me a couple of weeks to make the corrections and trim another 20-25 pages from the manuscript. Rather than put the revised version back in the mail, I suggested we meet somewhere for a drink. I found him to be a pleasant guy, perhaps a bit older than I. As I turned it over to him, I asked him pointedly what percentage of the writers he took on became published. "Ninety," he said matter-of-factly. He wanted to submit the novel to the trade ("literary," as opposed to the mass market) paperback houses. When we parted, I was certain that *Watson's God* would soon be in print, and all those years of lonely effort, as well as Karen's confidence and generosity, would finally be rewarded.

By then I had already started another novel, working title: *K-PAX*.

K-PAX, PART 1

I had been thinking for several months about writing a novel about a mental patient, someone who saw the world clearly, as a whole, in sharp contrast to most of the "sane" people running around loose, self-absorbed and paying no attention. In fact I had jotted down copious notes on the subject the previous summer on Grand Manan. When I mentioned my idea to our friend Andy, he suggested I read Oliver Sacks's *The Man Who Mistook His Wife for a Hat*. I scribbled the title at the bottom of the long list of books on my reading list. Even before "It's really good . . ." I had accumulated enough thoughts and jottings to begin writing the story.

Until that time I had written three novels in the third person, one (*2020*) in the first. I thought that *K-PAX* (the title came at night in bed—I didn't know they were the call letters of a TV station in Missoula, MT) would work better with a first-person narrative. I started my fifth novel by releasing my protagonist from the mental institution where he had been a long-time resident, and listening as he described his observations and encounters while traveling from place to place. After a few dozen pages, I could see this approach wasn't going to work. The book was becoming more and more of a diatribe cataloging what was wrong with humanity. The narrator seemed disdainful and arrogant, a holier-than-thou know-it-all. A novel whose main character ran around shouting, "You fools!" wasn't going to sell.

I checked him back into the hospital for further treatment.

The problem with setting the story in a mental institution was that I knew nothing about them, and even less about psychiatry in general. Fortunately, the Bobst Library housed plenty of tomes on the subject, and as a faculty spouse I was able to borrow them. I took out a few and began reading and taking additional notes. While I was learning about the myriad forms of mental illness I remembered the Sacks book and read it, along with Irvin Yalom's *Love's Executioner*. Both gave me a fair understanding of the doctor-patient relationship, i.e., how a psychiatric interview should go. Furthermore, I was delighted to find, in the former, the story that had haunted me since 1966, the one about the "idiot savant" twins, who could make huge computations and calendar projections in their heads, though they had difficulty learning to tie their shoes. It was just as fascinating to me then as it had been nearly forty years earlier. More importantly for the novel, perhaps, I learned from Sacks that if you can imagine a mental illness, no matter how bizarre, there is probably someone in the world who suffers from it. This gave me the confidence to create any kind of psychiatric patient I needed for the story.

Finally, it occurred to me to wonder what kind of "crazy" person would be likely to observe objectively what was going wrong with the Earth—someone who wasn't blinded by all our social customs and responsibilities, who hadn't been brainwashed by family, schools, churches, the media, government propaganda, and all the rest. In short, he had to be from somewhere else.

If there was anything (besides *2020*) that influenced the plot of *K-PAX* it was the brilliant film *The Day the Earth Stood Still* (1951). Klaatu was the kind of alien protagonist I wanted: someone who saw human beings for what we were, yet was dispassionate about the things we did. Someone who was indifferent, even unsympathetic, toward our mutual fate. Who came to tell us the options, but left it to us to decide between them. Thus, prot (for "protagonist") was born.

My studies of novels had also taught me that a narrator who is inferior, in a sense, to the main character somehow works to make the latter more believable (see, for example, *The Razor's Edge* or the Sherlock Holmes mysteries). On the other hand, the use of first person imposes some restrictions on the writing of a novel. The narrator is not omniscient; he only knows what he has experienced or heard personally. Counteracting this limitation, however, is the ease of telling the story. It becomes more natural, more like relating something one has witnessed. I was going for this kind of verisimilitude.

I made prot's psychiatrist the narrator ("narr" in pax-o) and called him "Dr. Gene Brewer," hoping readers would think the story was based on an actual case history. Dr. B wasn't difficult: I wanted him to be somewhat single-minded, maybe even a little oblivious, but nevertheless disarming and dedicated to his profession. He was essentially a "straight man" for prot.

The other staff members were probably based to some small extent on professional people I have known, but were otherwise made up. I composed a long list of possible patient types and weeded out the weaker ones as I incorporated them into the narrative. Some (Ernie, Howie, and perhaps Chuck) were based, to one degree or another, on my own psychological fears and hang-ups. On the other hand, the doctor's family (and their problems), his home life, and the structure and organization of the hospital itself were cut from whole cloth. I've never been inside a mental institution or raised any children. The only character in the entire novel who wasn't invented was our Dalmatian, Shasta Daisy (though I also used Karen's name for that of the fictional wife).

The story was propelled by the psychiatric sessions between prot and Dr. Brewer. Those were great fun to write, which I did, for the most part, in the summer of 1989 on Grand Manan (the year we began filtering our water). It was tremendously freeing to let prot say surprising things, to question all our basic assumptions. In fact, I wrote all these episodes first—by typewriter, since I had no computer there (I had finally learned to do away with handwritten first drafts). The rest was simply a matter of filling in the events taking place between those encounters.

I'm not sure where Robert Porter came from. The idea of prot arriving on Earth, making piquant observations, and then leaving seemed too slim, too facile, and not very original (cf. Klaatu). So I created an alter ego for him. I saw immediately that Robert would deepen both the character and the plot, make him more complex, more mysterious. When it was over I wanted the reader not just to decide for himself whether prot was an alien or merely a mentally ill human being, *but to wonder whether there weren't some questions we might never know the answers to.*

But there was an interruption. One Saturday afternoon, while cutting up some dead trees for firewood, I experienced a serious stretch of palpitations, accompanied by considerable belching. When I rested they went away. When I resumed chainsawing, they recurred. Same thing for jogging. This was different from anything I had encountered before; the premature beats had previously seemed to occur almost at random. From the Main House at Whale Cove Cottages I called Karen (she had returned to work), who contacted one of New York's top cardiologists, Bill Slater. He agreed to see me, and thought it safe for me to drive back to New York for an exam. After a long, sleepless night listening for the knell of death, I drove to the Grand Manan hospital to confirm the notion that I was well enough to travel. An EKG showed nothing extraordinary (perhaps because I wasn't exercising). Dr. Dapena called Dr. Slater to report this finding, and I heard him say, "He *looks* all right." In a few hours (and many more PVC's) I was on the ferry to Blacks Harbour. As soon as the boat started to move I felt better. I stayed overnight in Bangor—no problem—and the next day I ran around Washington Square Park several times—again uneventfully except for the usual little headache.

Dr. Slater gave me some propanolol in case the problem returned, but I never used it. It had been a freak occurrence, perhaps brought about by an allergy to spruce pollen, which was heavy that year. Or it might have been psychosomatic. In any case, when we returned to the island in August, I had no trouble chainsawing or anything else. My only concern was: when will it happen again?

As a (former) scientist, I love making graphs and organizational charts. I don't know how many other writers do this—maybe none—but I constructed a detailed checkerboard encompassing the four months of the novel's time frame, inserted the sixteen sessions in their proper places, and scattered various notes about the patients, staff, and family around the chart in such a way as to integrate and balance the appearances of the various characters and the situations they found themselves in. For example, if a certain patient appeared early on, I would space him/her out over the rest of the novel, telling bits of his story whenever he came up on the grid. Of course it was a very fluid matrix, and characters moved around in the story as the need arose.

I finished the first draft at the end of the year (1989) and handed it to Karen, who read it while I went out for a run. When I came back she was still reading, saying nothing. I waited, waited, paced around the living room. Usually after finishing one of my manuscripts she would smile and say, "I like it, but I don't know whether anyone will want to publish it." This time, as she turned over the last page, she declared, very seriously, "It's perfect—it will be taken immediately."

I went over it (adding details, filling out characters) two or three more times before completing the "final" revisions in early March, 1990, and sent it off to George Ziegler, who had had no success with *Watson's God*: although none of the seven or eight editors who had read it thought it was "involving" enough, several opined that I had some talent and two requested a look at my next work. Discouraging, encouraging. But step by step, I told myself, I was getting closer.

I wasn't sure George would want to further waste his time with me after that failure, especially with a book about a psychiatric patient who claims to be from another planet. To my surprise he, too, loved the novel. He dropped *God* immediately and started submitting *K-PAX* (after a few more minor revisions) instead. I was optimistic, as always, that the latter would soon find a home. I went back to see *A Chorus Line* and began thinking about the next effort.

Karen, in the meantime, was doing well in her massive undertaking to computerize the NYU Medical Center library. Realizing that a fresh breeze had come up, the students bestowed on her the honor of being a "favorite professor," awarded during a dinner dance at the Plaza Hotel. Although I don't dance well and hate social occasions in general, I got through the affair without too much difficulty, except for the dinner part. I had requested a vegetarian meal, but when the food was brought there was a steak with a couple of vegetables on my plate. I pointed out the error and the food was whisked away. I was confident that at a fine establishment like the Plaza, there had been a simple mistake and I would soon be getting a meatless substitute. When the plate came back, however, everything was the same except that the steak had disappeared, leaving a little smear of grease in its place.

That summer (1990), I began to look into the potential of the Green party in the U.S. One of the first articles I came across described a fundraising event, a meeting in which hamburgers and hot dogs (not veggie, but the real crappy things) were available. I wrote them a letter explaining the connection between meat-eating and destruction of the rainforests (among other things). The gist of the reply was that hot dogs were a popular food item. I lost interest in the Greens, who, like the Plaza, seemed to be missing the point.

Not long after that, George and I had lunch at an Indian vegetarian restaurant. During our discussion I asked him about the possibility of sending the manuscript to a movie studio. His unwelcome response was that it would never be made into a film.

Disappointed that he wasn't even interested in *trying* that route, I asked him, "Why not?"

"No car chases," he pronounced, taking a sip of his salty drink.

This was especially distressing because I had written it in what I thought was a very visual style, and had even made tongue-in-cheek references in the book to "inquiries from a Hollywood producer" for the story of prot. He wasn't impressed.

The rejections for the print version started to come in. The first was probably indicative. Joe Blades (Executive Editor at Ballantine) wrote:

"... It's tough, isn't it? I like much of this novel, but both my head and my heart recognize how very difficult this would be to place (both among my colleagues and in the reading world at large). I respect challenges (and it's already gratifying to be included in the "prologue/acknowledgments"—one of the many cute ideas at play here), but I think K-PAX is too, too fraught with obstacles . . . ."

Some were mildly amusing. Caroline Sutton at Ticknor & Fields reported that:

"... K-PAX . . . has a lot going for it, particularly Dr. Brewer's ability to make this all sound like *bona fide* nonfiction. I was remarkably wrapped up in prot's story, which unfolds quite tantalizingly. But I don't believe Dr. Brewer has integrated the/his story that well. It's convincing and has possibilities, but it isn't hooked into prot's part of the novel well enough to keep the reader going. And the ending, unfortunately, is predictable. But I would like to add that if Dr. Brewer is considering doing more nonfiction, we'd be very interested in seeing it. We are trying to broaden our base in nonfiction and it looks like we may even be doing a cookbook or two . . . ."

The *K-PAX Cookbook*, perhaps?
Senior editor Deborah Futter at Bantam Doubleday Dell said:

"... The story is wonderfully imaginative, highlighted by fascinating glimpses into the workings of the mind. Alas, I'm afraid the narrative is a bit stiff, *clinical* (emphasis mine); there's too much analyzing and not enough vivid scenes of conflict to make this as engaging a read as it could be . . . ."

An editor at Viking-Penguin (Andrew Something-or-other) was "very enthusiastic" about *K-PAX*—but thought it was nonfiction. He liked the glossary and everything else, and was "pushing" it at Viking. Also wanted to know who "Dr. Brewer" was and where he worked (there is no "Manhattan Psychiatric Institute"). But when he learned that the manuscript was merely a novel, he promptly lost interest.

Fortunately, George also sent it to Alfred A. Knopf, where senior editor Jonathan Segal had this to say:

"You are right about "K-Pax" being an unusual and surprising work. "prot" is indeed an amazing character and it's easy to get caught up in his story, but I'm afraid I have some reservations about the writing for this house, and whether the book would find its market (perhaps a film first and then a paperback would work better?) and for these reasons we won't be offering. It was a tough decision. Others may disagree and may be right to do so."

However, Segal's astute editorial assistant, Ida Giragossian, loved it. More about her later.

In November of 1990, a notice appeared on the bulletin board at #3 Washington Square Village. There was a six-and-a-half-year-old boy in #1 WSV who wanted to play chess with "anyone." I thought he must be a prodigy. When the sign was still up a week later, I called the number, and his mother brought him over for a match.

Christopher could play the game, but, unfortunately, not much better than most other six-year-olds. After he left I called his mother, Terri, and told her that I would have to discontinue the "lessons." A Britisher, she talked fast about how they didn't know anyone in the U.S., Chris needed an uncle, etc. So we played a little more, went to some movies and museums, saw a Broadway musical, a ballet, an opera, became the best of friends, and have been ever since. He was bright, even precocious: it was like talking to a small adult. In fact, he became the son I never had.

By this time, of course, I was working on my next novel. Whether *K-PAX* was to be published or not, I decided to have fun with this one. To give it one last try, gather all my leftover notes—everything I wanted to say in a lifetime of novels—to clean off my desk entirely and put it all together in a shamelessly satirical political novel called *The American Way.*

THE AMERICAN WAY

The novel begins with a disclaimer:

EDITOR'S NOTE: THIS NOVEL HAS BEEN EDITED TO PRECLUDE OFFENDING ANY MEMBERS OF THE UNITED STATES SENATE. FURTHERMORE, ANY RESEMBLANCE BETWEEN THE CHARACTERS DEPICTED HEREIN AND ACTUAL PERSONS LIVING AND DEAD IS PURELY ETC., ETC., ETC.

And goes downhill from there:

During the optimistic reign of President Calvin Coolidge, when everyone was getting better and better every day in every way, a very young baby was born in a small but rapidly-growing American town whose motto was (and still is): A GREAT PLACE TO LIVE AND WORK AND RAISE A FAMILY—ALL OTHERS STAY AWAY.

He was given a Christian name, of course, but, before he could figure out whom it referred to, his father began calling him "Coach." And, as is often the case with sobriquets, it stayed with him for the rest of his life.

Like all of us, he inherited the worst traits of both his parents. Thus, from the beginning, he exhibited that most dangerous combination of human characteristics: a humorless fearlessness. He was equally unintimidated by iodine and the Buckleys' German shepherd, and he thoroughly enjoyed lightning and thunder. Like the devil himself, fire-eyed and intangible, he would frighten his little brothers by suddenly appearing at their windows after they had gone to bed.

One black night he brought home a dead raccoon and left it in the kitchen for his mother, a deeply superstitious and pathologically docile woman, to discover in the morning. Dazed and staggering, she finally lost consciousness and fell, ironically, onto the deceased, awakening later amidst a stinking cloud of miasma and tiny winged insects.

After that, everyone got his own breakfast.

His first few years of schooling might best be described as boring. The only things of value he learned came from his pint-sized contemporaries: how to play poker and mumblety-peg, for example. The biggest bombshell, of course, was how babies were made (the school itself washed its hands of this unwholesome topic). Another was never to trust *anyone*, and as usual, it was learned the hard way—his best friend ratted on him for lifting a girl's skirt shortly after he had discovered how babies were made. His exhausted teacher finally stopped whacking the unrepentant Coach when it became apparent that he was totally oblivious to the punishment. And so it went, grade after grade.

Being fearless permitted him, at an early age, to observe dispassionately, and therefore to understand, what everyone else was afraid of: change, the unknown, and especially death, the ultimate change, the final unknown. With something approaching amusement he found that he was surrounded by terrified people—for every natural phenomenon or human activity there were multitudes who were frightened out of their wits by it.

By the time he was nine he had learned how most people cope with those otherwise debilitating fears: by tenaciously clinging, with the support and encouragement of the government (of either party), to unspecified "values," and to the fervent belief in an afterlife, as promised by one's religion of choice.

With this knowledge came the realization that great rewards accrue to those who are able to manipulate these desperate needs. The most powerful people he had heard about were the President and the Pope, both champions of the status quo. The ideas of chronic celibacy and constant prayer didn't particularly appeal, however, so he decided to become Leader of the Free World.

During the great Depression, his father, no longer able to sell enough insurance to provide for his family, succumbed to a secret lifelong ambition and ran off with a traveling carnival to become a geek, leaving his ill-equipped wife to raise their four children alone. But here is what makes America great: faced with overwhelming adversity she pulled herself together, did what had to be done, and each of her sons became pillars of their respective communities. The strain finally killed her, of course, but no matter—if it hadn't, something else would have.

As for the Coach, who loved and hated his old man with equal dispassion, the experience taught him another valuable lesson about life, shared by all who survived the economic downturn: the paramountcy of money. It was a lesson he never forgot, nor allowed his children to forget.

In high school a previously undetected heart murmur (precipitated by bouts with strep throat and rheumatic fever, which he ignored), precluded his participation in vigorous sports. Instead, he took up the less manly activities of golf and hunting, edited the newspaper and yearbook, and led the debaters to their first state championship, arguing successfully that "the President of the United States should be granted unlimited power to declare and wage war as he deems necessary to protect American interests at home and abroad."

His valedictory address was so fervently jingoistic that every male classmate—and many of their relatives—enlisted in his favorite military service the following

Monday morning. Sadly, the Coach himself was rejected because of his muttering heart and flat feet, and he was forced to work his way through college by playing poker every weekend instead . . . .

And so on. After failing to get himself elected to anything because he wasn't handsome enough, the Coach vows to further his conservative agenda by producing others of his ilk. He marries, fathers three sons (and a couple of unwelcome daughters) with the ultimate goal of seeing one of them become President of the United States, another Chief Justice of the United States Supreme Court, and the third, Speaker of the United States House of Representatives. Principles were not only disregarded, they were irrelevant.

I had hoped that the gross exaggeration of the characters (for example, his first son Duke, running for the presidency, uses his own son as a political football, booting him through the uprights during campaign rallies) made it a satirical, if not humorous, takeoff on American politics and politicians.

In January (1991), while I was working on the second draft, the United States started bombing the hell out of Iraq. Immediately the Empire State Building lit up in red, white, and blue, and stayed that way until the hostilities were declared "over." I called the manager's office and indicated my displeasure that the ESB seemed to be supporting Bush's (Sr.) conflict. The management replied that the lights meant that they were only supporting our troops, not the war itself. I asked him how you support the troops without supporting the war. "You're the only person who has complained," he retorted. A city of 10 million people and only one pacifist in the lot.

I finished *The American Way* in May. Karen didn't think it would "be taken immediately," or at any other time. Nevertheless I sent the manuscript to George Ziegler. He hated it, too.

I decided to submit it myself (George was still trying to find a home for *K-PAX*). I sent it to those editors who had written the nicest rejection letters for the latter, and waited for their expected declines. To my amazement, however, an editor at Atheneum, Courtney Hodell, actually liked it (she said). She requested some changes and said she'd be happy to take a look at the revised version, *something that had not happened before.*

I happily worked on it that summer on Grand Manan and sent it back to her in the fall. Unfortunately, she must have shown it to someone else in the interim, because now she didn't like it, but for different reasons. However, she thought it was, like *K-PAX*, "witty and crammed with imaginative twists." Frustrated to the extreme, I wrote back (I rarely respond to a rejection—what's the point?): "If you happen to know of any publishers who *are* interested in work that is 'witty and crammed with imaginative twists,' I would greatly appreciate your letting me know. In the absence of a response, I will assume there are none." As yet there has been no reply.

In October, Karen, Shasta, and I took a fall trip to Watkins Glen, where I proceeded to get a tick bite. I didn't notice it until the next day, when I was taking a shower. I couldn't get it off. Finally I pulled it from the back of my knee with a pair of tweezers and placed it in a pill vial.

We didn't know what kind of tick it was, but the site had a red ring around it, supposedly indicative of a Lyme Disease deer tick. Of course I already knew how serious an affliction this was—it can cause all kinds of arthritis-like and other symptoms, and even a heart block. I was sure I had the infection. I freaked out. The palpitations began and wouldn't stop. We came back a day early. As soon as we got to New York I called Eileen Hoffman and explained the situation. The next morning I was in her office, where she explained that the risk of the disease was small, even with a deer tick bite, and advised waiting for the lab results. Noting that I was considerably distressed, however, she prescribed an antibiotic (Doxycycline) and gave me the phone number of the same lab that had done the giardia testing three years earlier. But she was more concerned with the heart problem, and sent me home attached to a Holter monitor for a 24-hour period. Suspecting also that the premature beats resulting from the tick bite might be indicative of an anxiety disorder, she recommended a psychiatrist.

During the monitoring period there were probably hundreds of PVC's. The instrument, however, was defective and recorded no beats at all. The results indicated that I was already dead. The experiment was repeated a week later, but by that time my pulse was again quite regular, and there was no sign of any other heart problem.

The lab confirmed that the insect was indeed a female deer tick, and advised that there was a 15% chance of my contracting Lyme Disease. By then I had been on the antibiotic for several days. The gamble had paid off; for the time being, at least, I was safe from heart block and other tick-produced catastrophes.

Nevertheless I made the appointment with the psychiatrist, and we had three sessions during which I urgently poured out my life story. He recommended jotting down what I was thinking about whenever an irregular contraction occurred. But at this point they were occurring only rarely, and the interviews were discontinued.

In December, Kathleen Buckley was diagnosed, at seventy-five, with esophageal cancer (Jim had died of asthma shortly after we moved to New York). Since this particular affliction was my own worst nightmare, I empathized strongly with her plight. The recovery rate for this illness is quite small, and I was sure it was a death sentence for her. Early in 1992, however, she underwent successful surgery, and she lived to the age of eighty-eight, long enough to see her daughter Laura, a master chef, assume her loving care of the Whale Cove Cottages (now the Whale Cove Inn).

By the end of the year (1991), and with several more rejections of K-PAX and The American Way, I will admit that I was becoming a tad discouraged about finding a successful career in creative writing. I decided to part company with George, even though I thought he had done a good job. But sending out K-PAX and waiting for rejection letters was something I could do as well as he. Maybe even better, because I wasn't restricted by the one-at-a-time submission policy imposed on literary agents.

After another year of bashing, a total of nearly forty rejection letters, and with nowhere else to go, I essentially gave up on K-PAX. I had approached every possible publisher in New York and several elsewhere. Nobody thought it was worth the paper it was printed on. Perhaps, I realized, it wasn't.

But In June, 1992, while Shasta and I were on Grand Manan, Karen took a *phone call* (another first) from the aforementioned Ida Giragossian, Jonathan Segal's editorial assistant at Alfred A. Knopf. Would I please send *K-PAX* to her again—they had a new editorial director (Marty Asher) who might be interested. He wasn't, but for the next several months I found in the mail the occasional note from Ida suggesting that I send the manuscript to this or that editor. I complied every time—what could I lose but a few more stamps—with the usual results. One of these was John Silbersack at Warner Books. After a couple of months I called his office and spoke to an assistant editor, Christina Marciona. I asked the usual dread question; this time the answer was "*Maybe.*"

In a few weeks I called her again. She confided that *K-PAX* was "the most believable novel I've ever read," but was sorry to report that Silbersack's division was soon switching to "hard sci-fi." Evidently I had missed the cutoff by a few days.

Story of my life.

SHORT STUFF

Having decided I wasn't writing the kind of novels that anyone would want to publish, I concluded that, at fifty-four, I should probably try some other line of work. As an incentive, I threw out all my old manuscripts (I kept one copy of each) and rejection letters. But it was too late to go back to science or commercial flying, and I couldn't think of anything else I wanted to do (or any other talent I had that would interest anyone). In desperation I turned to writing fragments—the first fifty pages of novels. If an editor wanted to see the rest, I would write it—no need to waste my time producing an entire manuscript if nobody even wanted to take a look at it.

The first of these was an homage to my favorite work of fiction, *Platero and I*. I called it *Ben* (after Chris's younger brother) *and I*. Instead of the social outcast roaming the fields of rural Spain on his burro (Platero), my protagonist was a contemporary homeless man living with his dog (Ben) on the streets in the vicinity of an unnamed park (Washington Square) surrounded by a large metropolitan university (NYU).

I sent the partial to a horde of agents. While waiting for the rejection letters to come in I took some time off to campaign for the iconoclastic liberal Jerry Brown, who was running for president in the Democratic primary. Like my novels, his candidacy was doomed from the start. It was the first and last time (other than monetary contributions) I became involved in a political campaign.

I also started a nonfiction book called *Will We Survive?*, which I discarded after five or six pages—I hated it. Maybe, I thought, I should try the other route: see if I could get a story or two published. Establish a track record. I distilled a few out of *Watson's God* and *The American Way*, and went back to the library to research the short story periodicals. I sent each of the stories to what seemed to be the magazine of best fit. Nobody wanted even these capsules.

So I resurrected "The Boy Who Spoke with God," and wrote a couple more children's stories. One ("Branty") was about a flock of Canada geese who fly south for the winter only to find their home has become a real estate development. The other ("Lattie") featured an intrepid snowflake—though, in reality it was a metaphor for struggling writers everywhere. It begins:

> Lattie could not remember being born. His earliest memory was of a cold,
> dark night and of falling slowly, slowly toward the light. It was a pleasant feeling,

almost like floating. All of his brothers and sisters and aunts and uncles and cousins were tumbling gently with him, playfully bumping into one another from time to time.

With all his relatives blocking his view it was not easy to see the ground below, and Lattie had been drifting a long time before he noticed that the lights were getting bigger and brighter, and that some of them were moving. Like most young snowflakes he wondered what they were, where they had come from, and what sort of world he was falling into.

The lights were coming closer and closer and moving faster and faster. But he was unafraid because he was not alone. In fact, he couldn't wait to see what would happen next. Suddenly the beams were very bright indeed, and moving faster than the wind. He was blinded by a sudden flash, and then there was only darkness: he had been run over by a large truck!

Before he realized what had happened he was further pulverized by a small green car, a white van bearing the words BOB'S TOWEL AND LINEN SERVICE, and a long gray limousine with darkened windows. He began to feel very strange, for he was no longer a shiny white snowflake. Instead, he had become a muddy little drop of water . . . .

And ends:

. . . But he tried again. And again. And again. Then, one very cold afternoon on his thirtieth, or fiftieth, or seventy-eighth attempt—he had lost count—he found himself drifting out of a heavy black sky toward a wonderful white landscape dotted with big green trees. Nonchalantly (he had learned not to get too excited by prospects of any kind) he looked for a good place to land. Fully expecting to encounter a dog or a stream or worse, a fire down below, he gazed casually toward his destination. But below him and in every direction there was only stillness and beauty. He allowed himself a little thrill: could it be true? Could he have found his mountaintop?

Slowly he floated past the tip of a tall, broad spruce. Carefully he descended between its massive, sweet-smelling branches, and finally touched down as gently as a feather on the powdery ground.

At that very moment the sun came out. But it was a cold, distant sun and caused Lattie no concern. For he had attained his lifelong goal, fulfilled his destiny. He was so happy that he performed several cartwheels and one back flip. He had found his place in the world at last.

Neither this nor any of the other stories were deemed worthy.

We packed up and headed for Grand Manan. This was the summer I became a full-fledged vegetarian—no meat or seafood of any kind. It was also the first time that Chris, now eight, came to the island, and my first opportunity to be a surrogate father (his own father, an anthropologist, was mining for fossils in Africa). Chris's energy was amazing; he was never still. And he had eyes like a telescope. He could spot things on the rocky beaches that I would have combed right over.

But one afternoon I caught him in a lie. He tearfully denied it, to which I replied "Bullshit." From then on, everything was "bullshit" (though he couldn't pronounce it right and it came out "bullsit." One evening for example, he reported that he wasn't feeling too good. I asked him later how he felt. "Like bullsit." It was a wonderful August: he occasionally addressed me, inadvertently, as "Dad." (Later, he sometimes called his father "Gene.") And he never lied to me again.

At fifteen, Chris created my website. At seventeen, he obtained his Eagle Scout badge. He graduated from NYU with a bachelor's degree in computer sciences in May, 2005. We're still the best of friends. Check him out at *www.chrisharrison.net.*

In August, President Gorbachev was taken captive by hard-line communists demanding an end to *Perestroika.* A few months later, after a period of turmoil in which Gorbachev was reinstated and the Commonwealth of Independent States (which he opposed) was created, he resigned. A moderate pragmatist, he had presided over the democratization of the former Soviet Union and the end of the Cold War. The present and future generations are in his debt.

In the fall of 1992 our CD investment from the sale of the Mantua house had matured, and we decided to buy our own place in the West Village. But the prospect of moving again, on top of the chronic failure to write a publishable novel, might have been too much. I was experiencing a variety of gastrointestinal symptoms, beginning in the summer, which included increased esophagitis pain, a "froggy" sensation in my throat while swallowing, and soft stools, as well as the usual palpitations. One October afternoon, while looking at apartments, I suffered a difficult-to-describe "incident." It seemed as if the world suddenly became very intense, as if I were trying hard to focus my eyes on very fine print. While the real-estate agent droned on and on I began to hyperventilate, fought off a panic attack, and the episode passed. A few days later I visited Eileen Hoffman.

The incident, she assured me, did not portend anything ominous. For the GI problems she temporarily doubled the dose of Zantac. This helped, but not enough. My overall history, however, and the latest increase in esophagitis symptoms, pointed again to an anxiety problem. She sent me to a psychoanalyst.

Dr. Rabin listened while I gave him a preview of this memoir, and he made some good suggestions, but it soon became apparent that this wasn't what I needed. I asked him whether there were any drugs I could try. Since he wasn't an M.D., he referred me back to Eileen, who prescribed a mild sedative, Ativan (lorazepam). On the evening of February 24, 1993, a day that will live forever in my mind, I took one of the tablets. Within an hour I was no longer tense, uptight. For the first time since I was six, I wasn't afraid of being alive. I still realized that death could come at any moment, *but I didn't care.* It was one of the happiest moments in my life. I continued the Ativan, discontinued my psychologist. Eileen suggested that I take the drug only as needed; even so, it was quite comforting to know it was in the medicine cabinet.

We moved to the West Village at the end of April, 1993. The new apartment wasn't much bigger than the old one, but it had a third room, with built-in bookcases, which became my study. I still wasn't an author, but I felt more like one.

By this time I was already at work on my next novel "beginning." This one was about a young man who falls through a crevice while climbing in the Alps and finds a previously undiscovered community surviving under the mountains. I called it *Freeland*. Had I finished it, it would have been another political satire, this time about an underground civilization which had developed a rigidly hierarchical society in which farting played a major role in their efforts at both courtship and communication. As always, I sent partials everywhere: like a paper boomerang, they zoomed back again. I continued submitting the stories, too, as well as the beginning of *Ben and I*. It was already the summer of 1993.

In June, Karen was asked to become president of a national organization, the American Association of Health Science Library Directors, which sets medical library policy throughout the country. It was a great honor, and well-deserved. Even though I was failing with everything I wrote, I was very proud of her successes.

By the time we left for Grand Manan I was feeling considerable and persistent neck pain (the headaches I had long experienced while running were actually radiating from my upper spine). However, since we had decided the previous year that it was time to install a telephone, electricity, and a drilled well at our cottage, I proceeded to cut down a swath of trees (later used for firewood) from the road to the cabin to make way for the power lines. It took me two months.

At the end of August, after Karen had returned to the city and I was still on the island with Chris, there was a sleepover—two of his Grand Manan friends stayed overnight at the cottage. The next morning, while I was driving the other boys home, I suddenly felt my left hand and part of my arm go numb. As always, the first thing I thought was that I was having a heart attack. But, since Chris and I had tickets to a Paul Lauzon concert that evening, I did nothing about it, hoping the numbness would go away. It didn't, and I experienced that night the Zen-like sensation of one hand clapping.

The next day (a Sunday) I went to see Dr. Dapena. He advised me that I had a problem with either my heart, my brain, or my spine, as if it were my choice. Whatever it was (he suspected the spine), it was okay to finish out the trip and return to New York a week later as planned. During that interval the numbness diminished but never completely disappeared.

As soon as we got back to the city I visited Eileen, who suggested I make an appointment for an MRI. In the meantime, I should wear a soft cervical collar for a couple of weeks. The scan showed that I indeed had a pinched nerve, but that surgery wouldn't be required unless the problem returned or worsened (the collar had gradually eliminated the numbness, and most of the pain).

That fall I sent out a final batch of queries for *Ben and I* to a number of agents, including "Maia Gregory Associates," which asked to see a sample chapter (they are short so I sent the first three, a total of ten pages). Ms. Gregory herself responded:

"Thank you for sending the chapters of BEN AND I. They are touching little fragments. Are they part of a work in progress and how long do you estimate it will be? Do let me know if and when you have a complete manuscript."

I started to work on it immediately.

K-PAX, PART 2

In early October, 1993, Ida sent me an article she had seen in *Publishers Weekly* (Sept. 20) about an editor who had started his own imprint at St. Martin's Press. By this time I had become a bit jaded, even toward editors who were looking for novels that "can't be pigeonholed." Nevertheless, without the slightest expectation of success, I sent him a letter.

Bob Wyatt had come from Doubleday, where he had directed the mass-market division, and brought his assistant, Iris Bass, to SMP with him. Although the original *K-PAX* manuscript had gone to that house, it went to a different editor. When it was passed around there, however, Iris had read it and liked it.

Within a week I received a letter from her requesting that I "send over a copy of the completed manuscript, and we'll see if it's something for A Wyatt Book." I mailed it the same day, along with the required SASE, and began the long wait (anywhere from two to six months, usually) for the rejection package.

On October 23rd I took Chris to see *Cool Runnings*. By the end of the movie I was in tears. The film beautifully summed up the difficulty in overcoming the odds and achieving an unattainable goal. At that moment I realized quite clearly that I would never make a success of a writing career.

A week later, while I was at one of Chris's soccer practices (where I spotted Gregory Hines, whose son was among the players), our answering machine recorded a message from Bob Wyatt. He left a few sentences, which I listened to three or four times. The one that sticks in memory was: "I certainly want to make an offer." It was Halloween. He asked me to call him back at his weekend place in the Catskills the next morning, a Saturday.

I put down the phone, brayed for a minute, then called Karen, who was at an out-of-town meeting. When she stopped screaming I told her the rest: that I hadn't yet heard the actual offer, etc. She didn't care how much the advance might be, and neither did I. Whatever the ultimate outcome, a top New York editor had considered one of my novels worth publishing. Bob's call came three and a half years after I had finished *K-PAX*, and exactly fourteen years after leaving Case Western Reserve.

After a night of fitful sleep I called him and got the details. Yes, he wanted to publish *K-PAX*, which somehow reminded him of *The Little Prince*.

"As a hardcover or paperback?"

"Hardcover."

"When?"

"Probably next fall." Almost as an afterthought: "I can only offer you $4,000" (I hadn't asked about money; I would have paid *him* to publish it).

For those unfamiliar with the technicalities of a book contract, an "offer" is the amount a publisher agrees to pay an author as an "advance" against royalties (per cent of actual sales price, usually 15% for a hardcover book). If, for example, the writer is paid an up-front advance of $50,000, he gets no further income until his royalties exceed that amount. If sales don't live up to expectations, on the other hand, he keeps the entire advance. Four thousand dollars isn't a big offer, especially for worldwide rights (the bestselling authors can command millions), but eventually I would get all the royalties coming to me. It was no big deal, I thought. Only later did I discover that writers live on advances, not royalties.

At the time, however, despite all my earlier reading of *Writer's Digest* and other materials, I really didn't know much about the publishing world. There was always the fear, inherited from my mother, perhaps, that if I didn't have someone to count my change I might get cheated. I decided I ought to have an agent to take care of these esoteric matters (even though his/her main job is to sell your book). The first person I called was Ida Giragossian, to tell her the good news, thank her profusely, and ask if she would consider acting as my agent (I wanted her to have the commission). As an employee at a publishing house, of course, she wasn't able to do that, though she was extremely pleased and happy that Bob wanted to publish *K-PAX*. She said she would settle for an autographed copy of the novel.

The next person I thought of was Maia Gregory, the agent who had been mildly encouraging about *Ben and I*, and was still waiting for the completed novel. (Perhaps I should have gone back to George Ziegler, but his conservative approach wasn't what I was looking for.) I called Bob Wyatt again, told him I was thinking about getting someone to handle the publishing details, and asked him whether he knew her. "I *love* Maia Gregory!" he gushed. That was good enough for me. I phoned her and left a message.

A couple of days went by without a response. While waiting, my body turned against me once more. A row of red dots (pointed out by my wife) appeared on my back. I thought I might have been bitten several times by a nomadic insect or spider. Eileen had a different diagnosis: shingles. She prescribed a relatively new drug, Zovinax, and the affliction, a recurrence of childhood chicken pox, ran its course without serious discomfort.

I called Ms. Gregory again. Still no answer. I wanted to give her the benefit of the doubt (maybe she was out of town) and waited a few more days. I tried again on Saturday, and she answered. She seemed interested, but refused to commit herself until she had read the manuscript. I agreed to bring it over to her the following week.

Her "office" was her apartment, and "Maia Gregory Associates" turned out to be her. I guessed her to be well into her eighties, though she may have been somewhat younger. She complained about her secretary's not giving her my messages (there was no evidence for a secretary or anyone else), and kept dropping the name of Cass Canfield, a prominent New York editor, long deceased, as if she would go to him if Bob Wyatt didn't perform as expected. She claimed to handle "all rights" (foreign, paperback, film). I asked her about sharing her agency fee for *K-PAX* with Ida. She said she would speak to her about it. When I told her that Bob had offered an advance of $4,000, she quickly responded, "I can get you—at this point I imagined she was going to say $50,000, or even more—six." Nevertheless, I figured I had probably done the right thing, assuming, of course, she liked the novel. Finally she said she would offer me a drink, but she had "just come back from Paris and there's nothing in the house." I couldn't have cared less, but when she repeated this, word-for-word, I decided it must be a cue to leave.

Maia called me a few days later. "I love the book! I've talked to Bob, and got him up to $5,000!"

"Great!" I replied. "What's the next step?"

"We'll meet with him soon and work out the details."

"What about Ida?"

"It would be a conflict of interest for an editor to act also as an agent. So it wouldn't be ethical for her to accept an agent's fee."

I was sorry to hear that, but everything else seemed okay, and I happily got on with *Ben and I*.

Out of nowhere, however, a potentially disastrous snag sprang up. When I wrote *K-PAX*, I had named some of the characters after a few of my previous co-workers at CWRU. With publication coming up, it was time to get their permission (there would be no need for this if the book wasn't going to appear in print). I wrote to those in question, explaining that there was no similarity whatever between them and the characters (none of whom were mental patients) in the book, and if they would rather not have their names appear in the novel to please let me know. Three were absolutely delighted, one didn't respond (was on vacation, I later learned). However, from the colleague with whom I had shared an NIH grant, Nancy Oleinick, there came a registered letter which informed me, in part:

1 December 1993

Dear Gene:

I received your letter on Wednesday, November 24, 1993, informing me of the acceptance of your novel by St. Martin's Press and your use of my name for one of the characters in that novel. I am happy that you will finally be published, but I am distressed that you would use my name. It's a mystery to me why you would choose an exact name of a known person for one your characters without even consulting that person beforehand. If my name were common, perhaps it wouldn't matter, but "Dr. Nancy Oleinick" has to be quite rare. Accordingly, I am instructing you by registered letter to change the name of the character to something else. The name you choose should not even remotely relate to my name. To ensure that you comply with this instruction, I am also sending a registered letter to St. Martin's Press along with a copy of this letter . . . .

As Rosanne Rosannadanna used to say, "It's always something!"

December 7, 1993

Dear Nancy,

I am sorry that you were offended by the notion of my using your name for a fictitious character in K-PAX: THE STORY OF A MENTAL PATIENT. Everyone else I sounded out was delighted to find that his or her name would be appearing in the guise of a character in a novel.

You are wrong, however, in assuming that I did this "without even consulting that person beforehand." That is precisely what I did do, as my letter, which you received on Nov. 24, will attest. Inasmuch as the novel will not go to press for several months, it was quite unnecessary to take the extraordinary step of writing to the president of St. Martin's Press . . . .

I also called Bob Wyatt and explained the situation (he hadn't yet heard about the problem from the president). He told me he would check with SMP's attorneys and get back to me.

On Dec. 15, Karen and I invited Ida to lunch at The Four Seasons. It was hugely expensive, and we didn't spot any celebrities, but it was the least we could do and we all enjoyed the celebration.

In a note dated Dec. 21, Bob reported that the lawyers insisted I get rid of the names of any real persons. It was, in fact, company policy.

I had no problem with this, but it occurred to me that this was not a new or unique issue in publishing, so I sent off a Dec. 27 reply asking him whether the matter could be resolved to everyone's satisfaction through the signing of waivers by the half-dozen parties whose names had been used in K-PAX.

On Dec. 29 I found a phone message from Maia Gregory. I returned her call the next day. Bob is "very worried" about the use of real names. All of them have to be changed. A meeting is scheduled for 4:00 Wednesday (Jan. 5) to discuss the matter. She called me again later to emphasize that the meeting was *not* to sign a contract, and she urged a "conciliatory attitude." She must have thought I wasn't going to give up on the idea of using the names of friends in the novel. Aside from the fact that it would mildly distress those involved if I retracted my little gift to them, it was of no consequence to me whatever. But, though I willingly changed all the other names, I kept my own, and Karen's, and Shasta Daisy's, hoping none of us would be suing me for libel. (Karen later remarked that she was surprised I hadn't been sued by God, whose name was also mentioned in the book.)

Maia and I met with Bob in his office on the 18th floor of the Flatiron Building (at the intersection of Fifth Avenue and Broadway). It had gigantic windows, but they were so high off the floor that you had to stand on your toes to see the view. I gave him a copy of my letter to Nancy Oleinick. He read it, smiled, and handed it back without a word. Apparently I had been sufficiently conciliatory, and the issue was closed.

We chatted for a bit about what the jacket might look like (each of us, including Iris Bass, had a different idea), and Maia and I left. On the elevator she suggested a celebratory drink, and we found a nearby Indian restaurant. The waiter brought us an unordered plate of appetizers with the wine, fearing, perhaps, that we were planning to get smashed on one glass of Merlot and make a scene. She told me she was experiencing some sort of ophthalmological problem which caused one of her eyes to water uncontrollably, and she occasionally dabbed at it. As she got into a taxi she offered a cheek, which I kissed, and came away with the taste of salty tears, or worse. Despite my excitement and happiness, I'm afraid I spat on the street (after she was on her way), fearing she might have had some kind of eye infection.

A week later Iris and I met for lunch to discuss any questions I might have about book publishing in general, and that of *K-PAX* in particular. (Besides being Bob Wyatt's assistant, incidentally, she is a well-known expert on opera: see, for example, her book, *What's Your Opera IQ?: a Quiz Book for Opera Lovers*, Citadel Press, 1997.) I learned then that *K-PAX* had been re-scheduled for the winter list (January, 1995), a few months later than Bob had originally indicated, because a "similar" novel (*The Piltdown Confession* by Irwin Schwartz) was already on the fall list. I was disappointed, of course; not only was I eager, after hundreds of rejections, to get a book into print, but I had also assumed that a pre-Christmas publication date would be a boon to sales for *any* book. Iris patiently explained that there were far more books to compete with at that time and, as far as sales were concerned, it really didn't make much difference what time of year a book is published. I told her I was vaguely thinking about writing a sequel (several friends and relatives had mentioned, in the nearly four years since I had finished the novel, that they hoped to see prot return). "Bob doesn't like sequels," she replied immediately.

I told her about *Ben and I*. "Sounds interesting, but St. Martin's has just published a 'dog book'"(Lars Eighner's *Travels with Lizbeth*). My long career (I hoped) at SMP had barely begun and, it seemed, was already over.

Maia was unshaken to learn there would be a publication delay. I mentioned some of my other novels, asked whether she wanted to take a look. She told me she was not interested in seeing *Watson's God* or *The American Way* unless they were better than *K-PAX* (I had to admit they probably weren't), but she was eagerly awaiting *Ben and I*. I thought it strange that she didn't want to see even a sample of any others, but I assumed she knew what she was doing.

A few weeks later *two* contracts signed by her arrived in the mail. The one from St. Martin's Press seemed boilerplate. There was only one thing that bothered me about it: if there were a paperback edition, I would get half of any royalties, and the trade (hardcover) division the other half. As far as I knew this was standard procedure in the industry, yet it seemed somehow unfair. If Maia thought so, too, she didn't mention it.

The other contract was in the form of a letter *from me to her*, spelling out the terms of our own arrangement. Since I hadn't heard anything from her about a written contract, I had assumed it would be like the one I had with George Ziegler, sealed with a handshake. This one was good for three years, and "may not be cancelled, altered or amended except by an instrument in writing signed by all parties hereto." In it I agreed to pay her 15% for the marketing of my domestic literary rights, and 10% for foreign rights, as well as 10% "for any and all involvement and services rendered by me (sic—it should have read "you") in connection with the production of any spin-off derived from the manuscript, including, but not limited to, television, motion pictures, stage, radio, publishing, cable, videotape or any medium now or hereafter known." I should have shown it to my attorney, but, at that point, I didn't have one. Although I was suspicious of the deal, as was Karen, I signed the letter and sent it back. As far as I knew, most agents operated this way.

Despite the unexpected thorn, however, Karen and I decided to celebrate the upcoming publication of *K-PAX* with a week in the Caribbean. St. Maarten seemed an appropriate spot, especially when the most suitable accommodations appeared to be the aptly-named Horny Toad.

Bob didn't get to seriously editing the manuscript until June (1994), while I was on Grand Manan. Karen, who again stayed in New York for a couple of weeks due to work pressure, would bring the marked copy with her when she came up. In the meantime, we had a 150-ft. well drilled and electrical wiring installed to power the pump (and the telephone answering machine). The phone worked well, and the water was found to be safe. I happily settled in to await Bob's editorial comments.

In order to make the novel seem as much like nonfiction as possible, I had included a number of footnotes and references, some legitimate, some fictitious. By now, however, the aforementioned *The Piltdown Confession* had come out. It was in a similar style, and hadn't sold well. Bob thought I should drop all that extraneous material. I deferred to his better judgment, though with some reluctance. Looking back, however, I think it was a good suggestion, as the footnotes and parenthetical asides tended to interrupt the flow of the story. Bob had a few other comments and I was content, for the most part, to follow his excellent advice. He was pleased with the changes I agreed to, tolerant of those I did not. By now he had decided to feature *K-PAX* at the international book fair in Frankfurt in October.

Maia called in July to report that she was "thinking" of sending the manuscript to a Hollywood agent, and a few New York producers, all of whom, she estimated, "are about twelve years old." She also informed me that she was going to leave foreign sales to Bob Wyatt. "He enjoys it and he's so good at it," she gushed. At this point I was beginning to wonder what *she* did.

At the end of August, just before we returned to New York, the jacket copy with its innovative three-dimensional cover (the first for a work of fiction) arrived. With only one good eye I wasn't able to see the 3-D effect, but others described it to me. I was also informed that the pub date had been pushed back again, to the following March. I had little problem with that—another two-month delay seemed inconsequential by now and, besides, a couple of inquiries about a possible film tie-in for *K-PAX* had already come in.

The manuscript came back from the copyeditor in September. It took me eight straight days to go over it and agree or disagree with the hundreds of corrections and suggestions. It was also an opportunity to make "final" revisions before the book went to press. In early October, editor Wyatt went off to the 1994 book fair with *K-PAX* as his lead item. By then a foreign rights offer ($3,000—later raised to $5,000) had been made by Korea. "This is perfect," he told me. "Evidence of international interest to take to Frankfurt." By the time he got back he had secured substantial offers from France and Great Britain, as well as nibbles from several other countries.

On the 25th Karen and I hosted a dinner party (I took a long nap beforehand) for Ida, Bob, Iris, and Maia, and we learned that another offer had been made by Denmark. Brilliance would be doing the audio book. Except for my accidentally tipping over everyone's champagne glass as I was carrying the tray into the living room, it was a wonderful evening.

Karen read the corrected manuscript to me while I checked the galley proofs. There were, in fact, a few more typographical errors, as well as several additional words and phrases I wanted to change. (It's remarkable how each new scrutiny turns up a few more rough spots that weren't noticed before, but which make for an even better read once they are smoothed out. Although I'm as guilty as anyone of producing more work for the typesetters, some authors revise their page proofs even more heavily, with entire paragraphs added or deleted. Perhaps no writer has ever published a book without wishing there were a few more changes he could have made.)

K-PAX : a novel, was published in March, 1995. In late February, while looking for a future retirement location (a new hobby we were pursuing, and a chance to enjoy some long weekends), we happened to stop at a bookstore in Barre, VT. *K-PAX* was on the fiction shelf. With the yellow lettering on the spine's black background, it stood out from all the other books around it. I was tempted to ask the manager whether he would like me to autograph it, but didn't. We were content to enjoy the moment, to bask in the light at the end of the tunnel.

When we got back to the city we found it in most of the local bookstores: generally only one or two copies, sometimes a few more. Like most newly-published authors (there are jokes and cartoons about this) I sometimes "helped out" by making sure it was displayed prominently on the NEW FICTION table. Surprisingly (to me) it was usually shelved in the science fiction section—I had thought of it as a mainstream novel.

The reviews were generally excellent. Here is one of those capsule lists that often appear in later paperback versions:

"A blazing debut that looks set to become a cult classic."—Waterstone's magazine

"The crème de la crème de la crème."—The Guardian

"A compelling and intelligently crafted account . . . Brewer effectively blurs the edges between science fiction and medical journalism, leaving the reader with a sense of uncertainty that lingers long after the last page."—TimeOut

"It's interesting, irritating, tantalizing, and nicely told."—SFX magazine

"A fascinating, offbeat novel that is unexpectedly entertaining."—Detroit News

"This is a fine and fantastic story . . . suitable and very highly recommended for everyone from teens through adult."—Library Journal

"Offers its fair share of . . . pleasures."—San Francisco Examiner and Chronicle

"[A] fascinating novel . . . fascinatingly packaged."—Booklist

"Throughout, the narration's matter-of-fact, clinical tone makes this touching and suspenseful story all the more convincing."—Publishers Weekly

"A simply story, well-written, and keeps the reader guessing about prot's real identity right up until the end."—New Scientist

"Une oeuvre originale qui devrait conqerir public."—Le Figaro

"[A] cleverly structured and impressively well-written story . . . Fiction or not, Brewer stretches your senses."—Cleveland Plain Dealer

"The ending was most satisfactory."—St. John Telegraph Journal

"A mixture of *Starman*, Oliver Sacks, and *One Flew Over the Cuckoo's Nest*."—The Guardian

"Delightful . . . With *K-PAX* Brewer shows us that there is more than one way to have a happy ending and that there is no reason why reality can't meld to fit everyone."—Southern Book Trade

One of the neighborhood shops I had begun to frequent, The Biography Bookshop on 11th and Bleecker Streets in the Village, had stocked it. The other, The Three Lives, had not. I called the store and asked innocently whether they had *K-PAX*.

"No."

"Do you plan to order it?"

"No."

"Really? I've heard it's a wonderful book."

Dryly: "Is this the author?"

Only in New York.

When it was remaindered (the auctioning of unsold books) a year or so later, it had sold just under 4,000 copies, and foreign sales were still coming in. Not bad for an unknown author and a novel with a strange title that had been rejected forty-eight times. So far it's been published in more than a dozen languages and two dozen countries, and counting.

BEN AND I

The whole of 1994, the year before *K-PAX* was published, saw another deterioration in the state of my health. All the symptoms I had experienced over the previous decade or more seemed to have recurred and become more persistent. With a promising novel coming out I would have thought that the apparent anxiety underlying all of them would have diminished. Instead, it seemed, the opposite was true. Nevertheless, I pulled myself together every morning to write a few pages of *Ben and I*, which I finished in late April, a month after our return from the Horny Toad.

I composed the novel in a style similar to, if not as lyrical as, that of Jiménez's magical *Platero and I*, the illustrated story of a poet and his donkey. In fact, I read a chapter of that book every day before beginning to write. Mine was an unabashed homage to this work, as suggested not only by my title but by the epigraph: "In memory of Juan Ramón and Platero in the heaven of Moguer."

Using photographs I took of Washington Square Park and its surroundings as a basis, I did the illustrations myself.

Here is the opening:

1. Ben

I don't know how old Ben is, but when we go to the dog run in the park he is like a puppy. All the other dogs come at him, bouncing and yipping, while I fumble with his rope. They coax him to the center of the great arena, his ridiculous orange coat flashing from time to time like an enormous carrot among the blacks and browns of his entourage. They roll him over and the timeless Bacchanalia begins.

On the sidelines the spectators congregate to chat and watch the buffoonery. We never look at each other, and no one knows anyone else's name, only those of our furry companions. "Ben is happiest dog in pahk," the Chinese woman tells me, and it's true, despite his cocked eyes and general clumsiness. But this has nothing to do with me.

It was nearly a month ago, on a cold February morning, that I found him pressed against the wrought-iron fence enclosing my living quarters, shivering and asleep. I opened the swinging gate—it is never locked, though I wire it shut to confuse would-be interlopers—and invited him in to share my breakfast. Without a moment's hesitation he bounded down the half-dozen steps and sat immediately with one eye on my bananas, the other on the gate. One of his ears was bent back, giving him the absurd appearance of someone who doesn't know his socks don't match. Despite his enormous size and dearth of eye co-ordination he took the bites of fruit with the delicacy of a surgeon.

Everyone assumes we are homeless. That's not true. We have a home, we just don't pay rent. Although it suffers from a certain lack of amenities it is relatively warm in winter, cool in summer, and there is no doorman to tip. It is quiet and convenient to the park, churches, schools, shopping. Camouflaged by a pair of large plastic trash cans, there is ample room for sleeping, dressing, and storage of all our belongings, which consist of an extra set of clothing for myself, a few cans of food, a leaky air mattress, two blankets, a sketch pad, and the usual odds and ends. In exchange for these facilities we keep an eye on the empty flat, beneath whose sidewalk we sleep, for the absent owner.

Ben breaks away from the group and runs over to me. I know what he wants. It's okay, Ben, I tell him, and he lopes to a corner for his morning bowel movement. While I look for a discarded newspaper to pick up the steaming excrement he bounds away to find his best friend, Fricka. But the nameless guardians are beginning to leash their canine companions and return to their warm apartments, the latter to doze and wait, doze and wait, the former to pursue whatever endeavors their lives have led them to. I, too, must work; I slip Ben's rope around his great round neck and we leave the park. He trots animatedly at my side as if we are going to the fair, though he knows full well it is only to the savings and loan, where I hold the door for people to come in and deposit their money or take out what they have put in earlier. All morning we work the patrons, Ben accepting the occasional pat of a familiar hand and I the passing inquiry as to his health, though rarely does anyone ask after my own. "Have a nice day," I offer inanely to the tippers because they expect it, and to the penurious to shame them, though it rarely works.

By noon we are rich with nickels and dimes, enough for me to buy a day's meals from the Korean grocery and deli while Ben waits outside, his rope draped over the hydrant, never moving and never taking one or the other eye off the entrance until I emerge, greeting me as though I have just returned from a long and dangerous voyage.

It is an unusually clear day and we have lunch on the bench with the good view of the city skyline, Ben sitting attentively at my feet, waiting confidently for the last bite or two of my tomato and sprouts sandwiches, apple, and oatmeal raisin cookies. I give him a whole one. Ben loves oatmeal raisin.

Ben and I

The other main characters are Crazy Otto, who wanders the park looking for his dead son; Mabel, a schizophrenic who harbors a pathological fear of the "po-lice"; the Banger, an ex-con and brilliant chess player who spends his winnings at the nearby crack house; university students and other passersby preoccupied with their own problems; and the park's non-human denizens—assorted pigeons, squirrels, rats, and the regular visitors to the fenced-in dog run.

Many of the events seen and described by the narrator remind him of his past: his difficult relationship with a drunken father, the death of his mother, a timid younger brother whom he has helped raise and who is almost like a son, and a girlfriend who, despite her love and compassion, has refused to escape from her demanding parents and run off with him.

As time progresses and the narrator begins to better understand human frailty and need, he learns to forgive his father for his weaknesses. But his own life has become so difficult that he considers giving Ben to a local fire station whose mascot has died. Finally, on a snowy Christmas Eve, expecting nothing, he calls his former girl "just to hear her voice once more." Thus, he learns that his father is attending AA meetings and has remained sober for months, his brother has never given up hope for his return, and all of them want him to come home for Christmas.

I sent *Ben* to Maia Gregory. She called a couple of weeks later to gush that "the 'stories' are wonderful—lovely, touching, and perceptive." She wondered, however, whether they "held together." I told her about *Platero and I* (and later sent her a copy). She said she would hold *Ben* until fall, "so that it doesn't 'interfere' with *K-PAX*."

In September I mailed her a slightly revised version of *Ben and I*, hoping she would show it to Bob Wyatt soon, "while (according to Maia) he has high expectations for *K-PAX*." I thought of it as a "Christmas" book, and hoped it might be published a year or so later. She said she would send it on to him.

Bob had made his offer for *K-PAX* some three weeks after receiving the manuscript. By mid-November I was beginning to worry about what he thought of *Ben*. I phoned Maia, who had already heard from him (though she hadn't informed me of this): Bob was "unenthusiastic" about *Ben and I* and had suggested I call him to discuss his "objections." I did so immediately. He said he "just didn't think it is as strong as *K-PAX*." It was also, he thought, too "disjointed," and too "derivative" (he didn't say what he thought it was derived from). Even the title reminded him of *Ben and Me*, a book about a mouse. And there was Eighner's "dog book," already published by St. Martin's.

I called up Ida Giragossian, who "would like to see it." I relayed the request to Maia, who promised to give Ida "a chance at it." Otherwise, she wanted to wait until after *K-PAX* was published before submitting *Ben*, and asked for the names of the eight editors to whom I had sent queries or partials earlier.

Maia called in December: Ida had reported that Knopf "couldn't do anything with *Ben and I*." However, Scholastic Books, a "big and good" publisher of young adult fiction, wanted to see it. Two months later they, too, rejected it. Since (she asserted) I had "already sent *Ben* to every publisher in New York," she didn't know what else to do with it. I faxed her a list of twenty houses that hadn't yet seen it.

I wouldn't have cared if she had said it was a lousy novel. But she had claimed she "loved" it, yet she hadn't a clue as to who might want to publish it. I had thought this was what agents were supposed to have clues about; otherwise, what are they for? I couldn't fire her, however, because we had signed a three-year contract.

Frustrated by her inaction, I called in May (1995) to request permission to send it out myself. She had "no objection" to that proposal. Since *K-PAX* had just been published, I quickly found four more houses willing to take a look at *Ben*. An editor at Simon & Schuster actually called me a few weeks later to say she liked it and ask a few questions, but ultimately turned it down, as did all the others.

Maia phoned in September: she will re-read *Ben* to see if it can be "made salable." Two weeks later she was "still at a loss," and hoped I would consider making it into a "young adult morality play." Karen and I had lunch with her and Ida at the Russian Tea Room, where she promised to "construct a list of young adult houses" that might consider *Ben and I*. In a few days she faxed me the names of seven possible editors she had gleaned from *Literary Marketplace*, the reference many non-agented writers consult for the same purpose. I was beginning to wonder whether she was, or ever had been, a legitimate agent, or if I was her first client. In any case, I had learned another truth about publishing: even a successful, or potentially successful, author has no more standing than a mushroom. A published book might get your foot in the door but, unless it exudes the delightful aroma of bestsellerdom, it will get you no farther.

In the meantime, while Maia was not selling *Ben and I*, negotiations for a *K-PAX* film contract were underway.

K-PAX, THE MOVIE, PART 1

I had always supposed that one's literary agent shopped a potential film tie-in to the studios or producers. In my case, at least, it was St. Martin's Press who sent around the unedited "reader's edition" of *K-PAX*, some nine months before publication, not Maia Gregory. As far back as August 2, 1994, she had mentioned that there was already "some interest" in a film version of the novel (the inquiries, at SMP's behest, had gone to her). In the next month the overtures began to accelerate. At one point she told me she had already taken calls from ten different producers (mostly from television).

On Sept. 12, Maia called to breathlessly report an offer of $25,000 for a one-year option. (An "option" is similar to an advance for a book sale. A producer or studio makes a payment covering a certain period of time, usually a year, which gives him exclusive rights to buy the property at the end of that period, renew the option for another year, or return the rights to the seller. Whatever happens, the seller keeps the option payment.) She seemed nervous; her voice was shaky. The proposal had come from film and television producer Susan Pollock. With so much apparent interest in a movie version of *K-PAX*, my response was that we shouldn't make a hasty decision, and I suggested she ask for $50,000. I wasn't really unhappy with the offer; I just didn't think we ought to act precipitously. To my surprise, she replied that we should get an attorney for any further negotiations, something I thought agents were supposed to handle. She had in mind the firm of Leavy Rosensweig & Hyman, "the best entertainment lawyers in New York," whose services she thought she could get for $1,000.

On Sept. 14th, Ms. Pollock raised the one-year option offer to $30,000. The next day an inquiry came from director Jonathan Demme (*Silence of the Lambs* and many other films). On the 16th, Pollock raised the bid to $50K, plus another 50K for a second year if the option were renewed, and I learned she was "fronting" for Lawrence Gordon (*Field of Dreams, Die Hard, 48 Hours*) Productions, which was associated with Universal Pictures. A call had also come from Joe Roth at Disney.

On the 20th, Disney came in with an offer of $75K (first-year option) against 400K (the total purchase price) if the option were exercised, and an additional 100K if the book became a bestseller. There had also been "several" additional inquiries, primarily from television producers, none of whom could match the current offers.

But Pollock/Gordon/Universal came back with a comparable bid. Thus, on Sept. 21st, 1994, the deals stacked up like this:

	DISNEY	UNIVERSAL
1st year of option	$70K	$80K
	(or 200K outright purchase)	
2nd year	50K	55K
total purchase price	500K	550K
	(+ 100K if book becomes bestseller)	

At this point Demme, through Ed Saxon, who had produced many of his films, decided not to compete. Until then the deal was being handled by attorney Robert Harris. Since he was out of the office on the 22nd, the final negotiations were completed by senior partner Morton Leavy. Additional reports from Maia on that day:

9 A.M.

Final offers are expected today (except for certain details, like "% of gross sales," which would be worked out by Leavy). In her opinion, I would have more "control," and more "assurance" that the film would be made, with Disney.

11 A.M.

Final offers:

	DISNEY	UNIVERSAL
1st year of option	$100K	$100K
	(in both cases, the first draft of script must be finished during the first year)	
2nd year	70K	70K
		(not applic. to purchase price)
total purchase price	500K	600K
	(+ 100K if bestseller)	(+ 50 K "assoc. producer" fee)
	(+ 25K for book promotion in both cases)	

5:45 P.M.

Mort Leavy called Maia, who passed on the final result to me: the rights go to Lawrence Gordon/Universal Pictures. It's a "done deal." But here's the bad news: Leavy's firm would get 5% of everything I make on the film. This was the first I'd heard of any such arrangement, but at the time I was more concerned with my right to publish *K-PAX II* and *III*, which were being denied by the current contract. I asked her about the latter apprehension; she assured me I would retain the publication rights to all book sequels. The next day, on September 23rd, she called again: she was "rethinking the 5%" she was giving to Mort Leavy. That was the last I heard about this fee for a while.

The elation didn't last long. On the 24th, after Karen had described *K-PAX* to someone she knew, her acquaintance commented, "That sounds a little like *Man Facing Southeast*," a film neither of us had heard of. She called me immediately. Curious, and not a little worried about a movie with an apparently similar theme, I said I would try to find it.

The local video store did, in fact, have a copy, and I checked it out. We watched it that night with mounting trepidation. Not because there were some similarities in the plot (there were), but because we were afraid that Universal might want to opt out of our contract if they knew about this Argentinean "art" film. I called Maia Gregory on Monday to see whether she thought this might be a potential problem. She said she would take a look at the videotape herself and let me know. In the meantime, she assured me, "It's nothing to be concerned about. Similarities in plot and concept occur all the time. It's what you do with it that matters."

By then, Karen had spoken to an attorney friend of hers, who advised me to write down everything I thought was similar and different between *K-PAX* and *MFSE*, "just in case any problem comes up later." I did so at once. Here is the list I compiled the day after seeing the film:

SIMILARITIES   DIFFERENCES

protagonist

— young man in mental inst.   *prot*   *Rantes*
claiming to be from outer space
— no clue as to "true" backgd.   — traveled to Earth   — a laser projection (hologram)
— supernatural abilities   on a beam of light
— aware of society's social   — bouyant personality   — dour personality
inequities   — UV vision, can "disappear," — levitation
— perfectly fluent English   can smell tumors   — can "project" music
(Spanish), but also has   and drugs
own language   — can construct star charts
— a Christ-like figure   — aware of Earth's problems
(env., etc.)
— takes notes   — faces Southeast
— "disapp." at end (alter   — "dies" at end
ego catatonic)

	narrator/psychiatrist	*psychiatrist*
— middle-aged psychiatrist	— married, 4 grown children	— divorced, two small children
— amateur musician	— sings	— plays saxophone
	— up for hospital director	
	— upbeat and busy	— bored and depressed
	characters (K-PAX)	*characters (Man)*
	— reporter who helps identify prot	— sister who also claims to be an alien
	— inmates much more developed, direct interaction w/ prot	
	— *Robert!*	
	— family	
	plot (K-PAX)	*plot (Man)*
— patients wait for him to return (at end)	— unraveling prot's true identity before deadline	
— psych. takes protag. out of hospital	— prot is the only alien	— aliens everywhere
	— K-PAX!	
	— police work	

Some of the similarities were superficial at best. For example, prot had reported that sex on K-PAX was "accompanied by tremendous pain, nausea, and a very bad smell." This was an integral part of the plot of the book; it was based on prot/Robert's abhorrence of the sex act resulting from certain traumatizing events. The woman in *MFSE* coughed up a bit of purplish fluid (the obligatory vomit scene?) after sex, but there was no particular reason for this, it was apparently just thrown in "for effect."

More importantly, I thought, there were significant differences between the two stories. Prot came to Earth to tell us that we humans are destroying "the only home you have." Indeed, this was the reason I had created him. The purpose of the patient's visit in *Man Facing Southeast*, if any, was never made clear. I learned later (from several sources) that the writer/director, Elisio Subiela, was trying to say something about political repression in Argentina, a subject that had no special interest for me, nor for prot, who had no regard for *anyone's* petty politics.

Though my conscience was clear, I was still supremely uncertain about what Universal would think of all this. But there was nothing more I could do; I had reported the matter to my agent, who had consulted UP's representative, the executive producer (Sue Pollock) of the putative film version of the book. My subconscious mind, however, was not taking it well. The day after seeing the film, during a jog down to Battery Park to watch one of Chris's soccer games, I encountered some serious chest pain. I was pretty sure it wasn't a heart attack—I had been through all that before. Nor was it esophagitis, which—I thought—was under control. Was it the first indication of esophageal cancer?

I continued to jog even though I was sure to experience at least moderate chest pain (as well as the frequent neck/headaches.) Even while walking there was some chest discomfort. I was certain that the condition, whatever it was, would require me to undergo my worst nightmare, a gastroscopy, followed by surgery and nauseating chemotherapy, or (not much worse) a slow, painful death—a repeat of the terrors I had experienced with the swallowing difficulty more than forty years earlier.

On October 13th (1994), while most of my attention was focused on these unwelcome symptoms, Maia faxed me the draft of the Universal contract, "red-lined" (i.e., those terms which seemed unsatisfactory to our lawyers were highlighted) by Bob Harris, the attorney of record at Leavy et al. I was supposed to look it over and get back to her, which I did the next day with several questions. She referred me directly to Mr. Harris. I asked him about the "5% of gross" which Maia had mentioned earlier. In reality, it turned out to be 5% of *net profits*, which was a very different thing. Nevertheless, he thought it was a good contract overall, and I asked him to proceed with the negotiations, with particular attention to the clause allowing me to publish *K-PAX II* and *III* (in case I decided to write them).

On the 22nd, Bob sent over the "final" film contract, ready for signing. I read it over and called him back the next day, further dismayed by a 6- to 12-year holdback clause—regardless of what happened, I couldn't negotiate a film sequel with another studio for twelve years from the date of the contract, or six years after the movie was released—had I missed this before? He said he would ask UP about it. Five minutes later Maia phoned, roaring and fuming. "This is a great contract . . . best lawyers in the business . . . ," etc. I told her I didn't think it would hurt to inquire.

On the 28th, Bob reported that UP "won't budge" on the holdback period, but thought it wasn't a serious problem. A sequel would depend on the economics at the time, i.e., whether the first film made a profit. I signed the contract the next day and sent it back to him. The option payment, less 15% for Maia Gregory—ten for her, five for Leavy Rosensweig & Hyman—came a month later. (All payments for royalties, options, and advances, incidentally, go directly to one's agent. After a few days or weeks, the author gets his share from him/her.) The "done deal" meant that *K-PAX* could join hundreds of other projects in "development" (a.k.a. "development hell").

On November 16th, several weeks after I had notified her about the existence of *Man Facing Southeast*, Maia called to tell me that both she and Sue Pollock had watched it. "We both fell asleep," she said. "Don't worry about it." I tried very hard not to. She also asked me who I would put in the roles of prot and Dr. Brewer if the film were made. That got me to thinking about the entire cast. I came up with the following idealized list, not expecting the impossible, but to give any interested party an idea of character types I had in mind:

prot	Gary Sinise
Dr. Gene Brewer	John Lithgow
Karen Brewer	Kathleen Turner
Giselle Griffin	Jodie Foster
Russell	Donald Sutherland
Howie	Dustin Hoffman
Ernie	Jeff Goldblum
Mrs. Archer	Nancy Marchand
Whacky	Matthew Broderick
Ed	Tommy Lee Jones
Maria	Marisa Tomei
Bess	Cicely Tyson

When you dream, dream big.

November and December were filled with social events and gatherings. My chest discomfort became progressively worse, and the upper abdominal pain with accompanying chronic soft stools had returned—a recurrence of the irritable bowel syndrome. By the end of the year I knew that something more had to be done.

In January, during my annual physical exam, I reported everything to Eileen Hoffman, and asked her if there was anything better than Zantac for esophagitis. Happily, there was a relatively new drug on the market, Prilosec, a far more powerful acid reducer, which she prescribed. More importantly, perhaps, she sent me to see another psychiatrist, one of the best in New York. Finally, she told me she had decided to restrict her practice to women's health (Karen's for example). I would have to find another primary-care physician.

I first saw Dr. Kron, the psychiatrist, in January, 1995, a month or two before *K-PAX* was published. During that session we discussed my symptoms and what might be responsible for them. At the end of the hour I requested a diagnosis. "Well, you certainly have an anxiety disorder." I learned also that it is often an inherited condition, and that the medical and social apprehensions were part of the same syndrome. Moreover, the earlier "giardia" infection, and perhaps other afflictions (including, in part, most of the gastrointestinal symptoms), might really have been manifestations of acute anxiety.

"But why did it get worse now?" I asked him, "with my first novel about to come out?"

"It was probably precipitated by the events of last October" (watching *Man Facing Southeast* and wondering whether everything I'd worked so hard for was going to go up in smoke).

"What's the best treatment?"

He started me on Prozac.

I still find it astonishing to realize that most of the symptoms I had been experiencing for nearly a lifetime had been caused by anxiety. Though it seems obvious now, the chest pains, palpitations, and all the rest seemed so intense while they were happening that I naturally (or unnaturally) assumed they were heart, or other serious non-mental, problems. Of course that is part of the expression of an anxiety disorder. Furthermore, it's a disease, not a weakness or even cowardice. In my case, at least, the attempts to face my problems (learning to fly, for example) suggested just the opposite.

Equally amazing is the fact that anxiety (and the related affliction, depression) is often a result of a chemical imbalance (a low level of serotonin, primarily, or a shortage of its receptors) in the brain, and that any number of drugs can counteract it. With Prozac, I experienced virtually no anxiety at all. I happily stayed on it for five years.

The Prilosec, however, was less successful. Eventually I discovered that I was supposed to take it on an empty stomach, something the pharmacy had neglected to inform me about. When I began that regimen, those symptoms, too, virtually disappeared.

YONDERLAND

As soon as I had finished *Ben and I*, I went to work on *Yonderland*, which can best be described, perhaps, as a more youth-oriented version of *The American Way*. I finished the short novel in the summer of 1995.

It starts off this way:

> This is a story about a boy. Not an ordinary boy, because, if that were the case, he would be playing ball or computer games, and there would be no tale to tell. Nor is it a true story, but one that *could* have happened, and still might.
>
> The boy's name was Alex, and he was one of those kids who never seemed to be paying attention. He often missed what his teacher was saying because he was thinking about impossible things, or focusing his attention on irrelevant matters, such as a fly washing its face. When he asked questions, which wasn't often, they were usually of the annoying kind, the ones beginning with "why." "Your curiosity will get you in trouble some day," his mother predicted, adding the usual adage about the cat.
>
> To which Alex would reply, "That's all right. Cats have nine lives."
>
> Regardless of how many lives Alex or cats are allotted, the plain fact is that curiosity is like brown eyes: if you have it, there's not much you can do about it.
>
> His eyes were, in fact, brown, and with them he observed and contemplated his surroundings near and far. He would study the tiniest veins in a leaf and think about what it might be like to live inside them. He would gaze into the bright eyes of a calf and try to imagine what he or she was thinking about. He looked at the sky and wondered what was beyond the stars.
>
> Alex's parents, who were hard-working farmers, couldn't understand why he could never finish the simplest chore without wandering off after a butterfly or losing his concentration to the slightest change in cloud formation or far-off sound. He was always disappearing, sometimes forgetting to come in for meals. So they weren't worried the day he stumbled across a barely visible opening in the earth, at the base of an old, old maple tree on the far edge of the woods, and didn't show up for dinner, which is what lunch is called on a farm.
>
> The hole was barely wide enough for him to squeeze through. The hounds watched him disappear; they whined, but didn't follow him in. Grunting his way

headfirst down and down the long tunnel, he finally popped out, as if he were being born again, in a huge underground cavern. Except for the faint light coming from the passage he had just crawled through, the big cave was dark. So dark that he couldn't see the other side, or even the walls or ceiling.

Alex wasn't much impressed by darkness. He knew that everything was the same in the dark as in the light except that you couldn't see anything. But there was still hearing and feeling and smelling and tasting. The floor was dry, and it felt solid enough, so he set off toward the other side of the cavern without even glancing back at the opening he had come through, which he knew was there whether he looked or not.

It was a long time before he saw, in the distance, a faint light much like the one he had left behind. In fact, he thought he had gotten turned around and circled back to where he had started. The short, narrow tunnel smelled the same as before, too. So he climbed in and crawled up and up and emerged at the base of an old, old maple tree on the edge of a woods. From there it was a simple matter to find his way home.

It took him awhile to get there because he stopped to look at everything he encountered along the way: tall, green mushrooms with bites taken out of them; tiny, colorless flowers; giant dragonflies that flew backwards; and fat, waddling snakes with forked tails. No matter—there was no reason to hurry. But when he got to where the barn ought to be, it was gone. And when he looked behind where the barn should have been, there was no house, either!

At this point some boys might have become concerned, perhaps even alarmed. Alex merely assumed that he had made a wrong turn somewhere, and began to retrace his steps, though he paid more attention to a striped bird somersaulting across the sky than to the route he was taking. Suddenly a rabbit hopped by. Only it wasn't a rabbit like he had ever seen before, because it had no ears and no tail.

He decided to follow it.

From there, Alex proceeds to explore Yonderland, where every family is its own country, and the enemies of those who have eight children are those who have nine. Occasionally he hears a distant explosion resulting from one country annihilating another, and everyone around him murmurs, "Too bad," or "How sad." He comes across athletes transporting their money in wheelbarrows to the bank; politicians who answer every question they are asked, with: "Jobs, jobs, jobs"; lawyers who literally chase ambulances; diplomats who are concerned only with proper dress and table manners; groping clergymen. Whenever he asks who runs Yonderland, he is told, "Mr. Paragon," of whom there are statues everywhere. Midway through his travels he comes across a bookstore:

Humming a tune of his own creation, Alex came to a bookshop. Thinking there might be some information there, perhaps a map of the government buildings or a telephone directory, he stepped inside. When he opened and closed the door, a little bell tinkled somewhere. He opened and closed it several more times until he figured out how the mechanism worked, then turned to find a clerk staring at him. "Well? Are you going to buy anything? Or did you just come to ring my bell?"

"Uh—I'm just looking," said Alex, and he proceeded to look.

"Oh," sniffed the clerk. "One of *those*." He returned to the novel he was reading.

Alex soon discovered that the store had only three kinds of books. Along one wall stood tall stacks of romance novels, and on the other, mysteries. In back were the cookbooks. From the corner speakers came the anguished cry of a girl in unrequited love. The clerk, an owlish-looking young man wearing huge glasses, was reading *Murder in the Morgue*. He was as pale as freshly-squeezed milk.

Alex cleared his throat. When that elicited no response he coughed, and mumbled, "Excuse me, sir."

"Yes, yes, what is it?" said the young man without looking up.

"I was just wondering whether you have a map of Yonderland, or know how I can find a government office."

"Just let me finish this chapter, will you? Gloria is about to throw herself out a window."

Alex wandered along the shelves gazing at the romance novels, all of which had exactly the same cover and almost the same title. Every jacket pictured a semi-naked woman, head thrown back, in the arms of a tanned, muscular man. When he had seen all there was to see, he approached the high desk.

"Ah, Gloria, how could you do that?" the pale clerk lamented before looking up. "Yes? Have you decided?"

"Are these the only kinds of books you carry?"

"What other kinds are there?"

"I don't know. Aren't there other things besides mysteries and romance books?"

"Well, of course. We have a wonderful collection of cookbooks on the back wall."

"I meant books about science and things like that."

"Are you kidding? Nobody would buy such a book."

"Why not?"

"Because nobody would write one, that's why."

"Why not?"

"I already told you: because nobody would buy such a book. How about a nice whodunit?"

"No, thanks. But I'd like to see a map of Yonderland if you have one."

"Sorry. We only sell books." Yawning, the man returned his mystery to the shelves and pulled out another just like it. "How about a cookbook for your mother? There's a new one I just got in—*101 Ways to Make Stew*."

"I don't think so. Besides, I haven't got any money. But do you know where I can find any information about Yonderland?"

"What kind of information?"

"I don't know. Where I could find Mr. Paragon, or a list of schools, or a map—stuff like that."

"Got any sisters? They would love *Ashlee Meets Mr. Right.* Big bestseller."

"Sorry, I don't."

"Brothers? How about *The Tribulations of Jefferey?*"

"I don't think so."

"You certainly are hard to please." The clerk picked up his mystery, turned to page one, and was immediately engrossed. "It was a dark night, and stormy as well . . ." he muttered. Alex asked him whether he had a bathroom, but the man didn't hear him or the tinkle of the bell when he opened and closed the door several times on his way out.

"Come back any time!" the clerk called after him. Or try one of our other stores. THEY'RE ALL THE SAME!"

Alex continues his journey, visiting government buildings, factories, shopping malls, the university, a library. To find out who's in charge, the librarian sends him to a large corporation. On his way he visits a post office, where all the windows have "NEXT WINDOW" signs in them; an art gallery, where blank canvases sell for millions; a courtroom, where verdicts are decided by how popular the lawyers for either side are and how loudly the gallery cheers for each; a lottery carnival, where thousands of people line up to throw all their money away for a chance to "win big." The CEO of the corporation sends him to an advertising agency, where he is directed to the nearest TV news truck. The newscaster points him to a golf course, where the real power, the politicians of any party, are at constant play, and where an elderly lawmaker finally answers his question: Mr. Paragon is a composite of all of us.

At last he finds his way back to the cave, and comes out on the other side. He gets home just in time for supper, runs upstairs to his room to wash up. When he glances into the mirror, he finds that he looks a lot like the statues of Mr. Paragon.

A little over the top? Maybe. Maia didn't know what to do with this one, either. I sent it to a dozen or so editors, all of whom rejected it without comment.

1995 wasn't a very good year in other ways, either. Our New York/Grand Manan friend Pres Bowles was slowly dying of a rare cancer in her jaw. Early in the same year Rea Wilmshurst had undergone surgery for ovarian cancer. By summer, following chemotherapy, all traces of malignancy had vanished, according to her doctors. They were wrong.

After being turned loose by Eileen Hoffman, I sought another physician. The first one I tried was also affiliated with NYU. I told him about my chronic esophagitis, treated successfully with Prilosec. He asked me immediately whether I'd ever been "scoped" (invaded by a gastroscope). I don't know whether he planned to sign me up for one because I never went back.

A few days after that came a sudden and prolonged chest pain. I swallowed an Ativan tablet and called Eileen, who took me back within the hour for one final look. My EKG was unchanged, but I knew something was very wrong. A few days later, while having dinner with friends at the Zen Palate in New York, I suffered a full-blown panic attack (I hadn't yet reached the optimal level of Prozac), something I hadn't experienced for a long time. As always, I continued to nod and smile, and I don't think anyone knew I was "gone." Later, a barium swallow indicated my esophagus and stomach were okay, and a sonogram showed no evidence for a gall bladder problem. Eileen sent me back to Dr. Slater, whom I had seen following the "chainsaw palpitations" on Grand Manan a few years earlier. My heart was fine, too, but, to put the issue to rest, he scheduled a stress test. That was normal, also. By then the idiopathic chest pain (resulting from the fear of placing my fragile life in the hands of an unfamiliar physician?) had all but been forgotten.

On a couple of occasions we ran into Gregory Hines, who lived with his family only three blocks from our apartment—once on the street, once sitting on his front steps with his wife. We never met him when he wasn't smiling.

On Grand Manan, Rea seemed to feel fine, if somewhat weakened by the chemotherapy, and the prognosis was good. In November, however, she was back in the hospital with an intestinal blockage—the malignancy had returned. The same month Shasta began to show signs of arthritis, and Bob Wyatt informed me that, because of lower than expected sales of the hardcover version, he was "holding" on the paperback reprint of K-PAX.

By that time I was already well into K-PAX II.

K-PAX II, PART 1

We went to Toronto in January, 1996. Rea had a little device attached to her waist so that she could inject herself with morphine when the pain became severe. She was in good spirits, however, and talked openly about her illness without a trace of bitterness—she had lived exactly the life she had wanted, and expressed no complaints. Ten days later she was in a hospice. She died peacefully in March at the age of fifty-five.

We visited Rowell and Pres the following day to convey the news. Though she was bravely facing up to her own malignancy, Pres was confined to her bed. She was very happy to learn that Rea's death had been peaceful. Our final visit was on May 30th, the day before we left for Grand Manan. In July we received a call from Rowell: Pres had died (a nurse was present) while he was out for a jog in Central Park. Rea and Pres were terrific people and great friends. We still miss them.

Once I had decided to make *K-PAX* a trilogy, I thought of it in terms of a concerto: an adagio for Part I, an andante second movement, in which the themes of the first one were explored and further developed, and an allegro finish to the trilogy, at which time the mystery would be resolved. Though prot would still be a dominant character in *K-PAX II*, I wanted to delve more deeply into what had caused Rob's trauma(s) in the first place. This required a little more research. I knew that Robert had to have a sex problem, but I needed to figure out what had produced it.

During the five years when prot was gone, some of the patients described in the first book had left the hospital. I got out my old list of possible psychotics, added a few, deleted some, and selected those I thought would present interesting cases. When everything was in place it was only a matter of re-starting the engine and getting the wheels turning again. This was surprisingly easy: once I had written a brief recap of previous events I found myself back in the hospital interviewing prot, and the story essentially wrote itself.

I finished *K-PAX II* on Feb. 3, 1996, and sent it to Maia Gregory, who told me that Bob Wyatt wouldn't want to publish it for "economic" reasons, i.e., *K-PAX* didn't sell enough copies to warrant a sequel (her conclusion, not his). However, she had no objection to *my* sending the manuscript to him, which I did on Feb. 24. I got his response in April: he didn't think a sequel was "necessary." It was not a financial decision, he told me, but a literary one. I reported this back to Maia, who wanted to wait until the movie came out before re-submitting. I pointed out that it may *never* come out, and said I'd like to send it out myself. She had no objection to this, either.

Several inquiries elicited a common response: we don't do sequels if we haven't done the first book. Catch-something-or-other. I obtained the list of all the foreign publishers who had printed *K-PAX* and queried them, including Bloomsbury in London, publisher of the Harry Potter books. A few wanted to see the manuscript, but the result was generally the same—the original hadn't sold enough copies, and *II* couldn't stand on its own. But if the movie were to come about . . .

I told them they would be among the first to know.

LEGAL MANEUVERINGS

By April, 1996, I had concluded that Maia Gregory was doing nothing for me, and I was looking for a way to get out of my contract with her. I had come across a book called *The Rights of Authors, Artists, and Other Creative People*, by Norwick and Chasen (S. Illinois U. Press, 1992), and was gratified to learn that if I sold something *on my own*, she wouldn't be entitled to a commission *even though we had an agency contract.* Of course this would only apply to any future sales; she would still be entitled to a percentage of any income for *K-PAX* the novel, and the film as well if it came about during the current option period.

Coincidentally, because of the sudden income generated by sales of book and film rights for *K-PAX*, Karen and I decided to revise our wills. Our New York neighbor, Steve Peskin, who was president of the New York Bar Association at the time, suggested I contact the legal counsel for our apartment building, attorney Carol Buell. We showed her the changes we wanted to make in our previous documents. Hoping she could see a way out of my unfortunate relationship with Maia, I also left her a copy of my contract with her. Carol called me later that day. "Your agent is contractually entitled to 10%, not 15% on foreign sales. *In addition, you should not have to pay the 5% to your attorneys in the Universal deal.* According to your contract, Ms. Gregory is entitled to 10% of your income from the film, not 15%, so she has to share her fees with the attorneys."

I called Maia and reported what Carol had told me.

"I'm entitled to 15% of everything you make!" she huffed.

"Not according to my lawyer."

"Mort Leavy did a damn good job," she retored. "I thought you would be eternally grateful that I had—" She slammed down the phone. I *was* grateful that he and Bob Harris had negotiated an excellent contract with Universal, but not to the extent that I was willing to pay her more than she was entitled to, especially since she had done virtually nothing to earn it. She didn't buy me no peanuts.

On May 16, Carol sent Maia a letter setting out our position:

Dear Ms. Gregory:

As you know I have been retained by [Gene] Brewer, a writer with whom you currently have an exclusive agency agreement.

211

Mr. Brewer asked me to review your agreement with the intention of ending the exclusive agency period on May 1, 1996 rather than December 31, 1996. While he acknowledges that you have offered him some assistance, primarily by bringing in Morton Leavy of Leavy Rosensweig and Hyman to assist you in negotiating the film contract with Universal Studios, he has been dissatisfied with your representation of him in marketing his published work, *K-Pax*, or assisting him with his other works-in-progress.

I have advised him of the following:

1. The St. Martin's Press contract, which granted St. Martin's the exclusive rights to *K-Pax* and all subsidiary rights, throughout the world as well as all additional and subsidiary rights in the work was signed on December 16, 1993, well before the exclusive agency period in your agreement. The domestic and foreign rights as well as movie rights to *K-Pax* were not included in your agency agreement and any commissions received for compensation thus far on *K-Pax* are questionable in terms of the contract.

2. In the event *K-Pax* is deemed to be covered by your agency agreement, the compensation you have received thus far has been miscalculated. By the terms of your agreement you are to be compensated with a 10% commission for all foreign literary rights. You have retained a 15% commission on Mr. Brewer's foreign sales.

Additionally, by the terms of this agreement you were to receive 10% of any compensation for movie rights. Again, you have retained a 15% commission which was distributed, to the best of Mr. Brewer's knowledge, as follows: 5% to Morton Leavy, Esq. and 10% to Maia Gregory Associates. As you know, you informed Mr. Brewer that you were ill-equipped to negotiate a movie contract and suggested involving Mr. Leavy in the negotiations with Universal Studios. Mr. Brewer was very pleased with Mr. Leavy's work, however, there was no separate fee arrangement with Mr. Leavy. Accordingly, you have retained an additional 5% which is not provided for in your contract with Mr. Brewer.

My client would be prepared to discuss a settlement of these issues which must include a condition that the exclusive agency arrangement end on May 1, 1996 rather than December 31, 1996. In addition, the ambiguities in the terms must be clarified. I suggest you discuss these issues with your attorney. Mr. Brewer would like to resolve all of these matters as soon as possible.

Very truly yours,
Carol L. Buell

The letter elicited no response. She sent a followup letter on May 23. That one was stronger: it suggested that I was prepared to take Maia to court if necessary to resolve the dispute.

A few days later Carol called—she had received a letter from Maia's attorney, Ronald Lockhart, to the effect that she would agree to release me immediately from all subsequent sales, and to 10% for foreign publications, BUT she wanted a percentage of all subsequent and *derivative* sales related to *K-PAX*, as well as 15% of film rights (5% for Mr. Leavy).

On July 3, Maia returned the extra 5% retained by her on foreign sales, but refused to reimburse the extra 5% on the sale of film rights. Carol advised that I concede the latter in exchange for Maia's relinquishing her claim on all subsequent sales on *K-PAX* derivatives (a paperback version, any book and film sales for *K-PAX II*, etc.). I reluctantly agreed, and she sent a letter to Maia's attorney to this effect on July 11.

Karen and I went off to Grand Manan thinking this was a more than fair and reasonable settlement, and we presumed Maia would also. She didn't. A letter from her attorney in late August indicated that Ms. Gregory "sees no need to renegotiate the contract."

That summer we met another NY/GM couple, the Arensbergs, Fred a psychoanalyst, Leda an artist who creates fantastic mobiles, jewelry, and other works. Like the Bowleses, they became excellent year-round friends.

Shortly after our return from Canada (Sept. 3) I faxed Carol a letter indicating that I was unwilling to accept further delaying tactics on Maia's part, and was prepared to go to court. Since she is not an entertainment or trial lawyer, Carol recommended I call her colleague Rosalind Lichter, Esq., for further assistance.

I met with Roz the next day for a comprehensive discussion. She estimated the cost of litigating the dispute would be $20,000-30,000. I said I was willing to proceed. On Sept. 16th, she wrote a long letter to Maia's attorney, Ronald S. Lockhart, which reiterated the terms of my "contract" with her, and closed with:

> Gregory consistently breached her fiduciary duties to Mr. Brewer. It is well established law in New York that a breach of fiduciary duties by the party having the duty permits the damaged party to terminate any agreement.

> With respect to the option to purchase the movie rights to K-PAX, I understand that St. Martin's, not Gregory, submitted the Manuscript to a number of movie producers. Upon receiving telephone calls from interested producers (and I request that Mr. Brewer's file be sent to me forthwith), Ms. Gregory turned the whole matter over to the law firm of Leavy, Rosensweig. Although it is common in the movie industry for a literary agent to recommend to a client to retain counsel to review movie agreements, it is much less common to have an

attorney, when an agent is in place, as in this instance, to negotiate the business deal points as well as the contract/legal terms. Initially Gregory told Mr. Brewer that the legal fees would be somewhere around one thousand ($1,000) dollars. Without Mr. Brewer's prior approval, the legal fees were 5% of the movie deal—not coming out of Ms. Gregory's commission but out of the principal amount owed to Mr. Brewer. Once again, Gregory was unjustly rewarded for doing very little, if anything. Mr. Brewer had to pay even more money out of his own pocket.

In view of these circumstances, please be advised of the following:

Your client shall not be entitled to receive any further commissions for any income derived after May 1, 1996—either from any additional publishing royalties from K-PAX or any sequels or prequels of K-PAX or any other literary property of Mr. Brewer's. Secondly, Gregory shall not be entitled to commission any additional monies that may be due Mr. Brewer in connection with the Universal agreement or any film agreement, including but not limited to any income derived pursuant to the Universal Agreement or any extension or renewal thereof, including the 5% previous film commission that the law firm deducted which should have been Gregory's obligation.

In the event that your client does not agree to the aforementioned proposal by the end of the day of October 1, 1996, we shall seek declaratory and other relief in a Court of law having jurisdiction over these matters. Our claims will include, but not be limited to, a return of all commissions, paid to your client and for damages sustained by my client which includes your client's failure to exploit the paperback rights, and your client's failures to assist Mr. Brewer in any way.

The law considers an agent to be a fiduciary—a special position of trust. Gregory owed Mr. Brewer full loyalty and honesty. As far as my client is concerned, Gregory breached these duties in many instances.

Would you kindly call me so that this matter can be resolved outside of a court's jurisdiction.

Very truly yours,
Rosalind Lichter

This drew the following response, dated October 24th, from Mr. Lockhart:

Dear Ms. Lichter:

I received your letter of September 16th which I forwarded without comment to Ms. Gregory. I have no authority to respond on behalf of Ms. Gregory. I am not on retainer and represent her only when asked to do so.

Sincerely,
RONALD S. LOCKHART

! (Emphasis mine.)

Maia found a new attorney, Richard Dannay, presumably on retainer. He called Roz to ask what in her letter was negotiable, and a new round of letters and calls was initiated. After the dust cleared, the final deal, agreed to by both parties, was that Maia would keep the extra 5% (for Leavy Rosensweig & Hyman) for the 1994 film contract, receive $5,000 for any new (1996) contract with Universal Pictures, nothing for any new sales of derivatives of *K-PAX*, including a paperback version or sequels.

Roz called on Dec. 12 to tell me that "it's a done deal," i.e., she and Mr. Dannay had reached an agreement on these terms, and she would prepare a final settlement letter for Maia and me to sign. I wrote a check in the amount of $5,000, payable to Maia Gregory, on Dec. 26. This, along with the settlement document, was sent to Dannay on Jan. 8, 1997.

The response came on the 15th in the form of an amended agreement: Maia now wanted $10,000. Several other points were also changed. Roz faxed a reply on the 16th: Maia has until 6:00 p.m. to agree to the already agreed-upon settlement. She didn't agree, the $5,000 check was returned to me, and we waited for Maia to sue *me* if she chose.

K-PAX, THE MOVIE, PART 2

The Universal Pictures option was extended for a second year in November, 1995. The following April, at the beginning of the dispute between Maia and me, Sue Pollock called: "Mel Gibson's agent loved [*K-PAX*] and wanted Mel to [direct and star in] it." But he has a conflict. So they've "given" it to Tim Robbins. She had also spoken to Larry Gordon, who assured her that "it's on the fast track," though there's no script yet and little else had happened during the first eighteen months of the contract. She liked the idea of Gary Sinise as "prot" and asked to see *K-PAX II*.

In August, Bob Harris phoned me on Grand Manan: there is an unfinished script by Bryan Goluboff and Universal wants to renew the option for another two years. One of the terms of my contract stated that I could request, "from time to time," a look at the current screenplay for the putative film version of *K-PAX*. I asked him to find out whether the studio would send me a copy, even if unfinished, and to determine whether Disney was still interested. In the meantime, I authorized him to begin negotiations for a new Universal contract without the participation of Maia Gregory. I hoped he could get the holdback period for possible sales of stage rights and film sequels reduced as well.

The following is a summary of my notes of the time:

Sept. 11, 1996: Bob reported a call from Universal: what was the delay in negotiating a new contract? He thought this was a good sign; it appeared they were getting nervous. I again requested a copy of the unfinished Goluboff script and more information about him.

Sept. 27: A call from Sue Pollock: a deal with Jonathan Demme is nearly complete. The Goluboff script is unsatisfactory, but Demme may be able to work with him. Larry (Gordon) is very reassuring, still loves the project . . . .

Oct. 3: Universal will send the Goluboff script *when completed*. Disney is trying to figure out who was interested in *K-PAX* two years ago.

Oct. 9: a resume for Brian Goluboff arrived. His principal credit seemed to be adapting *The Basketball Diaries* to the screen. We rented it and hated it.

Oct. 16: Jeff Korchek (Universal attorney): "What's holding things up?"

Oct. 17, 12:30 P.M.: Disney has no recollection of *K-PAX*, but is willing to read it. We had a good laugh and decided to proceed with Universal. Bob will try to obtain a better deal than the $70,000 offered by UP for year three.

3:30 P.M.: new offer from UP: a) $100K for 3rd year, 50K taken off total purchase price, or b) 70K for 3rd year, 50 K added to purchase price. Bob suggested a compromise: 100K now, with 40K off purchase price; if that fails, he recommended accepting b).

3:45 P.M.: it's a done deal @ 100K for 3rd year, 100K for 4th year, 40K off the purchase price, and the holdback period was reduced by several years.

Dec. 5: signature copies arrived.

Dec. 9: all copies signed and returned.

I received the Goluboff script on Jan. 15, 1997. In my view he had turned a powerful story into a television soap opera. On the 16th I faxed Sue Pollock a desperate letter:

Dear Sue,

Yesterday I received a copy of Bryan Goluboff's screenplay for K-PAX and, of course, I read it immediately.

I won't annoy you with my comments here, but a couple of questions come to mind: What is the status of this script? Are you or Larry Gordon considering the possibility of another screenwriter? Or, if Mr. Goluboff is locked in, would you be interested in seeing a revised (by me) version of his script? Or perhaps a detailed criticism?

Please let me know at your earliest convenience. I, as much as you, want K-PAX to be a successful picture.

Best,
Gene

Sue called again on the 20th (she hadn't received the fax until then): The Goluboff script is "dead." She wants Richard deGravanese or Ira Stone to write the screenplay. Demme is out—was never a serious possibility . . . . (?) Universal wants K-PAX in the theaters by Christmas (1997)!

By then I was suspicious of everything I was hearing about K-PAX, the movie. Whether this had anything to do with my next medical problem I don't know, but soon after that call I came down with the mysterious "chronic fatigue syndrome." It probably started with a case of the flu, according to my new physician, Michael Palumbo, "but there seems also to be a psychological component." No surprise there. Whatever the cause, I fell in love with the bed: a nap every morning and afternoon, and the night came early.

It was during my first visit with Dr. Palumbo, which included a chest X-ray, that I learned I couldn't blame all my illnesses and disabilities on anxiety. The pictures showed several small calcium deposits in my lungs, probably resulting from a fungal infection (which would explain my breathing difficulty when I was in high school), and that one corner of a lung didn't fully fill up my chest cavity, suggesting that it had once collapsed, just as I had concluded in Memphis.

The CFS lasted half a year, but when I was awake I was working on another novel, this time a mystery.

MURDER ON SPRUCE ISLAND

I had long been thinking about writing a novel about Grand Manan, but wasn't sure how to go about it until Andy's mother, Barbara, suggested, as early as 1994, that I make it a mystery. I liked the idea (*K-PAX* is, among other things, a kind of mystery) and began the note-taking process. By April, 1996, I had a plot and a victim and plenty of suspects. The only thing I didn't know, when I began writing, was who the perp(s) was.

Thinking the Grand Mananers would resent people "from away" driving off the ferry and demanding to know where the murders took place, I didn't want to use the real name of the island, or identify any actual locations. Thus, North Head became Nor'east Head, Whale Cove Cottages became Porpoise Cove Cottages, and so on. The island itself I renamed Spruce Island.

The protagonist, Deputy Sheriff Louis Davenport, was sent to investigate the suspicious death of an unpopular guest at the Cottages. I would like to be able to say that I chose his name because he was a *much* softer-boiled version of Lucas Davenport, of the John Sandford crime novels, but it was pure coincidence (Karen had suggested I pick one that was soft and worn).

The novel begins:

A Call Comes

Special Deputy Sheriff Louis B. Davenport was on his way out the door for a long-overdue visit with his grandchildren when the telephone rang. Once. Twice. Three times. He hesitated. Four. Five. He dropped a frayed cardboard suitcase to the cement porch. Slowly, as though trapped in a bad dream, he grunted the door ajar and mumbled his way to the phone. In falsetto: "He's not here."

"Lou, boy! Glad you're still there!"

Davenport didn't like "Lou, boy," nor the sheriff's deep, commanding voice. Nor, for that matter, did he like the sheriff. He visualized the strong, deeply cleft chin, the confident smile, the involuntary jerks of the oversized head. "What's up, Loch?"

The sheriff slurped a mouthful of coffee that his special deputy knew was white with milk and thick with sugar. "I've got a deal here you can't refuse."

Davenport's rust-brown eyes scanned the dirty carpet, flicked up to the beige sofa with the hair stain on the arm. He fished for a Maalox tablet. "Something's happened out on Spruce Island, my friend. Ever been there?"

"No, I haven't."

"I was there once. Rained the whole damn weekend. Weird people over there. Stare at you like you're some kind of Frankenstein."

Davenport gazed at the wet spot on the ceiling. "What happened on Spruce Island?"

"Got a call from some woman runs a lodge called—uh—Porpoise Bay Cottages. Somebody found one of her guests at the bottom of a cliff. It would seem like an accident except for the note."

"Suicide note?"

"Just the opposite. Note said, 'YOU'RE GOING TO DIE.'"

"Why me, Loch?"

"C'mon, Lou. Most of the guys are off someplace for the holiday weekend. The rest have families they want to be with. You understand."

Davenport did understand. It was Tate's subtle way of reminding him that, despite his age and experience, he was low man on the pole.

"Here's the thing, Lou: why not pack up a bag and make it a working vacation?"

"Isn't there a deputy already stationed on that island?"

"There used to be, but we brought him back."

"How come?"

"Nothing ever happens out there."

Davenport refrained from stating the obvious. "What's the rest of the deal?"

"All right, all right. Full pay and expenses. I can't get away or I'd go myself. Got to give that damn speech at the Fourth of July shindig. You understand."

Davenport did understand. Sheriff Lochinvar Tate was running for Congress. "How do you get out there?"

"Only one way. Take the ferry from Milbridge. Leaves every couple of hours, if I remember right."

"Any other details?"

"Not many. They took the body to the island's only doctor for a prelim. Find him and away you go."

The torn curtain, the lamp with the ink stain on the shade. "Victim have a name?"

"Oh. Yeah. Let's see . . . slurp . . . SLURP! . . . name was Fairfax. Frederick. Older guy. Left a wife and a pack of dogs. The woman who called was a Rose Kelly. Got that?"

"Kelly. Rose."

"I won't forget this, Lou. You know, somebody's got to take over for me when I move down to Washington."

"Nobody could fill your shoes, Loch."

"Say a good word for me on the island, will you? I need every vote I can get. Got to run, Lou. Give me a buzz when you've got everything sorted out."

Davenport hung up, sighed miserably, stared at the smudges on the filamentous yellow curtain, the shiny spot on the broken TV antenna, the cobweb on the ceiling—imprinting them all in his memory, wondering, as he always did when starting a new case, whether he would ever see them again.

Davenport gets to the island and finds the doctor who is holding the body in the cool basement of his house/clinic/hospital. He is directed to the Porpoise Bay Cottages, Rose Kelly, proprietor, where the victim had been a regular summer visitor. From that setting the "special deputy sheriff" conducts his investigation. Among the suspects are the other guests, as well as a number of islanders.

There were maps, floor plans, a cast of characters, table of contents. No one who read *Murder on Spruce Island* could figure out whodunit, despite numerous clues, and that's how I wanted it. I began sending queries to mystery editors in April, 1997. There were many nice comments on the story (for example, an editor at Pocket Books reported that it is ". . . a good, well-paced mystery that kept me guessing until the end. Unfortunately, however, it's not right for our list."). No one else saw a commercial place for it on theirs, either.

For two or three years we had been looking for a place to live after we retired. These jaunts weren't very serious; they were an excuse for weekend getaways to various locations in the Northeast. That spring (1997), however, we found a place in Central Vermont that seemed perfect, made an offer, and bought it, with the proviso that we could pay half then, and the other half in November, when the film option was up for renewal—otherwise we would have to get a mortgage in addition to the one for the apartment in New York. (In exchange for this arrangement, the owners could remain through the summer while they looked for another house.) There was no guarantee this would happen; it was a gamble, and one that paid off. The other gamble didn't: Karen didn't retire for another decade. But I went there alone for a couple of weeks at a time—it's a wonderful place to relax, think, write.

In August we reluctantly decided it was time to put down Shasta Daisy. Although she still enjoyed her food, and having her ears scratched, she could no longer walk and was nearly blind and deaf. Like Daisy the Dog before her, she was almost fifteen. We took her to the vet in St. John, New Brunswick, on Aug. 21, 1997. She died quietly and with dignity, and we buried her along with all her toys in her favorite spot next to the cabin, where she had enjoyed the view of the bay and, at the same time, could keep an eye open for suspicious characters coming up the driveway.

That fall I went to work on *K-PAX III*.

K-PAX III, PART 1

B y the time I had finished *K-PAX II*, in early 1996, I already knew how the rest of the trilogy would play out. Despite not having a publisher for *II*, I began writing *K-PAX III* in September, 1997, not long after Bill Clinton, perhaps the best president we've had since FDR, admitted to having an affair with Monica Lewinsky after seven months of lying about it. While writing *III*, the movie contract was renewed for a fourth year, I had my first colonoscopy (no big deal, thanks to Dr. Kron and Prozac), took a trip with a visiting great-nephew on the Empire State Building's "Skyrider" (despite posted warnings), which further damaged my fragile upper spine, and accepted from our closest neighbors in Vermont a pup whose mother was an English setter and her father allegedly a German shepherd (though she most resembled a border collie). Whatever her parentage, she wasn't any kind of daisy, only a generic dog. Furthermore, she had a white stripe down her back. Karen named her Flower, after the skunk in the film version of *Bambi*.

I finished *K-PAX III* in December, 1998, the same month Clinton was impeached. But there wasn't a thing I could do with it but wait and hope that Universal would give a green light to *K-PAX*, the movie.

Top: Daisy the Dog
Middle: Shasta Daisy
Bottom: Flower

K-PAX, THE MOVIE, PART 3

A call from Sue Pollock on Sept. 23, 1997: the studio has hired another writer, Charles Leavitt, who is late with the first draft. There's no director or cast yet (they want a workable script first).

I received a copy of the Leavitt screenplay, along with his credits, in March, 1998. I was amazed to discover that, in his adaptation, a major character, Giselle Griffin, was missing. He had also changed some others (Dr. B's wife and children), but I realized that films are directed toward different audiences than are books, and have their own requirements. In fact, I liked the script, and told him so (by letter, with a few minor comments on the script). For the first time—notwithstanding Sue Pollock's regular glowing reports—it seemed that something might be happening.

My optimism was greatly enhanced by a story in *The Hollywood Reporter* (April 20, 1998) that Will Smith had signed on with Universal Pictures and *K-PAX*. He had formed his own production company (as many successful actors do), which had negotiated a working relationship with UP. Under this arrangement he was offered several roles, and prot was his first choice. I assumed, perhaps erroneously, that this would mean a relatively comedic approach to the role, which would have been fine with me as long as he did it well. But there was also talk that Smith, after his success in *Independence Day* and *Men in Black*, was leaning toward taking on more challenging roles. In any case, Universal was obviously serious about obtaining established stars for the movie; the film had finally clawed its way up from the depths of development hell, and was resting comfortably in development purgatory.

Bob Harris called in June: Will Smith is definitely committed, and discussions with directors are underway (though Smith can veto the selection, as well as that of his co-star). The budget is $50 million, of which Smith would like to have $20M.

Another call in July: Smith wants Barry Sonnenfeld, who is willing if the time and money are right. Carl Franklin is the alternate choice.

But by late October no further commitments had been made, and Universal decided to extend the option, for another 100K, to year five. By this time the studio had probably invested close to a million dollars (or more) in options, legal fees, etc., and seemed to be more than casually interested in proceeding with the project. I suggested that Bob ask for a 200K option, with a total purchase price of $1 million (I didn't expect to get this; it was merely a starting point for further negotiations). The studio came back with an offer of 100K for nine months. I told Bob that I would accept 100K for *six* months with 200K added to the purchase price. On November 9, 1998, evidently confident that K-PAX was a "go" with Smith, the studio decided to save some money in the long term and pay the balance of the total purchase price outright. Shooting began exactly two years later, only it was with a different actor playing prot.

THE PAPERBACK

Long before the Will Smith era I had sent out several queries about a paperback reprint of *K-PAX*, hoping something might be worked out with SMP if any interest were shown. Three houses indicated some, but only if the movie got a green light. For example, from Vintage Books:

Dear Gene,   Dec. 4, 1996

    Our editor-in-chief [Marty Asher, who had rejected the book earlier] looked at *K-Pax* for the second time. As he really likes the book, *we came very close to making an offer* [emphasis mine] for the paperback rights outright. But after careful consideration, we've decided to wait until the movie is a bit closer to being made. Can you please keep me posted on the movie's progress? In the interim, we will keep the copy of the book and reviews here . . . .

Sincerely yours,
Dawn Davis

In April, 1998, with Smith "committed" to the project, I immediately wrote to the three editors who had expressed an interest in obtaining the paperback rights. All preferred to wait until there was something even firmer.

By this time Bob Wyatt and Iris Bass had left St. Martin's Press, and they had asked me to keep another editor (Joe Veltre) informed of any developments with the film. I called him to see whether any fires had been kindled at SMP by the possibility of Will Smith's participation.

To my surprise, Veltre told me that "they (the powers that be?) definitely want to go forward with it," and that he would "talk to people and get back early next week." Three weeks later he called me with an offer of $10,000, *contingent on the film's being produced.* I told him this was an insult, and suggested ten times this amount if the film were made, or at least the 10K without the attached strings. With his offer, the rights would be locked up forever in a useless contract for which I would get nothing whatever if the movie languished forever in purgatory or slipped back down into the fires of hell. Again he said he would "talk to some people and get back." Though I placed several more calls over the next few months, a couple from our summer place on Grand Manan, and even requested an appointment, there was never a response.

On Nov. 10th I asked Bob Harris to intervene with St. Martin's Press—to try, if nothing else, to get a yes or no on a paperback deal. He said he would consult a lawyer he knew at SMP for advice on how to proceed. That attorney suggested that I speak directly to Bob Wallace, editor-in-chief of the trade division. I called him immediately and explained the situation to his assistant, Abby Rose, who assured me he would "get back to me as soon as possible." He called the next day, told me he would find out what was going on with the paperback, and let me know "by the first of the week."

On the 12th, while I was out, there was a phone message from Joe Veltre: "I hear you have a part II, and would be happy to read it if you want to send it to me." Not a word about a paperback contract. I called Abby, who said she would ask Mr. Wallace to call me. He didn't. Four days later I sent him a fax detailing the entire situation, and ending with:

> At this point you're probably wondering, "So what does the bastard want?" Well, here's what the bastard wants: 1) a new paperback editor, one who returns his calls and would seriously negotiate a reasonable offer, if one is to be made, and 2) some indication of whether SMP might be interested in publishing the rest of the trilogy in either hard or soft cover.

Wallace called a week after that to tell me that SMP *could* put out a *trade* (large-size) paperback. Otherwise, the mass market division will either put out a paperback or auction the rights. Said he would check with the head of "mass" and get back to me the next day (Nov. 24). I faxed him again on Dec. 11 to inform him of the rumor that Dustin Hoffman would be playing "Dr. Brewer," that the film would be directed (another rumor) by Fred Schepsi (*Six Degrees of Separation, A Cry in the Dark*), adding that if I didn't hear from him by Christmas I would assume that SMP wasn't interested in issuing a mass market paperback reprint of *K-PAX*.

A letter from Wallace, dated Dec. 21, 1998, arrived on the 22nd:

> I have looked at the contract on K-PAX. Since the book is still in print in hardcover and has not gone out of print, we do not have to make a decision at this time on auctioning the mass rights to the book. It is too early to be making any judgements in this regard.
>
> I hope that all is going well with the possible movie version of the book. It will be such good news for you if this happens.
>
> Please keep me informed of any developments.

I immediately faxed him back:

> Thanks for your letter of the 21st. In view of your response, should I feel free
> to submit the rest of the trilogy to another house?

I never heard from him again.

On Feb. 2, 1999, I informed Bob Harris that my latest semi-annual royalty statement indicated that exactly six copies of the hardcover had been sold during the previous six-month accounting period, and reminded him that the book had been remaindered nearly three years earlier. I asked him whether he thought I could get the paperback rights back. He said he would review my contract with SMP.

Bob called the next day to report that there was, in fact, a clause specifying that since I had declined their contingent offer of $10,000 on April 27, 1998, they were *contractually bound* to offer the paperback rights to auction, or return them to me!

He pointed this out in a letter to Wallace. On March 1, St. Martin's attorney Paul Slevin called to inform him that SMP would "neither auction nor revert the rights," and would send a letter "soon" to clarify their position. A week later, when no letter had yet come to either of us, Bob asked me to let him know in the event I hadn't heard anything by the end of the month. On March 30th he wrote to Slevin again. Two weeks later he received this fax from him:

> . . . As I told you when we spoke, the book remains in print so reversion is not
> appropriate. We have not formulated any firm plans at this point concerning the
> possibility of a mass-market edition of the book. If Mr. Brewer would like any
> further information concerning our intentions with respect to the book, he should
> feel free to call Bob Wallace directly . . . .

Exactly where we were five months earlier!

The next day (April 15, 1999) Bob wrote a follow-up letter to Mr. Slevin:

> I have your April 13 letter. You note that St. Martin's has not "formulated any
> firm plans" concerning the "possibility" of a mass market edition of the book. You
> may not be aware that back in June of 1998, Joe Veltre offered Mr. Brewer $10,000
> as an advance for acquisition of paperback reprint rights. The offer was promptly
> rejected by Mr. Brewer, who was then advised by Mr. Veltre that St. Martin's would
> reconsider the amount offered and get back to him. Notwithstanding several follow-
> up inquiries by Mr. Brewer, he never received the courtesy of a response. After my
> intervention, Mr. Brewer eventually heard from Bob Wallace in a December 21,
> 1998 letter wherein he wrote, "Since the book is still in print in hardcover and has
> not gone out of print, we do not have to make a decision at this time on auctioning
> the mass rights to the book."

I would point out to you, however, that Rider paragraph 5(h) of Mr. Brewer's publishing agreement provides that if the publisher makes an offer to the author which is not accepted and therefore no agreement is reached, "the Publisher will then seek to dispose of the mass-market reprint rights in an auction . . . ." To the best of our knowledge, and apparently confirmed by communications received from your company, St. Martin's has to date not sought to dispose of these reprint rights in an auction, as it was contractually obligated so to do by this provision. If in fact St. Martin's is not interested in promptly complying with this provision, then it should revert the reprint rights forthwith to Mr. Brewer. I would appreciate it if you would promptly confirm to me that St. Martin's will now proceed to auction the reprint rights at this time . . .

A *month* later, Bob sent a polite follow-up fax to attorney Slevin, including a copy of this letter, and requested a reply. Two weeks later Slevin called to inform him that SMP would auction the book "if that's what Mr. Brewer wants." I immediately notified the three houses that had been interested. All of them promised to look into their possible involvement in an auction.

While all this was going on, the impeachment trial of Bill Clinton proceeded in the U.S. Senate, where personal interests and ulterior motives flourish. The Republicans cleverly wanted to focus on sex, and the Democrats gullibly obliged them, thereby obfuscating the real issue: that Clinton had lied to a grand jury. I didn't give a damn that Monica had performed fellatio in the Oval Office, but perjury was definitely not a quality I desired in a president. It was quite revealing (and embarrassing) that the vote for acquittal came almost perfectly along party lines. It was the Senate itself that should have been impeached.

In May we visited my mother for the last time. She didn't recognize us, and died less than three weeks later. I still miss her sweet, doggerel singing voice. Mom was a simple soul, and I loved her very much.

The paperback auction finally began on July 20, while Karen and I were on Grand Manan. A call on August 4th from Jennifer Callan, subsidiary rights manager for the SMP trade division: only Berkley had made an offer ($5,000). St. Martin's responded with a bid of $6,000 (of which, according to my original contract, I would get half). There were no further bids, and the house won its own auction. Back to square one? Not at all. Regardless of whether the film materialized, the paperback version of *K-PAX* would at last be published.

But the war wasn't over. In late August I received an e-note from Matthew Shear, editor-in-chief of the mass market division: my editor would be Joe Veltre. I replied at once: ". . . I have tried to work with Joe Veltre before and would prefer a different editor . . . ."

Six weeks later (Oct. 7, 1999) there was a call from Mr. Shear's secretary: my new editor would be Marc Resnick. I called him, left a message. He phoned back *the same day*: a publication date hadn't been determined, but would be decided "soon."

And he asked to see *K-PAX II* and *III*! I don't think I shouted, "Hallelujah!" into the phone, but I was probably thinking it.

Top left: Kathleen Buckley
Top right: The view of the bay from our cottage on Grand Manan
Bottom left: Chris and Ben
Bottom right: Whistlewood

K-PAX II, PART 2

The next day I met with Marc. He seemed excited to be working with me on the *K-PAX* trilogy. "I'm not only your editor, I'm a big fan!" he gushed. By now I was suspicious of anyone in the publishing business (except, perhaps, for Ida Giragossian), but it was a good start to what might well become a long-term relationship. I gave him the manuscripts for *II* and *III*, along with some requested editorial changes for the *K-PAX* paperback.

On Nov. 8 (1999) he told me he liked *K-PAX II*, but wanted to change the title, and update the story to the present time. He also wanted to publish the paperback version of *K-PAX* "simultaneously" with the hardcover edition of *II*. The offer of a $5,000 advance for world rights to the latter came on Dec. 1. I knew it was another "steal," and asked for $10,000. He came back with a final offer: $7,500. I took it. This time I didn't call an agent. I sent the contract to my attorney, Bob Harris, for his approval.

I resisted updating the sequel because the dates just didn't fit the story. Marc accepted that, but insisted that I get "K-PAX" out of the title. I presumed he thought the word had been responsible for the poor U.S. sales of part I. Though I disagreed with that, I e-mailed him some alternatives:

1) *For Whom the Bell Tolls*
2) *Catch-22*
3) *The Grapes of Wrath*
4) *Catcher in the Rye*

He didn't like any of these, and came back with:

1) *Macbeth*
2) *The Sun Also Rises*
3) *The Hobbit*

At least, I thought, he has a sense of humor.

We settled for *On a Beam of Light*. Worried about whether anyone who had read the first book would know that *Beam* was a sequel to it, I suggested a subtitle: Book II of the *K-PAX* trilogy. He vetoed that, too.

In January of 2000 my libido began to droop and, by spring, was almost flaccid. Recognizing this as one of the side effects of Prozac, I visited Dr. Kron again and came away with a new anti-anxiety medication, Effexor. It perked back up. But I was only on this one for a couple of years when it fizzled again. (NB: this does not mean that Effexor is inferior to Prozac, or other meds, in any way. Results vary with the individual.) Next drug: Zoloft, which I've been taking for four years to date. I'm still medically fearless, and there have been no unwelcome side effects so far . . . .

The paperback edition of *K-PAX* (including a "teaser"—a chapter from *On a Beam of Light*) was scheduled for publication in January, 2001 and *Beam* (in hardcover) for February or March. *K-PAX III*, Marc indicated, would be published about a year later, along with the paperback version of *II*. I gave him partials of *Watson's God*, *Ben and I*, and *Murder on Spruce Island*. It was at around this time that he told me about his actual editorial interests: war history and games. Well, I thought, at least it wasn't cookbooks.

When Karen and I began to edit the proofs (she reading, I checking), we discovered that someone had made some arbitrary changes in the text of the paperback—ages, dates, and the like. Marc, too, was flabbergasted—the type had to be re-set. Nevertheless, the original pub dates were met.

In October Marc and I had lunch at Cal's (an upscale restaurant near the Flatiron Building) with Joe Rinaldi, "the best publicist in the company," who had all kinds of plans for radio/TV interviews. I was delighted to learn that the books were finally going to get some publicity. I never heard from him again, either.

Marc did very little editing on *K-PAX II*, but there was one scene I liked that he insisted on eliminating. Dr. B invariably has only cottage cheese and crackers for lunch, otherwise he would fall asleep afterward. So, when Giselle accidentally spits a bit of her sandwich onto his plate, he hungrily goes for it. "Too gross," he explained. So much for a sense of humor.

He didn't like any of the partials I sent him, either. With his knowledge and permission, I went over his head and called the president of St. Martin's, Sally Richardson. Not because I was annoyed by his lack of perspicacity, but because I was seriously worried that if some other house published them, SMP might come down on him for letting them slip through. She agreed to read one of them, *Watson's God*. A few weeks later she called back. "I read your manuscript, darling," she said, "and I didn't get it. So I showed it to another editor here, and *he* didn't get it. It's too quirky and original."

Were they looking for ordinary and derivative?

With *K-PAX II* and *III* safely on the road to publication (I thought), it was time for another change of pace. I decided to write a courtroom drama.

WRONGFUL DEATH

I've always been fascinated by courtroom dramas, perhaps because of countless Saturday evenings eating hamburgers and butterscotch sundaes while watching *Perry Mason* when I was in high school. When I decided to write an animal rights novel, it seemed reasonable to base it on a lawsuit resulting from the death of a patient who had been given a drug alleged to be safe through animal testing. I began researching my twelfth novel, *Wrongful Death*, in June, 1999.

One of the grossest misconceptions about medical science is that the production of pharmaceuticals requires preliminary testing in animals for the sake of (human) consumer safety. Nothing could be further from the truth. In fact, animal-tested prescription drugs are regularly taken off the market because they have been found to be unsafe or ineffective in humans. Recent examples include Vioxx (Merck) and Celebrex (Pfizer), but there are hundreds of others. Almost as ridiculous, perhaps, is the trashing of thousands of potentially life-saving drugs because they happen to be toxic in mice or rats.

The common adage is "a man is a dog is a rat," meaning that all animals share the same basic biochemical processes, and therefore something that is found to be safe in rats will be equally harmless in humans. But living organisms are far, far, more complex than that. Safety and effectiveness depends on several very subtle anatomical and biochemical parameters. Something that works well in mice without doing them too much damage might be disastrous (and often is) in people. The list of such catastrophes is long, and rather than go into the gory details here, I refer the reader to *Sacred Cows and Golden Geese*, by Ray and Jean Greek (Continuum Publishing Group, New York, 2002). We now have the healthiest mice and rats in the world; it's time to initiate the safe treatment of disease in humans based on more modern criteria.

Wrongful Death is a story about a child who dies after taking a new and presumably safe diabetic drug. Since most of the action takes place in a courtroom, I decided to write the novel without narrative. All the background and character descriptions would be brought out in the dialogue. Unorthodox, yes, and maybe even quirky and original, but orthodox novels are already available by the trainload.

The lead attorney, Marcus Allen, Jr., is reluctant to take the case (a lawsuit against Mercer Pharmaceuticals, Inc.) at first. For one thing, he knows very little about the pharmaceutical industry and its practices. For another, he's sure he can't win it. The senior partners, however, in their weekly group meeting, encourage him to proceed:

"You took the case?"

"Well, not in so many words."

"But you encouraged them."

"Not really. I told them it would be very difficult. In fact, I intimated that it was practically hopeless."

"It's hopeless, period."

"I couldn't agree more, Sammy. I don't want the damn case. But I told them I'd talk to Bill and Lew about it. And Dad, of course."

"I disagree. No case is hopeless. There are too many unknowns. The judge, the jury, undiscovered evidence . . ."

"Bill, you know goddamn well it's hopeless. Pass those donuts down, will you?"

"On the other hand, maybe the parents are right about the damn drug."

"Right or wrong has nothing to do with winning, folks."

"There have been more hopeless cases. You've won a couple of them yourself."

"What about *A Civil Action*? That was a hopeless case."

"Yeah, and the guy lost. And after that he was—what—selling used cars for a while, something like that?"

"It sounds like a sucker to me."

"A sucker?"

"It sounds like one of those cases that will suck all of us into it. All our resources will get tied up in this damn thing. I'm opposed."

"We haven't asked for a vote yet, Sammy."

"Marc, can you get them to take an hourly arrangement?"

I doubt it. I don't think they're very well off. But they seem to be pretty dedicated to carrying this thing out, regardless of how—"

"Sorry I'm late, folks. What have I missed?"

"Your son here was telling us about Calvecchi v. Mercer. Says he doesn't want the case. Has he filled you in on that?"

"He mentioned something about it, yes."

"What's your take on that, Marcus?"

"I can see both sides of the question. Anyway, it's up to Bill and Lew. I'm 'semi-retired,' remember?"

"Ladies and gentlemen, we've heard the negatives. Let's look at the positives. We've had some bad publicity lately. Not to mention a couple of other setbacks. I won't name names here, but you all know what I'm talking about. This might be just the kind of case we need right now, win or lose. It's the type of thing that will get us in the papers, on the nightly news. It's something everyone can identify with, even people who don't have children. All of us are at the mercy of their doctors, their medications. There's a lot of concern out there about that, especially in view of the cutbacks and belt tightening going on right now. Stingy HMO's, hurry-up visits, prescription mixups, hospital errors, overpriced drugs . . ."

"On top of that, it's going to the biggest human interest story going. Did everyone here read about this case? Have you seen the little girl's picture? She was beautiful. Smart. Limitless potential. She's going to have the sympathy of every American who doesn't kick dogs in the streets."

"Is there any more coffee?"

"And the other side of that coin is Mercer & Co. They're going to get the worst publicity in their history."

"And the best lawyers money can buy."

"Marc, have there been any other deaths resulting from the use of the drug?"

"I haven't looked into that yet."

"What's it called, anyway?"

"Mercipine."

"Perfect! They attached their own name to the damn thing."

"No doubt they meant it as a double entendre."

"Obviously."

"They might very well be eager to settle. Get the whole thing behind them."

"Good point. I say we let Marc, Jr. find out how widespread this is. If it's another thalidomide, we go for it. If the girl is the only casualty, it's a waste of time."

"Not if we can get a settlement right off the bat."

"Any volunteers to help Marc on this?"

"It's his case. Let him do some research on it before he takes on a partner."

"What if they can't afford the hourly fee?"

"Ladies and gentlemen, I think we should respect plaintiff's wishes for a percentage arrangement. Any further discussion? Good. Now who wants to help Marc out with this? No takers? Okay, let's look at it the other way. Marc, who would you like for an assistant in this case?"

"Wait a minute! Do I get a vote on this? I don't have the experience for a medical lawsuit against a giant drug company like Mercer—"

"Marc, you've been with us for six years. When will you be ready to handle something like this?"

"Maybe in another year or two . . . ."

"Perfect. It'll take that long to get it into a courtroom."

"Okay, okay, I'll take it on and I'll do my best. But only if Dad helps me out on it. He's the most experienced lawyer we have in medical malpractice suits."

"What about it, Marcus?"

"Son, right now I've got four cases up my nose and I'm supposed to be phasing out . . . ."

"So have I."

"All right. But only if you're lead attorney. I'll help you in any way I can, but it's your case."

"Any other business, ladies and gentlemen of the bar? Very well, let's go kick some ass!"

Following extensive research and the taking of depositions, the case goes to court, where each side presents its witnesses. While the trial is proceeding, of course, subplots are developing. Marc, a Caucasian, begins to fall in love with his partner, a brilliant young Afro-American attorney, who wants nothing to do with him (she doesn't like lawyers); his father is hospitalized with cancer; Marc can't seem to make progress with any of the girls he dates; he promises to spend more time with his troubled little brother and reneges on it. The case, which has exhausted him, finally comes down to closing arguments, and the case goes to the jury. I won't tell you who won it, only that there is an unexpected twist at the end . . . .

I finished *Wrongful Death* in May, 2001, and queried the usual suspects. None of them wanted it. As it happened, I also ran across an agent who was sympathetic to the plights of animals in research and testing (and she liked *K-PAX*). Her response: It would be hard to sell as is. Might appeal to commercial houses if it were in a more conventional style.

Rightly or wrongly (or perhaps stupidly), I declined to make it more "conventional"— that's not what I do. John Grisham and others had already cornered that market and, besides, I had plenty of other projects to pursue.

K-PAX ONSTAGE, PART 1

More than a year earlier, on Feb. 26, 1999, I had received a call from an award-winning British director, Kate Raper, who was interested in adapting *K-PAX* to the stage. In view of the doldrums the film was becalmed in, this seemed an attractive idea. After some correspondence back and forth (how and where would it be staged, would I like to be co-author, etc.), I asked her to send me a scene outline, which she did in August. I had no problem with her staging, and suggested she should be sole author. In September she sent me a few pages of dialogue and, when I reported that I liked that, too, she sent (in October) an official proposal to stage the play at a London theater. I showed this to Bob Harris, who advised postponing consideration until the holdback period for stage productions expired later in the year (Nov. 29). Kate's proposal, after vetting and revisions, was forwarded to Universal Pictures on Jan. 5, 2000.

According to the terms of the movie contract, UP had fifteen business days in which to match any stage offer. If not, I would be free to pursue the project. At the end of the three-week decision period, Masako Ichino, Director of Business Affairs, called me. Apparently concerned about the effect of the play on the success of the putative film, the studio wanted to extend the holdback period for stage productions another *six* years, for which I would receive $50K (if the film were made during that time), or $25K if it were not. I declined, saying it wouldn't begin to cover my losses if the play became successful, and, furthermore, the concept seemed backward—if the film were made, I wouldn't need the compensation as much as I would if it were not.

They sicked one of the *K-PAX* producers, Lloyd Levin, on me. In a telephone conversation, he indicated that "many people would be very upset" if the stage play were to go forward, that UP was very enthusiastic about the film, there was a meeting scheduled with M. Night Shyamalan, director of *The Sixth Sense*, who could sign on at any moment, etc. I explained to him that, if I agreed to another six-year holdback period, I could end up with neither a movie *nor* a play.

On Jan. 31, the *President of Productions* (emphasis mine), Kevin Mischer, called. The offer would be increased ($25K now, $50K if the movie were made within eighteen months). I told him the same thing I had told Levin: there was no guarantee the movie would be made and, without the play, I could end up with nothing (a stage production could be worth far more than $25,000). I counter-proposed that I would accept an additional holdback period if they paid me the $75K in case the film were *not* made within eighteen months. He said he would get back to me. On the same day, a fax from one of UP's endless attorneys, Anthony Zummo (a former Marx brother?) arrived. It asserted that Kate Raper's proposal was insufficient in that it did not specify how much the monetary offer for the stage rights would be (except in terms of a percentage of ticket sales).

On Feb. 7, Bob responded to this nonsensical assertion by pointing out that ticket sales formed the basis for royalties for *any* stage production. Two days later, Universal threatened to sue me if the Raper production went forward. When Bob responded to this threat, Mr. Zummo averred that he would "speak to the business people" and get back to him.

Three months passed without a word. In the meantime, Kate Raper, worried about a possible UP lawsuit over stage rights, sought advice from her own solicitor. On May 4, she withdrew from the project pending a resolution of the threat from Universal. Finally, on June 2nd, nearly four months after their initial warning (bluff?), Universal agreed to let Kate go ahead with the play. I reported this development back to her. By that time, however, she had several other projects underway, and wasn't able to take on *K-PAX!*

Totally disgusted by this turn of events, I asked Bob whether a lawsuit against Universal might be possible. He advised against that approach, but said I might be able to get the money that had been offered for the holdback extension, or to get UP to eliminate the "matching" clause for stage productions from the original film contract. But Universal would agree to neither. Instead, the studio came up with the same offer ($50K/$25K) I had declined earlier. I rejected it yet again. The whole unpleasant episode had resulted in nothing less than a lost theatrical opportunity, nearly $4,000 in legal fees, and a profound distrust of any major film studio.

K-PAX, THE MOVIE, PART 4

Meanwhile, back at Lawrence Gordon Productions, little was happening with Will Smith and *K-PAX*. Even though he was firmly "attached" to the project, he decided to make *The Wild, Wild West* and *The Legend of Bagger Vance*, instead.

There were some encouraging signs, however. Producer Levin called me on Sept. 30, 1999 to report that Larry was bringing Smith and director Jonathan Demme together to discuss the latter's possible involvement with *K-PAX*. The studio would like to begin shooting by February, 2000, he told me, and, if all went well, the film should be in the theaters by the end of that year. The movie "has always had a green light," he said, "and could have been made many times in the past few years. But everyone concerned wanted a first-rate film with a top director." He requested that I send him copies of *K-PAX II* and *III*.

Bob Harris had also received a call from Demme's office requesting a look at the sequels. And one from Kate Petrosky, an assistant to Kevin Spacey, asking for the same. I returned her call immediately: Spacey's interest, she reported, was primarily that of producer/director (possibly also playing prot). I reminded her that Will Smith had signed up for that role, and asked her whether Kevin might be interested in playing "Dr. Brewer." She gave me the telephone number of his manager, Joanne Horowitz, and asked me to forward it to Larry Gordon's office. That was the last I heard from Trigger Street Productions for almost a year.

Variety (Oct. 26, 1999) reported on the meeting between Will Smith and Jonathan Demme, who had "cooled" on the project ostensibly because of "script problems." Smith was still attached, Demme was not.

By the spring of 2000, I think Universal was becoming a bit impatient. So when Smith decided to make *Ali*, they began to look elsewhere.

On July 24, 2000, there was another article in *Variety*, "Softley touch sells Spacey," by Michael Fleming:

> Kevin Spacey has committed to star in "K-Pax," a Universal drama to be directed by Iain Softley ("The Wings of the Dove") from a script by Charles Leavitt. Filming will begin in the fall.
>
> Adapted from a novel by Gene Brewer, "K-Pax" concerns a mysterious patient at a mental hospital who claims to be from the planet K-Pax. A psychiatrist trying

to help the patient notices that he has a positive effect on the mental health of the other patients.

Pic, to be produced by Lawrence Gordon and Lloyd Levin and exec produced by Charles Leavitt [sic—should have read Susan Pollock], has long been a priority project for the studio, and nearly got made with Jonathan Demme directing and Will Smith starring.

For months Spacey has been rumored to be negotiating for the film but maintained that it was one among many offers. He committed late last week once Softley was brought into the fold . . . .

You might suppose that I would have been notified by the studio, but I wasn't about to complain. The picture had not only risen again from hell, but there was a bright green light shining down from heaven. It was scheduled to open on December 25, 2001.

By September, Jeff Bridges had signed on to play the psychiatrist. With all the major players in place, things now happened very quickly: the rest of the cast and crew were brought aboard, locations arranged, the shooting script finished. Filming was scheduled to begin on Nov. 13th in New York. The budget was still set at $50 million.

I faxed Anthony Zummo on Oct. 16 requesting a copy of the latest draft of the Leavitt screenplay. On the 25th, I got a call from the secretary of another attorney, Mark Torpoco, who had taken over Mr. Zummo's duties vis-à-vis *K-PAX*: the most recent script would be forwarded "as soon as we get it." I called her back on the 30th to ask whether a shooting schedule was available, and was referred to Diane Ward (production co-ordinator). From Ms. Ward I requested travel expenses to visit the set in Hollywood. She said she would ask producer Robert Colesberry and get back to me. I called her again on Nov. 6th; she referred me to Mr. Colesberry's assistant, Kia Hellman (in the New York office), whom I phoned on the 7th. Mr. Colesberry called me on the 8th: there is no shooting schedule yet, and I would have to be cleared by Iain Softley to be on the set (in New York).

On that same day the American people elected Democrat Al Gore to be our next president. Unfortunately, the vote of the archaic Electoral College rested on the outcome in the state of Florida, which was rife with irregularities and too close to call. After weeks of lawsuits and recounts, the U.S. Supreme Court stepped in and, in one of the most bizarre episodes in U.S. history, arbitrarily decided the election in favor of George W. Bush, Republican. There must have been shit-eatin' grins all along the high bench after that one.

Kia called on the 10th: I was invited to the set on Nov. 19th or 20th (the only days Spacey and Bridges would both be filming). Because it would be "crowded" in the Rose Planetarium of the American Museum of Natural History, I wouldn't be allowed to bring anyone else. She called again on the 17th: shooting on both evenings would begin at 7:30 and continue until 2-3:00 A.M., maybe later. She suggested I show up outside the planetarium on the 19th and ask for her.

This is from my diary for that night:

Sunday, Nov. 19, 2000

The nighttime (7:30 P.M.) view of the Planetarium from 81st Street is quite beautiful, with blue and white lights illuminating the silvery dome behind a huge wall of glass. Inside the building a dozen or more crewmembers, all wearing identification badges labeled "K-PAX, BACKGROUND," are milling around. I don't have one, so a security guard stops me immediately and asks if she can help. I explain that I have been invited to come, and am looking for Kia Hellman. The guard has no idea who Kia is but lets me stay, though she glances at me from time to time to make sure I'm not getting into any trouble. After a few minutes of supervised wandering a guy comes up, introduces himself as "Dave," the publicity director for the film. I say, "Gene," and he replies, "I thought so."

Dave (Fulton) takes me outside to look for Kia. He introduces me to Ken Regan (who is doing the still photography, mainly for publicity purposes), producer Bob Colesberry, the cinematographer (John Mathieson) and the director (Iain Softley), who are beginning to accumulate for the one outdoor scene. Iain asks me how I got the idea for *K-PAX*. I mumble something about *The Man Who Mistook his Wife for a Hat*. He nods and wanders off. I also meet the costume designer, Karen Golden, and Softley's assistant, Katie Finch. We all congregate along the back fence waiting for a camera track to be set up, and rehearsals for the scene finally begin. During the wait Karen Allen strolls by. She knows Ken Regan quite well, and he introduces me to her. What a smile! She waves a new CD by Jeff Bridges (NB: it's great; you can order it from his website (jeffbridges.com—while you're there, make a contribution to the alleviation of hunger in America). After telling her that *Starman* is one of my favorite movies (another big smile and a "Thank you!"), I drift off to let her speak privately with Ken.

Eventually Kia shows up ("just to say hello"—she's not scheduled to be there), and Executive Producer Larry Gordon somehow recognizes me and introduces himself. "Been a long wait," he volunteers before continuing his tour of the personnel. A taxi carrying four stand-ins drives up in front of the building, people get out, lighting is adjusted, and all this is repeated 5 or 6 times. With each run, the camera dolly is pushed down the track and stopped by two other guys just before it rolls off the end. Though I'm wearing my heaviest coat, I, like everyone else, am freezing (it's 30F and windy). I spot Iain huddled against the back fence watching the setup. More pleasantries: he loved the story, etc. As I leave him (I presume he has better things to do) I casually remark: "I've got one word to say to you . . . ."

"What's that?"

"Cameo."

He bursts into a hearty laugh.

As I'm wandering the lawn I again run into Colesberry. He tells me about a scene near the end of the film, already shot, in which the psychiatrist pushes the catatonic Robert around in a wheelchair on the roof of the hospital. Two alternatives were filmed: in one, Robert smiles as his psychiatrist informs him of Bess's disappearance. He smiles in the other one, too, but only a little. I protest mildly (I didn't want to be thrown off the set before shooting even began), "But that destroys the mystery, doesn't it? If this is Robert, and prot is back on K-PAX, he wouldn't be smiling, would he?" Colesberry seems to consider the idea, but in the finished film the scene (slight smile version) wasn't changed.

I also come across Sue Pollock—the producer who started it all—a pleasant, middle-aged woman, not at all like the hyperactive, chain-smoking executive I had been expecting for such a high-powered position.

During the last couple of rehearsals Jeff Bridges and Kevin Spacey appear, study the monitors, and discuss the scene with Softley. Suddenly I hear Iain say, "That's Dr. Brewer over there." Spacey *runs* over to introduce himself and shake hands, and thanks me for the appreciative letter I wrote to him. He is wearing a ragged old corduroy jacket; a tuft of hair sticks up from the front of his head. Perfect, I think. To Bridges I say, inanely, "Dr. Brewer, I presume." No one has told me that the name of the psychiatrist has been changed to "Powell." I assume that's the last I'll see of either of them up close.

They finally do the scene with the taxi. "Cameras rolling!" "Quiet!" "Scene 34, take 1!" Softley, a Britisher, shouts, "ACK-see-un!" The cab pulls up in front of the building, the actors (Bridges, Spacey, Vincent Laresco and Ajay Naidu) get out and stroll inside, "prot" gazing with interest at the dome. "Cut!" yells Softley, just like in the movies. I ask Sue about the horns and sirens in the background. "They'll take that out," she explains patiently. Another take: "That's a wrap!" and everyone gratefully hustles into the relatively warm interior of the planetarium. It's already 10:30.

By the time we get inside, the cameras have been set up for the next scene, which takes place in the "Solar System" corridor. I flatten myself against the window to the right of the camera. Several rehearsals (with stand-ins) later, lighting adjusted, Spacey and Bridges reappear and do five takes of the scene where they're strolling down the corridor toward the cameras, prot gazing curiously at the planets hanging above. "Navarro" jokingly remarks, "I guess this is your neighborhood, huh?" Prot smiles wistfully at him. In one of the takes, Spacey offers an ad lib which doesn't appear in the final cut, but does in another scene. I wonder how many lines like these he and other actors have wriggled into their films.

When this scene is wrapped, there's a 15-minute break. Spacey and Bridges immediately head for me. I say, "I hope you don't mind my being here." "No, certainly not, not at all—great having you here!" Kevin wanders off to find some food. Jeff brings out a panoramic camera and begins taking pictures of everything around him, including me. I take the cue and gaze toward the heavens. He hands me the thing, which I gingerly accept (it's very heavy and looks expensive), and invites me to look through the viewfinder. I'm tempted to take a picture of *him*, but I think better of it: maybe there's a rule against this, or it's unethical or something. In any case, I don't want to overplay the "Jeff is my new pal" business. Besides, what if I dropped the damn thing? He explains, almost apologetically, that this is the first time he's gone right from one movie to another, and admits he's "not fully prepared yet." If so, it didn't take him long to gear himself up.

There's a request for everyone to move to the other side of the set for the next scene. I find Bridges and Spacey munching vegetables and playing a game called "Pigs." Spacey is rolling the rubbery dice-size animals and Bridges keeps score. At one point a makeup person brushes up Spacey's little tuft of hair. They invite me to join in. Not knowing how to play, I tell them I'll just watch. They seem to get along well. I never do figure out the game, which I suspect is a sham, but they seem to be having a great time. Kevin confides in me as he passes by afterward, "Now you know what we do on the set instead of behaving appropriately."

While the cameras are being set up for the next scene, the set dresser, Wayne Leonard, comes up to discuss the possibility of life outside the solar system and give me his "K-PAX Background" badge to get into the planetarium the next night without being accosted by Security. The sound engineer, Mark Weingarten, supplies me with headphones, and cameraman Dave Dunlop hands me a schedule of the night's shooting. There are cables everywhere. The only precaution with being on a movie set (besides staying quiet and out of the picture) is not tripping over one of them.

In this scene Dr. Powell and his brother-in-law, Steve (an astronomer admirably played by Brian Howe) are coming out of the dome. Dr. Powell: "What the—What went on in there, Steve? I mean . . . he could be a savant, couldn't he? There are people who can make perfect replicas of a Rembrandt painting, and they can't learn to spell their own names . . . ." Steve puts a hand on Powell's shoulder and escorts him down the corridor. "I don't know what I believe, Mark. But I know what I *saw*." Six takes of that scene. After almost every one, Bridges hurries to the monitor to watch a replay. He's a perfectionist who studies every take to see how to make it better. When Spacey's on camera, he does the same.

During the lengthy setup for the next one I search out Colesberry and ask him whether anyone would mind if I showed up again with my wife the next night (the final night of filming in New York). Despite my presumptuous comment about the wheelchair scene, he tells me that wouldn't be a problem, perhaps pleased that I hadn't jumped up after every scene shouting, "You idiots!"

By now it's after 2 A.M. and I decide to call it a night. I find out later that shooting continued until about 4:30. Exciting as it was, it had been a long day. I've never been on the streets of New York at that hour, and am surprised to find plenty of available taxis. I'm home by 3:00. Karen wakes up, demanding to hear all about it. I tell her she'll find out for herself tomorrow (tonight).

Monday, Nov. 20

The next day she isn't feeling well. Nevertheless, she goes off to work. By the time she gets home, her abdominal pain is worse. She doesn't tell me about this, however, and we're on the set promptly at 7:30.

Wearing my "K-PAX Background" badge, Karen and I have no trouble getting past the guards, where we are greeted by Wayne, the set dresser, who chats until Bob Colesberry comes up. I introduce him to Karen, and he moves on toward the cameras. The first scene is a followup to last night's "What the—" scene, in which Steve explains to Dr. Powell that prot knows more than he should know about "his" star system, while they proceed down the same corridor as before. After that is wrapped, Jeff comes over to say hello and meet Karen before moving on to prepare for the next scene. We mosey up a ramp to the next floor (actually about half a floor), to watch the setup.

The cameras turn 180 degrees to focus on a well-lit glass-fronted elevator coming down from the sixth to the second floor. It contains stand-ins for prot and some of the scientists. Several rehearsals are necessary to get the lighting right. The elevator comes down, goes up, comes down again. Sue Pollock appears, along with her son Robert, an extraordinarily pleasant young man who loves movies. She chats with us about the process and how everyone thinks it's going to be a great film. We also meet Brian Howe and Ajay Naidu ("Dr. Chakraborty"). I tell the latter that he's exactly what I had in mind for the character. "Thank you," he says. "That means a lot to me." Suddenly we hear Bridges down below calling our names: he wants more pictures. We patiently oblige. He yells, "Thank you!" when he's finished, to which we reply, "Anytime!" Shooting finally begins. No dialogue, just the elevator coming down with Bridges strolling into view at the end. It doesn't get into the film.

The next scene takes an hour or more to set up. Brian suggests that "it's not possible, of course, that prot comes from another planet."

"How can you be so sure?" I reply.

At that moment Iain passes by, overhears this and pipes up, "What about Bess?"

"Exactly," I add, superfluously. And I thought: Iain gets it!

While we're waiting for something to unfold, Kevin spots us and ambles over to greet Karen and me: "Hi, how are you, glad you could be here," etc. He is called away by the director. In the scene, Dr. Powell approaches the planetarium dome towing prot (who is still gawking around at everything), Chakraborty, and Navarro. He is greeted at the entrance by the four astrophysicists. (By now we know the ropes and grab our own headsets—they're lying around everywhere.) Powell introduces prot to Steve, who presents him to his colleagues. Prot looks them over, points to them one at a time, and says, "Dr., Dr., Dr., Dr . . . . How many doctors are there on this planet?" Steve laughs and they all go inside the dome. "Cut!" There are six takes of this scene.

"Lunch" (it's almost midnight) time. We traipse through the planetarium garage and out into the cold for several blocks to a school cafeteria, where food is produced for everyone except the director and the stars (who presumably are dining in their respective trailers). In 45 minutes or so everyone heads back to the planetarium and begins setting up for the principal scene inside the dome. This is where prot will draw a picture of the orbit of K-PAX around its parent suns, which will perfectly match one calculated by a computer (a technician is already lining this up). But there isn't a camera in sight yet, so we head back down to the previous scene and find they're shooting a few more takes! A chubby guy comes around with little Hershey candies, followed a few minutes later by a tray of cookies. "Try one of my cookies," the Santa Claus-like caterer implores everyone. Having had pie and cookies at the cafeteria, we pass. Most of the crew does not.

Helen Hunt appears just in front of where we're sitting (on tall chairs labeled "Mr. Colesberry" and "Mr. Softley"). She studies the monitors. Between takes, Kevin strolls over to greet her and immediately introduces her and his assistant Dana to Karen and me. I tell her, "I thought you were twenty feet tall!" Inane, perhaps, but she gives me a huge smile nevertheless. Kevin grabs a cookie, eats half of it before being called back, sets the other half on the monitor. He does the scene, where he meets the four astronomers who have come to determine what he knows about space, with one too many "doctors" ("Dr., Dr. Dr., Dr., Dr . . . ."), returns and finishes the cookie. "I couldn't stop saying 'Doctor,'" he confides to Ms. Hunt, and starts on a bottle of water. Dana asks for some of it. He hands it over with: "Strange custom you have on this planet, sharing water." Dana replies, "You might not get it back, though." Kevin: "*That* I understand!" as he hustles back to the cameras.

When this scene is finally in the can we head back up to the dome, where Camera A is just being set up for the superb planetarium scene. Karen finally confesses that her abdominal pain is becoming quite unpleasant. Reluctantly, we call it a wrap.

She saw Dr. Palumbo the next day and we learned that she was suffering from a case of diverticulitis. He gave her an antibiotic. Three days later she had a CAT scan and was prescribed another drug. Three days after that I began jury duty. When I returned home that evening I found a note: Karen was in the hospital, where she stayed for five days with an antibiotic drip. A surgeon was on call in case this treatment failed. At the end of the stay she was given another CAT scan, sent home, and admonished to eat more fiber. Five years later there has been no recurrence.

Totally hooked on filmmaking, I lobbied Kia Hellman for a chance to go to Hollywood to be on the "Ward Two" set (we'd have happily paid for the trip ourselves). She called on Jan. 8, 2001—Universal has approved our visiting the set in Hollywood!

According to my notes:

Sunday, Feb. 4, 2001

A limousine arrives for us *at our apartment*. The driver escorts us to the *VIP lounge*, where we wait for our plane to depart. We are flown *business class* to Los Angeles, where we are *picked up at the airport* by another limo and taken to our hotel in West Hollywood. In a few minutes a *bottle of champagne* is brought up, a gift from the management.

At 9:00 the next morning a *courtesy car* collects us and takes us to the set (for the remainder of the visit we are *provided with a free rental car*). I try to tip our driver for the ride but he declines, explaining that he is well-paid for his services.

Monday, Feb. 5, 2001

Heather greets us with a smile and escorts us into the studio (as soon as the red light, indicating filming is in progress, goes off), through the commissary, where snacks are available at all times, and upstairs into—a hospital! In front of us is a perfect replica of a nurses' station down to the last detail of paper clips, rubber bands, notices pinned to the walls, drawers labeled with various medications, etc. To the right of that is the big day room, where card tables are set with chess and checkers. Heavy plastic chairs and sofas line the walls. Off to one side of that is the game room and an examination room, and to the other are the art and TV rooms. Two parallel corridors lead from the day room past the nurses' station to the patients' rooms, each equipped with a bed and a desk and chair. In the examination room are cabinets containing medical supplies (even though none of them will show up on camera). We are immersed in authenticity.

We say "hi" to Mark (sound) and David (camera) and someone places a tall director's chair to which my name has been attached! alongside others in front of the two television monitors. The other chairs are never fully occupied, so Karen takes Colesberry's and we watch the next take of the current scene, in which the usually frenetic "Howie" (David Patrick Kelly) is sitting quietly by the day-room windows overlooking a sunny garden. A puzzled "Dr. Powell" sits down beside him and asks if he's looking for something.

"The bluebird," Howie replies.

"The bluebird?"

"The bluebird of happiness. It's a task 'prot' gave me. The first of three . . . ."

We watch this scene on the monitors, after which Jeff Bridges comes around to study the replay, greets us warmly, introduces us to Iain Softley's son (an eight-year-old who is videotaping a film of the making of the film), and returns to work. Jeff studies the replay for a few minutes before hurrying off for another take. Softley, too, says hello and shakes hands, as does John Mathieson, the cinematographer. We act as if we belong; we are, in fact, old hands by now.

For the next take we hustle into the "TV room" to watch the action through its window, live. Assistant director Peter Kohn: "Cameras rolling! Quiet! Background action!" Softley: "ACK-see-un!" We watch the scene again, the same take but with slightly different movements and inflections. Howie: "I don't know what the second one is yet—he'll tell me . . . ." "Cut!"

At this point Susan, a production assistant, pokes her head into the room and says to me, "You're wanted in 'Hair.'"

"Hair?"

"You're going to be in the next scene. They want you in 'Hair and Makeup.'" I almost knock her over getting past the nurses' station, downstairs through the commissary, out of the building and into the adjacent one, which houses "Wardrobe" as well. Kathleen hands me a pair of blue sweatpants, orange socks with loose-fitting carpet slippers, a gray T-shirt, and an outer shirt several sizes too small. I quickly change into this garish outfit, stomach hanging out, and am taken around the corner, where my hair is sprayed but left in disarray by Enid, and my face aged somewhat and a large bruise painted on the back of my right hand by Sue, on leave from "Dawson's Creek." "Can you find your way back?" she asks me. I shoot out of there straight to the set, where someone takes a Polaroid picture so my appearance can be duplicated the next day, if necessary. I speak to the technical advisor, psychiatrist Alessia Gottlieb, who advises me "not to overdo it." I decide to play it cool. This is my first film role, and I want to get it right.

By this time the cameras have been shifted around for a different take on the previous scene. Kevin has appeared and cordially greets Karen and me, apparently not noticing that I have been converted to a medicated paranoid schizophrenic. We wait some more while the cameras are moved back for the "Bluebird Scene." Stand-ins stand while lighting is adjusted and readjusted, the director studies the layout, sound is tested. While all this is going on the background actors (patients) take their places. Finally Scott Robertson, the second assistant director, leads me into the game room and instructs me to step out when the commotion starts and mingle with the other patients.

From down the corridor Peter shouts: "Okay, let's go! Quiet, please! Red light! Cameras rolling! Background action!" "ACK-see-un!" Then all is quiet. Howie stands at the windows looking out. Suddenly he murmurs, "Bluebird . . . Bluebird . . ." He becomes more animated. "Bluebird!" He starts running around, jumping onto the furniture, shouting "Bluebird! Bluebird!" Head nurse "Betty" (Conchata Ferrell) runs in and asks him what's the matter. He dances her around and takes off down the left corridor shouting "Bluebird!" At this point I shuffle in, "acting" curious but afraid of what's happening, my mouth hanging open and glasses awry. The other patients are starting to come out of their rooms. In the background we hear Howie knock over a supplies cart and then continue around through the other corridor and back to the day room. Security officers "Navarro" and "Simms" (Mark Christopher Lawrence) barge in. "Disturbance on Two!" Navarro shouts into his no-doubt-authentic communicator. By now all the patients are running around shouting, "Bluebird!" "Bluebird!" Powell appears, spots Betty with Howie back at the windows, and yells, "What the hell's going on, Betty?" He comes up to see for himself. "Hospital Director" Alfre Woodard hurries in to demand, in turn, "What's going on here, Dr. Powell?" Powell turns and quietly replies, "It's just a bluejay. Just a bluejay . . . ." "Ernie" (Saul Williams), who has been afraid to leave the ward for years, asks Powell if they can go out to see it. He tugs Powell toward the corridor, where they run into "Mrs. Archer" (Celia Weston). "Bluebird?" she inquires, gliding elegantly to the windows. Prot appears, smiles knowingly at Mrs. A and Howie. "Cut!"

It's time for lunch. Susan tells us where to find it. There are trailers set up along the street, and the crew and actors are lining up for the free food, which is hot, plentiful, and very good. We haul our bulging plates into the "mess hall," which offers all kinds of salads and fruits, and half-a-dozen desserts. On this first day we sit timidly off by ourselves. Everyone is there; conversations revolve around the movie business. As soon as we're finished we hurry back to the set, not wanting to miss anything. Our director's chair has followed the monitors to another location so that the cameras can be rearranged. Mathieson is running around with his light meter, otherwise not much is happening, and won't until the major players have returned. People start to drift in. I begin to collect autographs for a teenage friend. Unbelievably, someone asks for *mine!* By now we're beginning to recognize the cast and crew, and strike up conversations with some of them. Josef and his teddy bear, "Dr. Zoloft," Julie, Leo, Clete, Lydia, Tracy, John, David (Howie), Peter Gerrety (Sal), Saul (Ernie), and others. All very interesting people, all have read the entire script, and most the book. Some had questions (e.g., is he really an alien?), many of which were quite perceptive (if prot responded to hypnosis, why not to the antipsychotic drugs?). A few of them thank me for writing *K-PAX.* Many of them seem grateful to have a job; being an actor (or crew member) seems to offer little more security than being a writer. A few more autographs and we take our places.

Finally the directors, producers, and principals are back (they watch the "dailies" during lunch). "Quiet! Quiet please! Cameras rolling . . . !" Same scene, different perspective. Four or five takes and the equipment is moved somewhere else for another half-dozen from that angle. While waiting, "Sal" ("Chuck" in the book, but screenwriter Chuck Leavitt changed the name for some reason) keeps everyone entertained. At one point Bridges brings out his "pigs" and he has a go with Peter and Saul. Another take and another . . . . Karen reports that producer Bob Colesberry has told her I was the only one who looked like a real patient (i.e., wasn't overacting) in the scene. That's true—I wasn't even underacting, just trying to stay out of the way.

It's after eight o'clock: "Checking the gate" (the lens cover, looking for dust), and "That's a wrap!" We all traipse down and out, I get back into regular clothes, our driver picks us up, and we are transported back to the hotel, tired but still tingling.

Tuesday, Feb. 6

I've been instructed to show up at 7:30 A.M. Today we have our own car, and we drive to the set early. An attendant parks it for us and we find our way to the breakfast line. Again, a large variety of good food. Back to wardrobe, hair, makeup, and onto the set to wait for shooting to begin. We continue our autograph collection, but apparently no one believes the signatures are for someone else, and many of them jot a little note to me. Filming starts with the scene of Howie in the back hallway knocking over the supplies cart. Over and over he flies around the corner shouting "Bluebird!" and ramming into the cart. Cans and boxes and syringes go flying. It is filmed from front and back. Prot steps out of his room after each pass and crunches through the mess, following Howie to the day room.

At last we return to yesterday's scene. This time I'm instructed to come out a different door (same room). The cameras are set up on one side, then the other. Another dozen takes from different angles.

At lunch we strike up a conversation with Ajay Singh, and ask him where he grew up.

"Near Chicago."

Karen tells him about her brother Gary and his family in Evanston.

"What are their names?"

Of course he couldn't possibly know them, but she tells him "Schultz."

"Do they have a son named Steve?" Impossibly, he went to primary school with her nephew.

There are five windows overlooking the garden, each with its own set of venetian blinds, which must be adjusted for every take. Mathieson is everywhere with his light meter. I shuffle in and out.

Although I'm still wide-awake, the lunchtime feast is doing a number on my digestive system and I'm grateful to be left alone in the game room. But after a couple more takes, as I'm standing by myself in the day room, I give in to the pain and pressure and break a rather unpleasant wind. As luck would have it, Jeff Bridges spots me standing alone and comes over to ask me where my wife is. Exceedingly embarrassed, and probably bright red, I tell him she's watching the monitors. Jeff, a classy guy if there ever was one, pretends not to notice the foul air he's breathing. In fact, someone runs up to take a picture (for "Hair and Makeup," I suppose) and he leans close to me for the shot. I wish fervently I had died one of the horrible deaths I have feared all my life. But we chat a little more and he asks, "Are you both enjoying yourselves?" I tell him we are. He smiles and starts to leave. As an afterthought, I ask him, "Are *you*?" He thinks for a moment. "Sometimes," he says, before taking his place again by the window. "Depends on the scene." By now the air is clear.

Peter Kohn: "Let's go, let's go, let's go!" Howie runs the corridors, the patients get excited. Sal reminds me on one pass that I "stink." I have to laugh, maybe ruining the take. At some point, while waiting for a scene to be set up, camera operator Paul Babin tells me he's "tired" and invites me to take his place. I climb up and attempt to follow him with the camera as he proceeds down the corridor and out the door. In a minute he comes back; I try to keep him in the viewfinder. With two wheels, one for up-down, the other for left-right, it's surprisingly difficult, even without worrying about focusing. "Don't give up your day job," he advises. Jeff Erdmann, the boom operator, also lets us try our skills. It's not so heavy, but holding a twelve-foot carbon fiber rod over your head for several minutes can be very wearing, especially for windy outdoor scenes.

It's already 7:30 P.M. Another 12-hour day that seemed to last about 5 minutes. A change of outfits, someone brings our car, and we drive back to the hotel, too tired for dinner. An actor's life is an exhausting one.

Wednesday, Feb. 7

Today I'm instructed to get made up before breakfast: we're running behind schedule and Softley wants to finish the scene by lunchtime. Cameras move here and move there; another several takes for each setup. Mathieson flies around with his light meter. Lunch comes and goes. At one point the action is all in pantomime. "Tone it down a bit, please, Julie." When this is finished, there are a couple more run-throughs with sound only. "Bluebird!" Bluebird!" "Bluebird!" Softley directs, his arms waving like a conductor's. Some individual speaking parts are then recorded, and the scene is over. "Checking the gate." We all wait. "That's a wrap!" Some muffled cheers and applause. Not a big deal. All in a day's work. I'm told that I can return to Wardrobe. I take my time, wishing it would go on and on.

When I get back, Karen and I find our chairs positioned in front of the monitors (the scene takes place in prot's room and there isn't space for watching onsite). In this scene Melanie Murray ("Bess") shuffles down the corridor and whispers to prot: "I know who you are. You're the bluebird!" In the meantime, Spacey is diagramming the night sky. His window is a green backdrop, on which the stars will be superimposed later. After a couple of takes, ". . . You're the bluebird!" he turns to her and says, softly, "All right, Clarisse!" in the voice of Anthony Hopkins, breaking everybody up. "Cut!" Several takes later, the gate is checked, another day is wrapped, and we go "home."

Thursday, February 8

Our final day on the set. We don't have to be there at any particular time, and we miss breakfast. But the commissary is stocked with bagels, cereal, fruit, donuts, etc., so we do well enough.

Today we can relax. We wander around getting the last of the autographs, chatting about movies and books, checking out all the backstage areas we missed earlier. The first scene is a repeat of last night's "I know who you are," except that the camera points down the hallway at Bess rather than prot. There are three or four shots of that, and a few audio takes of her voiceover.

While we're waiting for the cameras and lights to be ready for the final couple of scenes of the day, Karen manages to get a photo of me with Kevin, who is playing ping-pong with Iain's son. All our goals having been accomplished, we retire to the plastic chairs to wait for filming to begin. I bring out a copy of the book to show someone the 3-D cover, and a crowd gathers around to study it. Some can see it, some can't, but the challenge generates a lot of interest.

The next shot is set in the day room. Prot is playing chess with Ernie. Several other patients lounge around. In front of the window a group therapy session is going on. "Maria," a multiple personality (Tracy Vilar) bursts out of the art room wearing a nurses' uniform. "How are we doing this morning?" prot inquires as she breezes past him. "Oh, just fine," she replies cheerfully, and exits into the game room. Navarro, following along behind her, points at prot. "My man!" Prot points back (in later takes he doesn't). The art room is empty, something Sal has been waiting for. He gets up from his table, whispers "Psssssst!" (Softley calls this "the Pst scene"). Prot turns around to look. Sal disappears into the art room, pokes his face and hands through the blind slats, watching prot, who comes to see what he wants. "Cut!" Another five or six takes of this. At one point, Spacey gives us a thumbs up: everything is going well.

During the lunch break (I eat less on days three and four) someone insists that we move to the head of the line. We apologize profusely, but no one seems to mind. The meal—we're sitting with John ("Russell") Toles-Bey and his two kids—is interrupted by Susan, who tells us we're invited to watch the dailies (yesterday's takes) two blocks down the street. We pick up our trays and hustle to the trailer, barge in, and settle down in a tiny theater with our half-eaten lunches to watch the filming on a real screen. All the VIP's are there, and the show begins. Everyone is having a good time, and they all seem to like what they see. One scene has Howie running through the back corridor shouting, '"Bluebird," etc., and knocking over the supply cart. The camera stays on a metal pan that has fallen to the floor, spinning like a top. When it slows down, a hand reaches out to keep it going. The take doesn't make it to the big screen.

Next scene: Sal checks to make sure no one else is coming into the art room. He asks if prot can show him how to do "that light travel thing." Prot asks him why he wants to know. Sal tells his story, how bad everyone on Earth smells—he wants to go to K-PAX. It's a very moving scene (unfortunately, some of it had to be cut). By now it's six o'clock and we have to leave to meet screenwriter Leavitt and his wife Madeline for dinner. We try to sneak out without disturbing anyone, but some of the cast and crew spot us and come up for final handshakes, hugs, kisses, farewells. They have been wonderful to us, and we miss them all before we're even out the door.

Top left: With Kevin in the game room
Top right: In costume, with Jeff in the day room
Bottom left: Watching the monitors
Bottom right: With Tracy Vilar, cast and crew

I ended up with three appearances in the final cut, each a few seconds long. But it's a start. If anyone makes an offer for me to appear in another motion picture, I'm prepared to accept, especially if it's a starring role.

A few weeks after we returned to New York, an ominous note: *K-PAX* has been booted from its Dec. 25th opening up to October 5th . . . .

K-PAX III, PART 2

With *K-PAX II* soon to be published (in March, 2001), I called Marc Resnick to determine the status of *III*, which he had told me he wanted to put out about a year after *II*. To my amazement, and despite the "major motion picture" tie-in, he said he was waiting to see how the latter "performs." He added that he would have no objection to my showing it to other houses, knowing, of course, that it would be impossible to find a publisher for it without the rights to *I* and *II*. He asked me to keep him "informed." How could anyone publish only the first two-thirds of a trilogy, I wondered, especially with movie potential and foreign sales, as well as the possibility of a boxed set of the three books for holiday giving? Easy, I learned.

I sent it around anyway, and all the editors told me exactly what I expected. By now, however, *K-PAX II* had appeared in Great Britain and had sold well (as had *K-PAX*). I e-mailed my editor at Bloomsbury, Mike Jones, and asked him whether he would consider finishing the trilogy. He asked me to send him a copy.

On April 17, Mike made an offer of 20,000 pounds (ca. $35,000) for world rights to *K-PAX III*. I called Marc to inform him. He requested a week to reconsider his position ("the bosses are all at a sales conference"), but he wasn't optimistic. While we were on the phone I asked him whether he anticipated that *III* would lose money for St. Martin's Press. No, it will make money, *but not enough* (somewhere between $10,000 and $100,000, he told me). Two weeks later he called with an offer of $7,500 (the same as for *On a Beam of Light*). By the time the phone reached the cradle I was signing the contract with Bloomsbury.

K-PAX III came out on July 1, 2002; within a couple of weeks it went into a second printing. It is still in print and still selling.

THE MOVIE SEQUEL, PART 1

After treating us so well on the set, both in New York and Hollywood, the studio decided to play hardball with the sequel. On March 1, 2001, when *On a Beam of Light* (part II of the *K-PAX* trilogy) was published by St. Martin's Press, negotiations for the film rights were initiated. According to the terms of my contract, Universal had 30 days to make an offer or release the rights to me. Bob Harris called me on the 22nd: UP attorney Mark Torpoco had informed him that the studio planned to make a "small offer" for *K-PAX II*, and reminded Bob that that the studio "owned" the characters in the movie. In other words, if I didn't accept their offer, they would be free to make their own sequel. Moreover, the original *K-PAX* contract stipulated that, even if I could find another studio to produce *II*, the rights to any *subsequent* films in the series belonged to UP.

A written offer for an option to make the sequel came on March 26th. It was for two years, $25K for each year, far less than they paid for the first film. Torpoco indicated there was a "cash-flow problem" at Universal (despite their record billion-dollar income for the previous year). I didn't care so much about the size of the offer, but the guile was both disappointing and annoying, particularly since the offer came only four days before the negotiating window closed. I declined, citing this and other points of concern, such as who would write the screenplay if Chuck Leavitt declined (I didn't want another Goluboff fiasco). On the 30th, the studio came back with another offer: $35K for the first year of the option, $100K for the second year, and *maybe* I would have the opportunity to write the screenplay myself (if all their contracted "A-line" writers opted not to participate). I declined again. The $35K became their final "obligation" offer—if the negotiations fell through, I would be able to accept any higher offer from another studio without giving UP the opportunity to match it.

I was gambling here. Post-production was barely underway, and *K-PAX* wasn't scheduled to premiere for several months. No one knew how well it was going to do in the theaters—it could have been another *Forrest Gump* (to which *K-PAX* has sometimes been compared) or a dud. The studio was hedging its bets; all I wanted was fair treatment.

It wasn't until April 2nd, after the negotiating deadline had passed, that I heard again from Universal: the offer rose to $50K for the first term, but that period would be extended to eighteen months, and nothing was said about screenwriters. (Evidently the studio had enjoyed a windfall: they had only $25K in the bank six days earlier.)

I respectfully declined.

On April 10th it was back to 35K for the first year, but with substantial bonuses if *K-PAX*, the original movie, made a fortune—$100 million domestic or $250 million worldwide—at the box office (this, of course, would cost them nothing if *K-PAX* were only moderately successful).

I said no to this apple pie in the sky.

On April 17th I called Kevin Spacey's assistant, Bernie Morris: Would Trigger Street Productions be interested in purchasing the rights to *K-PAX II*? He spoke with Kevin, who seemed to be interested, but the budget would be beyond their resources and they would have to go back to Universal Pictures for financing in any case.

By this time another of the studio's endless attorneys, Jeff Daitch, had taken over the negotiations. Bob asked him on the 18th whether UP could offer $35K for a shorter option period. (No.)

April 22: I agreed to the $35K for one year if the second option period were eliminated; i.e., a new contract would have to be negotiated at the end of year one.

May 9: Daitch agreed to eliminate the second year, but only if the first year (now $40K) were extended to an 18-month period.

May 15: I proposed to accept the $35K, and the rest of the contract, if this amount were not applicable to (deducted from) the total purchase price (now $1 million).

May 22: Daitch agreed, but only if the option were exercised during the first year.

May 23: I agreed, provided the first option period would be effective May 1.

May 24: Daitch agreed to this, and I accepted the offer. The contract was a done deal except for signing. A letter from Daitch, confirming the agreement, was signed by him on May 31st, 2001.

A month passed before we heard from Daitch again. In the meantime I joined Karen, who was at a meeting in Orlando, for a few days of vacation and to visit former laboratory assistant Peggy Busacca and her family. At Epcot Center on May 31, again despite warning signs that people with neck problems should stay off, I stupidly took a ride on the "test track." A day later, after a round of miniature golf, my left shoulder and neck were agonizingly painful, so much so that I couldn't sleep that night. Even so, we were thrilled to get the VIP tour of the NASA facility at Cape Canaveral, where Peggy's husband Mario works. By the time we returned to New York on June 3, I couldn't lift my left hand higher than my shoulder. I called Mike Palumbo and he prescribed Vioxx (its potentially devastating side effects hadn't yet been revealed to the public). It didn't help the pain in the slightest. I went to see him and, a week later, had an MRI: two discs were out of place and pressing on a spinal nerve. A few days later I saw a surgeon and was tentatively scheduled for an operation to remove the discs and install new bone and metal rods. I decided to get a second opinion. Dr. Cooper agreed that I needed to have the problem corrected and, since I liked him better than the first guy, I scheduled the surgery with him for July 9th.

During the month of June, however, the pain gradually subsided, and I was able to raise my arm higher and higher. After the pre-surgical testing on July 3rd, I stopped by Dr. Cooper's office and gave him a progress report with demonstration (I raised my arm straight up with little pain). He shouted, "Cancel the surgery!" Of course I thought he was joking—many surgeons have a strange sense of humor—but no: the discs had slipped back where they belonged. Not only that, he told me, it was no more likely they would be displaced again than for someone on the street. A miracle? No, but the self-repair of a nerve compression injury is surely an infrequent occurrence. Ironically, I had no anxiety about going in for the procedure. Zoloft and I were no more terrified of the surgery than anyone else, perhaps less so. In fact, I was almost looking forward to the experience. If there had been any doubt before this episode, I knew then that I had truly been cured of my anxiety disorder, at least consciously, and for as long as I was taking this or a similar medication.

To date I have had no recurrence of the slipped discs, or even of pain while jogging. On the other hand, I no longer jump onto every juvenile circus ride I encounter.

On July 7th (2001) the new Universal contract, with all the terms we had agreed to, arrived. However, Universal had attached some new provisions, which Bob referred to as "problems." He reported his concerns to Daitch.

Three more weeks passed. On July 31st, a "revised final" contract from Mark Torpoco (Daitch's boss) arrived. Amazingly, he had made several additional changes to the text. Bob conveyed his annoyance back to Torpoco.

On August 7th we learned that the theatrical opening for K-PAX had been moved again, this time from October 5th to October 26th, to avoid a conflict. Another bad sign?

Two more *months* went by. During this period, unfortunately, the negotiations were trivialized by the events of September 11. We happened to be on Grand Manan at the time, and heard the reports by CBC radio. It was an unbelievable tragedy, one of immense magnitude. The reaction of the American people was, at first, enormously gratifying. Police and fire departments all over the country sent help to the overwhelmed forces in New York City. But when things began to get back to "normal," we were distressed to discover that the long-term response of the majority of American citizens was one of revenge, of killing whomever it took in order to get to Osama Bin Laden. Someone asked me what prot would have said under these circumstances. I replied that the first question he would ask would probably be, "Why do so many people around the world hate America so much?" In the rush for retaliation, very few others have asked this question. Until our government (and the media) deals with this reality, it seems to me that anti-American terrorism can never be eradicated.

On September 28th, four weeks before the K-PAX premiere, Torpoco informed us that Universal wanted the right to match *any* offer for the sequel, which was where we had started seven months earlier.

Frustrated that the studio appeared to be stalling, and indeed reneging on the terms I had agreed to on May 24th, I said no. Aside from the studio's apparent duplicity, I firmly believed that, even if I agreed to all the terms, UP would come up with additional demands until it got what it wanted. Bob faxed my decision to Torpoco.

Still another month crept by. On October 25, 2001, the day before the scheduled theatrical opening, Jeff Daitch called Bob Harris: Torpoco was out of the picture, Daitch was back. He wanted to conclude the negotiations as soon as possible (I thought they had been concluded long before). My response (on Oct. 30), was that I would be happy to weigh Universal's latest offer against any others that I might receive. When Bob reported this to Daitch, he hung up. Final result: after eight months of deviousness and procrastination, Universal had managed to save $35,000 (while spending far more in legal fees) without even knowing how well *K-PAX* would do at the box office.

I decided that if I were offered a starring role in a major motion picture, I might not accept it.

K-PAX, THE MOVIE, PART 5

Despite the general antagonism, Karen and I were invited to the Hollywood premiere, though we were told there would be no cast party because of security concerns. This time we went *first class*! I invited brother Bob and his wife Christina, along with a couple of friends, Lois Weinstein and Joel Ax (Lois had been one of my staunchest supporters from the beginning) to come with us. We were put up at the Four Seasons Hotel, all expenses paid, including wonderful meals. Our room was on the second floor facing the courtyard; one of the highlights of the trip was getting a close-up look of Cameron Diaz at a photo-op just below our little balcony. As a bonus, there was a minor earthquake that night, 2.9 on the Richter scale.

On the evening of the premiere (October 22, 2001), the six of us were picked up by a stretch limousine and taken to the Mann Village Theater in Westwood. We arrived to find a well-lit press podium with Kevin Spacey being interviewed. From that a long red carpet stretched to the door of the theater. Across the street, perhaps a hundred movie fans were screaming for their favorite actor(s). We watched all this for a while, took some pictures. I shook hands with Hailey Joel Osment (there with his mother), a friend of Kevin's since *Pay It Forward*, and told him I admired his work. The kid lit up with a genuinely happy smile, though he didn't know me from a cellular phone. Finally, we all went into the theater. Amazingly, no one took my picture or shouted my name along the entire red-carpeted stroll.

Inside, we were shown to seats surrounded by the some of the actors: the magnetic Conchata Ferrell; the wonderful Brian Howe (Dr. Steve Becker), the amazing rapper, political activist, and fine actor Saul Williams (Ernie). Chuck Leavitt and his wife and son were right in front of us. When the various names appeared as the credits were rolled, there were shouts and applause; everyone was having a good time. Judging by the reaction of the crowd after the film was over, it was going to be a great success in the theaters.

After the screening we met Jeff Bridges, who was greeting the attendees at the top of the aisle. I performed the introductions for our party, asked him what he was doing at present ("nothing"), and joked that he only worked when he ran out of money, which elicited a chuckle and a confirming nod.

Outside the auditorium we found Kevin in a rare moment of being alone. I thanked him for his superb performance in the— "No, thank *you*!" More introductions, then it was on to the post-premiere dinner party (it was scheduled after all) at Wolfgang Puck's "Spago," where we met Mr. Puck himself. We wandered around in a daze for a while, chatting with some of the actors and the director (Kevin had just given him a large framed photograph taken on the set). I thanked Iain for the terrific job he—"No, thank *you!*" He told us his next film would take him to El Salvador. We wished him the best of luck and went for the gourmet food.

Finding no obvious place to eat it, we asked a waiter where we could sit, and a card table was set up for us. It was only later that we discovered we were among the special guests with a table of our own, next to the Leavitts. We sipped champagne for a while (some of the cast and crew stopped by, as well as Kevin's assistant Bernie Morris, and the movie's website creator, Parker Bennett) before schmoozing again. If I had any social anxiety, I didn't give a damn.

Though we hadn't had the opportunity of meeting Mary McCormack ("Rachel Powell") on the set, she jumped up from her table for a kiss/hug. Brother Bob, the semi-professional actor, was very much taken with both Ms. McCormack and her performance, and insisted on having his picture taken with her (he has a good eye for beautiful women). More mingling, more wine, more food. The party was still swinging when we left at 1:30 A.M. (4:30 in New York).

At the premiere.
Top left, First row: Chuck and Madeline Leavitt with son David.
Second row: Sister-in-law Christina, me, Karen, friends Lois Weinstein and
Joel Ax. Behind us: Mary McCormack.
Top right: Saul Williams and Conchata Ferrell.
Bottom left: Outside the theater.
Bottom right: Jeff Bridges greeting attendees.

Top left: Brian Howe and friend at the premiere dinner.
Top right: Kevin with a bearded Larry Gordon.
Bottom left: Brother Bob with Mary McCormack.
Bottom right: The party in full swing.

The next day we flew home, again in first class, just across the aisle from the ABC newscaster Elizabeth Vargas, who, like Helen Hunt, is smaller than she appears on television. Though, like the latter, very attractive.

The film opened in the theaters on October 26, 2001, to mixed reviews. Probably the nastiest of them all was by The New York Times resident critic, A.O. Scott, who wrote his report as if he hadn't seen it:

Now Arriving on Track 10: The 3:15 From Outer Space

In "K-Pax [sic]," Kevin Spacey plays a character—either a profoundly disturbed mental patient or a being from a distant galaxy [sic]—who regards the strivings of ordinary earth folk with an amused detachment that combines smug superiority and gentle pity. So what else, you may ask, is new? Mr. Spacey's gift for irony, his attraction to roles that hide emotional distress behind a cloak of knowing composure, is starting to look like a vice.

Here, as in last year's vile "Pay It Forward," he lends his keen intelligence to a dubious therapeutic cause. "K-Pax" is a draggy, earnest exercise in pseudo-spiritual uplift, recycling romantic hokum about extraterrestrial life and mental illness with wide-eyed sincerity . . . .

. . . The K-Paxian civilization has evolved far beyond our own, so what do these beings have to teach us? "Get it right this time. This time is all you have." Can they send us some screenwriters, or are the ones we have aliens in human form?

Of course, there is also the possibility that Prot [sic] is just a severely deluded, terribly traumatized earthling, and the one thing "K-Pax" does get right is its handling of this ambiguity. Though the individual scenes are atrociously written— and dragged out so that every possible emotional cliché can be ticked off the checklist—the story is cleverly structured and allows us to entertain two contradictory possibilities without seeming egregiously illogical.

There are some lapses, though. Prot finds the expression "take a seat" incomprehensible and the New Jersey city of Hoboken difficult to pronounce, yet he seems well acquainted with American cinema. "Don't worry, doctor," he says to Powell, "I won't jump out of your chest."

But his divided identity does allow Mr. Spacey to jump out of his skin, to break through his sly reserve in a moment of wailing, screaming anguish tailor- made for the video screens on Oscar night. Mr. Bridges looks on with evident concern, and it's hard to watch these two actors plow through the nonsense of "K- Pax" without feeling that a terrific opportunity has been squandered. Mr. Spacey uses his quick verbal intelligence and his easy smirk to deflect emotion and then, in unexpected and often untrustworthy ways, to reveal it. Mr. Bridges's cunning works in the opposite direction. His plain-spoken naturalism is often an especially effective form of guile. If Mr. Spacey's characters are often more sincere than they seem, those of Mr. Bridges are smarter than they let on.

Unfortunately, the premise of "K-Pax" is so tired, and the direction so plodding and uninflected, that the actors rarely connect with each other. Iain Softley, the director, whose adaptation of "The Wings of the Dove" shook loose some of the novel's mannerisms and excavated its gothic psychosexual subtext, almost succeeds in giving some resonance to Charles Leavitt's relentlessly shallow script (from a novel by Gene Brewer). The problem is that, in spite of some dreamy visual motifs (there are a lot of orbs and spheres, perhaps to illustrate a remark Prot makes about soap bubbles), his approach to the story is stubbornly literal minded . . . .

But what can you expect from a man who doesn't know a capital from a small letter, a planet from a galaxy?

On the other hand, Ebert and Roeper, who actually watched the movie, gave it two thumbs up. The former even went so far as to compare *K-PAX* with *Man Facing*

Southeast, noting the similarities but concluding that these were two entirely different films. Several other reviews were also positive, some enthusiastic. Still others, though less mean-spirited than the New York Times, were vaguely disappointed, opining that the producers "couldn't make up their minds" about how to end the movie. Which, of course, entirely missed the point. The ending was *supposed* to be ambiguous: to let the viewer decide for himself, to underscore the uncertainties people have in knowing what to believe, to leave room for reasonable doubt, as well as individual hope.

Since the story was about a man claiming to be an alien, and set in a mental institution, it was compared, sometimes unfavorably, to films with similar themes or settings, e.g., *One Flew Over the Cuckoo's Nest*; *Don Juan deMarco*; *The Brother from Outer Space*; *Mr. Jones*; *The Man Who Fell to Earth*; *King of Hearts*; *The Day the Earth Stood Still*; *Starman*; *E.T.*; *The Fisher King*; *Wings of Desire*; *Happy Accidents*; *The Green Mile*; *Ghidra, the Three-Headed Monster*; and yes, *Man Facing Southeast*, implying a lack of originality (never mind that dozens of action pictures and romantic comedies, all amazingly like their thousands of predecessors, are produced every year).

The bottom line is that the critics either loved it or hated it—ironically, I suspect, because of its uniqueness. In any case, *K-PAX* was the #1 box-office attraction it's first weekend (October 26-28, 2001) in the theaters.

One of my greatest disappointments was the total absence of Academy Award recognition. Kevin's performance was virtually perfect, and so was Jeff's in the more difficult role of "straight man." I also expected director Softley and cinematographer Mathieson, and perhaps a couple of the supporting actors, as well as screenwriter Leavitt to be nominated for their solid work on the movie (not to mention composer Edward Shearmur for his beautiful and felicitous music). However, Universal decided to push Ron Howard's film, *A Beautiful Mind*, the one that bumped *K-PAX* from the Dec. 25 opening, instead. While *Mind* is certainly a good movie, it doesn't have the originality and depth of *K-PAX*, which we saw half-a-dozen times in theaters and, each time, the audience glued its collective eyes to the screen and didn't utter a word (laughter excepted) until it was over, a clear indication of a fine production. Often, there was applause at the end. No doubt money and politics exerted heavy influence in UP's decision, but it's a great shame that the principal players in *K-PAX* weren't better recognized for their outstanding achievements.

Having said that, I'll add that there were a few smaller disappointments for me, personally, with the film itself. For example, one of the pivotal characters (Giselle) in the book was left out of the movie. Also, an excellent chance for some gripping action was lost because, incomprehensibly, there was no scene showing Howie trying to "kill" Ernie, only the aftermath. And why a bluejay—couldn't they find a bluebird anywhere in Southern California? Worst of all, Robert Porter was discovered in prot's room at the end of the film, rather than having transported himself to Bess's. That little excursion in itself probably would have made the ending less "ambiguous" for the reviewers. And to make Robert look different from prot, they gave him a nose job—whose crazy idea was that? Then there was that little smile, which meant—what?

There were a few technical problems as well. Dr. Chakraborty tells Powell that prot can see UV light "up to 300-400 Angstroms" (since humans can only see light from 4000-8000 Angstroms, it should have been "*down* to that wavelength (I would have been happy to serve as technical advisor free of charge, but wasn't asked); "Natalie" loses a tooth early on, and later it miraculously grows back in; the house in the desert was far too rundown five years after being abandoned; the river Robert tries to drown himself in was a placid stream despite earlier assurances that it is a roaring river "even in July." But these are minor complaints. Overall it was a magical film that, I think, beautifully conveyed the spirit of the book, something rarely achieved in Hollywood.

As soon as the movie was released, the e-mail started to come in from all over the world, several hundred messages in the first couple of months. To date, more than a thousand viewers/readers have written to me about *K-PAX*. Some implored me to tell them whether prot was really an alien or just a mentally-ill human (I referred them to books *II* and *III*), or whether the story was fiction or non-fiction (even though it says "a novel" on the front of the book). If prot is not a real person, many wondered, where did I get my "inspiration" for him and for the story? (the same place all original ideas come from: the imagination, which is constructed from the sum total of one's life experiences). And am I like Dr. Brewer? (no, I'm more like prot, but probably there's a little of me in all the characters). Others asked what I thought of the movie. And, of course, many people wondered whether I think there is life elsewhere in the universe (yes, it's likely that the Milky Way alone is crawling with life, but Homo sapiens is, I suspect, a rarity). A dozen or so thrashed me for stealing the plot from *Man Facing Southeast*. It's quite amazing how a stranger can *know* that a writer has plagiarized someone else's work even when he hasn't (this phenomenon may be similar to religious faith, in which belief is equated to truth). The same mindset prevails at the trials of celebrities: fans gather to demand their hero(ine) be turned loose because he/she is a star, or at least a famous person, and therefore couldn't possibly be guilty.

One e-letter was sent by an astute reader who couldn't understand the connection between Dr. B's wishful thinking about Giselle, and Brown's syndrome, an affliction I thought I had made up. It turns out there is one by that name, a disease of the eye. Live and learn.

The most gratifying correspondence came from dozens of fans who told me that the book(s) made them think differently about the Earth, vegetarianism, and our treatment of non-human animals. These alone made all the work and frustration worthwhile.

Several requests for radio and newspaper interviews also began to arrive, and a few for speaking engagements, one as "special guest" at a writer's conference, where I used to go for advice from someone like myself. I was happy to comply with them all.

The domestic box-office receipts were $50 million, two million more than the film's final cost. A successful project, right? Wrong. In Hollywood, basketfuls of the income go for intangibles, including advertising, revenue-sharing (with theaters and distributors), and incidentals like travel and promotion by the stars (though rarely the writers). So does the studio lose money on all this? No. It takes a percentage of every dollar for "overhead" before the balance sheets are figured, and it's a long time before any "profits" are realized. Even Winston Groom, the author of *Forrest Gump*, had to go after the studio (Paramount) to obtain his rightful percentage of the film's income.

Some months after the domestic run, *K-PAX* opened in a couple dozen countries throughout the world. Despite the popularity of the book (it was a bestseller in Great Britain and Poland, and a near-bestseller in France, for example), the worldwide box-office receipts were disappointing and, in some cases, dismal. Why? Because in order to hold down expenses, the studio hired an incompetent German tax-sheltered company to distribute the film in Europe and Asia. In November, 2002, in fact, producer Larry Gordon sued Universal for its botched foreign distribution of *K-PAX*, claiming that the alleged fraud cost him millions of dollars. As of this writing, the case is still in the courts.

When the videotape/DVD came out, however, *K-PAX*, the movie, at last became a popular success.

PROT'S REPORT and THE K-PAX TRILOGY

I had long planned to compile the report on planet Earth that prot had been writing in *K-PAX*, hoping to get it published as a small paperback pocket edition. It was basically an interweaving of his experiences at the Manhattan Psychiatric Institute with his assessment of human civilization and why our evolution had been such a disaster for all other species, as well as for the Earth itself.

I finished it in May, 2002, the same month that Flower became a vegan. When Karen read it she said it wasn't fair to my readers: half of it was simply a retelling of *K-PAX* from prot's point of view. She was right. I started over with a different slant, and finished the "revised" version in July.

No one wanted to publish it, not even Mike Jones (he liked it, but thought it was too short to stand alone). By this time, however, Bloomsbury was contemplating putting out an "omnibus" edition of all three books bound together. He thought it would be a good idea to include *Prot's Report* as a "tag-on" to the trilogy. I thought this would be an insult to those who had already bought the three individual books: to read the report they would have to buy them again in the form of the omnibus. He countered that he would simultaneously publish it (the report) on their website (www.Bloomsbury.com) when the trilogy came out. Better, but I still thought that many fans would prefer to have it in hard copy.

At about the same time, however, *Vegan Voice*, a terrific Australian animal advocacy magazine, published an interview with me. Its editor, Sienna Blake, suggested a serialization in that periodical, and *Prot's Report* first appeared there. Moreover, another good friend from New York and Grand Manan, Leda Arensberg, pointed out that if it weren't published as part of the trilogy, my readers would also be cheated by not having access to it at all. My compromise with Mike was that he could have it for the omnibus edition, but I would retain the North American rights in case an American publisher decided to publish it later on. St. Martin's Press agreed to a 50:50 split on profits from the trilogy. It was published in December, 2003, and became another bestseller in Great Britain (it can be ordered by any bookstore, or from *www.amazon.co.uk*).

THE MOVIE SEQUEL, PART 2

Even though Universal Pictures had little interest in making a sequel to the film version of *K-PAX*, I nevertheless began writing a screenplay for *K-PAX II: the Return of Prot*, hoping that other movie or television studios might be more receptive, including those in England, France, or Poland, where *K-PAX*, the novel, had done well. These would also have the advantage that viewers might be more willing to accept different actors from those appearing in the original film. Before going that route, however, I wanted to give the original players a chance to see it in case they were interested in pursuing the project.

Although I adapted it from the book (*On a Beam of Light*), I was also forced to use the original film as a starting point, with the characters imposed by Chuck Leavitt and Universal Pictures. Thus, it started off this way:

1   INT. A COTTAGE SOMEWHERE IN THE ADIRONDACKS—MIDMORNING   1

PSYCHIATRIST MARK POWELL (**Jeff Bridges**), his WIFE RACHEL (**Mary McCormack**), and DAUGHTERS GABBY (**Natasha Dorfhuber**) and NATALIE (**Tess McCarthy**) sit in the living room playing CLUE on an old card table. The fireplace is unlit. Facing it is a worn sofa and an overstuffed chair. Along another wall is a bookcase holding rocks, photos, and paperbacks. Books are also strewn on the furniture and floor. A rocking chair with reading lamp occupies a corner. EVERYONE is wearing shorts and T-shirts. SHASTA, an aging GOLDEN RETRIEVER, is snoring on a daybed next to the front window. Outside, a gentle rain.

NATALIE

Shasta, turn over!

SHASTA opens her eyes, licks her lips, gets up and repositions herself with a grunt.

GABBY

It's your turn, Dad.

POWELL

Huh? Oh.

POWELL picks up the die, rolls it flamboyantly.

> POWELL
>
> Okay. Uh—hm. Let's see—
>> (moving his piece into the conservatory)
>
> Okay, I'm going to say—
>>> (beat)
>
> —the foul deed was done in the conservatory by Miss Scarlett with a—
>>> (consulting his notes)
>
> —with a knife.

> NATALIE
>> (whining)
>
> Daaaaaddy! You did that the last time!

> GABBY
>
> You're not concentrating, Dad.

O.S. A bluejay squawks.

> RACHEL
>
> What are you thinking about, hon? You're supposed to be on vacation, remember? You agreed that you—

> POWELL
>
> You're right. I'm sorry. It's just that—

> RACHEL
>> (interrupting)
>
> It's prot, isn't it? You're thinking about prot again, aren't you? I knew we shouldn't—

> POWELL
>
> It's just that he's due back today . . .
>> (shrugs)

> RACHEL
>
> You don't know that, Mark. He said he *might* be back. In *about* three years . . .

> POWELL
>
> You don't know prot. When prot says "about," he means within a second or two.

NATALIE

But *Daddy*, we're on vacaaaation!

POWELL

I know that, sugarbabe, but—

The phone rings. SHASTA barks. EVERYONE stares at POWELL. After a few seconds POWELL smiles sheepishly, shakes his head, and gets up to answer it. SHASTA runs to join him, barking.

POWELL

Hello?

Later, when prot has recovered from his "journey":

6   INT. POWELL'S INNER OFFICE—DAY   6

POWELL sits at his desk across from PROT, who has just finished a ripe banana. PROT'S mouth is still full. The lights have been dimmed: no dark glasses.

POWELL

So—how are you feeling today?

PROT
(cheeks stuffed, bits of fruit spraying from his mouth)
Just fine, Mark. Completely recovered from the trip. How about yourself?

POWELL
(suppressing a grin)
Much better, now that you're back.

PROT
(swallowing the last of the banana)
Really, Dr. P? Have you been ill?

POWELL

Not exactly. Frustrated, mostly.

PROT

Maybe you should see a psychiatrist.

POWELL

Actually, I've consulted with some of the best minds in the world on the subject.

PROT

Does it have anything to do with your relationships with other humans?

POWELL

In a way.

PROT

I thought so.

POWELL

To be honest, it concerns you and Robert.

PROT

Really? Have we done something wrong?

POWELL

That's what I'd like to know. But let's begin with your telling me where you've been for the past three years.

PROT

Don't you remember, Marko? I had to go back to K-PAX for a while.

POWELL

And you took Bess with you?

PROT (becoming a little bored) gets up and examines a framed photograph on the wall opposite the windows. It is the EARTH as seen from SPACE.

PROT
(musing)
Too bad. It's such a beautiful place . . .
(coming back to reality)
I thought a change of scene would do her good.

POWELL

And she's still on K-PAX?

PROT

Of course.

POWELL

(doubtfully, drumming his pen on his chair arm)

Can you prove to me that Bess is on K-PAX?

PROT

(immediately)

Can you prove to me that she is not?

POWELL

(resignedly)

And how is she doing?

PROT

Like a fish in water.

POWELL

Why didn't she come back with you?

PROT

Are you kidding? Would you want to come back here after you've seen Pa-ree?

POWELL nods, throws his yellow pad onto his desk.

POWELL

Well, did anyone else come back with you this time?

PROT

No. I wouldn't be surprised if no one ever did.

POWELL

Why is that?

PROT

They read my report.

POWELL

(becoming more frustrated)

Tell me, prot: If you think our planet is such a shitty place, why do you keep coming back?

PROT

Your memory isn't very good today, is it, Mark? Robert needs my help once in awhile. As soon as I delivered my report I hurried on back here. Besides, I promised certain beings that I would come back for them on my next visit.

POWELL

Come back for them? You mean to take them to K-PAX?

PROT

Where else should I take them?

POWELL
(sighing)

I see. And how many—uh—beings are you planning to take back with you?

PROT

I came prepared this time, Dr. P. I can take as many as a hundred others with me when I return.

POWELL
(sitting up straighter)

What? A hundred?

PROT

Your hearing seems to be going the way of your memory, *mon ami*.

POWELL
(ignoring PROT'S comment)

Who are you planning to take with you, for example?

PROT

Oh, I won't know that until the time comes.

POWELL

And when will that be?

PROT

Ah. That would be telling, wouldn't it?

POWELL
(flinging his pen onto the desk)

You mean you're not even going to tell me when you're leaving?

PROT

By George, I think you've got it!

POWELL

Why the hell not?

PROT

Because if you knew when I was leaving, you'd watch me like a cat watches a bird on this carnivorous world.

POWELL
(giving up)
All right. (pause) Have you spoken with Robert since you've been back?

PROT

Of course. He was the first human I ran into.

POWELL (rubbing his nose)
How is he feeling?

We see a little particle hanging from POWELL'S nose.

PROT

Like a sack of mot excrement.

POWELL
(pausing, considering how to put this)
Prot, I'm going to give you a task. Like you gave Howie three years ago—remember?

PROT

Certainly.

POWELL

I'm going to ask you to help Robert. Like you helped the other patients when you were here.

PROT
(smiling warmly)
You never give up, do you, doc?

POWELL
(smiling back)
We try not to. Okay, I'll let you off the hook for today.
(standing)
See you next week?

PROT
(also standing)
Put plenty of fruit on that hook.

POWELL
(reconsidering)
Is there anything else you want to tell me before you go?

PROT
You have a rutad hanging out of your nose.

POWELL reaches for a tissue, removes the offending particle. He tosses the tissue toward
a wastebasket, misses, gets up from his desk, picks it up, and throws it in. PROT wags his
head gently, smiles at POWELL, who smiles back. As POWELL and PROT regard each
other fondly as

FADE TO BLACK.

Much later:

50 EXT. BRONX ZOO—DAY   50

Most of the WARDS ONE and TWO PATIENTS (and some of WARD THREE) stroll
in a group toward the great ape enclosure, shepherded by GISELLE, NAVARRO, SIMMS,
BETTY and OTHER STAFF. A couple of POLICE OFFICERS bring up the rear.
BERT finds JACKIE, takes her by the hand.

BERT
Prot wants you to stay with me, kiddo.

JACKIE
(all smiles)
Okay!

As they approach the outdoor enclosure, a commotion begins among the CHIMPANZEES. They all run to the bars leaping and screaming. Prot breaks from the pack and lopes toward them. Taking the cue, all the OTHER PATIENTS start to run, too.

NAVARRO

(into walkie-talkie)

Uh-oh. Guys, I need some help up here!

The POLICE OFFICERS run toward the front of the group.

OFFICER #1

(shouting)

Okay, people, take it easy. The monkeys aren't going anywhere . . .

NAVARRO (running ahead)

Prot! Stop!

PROT ignores him and rushes toward the enclosure. The CHIMPANZEES are beside themselves. PROT climbs the outer wall and approaches the inner cage. He begins to make apelike sounds. The CHIMPANZEES quiet down immediately. One of them pokes a tentative finger through the bars. PROT takes the finger in one of his own. (**NB: This is the principal poster shot.**)

PROT

(lips protruding)

Mmmmmmmm. Ummm. Um! Roooooooo! (Etc.)

CHIMPANZEE #1

Ruuuuuuuup! Ruuuuuuuup! (Etc.)

As the conversation proceeds, the OFFICERS and STAFF stand watching, mystified. The PATIENTS jump, laugh, clap their hands. The OTHER CHIMPANZEES gather around prot, fingers poking through the cage. PROT touches every finger and says something to each of them.

FADE TO BLACK.

Near the end of the film prot visits the set of *The Late Show with David Letterman*:

71 INT. CBS STUDIOS—EVENING   71

Two smiling young ASSISTANT PRODUCERS escort PROT, POWELL, GISELLE, and NAVARRO to a corridor.

FIRST ASST. PRODUCER

Okay, I'm going to take Dr. Powell and Ms. Griffin to the Green Room. Sandra will escort prot and his "chaperone" to makeup.

PROT

See you later, doc.

POWELL

Uh– Break a leg!

PROT
(shaking his head)
You humans are such cards!

72 INT. GREEN ROOM—A MOMENT LATER   72

The FIRST ASST. PRODUCER escorts POWELL and GISELLE into the room.

ASST. PRODUCER

Here's your remote—your monitor's up there. We have coffee, doughnuts, chips, and there's wine and beer in the fridge. That's the bathroom. Is there anything else I can get for you?

POWELL and GISELLE stare up at the monitor. LETTERMAN (**David Letterman**) is talking with a STARLET. The volume is too low to hear the conversation, but she is obviously the quintessential "dumb blonde."

POWELL

Is the coffee decaffeinated?

ASST. PRODUCER

No, but I'll get you some.

POWELL

Never mind.

ASST. PRODUCER

Are you sure?

POWELL

I'm sure.

                              ASST. PRODUCER
It's really no trouble.

                                 POWELL
I'll just have a little of the regular.

                              ASST. PRODUCER
Well, if you change your mind, give me a buzz. There's your buzzer.

                                 POWELL
Thanks.

                              ASST. PRODUCER
                                 (exiting)
No problemo.

GISELLE stares at the monitor and stuffs a handful of potato chips into her mouth.

                                 GISELLE
Oh, I hope this isn't a disaster!

                                 POWELL
I just hope Rob doesn't wake up for a while.
                        (pouring coffee into a mug)
I'm going to regret this.
                                  (beat)
Want some coffee?

                                 GISELLE
Wait! Turn it up! Turn it up!

POWELL, spilling coffee, fumbles for the remote.

                                                              CUT TO:

73 INT. LETTERMAN SET—SAME   73

DAVID LETTERMAN sits behind his desk. The STARLET has made room for PROT.

                                LETTERMAN
Our next guest has come quite a way to be on the show tonight. A
thousand light-years, to be exact. Please welcome

(beat)
prot—a visitor from the planet K-PAX!

PROT comes from backstage wearing his dark glasses. He looks uncertainly at the hooting and clapping AUDIENCE. LETTERMAN offers a hand, which PROT shakes vigorously.

LETTERMAN

Welcome!

PROT

I will have a seat.

LETTERMAN
(chuckling, surprised)
Sure. Make yourself right at home.

PROT

I am a citizen of the universe. Wherever I am is home.

LETTERMAN

Well, welcome to this neck of the universe.
(checking notes)
Maybe you can answer a question that seems to plague a lot of us Earth people . . .

PROT

You have a lot of people to plague.

Chuckles from the AUDIENCE.

LETTERMAN
(grinning)
You may be right about that. But here's the question: Has Earth been visited by flying saucers?

PROT

No.

LETTERMAN
(when no elaboration comes)
How do you know that?

PROT

Alimentary, my dear canal. Travel between the stars in a saucer would be like hopping a trillion times around the Earth on a pogo stick.

LETTERMAN

(turning to AUDIENCE)

Is that in the Guinness Book of Records?

Laughter from the AUDIENCE.

LETTERMAN

So you're the only alien visitor we've had?

PROT

So far.

LETTERMAN

And that's because you travel on a beam of light.

PROT

That's one reason.

LETTERMAN

Sounds like a clean type of fuel. How long have K-PAXians been able to do this?

PROT

Only for a few billion years.

LETTERMAN

Only a few billion . . . So you're still working out the kinks?

PROT grins but says nothing.

LETTERMAN

Could you tell us a little about your home planet?

PROT

Sure.

The AUDIENCE titters.

LETTERMAN
(grinning broadly)

Great! Please do.

PROT
(dreamily)

K-PAX is a beautiful planet. Not like Earth, of course, with all its color and variety. But there are certain compensations . . .

LETTERMAN
(sipping from a mug)

Such as?

PROT

Well, we don't have any mosquitoes, for one thing.
(beat)
And no famines, no serious diseases, no wars . . .

LETTERMAN

You mean no one has destroyed your World Trade Center?

The AUDIENCE applauds politely.

PROT

We don't have trade centers of any kind. No *money* of any kind. Ergo, no graft, no greed, no corruption, no wealth, no poverty, no taxes . . .

LETTERMAN

No taxes? Sounds like my kind of place. What sort of work do you do there?

PROT

No one works on K-PAX.

LETTERMAN

So you're with a road crew?

AUDIENCE laughs.

PROT

I'm not with any crew. Work is when you do something you don't like. You don't call what you do "work," do you?

Hoots from the AUDIENCE. LETTERMAN mugs.

LETTERMAN
Well, I admit it beats cleaning latrines.

Laughter.

LETTERMAN (CONT'D)
So you got here on a beam of light.

PROT
You'd be surprised how much energy there is in a beam of light.

LETTERMAN
You wouldn't want to give us a little demo of that, would you?

PROT
Why not?

PROT stands, takes a little flashlight and mirror from a jacket pocket, holds the mirror at arm's length in his left hand, shines the light on it, and immediately disappears.

The AUDIENCE gasps.

BACK TO:

GREEN ROOM.

GISELLE
Dr. P! He did it!

POWELL
(shaken)
It must be some kind of trick . . .

The CAMERA pans around crazily looking for PROT, finally finds him in front of the microphone reserved for standup comics. He puts away the flashlight and mirror, and pulls MILTON'S funny hat from another pocket.

BACK TO:

SET.

PROT
(sticking the hat on his head)
Good evening, ladies and germs.

The AUDIENCE is still murmuring.

PROT (in the voice of W. C. Fields)
Man goes into a bar, has a few drinks, falls asleep. While he's dozing, someone rubs limburger cheese all over his upper lip. Man wakes up, sniffs, goes outside, sniffs some more, comes back in. "'s no use" he says. "Whole damn world shtinks!"

The AUDIENCE doesn't laugh.

PROT
Am I going too slow for you folks? Who is your leader? All right, how about this one:
(in the voice of Cary Grant):
Who are the first to line up for wars? To pull the executioner's switch? And to murder their fellow beings because they taste good? Give up? The pro-lifers!

No laughter.

PROT
(chin on hand à la Jack Benny)
Well!

After a beat, PROT shrugs and returns to his seat.

LETTERMAN
(soberly)
How in the world did you do that?

PROT
I learned that routine from one of the patients at the hospital.

LETTERMAN
No, I mean: how did you get from here over to there?

The band begins a soft rendition of "Two Different Worlds."

PROT
Didn't we already discuss that?

The music comes up.

LETTERMAN
Don't go 'way, folks—we'll be right back!

CUT TO:

74 INT. WARD TWO—SAME   74

All the PATIENTS are crowded around the TV room, cheering, as the scene fades to a commercial message. BETTY and other STAFF laugh/cry, too. MANUEL nods confidently.

CUT TO:

75 INT. BECKER HOME—SAME   75

BECKER sits in front of a TV set with a beer, his big toe bandaged, leg propped on a footstool. His mouth has fallen open.

CUT TO:

76 INT. POWELL HOME—SAME   76

RACHEL laughs. The GIRLS jump up and down, hooting.

BACK TO:

GREEN ROOM.

A commercial is playing on the monitor. The HOSPITAL'S 800 number is superimposed at the bottom of the screen.

GISELLE
Now do you believe him, Dr. P?

POWELL, his eyes glued to the screen, says nothing.

BACK TO:

LETTERMAN SET.

LETTERMAN holds a SMALL DOG on his desk.

LETTERMAN
My spies tell me that you can talk to animals. Is that right?

PROT
So could you if you wanted to badly enough.

The dog barks. PROT barks back.

LETTERMAN
What's he saying?

PROT
He's saying he needs to take a [bleep].

As if on cue, the DOG crouches and defecates. The audience, now on firmer ground, roars.

LETTERMAN
(holding the dog with one hand, pinching his nose with the other)
Oh, God! And I thought mine was bad! OH MY! WILL SOMEONE PLEASE TAKE THIS ANIMAL AWAY?

The ASSISTANT PRODUCER runs out with a roll of paper towels and a can of air freshener. He picks up the mess, sprays the air, grabs the dog, and exits. The AUDIENCE is still howling.

LETTERMAN (CONT'D)
Ah, that's better. *Much* better! Whew! Okay! We've established here that our guest, prot, can talk to animals. Can we roll the slo-mo now?

BACK TO:

GREEN ROOM.

On the monitor, prot's "disappearing act" is re-run in slow motion.

LETTERMAN (V.O.)
Can you slow that down some more?

The tape moves frame by frame. Prot still disappears.

After the show it's not prot who returns to the Green Room, but Robert Porter. The film ends with Milton flying around the hospital lawn and Robert helping Powell bury the ashes of Dr. Villers and her husband. Prot doesn't make another appearance, though the patients know he'll be back one more time.

Want to see this movie? Me, too.

Karen's father, Gordon Schultz, died in August, 2002, in a nursing home at the age of ninety-two. In one of our last meetings, in an attempt to lighten the tension my leaving the sciences (i.e., quitting a good job) had created, I said, "Lefty, you never thought I'd amount to anything, did you?" He looked shocked, then began to quiver, and finally to laugh heartily. He knew exactly what I was getting at. Whatever his beliefs and prejudices, he was a very good father-in-law.

I finished the script in October and sent queries to Universal, Larry Gordon, Kevin Spacey, and Jeff Bridges (who had expressed a strong interest in making a sequel from the beginning). Universal didn't even want to look at it, but the others requested that I send them a copy of the script.

On Oct. 21, 2002, Michael Levy (another associate of Larry Gordon's) called me. "It's great," he told me, "everything's great, but we don't think Universal wants to make the sequel." I asked him if there were any other options. He said he would find out.

Levy called back on Oct. 29: he had spoken with Jeff Daitch. "Any negotiations would have to involve Universal Pictures," he asserted. "No other studio would want to proceed without the rights to *K-PAX III*." I told him I would speak to Bob Harris.

Bob told me this was a common situation in Hollywood. If another studio wants to make *K-PAX II*, they can do it and negotiate later for *III*. He said he would explain this to Michael Levy. When he did so, Levy told him he would speak again to Larry Gordon.

Levy called me back a couple of days later: Larry respectfully declines. He's happy with *K-PAX* and its ending, and wouldn't want to revisit the project.

I e-mailed Jeff Bridges: If Kevin is interested, I asked him, would you consider doing the sequel with another studio? He sent back: "I'd be willing to explore it."

I reported this to Bernie Morris, whose assistant sent me a note a few weeks later: Kevin is traveling in Europe and may have misplaced the screenplay. Could you send another copy?

In February, 2003, Spacey finally decided not to make the sequel. He gave no reason, but he had just taken over as director of London's Old Vic, and was involved in a couple of other movie projects as well. Or perhaps he hated the script.

In any case, over the next few months I tried several other producers and studios in the U.S., Britain, France, and Poland. I also called Jeff Daitch and offered him both *II* and *III*, which would have solved the problem of rights to a *second* sequel. He seemed quite interested, said he would get back to me. The suits, however, were not. I even tried (through Bob Harris) to find an agent. No one saw any potential in the project even if the rights to *K-PAX III* could be obtained.

Daitch soon left Universal. Probably a coincidence.

A final note: Bob Colesberry died during heart surgery on Feb. 17, 2004. He was a fine producer and a good man.

THE LAWSUIT

Less than two weeks after the opening of the film version of *K-PAX*, Bob informed me that lawyers for Jason Laskay had "asserted a claim" against the movie, charging plagiarism of his script for *Man Facing Southeast*, to which he had apparently obtained North American rights from the Argentinean writer/director Eliseo Subiela.

St. Martin's Press offered to handle my defense, without charge, through their associated law firm in Los Angeles, Sidley Austin Brown & Wood. But there was a catch: according to a letter agreement sent to me for signature, "St. Martin's will retain control of the conduct of the defense (subject to consultation with you with respect to issues that directly affect your interests). *Without limiting the generality of the above, St. Martin's will have the sole right to make decisions concerning settlement* (emphasis mine). This meant that SMP could settle out of court with Laskay, leaving a clear implication of guilt, which I could do nothing about. If it came to that, however, I would be able to crawl out from under their legal umbrella and hire my own litigating attorney. Bob said he would try to clarify SMP's position, and advised me to hold off signing the letter until he did so.

In a Feb. 14th, 2002 conference call, I spoke with Gail Title, Esq., who was representing Universal Pictures in court; an associate of hers, Kristen Holland; and Bob Harris. Some interesting revelations came out of that conference. For example, Laskay was claiming that Maia Gregory had told him, in a telephone conversation, that I had adapted *K-PAX* from *Man Facing Southeast*! (One wonders whether she was demanding 15% of any monetary settlement.) The other was that it was going to be a long haul: there had already been contact with lawyers for the original director—if Laskay lost, Subiela would probably sue everyone as well. Ms. Title wanted me to send *everything* to her: all my unpublished manuscripts, correspondence, notes, diaries, etc. prior to writing *K-PAX* (to show the kinds of themes I had been exploring for years, even before *MFSE* came about). Karen and I spent the rest of the day photocopying everything in my cabinets, and we sent off forty-two pounds of documents on the next.

In late March, Bob reported that Universal had asked the court for a summary judgment, and this was granted. The judge indicated there was some missing documentation, and offered Laskay a chance to amend his claim. On the appointed day, his lawyers didn't show up! The case was "dismissed without prejudice," though

Laskay was given ten days to refile, which he did. Universal argued that the documents supplied by the plaintiff had no connection to the original film (*MFSE*). Another motion to dismiss; a decision was due on June 10. Bob called again on the 19th: the judge threw out the claim again, but allowed Laskay to take depositions so that he could demonstrate clear title to the rights for *MFSE*. If he were able to do this, I would be subpoenaed. No problem: I was eager to have my day in court. But I heard nothing more about the case for another year.

It turned out that Laskay had filed a similar lawsuit in 1997 against the principals involved with the film *Don Juan DeMarco*, which is also unrelated to *Man Facing Southeast* except that, like *K-PAX*, the main characters are a psychiatrist and a mental patient. I was encouraged to learn that the case against *Don Juan* had been thrown out in 1999 and Laskay had been fined $150,000 for wasting the court's time.

In a maneuver worthy of a modern-day celebrity, Laskay went to the Internet to appeal to his supporters, if any, to write to the judge to support his claim! I don't know if any such letters came forth, but it didn't help him in this case. Nor do I know whether he (or Maia Gregory) got any money in a settlement with Universal Pictures. But on April 2, 2003, he withdrew his lawsuit against me. Except for a few phone calls to Bob Harris, it didn't cost me anything. In fact, if anyone buys this memoir, I might come out ahead.

Unless, of course, Mr. Subiela decides to try his luck. . . .

K-PAX ONSTAGE, PART 2

In September of 2002, while I was on Grand Manan working on the movie sequel, another offer to do a stage version arrived, this time from a theater in Shaw (near Manchester), England. I asked the producer, Jason Sharp, for details. He was prepared to offer a modest ($1500) license fee for a two-week run. I checked the theater's website (*www.playhouse2.com*) and was impressed: they were doing a number of interesting productions that season (2002-2003), all in a beautiful 160-seat theater.

Flushed with the fun I was having adapting my own novel to the screen, I e-mailed a reply setting out the conditions: okay, but I will write the adaptation and play "Dr. Brewer" in the stage production. I didn't expect him to agree, and I had my hands full anyway with a screenplay already underway and plans for a fourth novel in the *K-PAX* series. But he did, and he wanted to stage it the following September-October, a year from the inquiry. I warned him that Universal Pictures might try to delay or prohibit it. He wasn't deterred. After a number of other details were worked out I showed Jason's offer to Bob Harris, who called Mark Torpoco at Universal to determine whether, since the film had come out over a year before, UP still cared about "matching" any offer for a stage adaptation. They did. I requested a formal offer in writing from Jason and forwarded it to Universal on Nov. 11. This time there was no objection, so I started adapting *K-PAX* for the stage.

There were twelve characters and two acts. The first ended when prot informed Dr. Brewer that he would soon be leaving the Earth; the second began with Howie strangling Ernie almost to death. The scenes were set in Brewer's office, in Ward Two, and in the staff conference room. Between the scenes were several "entr'actes," in which the characters, one at a time, spoke directly to the audience.

In January, 2003, I sent the first draft off to Jason and director Steve Bennett, who was quite enthusiastic about the author's playing one of the two lead roles in the play (though probably not as excited as the author). In the meantime, Karen and I went to France and Poland to launch the publication of *K-PAX II* in those countries. The Paris trip turned out about as expected: we met the staff at Éditions l'Archipel; there was a party to which several writers, radio personalities, reviewers, and translators were invited; and I did a reading at W.H. Smith, an English-language bookstore, for eight or nine people. It was a pleasant visit, but not out of the ordinary.

Poland was an entirely different story. From the moment we arrived we were treated like celebrities. *K-PAX*, published by Znak in Cracow, had been a big hit and *K-PAX II* was already high on the bestseller lists. We visited five cities, where discussions of the books were attended by fifty to two hundred people, with long lines for autographs. There were also several radio and television appearances (one for a *nationwide* interview program), and an organized exchange of ideas over the Internet. My impression, based on the questions I fielded (translated by the wonderfully capable Maria Gardziel, who, with her husband Andrzej, had also translated the books), was that the Polish people were just coming out from under communism and were enthusiastically considering all kinds of brave new worlds. Some of the questions were about psychiatry (these were usually taken by Andrzej, who is a psychiatrist). It seemed to us that mental illness was still languishing in the shadow of the Dark Ages in Poland, and audiences were eager to know whether things were different in the West.

Whatever the reasons for the books' popularity, it was quite gratifying to be greeted by an enthusiastic audience at every stop. And the food was excellent, too. I don't know whether I'd like to live there, but Poland is a wonderful place to visit.

The downside to the trip, however, was the space shuttle Columbia disaster, the third major tragedy in the U.S.'s manned space program, and yet another example of cost-cutting and shoddy work by the National Aeronautics and Space Administration. I wondered when the American people were going to cry, "Enough!"

Shortly after our return to New York, Znak obtained the rights (from Bloomsbury) to publish *K-PAX III* in Poland. Since everything seemed to be going so well there, I sent the house a copy of "The Boy Who Spoke with God," and planned to send a few of my unpublished novels later on. Without warning or explanation, however, *K-PAX II* suddenly disappeared from Polish bookstores. Not long thereafter, despite having paid for the right to publish it, Znak decided not to release *K-PAX III*. Since both *K-PAX* and *K-PAX II* were bestsellers, it couldn't be for economic reasons. Ninety-five percent of Poland's citizens are Catholic; did someone finally come to realize that prot has little use for organized religion? Or had the house perhaps been frightened by the appearance of God in "The Boy . . ."? The answer remains a mystery not only to me, but to the Gardziels and hundreds of Polish fans, who keep writing to me asking when and where they can find the third book in the trilogy (it will be published in 2006 by Ksiaznica).

In March, 2003, after considering Steve Bennett's comments about the stage adaptation, I sent the second draft to him and prepared to fly to Manchester right after Labor Day for rehearsals. That was the month the G.W. Bush Administration decided to invade Iraq *because it harbored "weapons of mass destruction."* This operation was wrong for several reasons (poor intelligence being only one), but the main logical fault, which the media have ignored in their obsession with televising the bombs annihilating their targets, is that this isn't a good reason to attack another country. *Many* countries have WMD's, including England, France, Russia, and several others— should we go after them, too? Worse, the *United States* has more of them than all the other countries put together. Should the rest of the world invade *us*? Worst of all, why hasn't anyone asked these questions?

Top left: Television interview, Torun.
Middle left: Internet dialogue, Cracow.
Top right: Book signing, Wroclaw. Co-translator Andrzej Gardziel is at my left.
Bottom left: part of interview audience, Cracow.
Bottom right: newspaper interview, Warsaw. Co-translator Maria Gardziel
is at my left.

In April I started to feel some lower abdominal pain whenever I coughed or sneezed. A couple of weeks later, after returning from a jog, I discovered that there was some numbness in the same area. After forty-eight years of putting it off, it was time to get the hernia repaired.

I heard nothing from Steve or Jason for weeks. Finally, on May 21st, there came disheartening letters from both of them: Steve had been badly injured in a car accident and, as if that weren't enough, his fiancée had become seriously ill and required round-the-clock care. The play would have to be postponed for at least a year.

The hernia surgery took place on May 29. I had no trepidation whatever about the procedure, which was done with a local anesthetic and a tranquilizer, Versed. The surgeon told me later that I had enjoyed "quite a conversation" with the anesthesiologist, but I remember nothing about it; somehow, the latter drug doesn't allow memories to form. I'm still amazed by that experience: if you don't remember something, did it happen? Perhaps this is what death is like . . . .

In July my good friend and neighbor (and author of the powerful play *I Can Cry*), Miri Ben-Shalom, arranged a staged reading of my adaptation on Oct. 26 at the Genesius Guild, a non-profit organization which supports and promotes new playwrights. The purpose of the performance was to give the directors of the group a chance to determine whether they might want to do a later staging. I would be reading the part of Dr. Brewer.

In August we learned that Gregory Hines had died of cancer in California. He was invariably bright and pleasant, as well as a great dancer and actor, and our neighborhood (and the world) is much poorer for his untimely departure.

On Sept. 24th, again on Grand Manan, there came another e-mail query about a stage version of *K-PAX*, this one from a London fringe theater group called Act Provocateur, Intl. They were thinking of adapting their own production, but readily agreed to consider my finished script, as well as my coming to perform in the play, at least for the opening nights. If successful, they wanted to take the play to the 2004 Edinburgh Fringe Festival.

I sent them the adaptation I had written for the Shaw group. Too many characters and too many sets, said their director, Victor Sobchak. I told him I would try to come up with a smaller version by the end of November.

By then I had begun to prepare for the reading in New York. Much to my dismay, I discovered that I couldn't be both an actor and a writer. Learning lines—even my own—took far too much time. I gave up the idea of performing (except for the New York reading) and decided to stick to writing. The presentation went well, however, and the Genesius Guild expressed an interest in workshopping the play for staging it the following summer. Not long after that, unfortunately, this benevolent organization, like many others that have tried to support the arts in America, closed its doors for lack of funds.

On Dec. 1, 2003, I sent the revised script (eight characters, two sets) to Act Provocateur. Victor had some additional minor suggestions, and I e-mailed him the "final" version on Jan. 14. By then I had written to Universal Pictures, which had no objection to AP's doing the play.

Karen and I were invited to London for the Feb. 11 opening, air fare and accommodations to be paid for by the sponsor with the help of my British publisher, Bloomsbury.

The opening was enthusiastically received, the play ran for three weeks, and there were a couple of reviews, both good. It was soon accepted for the Edinburgh Fringe Festival and, in August, we went there as well. Unfortunately, the venue required that the play be cut from a hundred and twenty minutes, including intermission, down to sixty without a break. A skeleton of its former self, it was not a great success in Scotland.

But by this time I had already started another novel (working title: *fled: Part IV of the K-PAX saga*).

K-PAX IV

I have always wondered why light travels at 300,000 km/sec., and not some other speed, and why it flies out in all direction from a given energy source. Just before starting to write *K-PAX IV*, I read a book that suggested the speed of light is not constant, but has varied during the evolution of the universe. It suddenly occurred to me that perhaps light travels at the speed it does because that is the rate of expansion of the universe, i.e., the photons simply go along for the ride.

In March, 2003, I posted this hypothesis both on my website and on one called www.space-talk.com:

ON THE SPEED OF LIGHT AND THE EXPANSION OF THE UNIVERSE

In his new book, *Faster than the Speed of Light*, Dr. Joao Magueijo suggests that his variable speed of light (VSL) theory explains many of the mysteries of the Big Bang universe in much the same way as does Alan Guth's inflation (variable expansion rate of the universe) theory. I suggest that both are variations on the same theme, namely, that the speed of light is a direct function of the expansion of the universe. That is, the speed of light in the early universe varied *because* of inflation and, furthermore, it varies today in intimate proportion to the present expansion rate. To put it another way, **light travels because the universe is expanding.**

The principal ramification of this hypothesis is that photons do not *travel* through space-time—they are dragged along *with* it. According to this proposal, the speed of light (and other electromagnetic radiation) through space is an illusion; it is, in fact, 0 km/sec. It is the universe which is expanding at the present rate of 300 kkm/sec., and taking these massless wave/particles with it.

I suggest further that objects with mass are *not* pulled along at the same rate by the expansion. Indeed, such objects resist this "force," and therefore tend to slow down the universe's expansion rate. This can be observed, for example, in the effect of celestial objects on the path of photons in space-time and, in particular, the gravitational effect of black holes. Thus, the latter do not prevent light from escaping them; they prevent space-time itself from expanding around them.

It follows also from this proposal that if the expansion rate of the universe is increasing, we will eventually be able to see objects that we cannot now see and, conversely, if the universe is slowing down, that such objects will twinkle out. If the expansion rate becomes zero, and therefore photons stop moving with space-time, we will be able to see nothing at all. This concept is in direct opposition to predictions currently associated with the rate of expansion of the universe. The correct interpretation is experimentally verifiable by currently available methods.

With this proposal in mind, I began writing *fled: Part IV of the K-PAX saga.*
At the end of part III of the *K-PAX trilogy,* prot departs for his home planet vowing never to return to Earth. But his world is loaded with denizens of various other species. I decided to bring one of the orfs (a progenitor of prot's species, the dremers) for a visit:

PROLOGUE

This book can be understood and enjoyed by those who have not yet read *K-PAX* (1995), *K-PAX II: On a Beam of Light* (2001), and *K-PAX III: The Worlds of Prot* (2002). To fully appreciate the context, however, I urge you to read this series prior to, or immediately after, reading *fled.*

The aforementioned trilogy describes the appearance, in 1990, of a man who claimed to have arrived "on a beam of light," from the planet K-PAX, some 7000 light-years from Earth in the constellation Lyra, and records my attempts, as a staff psychiatrist at the Manhattan Psychiatric Institute, to determine his true origins and treat this apparent delusion, which continued until the time of his "departure" in 1997.

For those of you who *have* read the *K-PAX* books, it should be mentioned at the outset that "prot" makes no further appearance in the present work. This should come as no surprise, as he himself stated that he would not be making a return trip to Earth.

Six months after prot's departure I retired, and my wife and I moved out of the suburbs and into a lovely cedar-shingled home in the Adirondack Mountains in upstate New York. For the past several years we have enjoyed all the things we would have liked to do but never had time for—travel, reading, gardening, socializing with family and friends. I even took up flying, a hobby I enjoy very much (to the horror of my son Fred), but which turned out to be far more expensive that I had imagined. (Q: What makes an airplane fly? A: Money.) And, owing, no doubt, to prot's influence, astronomy. For a retirement present, Karen gave me a four-inch reflecting telescope, and over the past several years I have become quite familiar with the planets, stars, and nearby galaxies that surround us. But my interest in the stars led me to wonder about the origins and meaning of it all, and the wonders of cosmology itself absorb most of my reading time.

The entire family, incidentally, is doing fine. Karen is totally free of cancer cells and is feeling better than ever. Abby is now the mother of college men, Rain into computers, and Star wants to be an actor, like his uncle Fred. The latter has found a niche in Broadway musicals, especially after his long-running success in *Les Misérable*, and has appeared in two major films as well. Jennifer is the busiest of the brood, intimately involved in the testing of the first vaccine against AIDS, though Will runs a close second as the newest member of the psychiatric staff at MPI, and he loves to discuss his patients with me as do I, of course, with him. He even takes my advice from time to time! I have been told that he looks a lot like me, and I suppose that's why we have children: to do it all over again, in a sort of vague and distant way. (On the other hand, I've also been advised that everyone with a beard looks a lot like me.) I should also mention that we have another member of the family, this time a mixed-breed dog obtained a few years ago from the local animal shelter. Flower is five now, in the prime of her life, and she's all dog, a clumsy, hilarious, canine oaf, whom we love dearly.

As an aside, by the way, the film version of *K-PAX* didn't do as well at the box-office as had been expected and, as of this writing, a movie sequel is still up in the air. There's a ray of hope in the strong video sales and rentals, however, and as prot pointed out on numerous occasions, anything is possible. Whatever happens, I think the movie was a good adaptation of prot's story, and brilliantly played by both Kevin Spacey and Jeff Bridges (as well as the rest of the cast). Karen and I were privileged to meet them during the filming (look for me at the end of the "bluebird" scene), and both are fine gentlemen as well as great actors.

But I digress. The point is that when prot departed the Earth at the end of '97 I was pretty sure we would hear no more about K-PAX, certainly not in my lifetime, and especially not from an entirely different denizen of that faraway planet.

As usual, where alien visitors are concerned, I was wrong.

CHAPTER ONE

When she arrived I was in my study answering some e-mail. There was a knock on the back door. Actually it was more like someone was banging on it. Flower ran from the room, barking as usual (she even barks at falling leaves). Karen was out doing some shopping, and I thought it was probably her standing at the door, her arms full of grocery bags. I left a note unfinished and hurried to open it. But when I looked through the window in the upper part of the door I saw something so strange, so unbelievable, that I froze. In fact, I attributed the apparition to some mushrooms I had eaten the previous evening, which sometimes make me a feel a little peculiar.

The hairy creature standing outside smiled grotesquely in at me. I stared back. Finally she yelled, over Flower's barking, "I have a message from prot."

Still stunned, I opened the door a crack. That was all she needed. She pushed her way into the kitchen and looked around with interest, as if we weren't even there. Flower, for her part, gave her a good sniffing and ran to get a toy to play with, as she does for every visitor we have. I couldn't help but notice that this one was wearing nothing. Finally she looked at me with her huge black eyes and said, "Prot told me you would put me up."

I managed to squeak, "Put you up?"

"That's what he said. It means you will give me food and some space in your dwelling for a while."

"I *know* what it means."

"Well?"

"All right, all right—I'm thinking about it." She was literally blanketed with hair. Except for her face, and even that was quite fuzzy. "Are you from K-PAX?"

"Of *course* I'm from K-PAX. Otherwise I wouldn't know prot, would I?"

Despite her hirsute appearance and somewhat belligerent manner, I found myself drawn into the conversation whether I liked it or not. Apparently K-PAXians of whatever nature had this effect on people. "Not necessarily. You could have met him on one of the other planets he has visited."

Flower came back with her squeaky toy, which this—being—grabbed and tossed back into the living room. "Not likely. He's retired from traveling. Says he's seen enough."

"So he sent you."

"I didn't say he sent me. I said he sent a message."

At this point Karen drove up. I told our new guest to make herself at home, that I would be right back, explaining, "I have to help my wife with the groceries." Of course I wanted to prepare her for what she would find inside. Our visitor gazed out the window with curiosity—evidently she had never seen anything as primitive as a motor vehicle before—but she nodded and wandered on into the house, Flower following hopefully with her toy.

I ran outside. Karen was already opening the car door. "Just a minute," I yelled.

"What? What's the matter?"

"There's something I need to tell you."

She got out of the car. "Fine, but help me with the groceries first, will you?"

"We have another visitor from K-PAX."

She seemed amused. "Really? Who is it this time—prot's mother?"

"She's not related to prot, as far as I know. I don't think she's even the same species."

"No kidding! Well, help me with these bags and let's go in and meet her." I should mention here that nothing on Earth fazes my wife. Even something from a distant galaxy, forty feet tall and with seventeen eyes, would have to work hard at it.

I grabbed a couple of sacks and started toward the back door. There was no point in trying to describe the alien creature. She would see her soon enough.

We set the bags down on the kitchen cabinet. Karen looked around. "Well, where is she?"

"She must be in one of the other rooms."

"This isn't one of your mushroom dreams, is it?"

"I have a feeling I'm going to wish it were."

At that point our visitor reappeared. "Why do you need all those rooms?" she demanded.

"Because we have a big family."

"Oh, yes. Prot told me about your attachment to 'families.' Very peculiar, don't you think?"

My wife was still unfazed. "What should we call you?"

"Call me ishmael."

Neither of us responded.

The ape-like creature burst into laughter. "He *said* you had no sense of humor! Actually, my name is "fled."

We stared some more.

"You were expecting someone else?"

Karen said, "We weren't really expecting anyone. But please—sit down. Are you hungry? Has Gene shown you the facilities?"

"No, but if you mean toilets, I found three of them. Isn't one enough? And yes, I'm very hungry. I haven't eaten in months. *Your* months, of course."

"Of course," I murmured dismally. I was already contemplating a long period of disruption, confusion, and possibly even debacle. I excused myself to make use of the facilities.

*　　*　　*

While I was sitting there I ran over in my mind some of the ramifications of what I had just seen. K-PAXians seemed to sleep wherever they found themselves and eat whatever was around. What did she mean by our "putting her up"? Would she want a room of her own or, since it was spring and already growing warm, would she prefer to sleep outside in a tree? What did her species (whatever it was) eat, anyway? Could we get her to wear clothes, and if so, would she look as silly as a performing chimpanzee? But if not, would she be subject to stares and ridicule for going around naked?

More importantly, perhaps: why did she come here? How long was she planning to stay? I remembered her opening statement: "I have a message from prot." What was the message—another attempt to get *Homo sapiens* to behave ourselves? No, that was wrong; prot never made such an appeal. In fact, he didn't seem to care much what happened to us. He was, he said, merely making observations about the Earth (see "Prot's Report to K-PAX" in *K-PAX: The Trilogy*, Bloomsbury, London, 2003).

It briefly occurred to me to wonder how we would know that she really came from K-PAX. But of course she couldn't have come from *here*—we have no talking (in the usual sense) apes on this planet, as far as I know. I laughed, hollowly to be sure; I was going around in the same circle that I had traveled with prot fifteen years earlier. While reaching for the toilet paper, I came to an understanding with myself. This time I wouldn't fight it. I would just accept her statements at face value and see what came of them.

When I got back to the kitchen our unannounced guest was digging into a very large bowl of uncooked kidney beans. Not with her hairy fingers, but with protruding lips. She was obviously enjoying them, washing them down loudly with swigs of apple juice. Flower sat beside her chair patiently waiting for something to fall, as if this—ape?—had lived here all her life.

While I waited for her to finish, Karen filled me in on what I had missed. Fled had told her that Robert and Giselle were as happy as gonks (clamlike beings), and that "baby" Gene, nearly nine years old (Earth years, of course), was becoming, like his father, quite an expert on K-PAXian flora and fauna. Oxeye, too, was still fit and energetic at fourteen, having a whole planet to run around in. He even had a playmate, another Dalmatian prot had apparently rescued from a pound "seven thousand jarts west of here." Gene, himself, had a girlfriend about his age, formerly from Ukraine. Bess was fine, too, though fled didn't see her much—our former psychotic depressive spent much of her time visiting other worlds. As a retired psychiatrist I was tempted to conclude that this was her attempt to make up for her childhood years tied to the family tenement apartment cleaning and cooking for her parents and siblings. But who knows anything about the mind, human or otherwise? During prot's visit it became painfully obvious to me that I certainly didn't.

Indeed, all the hundred beings he had taken back with him to K-PAX were doing very well. There was a little homesickness, of course, but not one person (mammal, insect, whatever) had requested a return visit to Earth. Since *K-PAX III* was published, I've had literally thousands of e-mail messages requesting a placement on the passenger list for the next trip to that idyllic planet. Thus, it occurred to me to ask fled whether she planned to take anyone back with her if and when she returned. When she finally finished crunching the bowl of beans, I did so.

She sat back and—you guessed it—burped loudly, as though she were in some bad movie. She replied to my question before I could ask it. "Yes, I will definitely be going back to K-PAX. And when I do, I will be taking 100,000 of your beings with me. If that many people want to go, of course."

I paused to let that sink in. "Did you say 100,000? And did you say *people*? Not giraffes or turtles?"

"Prot told me your hearing was going. I repeat for the deaf among us: I can take 100,000 people back with me when I go."

"But– But how?"

"Well, I'm happy to see that you're still curious about math and science, gino. Prot was afraid you'd turn into a robot like most sapiens. It's simple, really. All I need is a place big enough to hold everyone.

"You mean . . . a football stadium or something like that?"

"That would do nicely. The dimensions have already been programmed. It's just a matter of setting a time."

"And may I ask when you might set that date?"

"Sure. Why not?"

"Well, what date have you selected?"

I have reserved six windows for the trip, each one month apart. We'll leave on the next opening after all the arrangements are made. The first one is a month from now. Do you think we can gather together everyone who wants to go by then?"

We? I thought. "I haven't a clue," I said, rather fatalistically, I suppose.

At this point the telephone rang. Karen answered it. It was Will, just checking up on us on a Saturday morning in May. It suddenly occurred to me that perhaps fled would be comfortable living in the Institute while she was on Earth. We could keep an eye on her there, she would be safe, there would be food and a place to sleep, and patients who might be delighted to learn that the "legend of K-PAX" had come true again at last, though none of them had ever doubted it would.

"Sure," fled said. "I'll stay where prot did when he was here."

But I hadn't said anything yet. "You— You can read minds?"

"Of course."

"But prot couldn't do that, as far as I know."

"Well, don't tell him I said this, but we trods are a little more advanced in some ways than the dremers. Being hairless is of very little advantage in the brains department."

Very slowly I got up and took the receiver. "Will," I said, probably a bit too desperately, "How would you like a new patient?"

*   *   *

Fled sat in the front seat with me as we drove into the city. She laughed heartily when we started out, presumably at the primitive type of conveyance she was riding in. "You just sit here in this little room, is that it? And the thing moves along by itself on those little round feet? Weird!"

"Well," I corrrected her, "it's not that simple." I started to explain how a car operates, but found that I had forgotten most of what I had learned in driver's ed half a century ago. I did mention, however, that the energy came from the oxidation of refined hydrocarbons, and somehow this turns the driveshaft and, finally, through a system of gears, the "feet."

She laughed again. "And I suppose one of your 'airplanes' works the same way?"

"Uh, not exactly. The fuel part is similar, but the propeller or jet engine pulls the plane forward."

"So what makes it fly?"

I started to tell her, but she interrupted: "Besides money, of course."

"It has something to do with the shape of the wings. Actually, there are a couple of different theories on that . . . ."

When we merged into traffic on the interstate, I glanced over at the passenger in the pickup truck passing us on our left. I couldn't hear anything, but I could see that she was screaming. She turned toward the driver and suddenly the truck accelerated to about 90 mph and pulled away from us. Fled laughed again.

I started again to explain how the shape of the wings lifts a plane into the air. "Never mind," she said. "I get it." After a moment she added, "One day I'll take you for a ride in the sky with me."

A chill shot up my spine. On the one hand, I thought, it might be fun. On the other, what effect would that have on the anatomy of a sixty-seven-year-old human? I realized that Karen would go with her in a heartbeat.

"Her, too," fled promised.

Not knowing whether I'd ever have a chance like this again, I brought up some of the questions I had about cosmology—if the universe recycles over and over again, where did it come from in the first place, and when would the reverse process begin? And can quantum theory and general relativity ever be reconciled?

She yawned. "That stuff doesn't interest me."

Thoroughly disappointed, I asked her what did.

"The Earth."

"Why the Earth?"

"Who knows? I'm not a shrink." She glanced at me accusingly before continuing. "Some of your people study the history of other countries, right? I'm interested in the history of other PLANETS."

"So why are you planning to take 100,000 of us back to K-PAX with you? To study us?"

"Not at all. Prot told me that most of your beings want to get off this WORLD. I thought: what the hey? As long as I was here, I'd try to help some of them out."

"So what sorts of things do you want to know about the Earth?"

"For one thing, why are so many of you trying to kill it?"

Oh, God, I thought. Here we go again. "Well, if that's the case," I argued, "aren't you afraid that if you took some of us back with you, we'd kill K-PAX, too?"

"Ah. Perhaps I should explain that this won't just be a lottery. I'm only taking back those who haven't been carried away by the fear that keeps most of you in the grip of the fernads among you."

"Fernads?"

"You could translate that as, 'assholes.' Or," she added with a pleasant grin (it was more like a grimace), "'anal orifices,' if you prefer."

"Ah." While she gazed at the suburban landscape, I thought: How would she determine whether each of the people she planned to take agreed with her philosophy?

"Well, you can eliminate anyone with a cell phone in his ear, for example."
Instinctively I felt my jacket pocket, wishing I had turned mine off. When I glanced
at fled, I found her grinning toothily.

We "talked" on about prot and Robert and Giselle, and I learned that my
namesake had a little sister now. "That must be quite a rarity on K-PAX," I pointed
out. "Given your reluctance to have—uh—sexual relations."

"Oh, that only applies to the dremers. And a few other species. The rest of us
can't get enough of it."

I changed the subject. "When you got here, you said you had 'a message from
prot.' What was it?"

"Nine suggestions."

"*Nine?*"

"Nine."

"What are they?"

"Prot advised me not to tell you until later."

"Why not?"

"He thinks I should tell everyone at the same time."

"You mean go the UN? Something like that?"

"Something like that."

"That's awfully science fiction, don't you think?"

"Except in sci-fi they never make it to the UN."

The city of New York came suddenly into view. "Whoa!" she exclaimed. "It's
just like prot said. Except that the world trade center is gone now, of course."

"Of course," I responded helplessly.

*   *   *

When we got to the hospital I parked right in front of the building and
hustled fled past the gate and inside as quickly as possible. The guard's mouth was
still open when we hurried through the big front door.

Fled was far more outgoing than prot had ever been. She waved and smiled (at
least I think it was a smile) at everyone milling on the lawn or in the lounge. A few
of the patients waved back, but even they seemed confused by what they had just
seen. A couple of them tried to follow us upstairs, but I summoned a bug-eyed
nurse to take them back to what they had been doing.

I had warned Goldfarb that we were coming, but even she was shocked by the
appearance of our guest. Nevertheless, she managed to return fled's grimace and
offered a hand, which our newest visitor took. Evidently she had been coached by
prot on the proper protocol with respect to introductions.

After we had all sat down, and fled was staring at everything around her, I put
it right to Virginia: did she have someone to look after prot's K-PAXian friend? I

presumed Will had spoken to her about this. By now she had regained her composure, and she smiled broadly as she replied, "I was thinking *you* might look after fled."

It hadn't even occurred to me that she would come up with this nutty idea, and I told her so. I protested further that I was retired, and didn't even live close to the city anymore. Goldfarb wasn't daunted. She never is. "That's precisely it. No one on the staff has room for another patient. You do, and you come in once or twice a week anyway. Why not do something useful while you're here?"

"What about—?"

"Your son has more than he can handle. So does Thorstein and Chang and Menninger and Rothstein and Rudqvist and Roberts. We have more patients than we've ever had, and none of them seems to want to leave. They're all waiting for someone from K-PAX to come and get them. And who knows more about alien visitors than you do?"

My last feeble defense: "I don't have an examining room."

"You can use mine. It has a separate entrance and I don't have that many patients anymore."

She had me and she knew it. And if the truth were known, I rather missed the direct interaction with the patients.

"I'll have to clear it with Karen." But I knew she would have no objection to getting me out of the house a couple of days a week.

When I turned to look at fled, I saw that she had fallen asleep, her feet curled around the legs of her chair.

It was good to get back to the idealistic world of K-PAX, but the Laskay lawsuit and the e-mail asking me where the ideas for *K-PAX* came from kept working their way into my thoughts. How did I become a blatant L-word? Why do I have a burning desire, or any desire at all, to try to do something about the rapid deterioration of the world we all share? Why do I have such compassion for the suffering of animals, including humans who are mistreated and abused? It occurred to me that this might be a fertile area of exploration for me, both personally and as a writer. Moreover, I had never written a non-fiction book, and the challenge excited me just as had the tentative branching into writing for the stage and screen. I temporarily shelved *K-PAX IV* and began to work on *Creating K-PAX*.

Fortunately, I had been keeping a diary for the previous twenty-four years (ever since leaving the lab). For events that took place before that, I had to rely on memory (mine and that of my siblings) and a few photographs and documents. Before I forgot everything I still knew, I began to jot down some notes . . . .

THE FUTURE

"Alejandro"

On breaks between my writing ventures, I sometimes re-submit my unpublished novels and stories, hoping there has been a change in attitude by the publishing world. In the summer of 2004 Sarah Shumway at Dutton Children's Books came down on the side of "The Boy Who Spoke with God" 's being too adult for their audience. However, she asked me whether I'd be interested in contributing a "young adult" story to an anthology based on drawings by artist Scott Hunt. It was an interesting idea: for each drawing, two authors would be asked to write a tale about it independently; the book would be called *Twice Told*. I told her I would give it a try.

I had never written for young adults, a specialized audience, and my first attempt, ironically, was too juvenile. Sarah patiently explained what was wrong with it, made some suggestions, and I tried again. This time it was more successful. A few relatively minor revisions and it was finished. The anthology appeared in the spring of 2006.

Other books

In *K-PAX V*, Giselle will bring Gene back to Earth for a return visit. I know also what will happen in *K-PAX VI*, but for now it will remain a secret. Star dreams.

Between *IV* and *V*, I have in mind a September-May romance novel set in Vermont. I don't yet know how it will shape up, but I've begun to think about it.

And finally, between *V* and *VI*, I'm planning a (humorous?) book of essays summing up what I have learned about the nature of human beings and their pathetic attempts to govern themselves.

Or, if no one buys the present catharsis or wants to publish *K-PAX IV*, I might just retire and enjoy my "golden" years.

We'll see how it all plays out.

Beyond writing

After I put away my pen, there are plenty of other things I'd like to do. I want to learn to play the organ, study history and astrophysics, read all the unread books on my shelves (including the Great Books), and take a bigger role in helping to free the world's nonhuman animals from further oppression. To sing the role of Emile DeBeque onstage, as brother Bob has already done very well. Learn French, maybe, or parachuting. Take up flying again. Go places.

But there may be a problem. George W. Bush, the worst president in America's history, was re-elected on Nov. 2, 2004. Unfortunately, he didn't have much competition. The Democrats put up another war hero who was prepared to "stay the course" in Iraq, regardless of the consequences: business as usual. The media, in its pop-culture way, ignored everyone else, including the candidate with the most right answers, Dennis Kucinich. My second choice was Howard Dean, who had the temerity to oppose the "liberation" of Iraq by America's "right thinkers." I voted for Ralph Nader, the best of those on the ballot, because I was tired of choosing between the lesser of two evils. In a sense, all of us lost that election.

In view of the outcome, one wonders whether a President like Bush is the inevitable outcome of a democracy, where ignorance and superstition are fostered and encouraged by interests that profit by them. And whether little Georgie W. spent his childhood dreaming of ways to make the rich richer, the national debt bigger, and the whole world a factory, regardless of the environmental consequences. Because of these and other "values," America is rapidly becoming one of the most backward nations on Earth.

Yet, I am eternally hopeful. I hope that by November, 2008, the U.S. hasn't decided to unilaterally invade some other nation and bring Americanism to their people whether they want it or not. I hope that the concerns of big (and small) business don't completely overwhelm our small planet's not-so-abundant resources. I hope that a future president will tell the American people that it's time to stop torturing and killing animals for any reason, particularly for food. And I hope that the world's human population as a whole stops trying its damndest to multiply and subdue the Earth, which is already begging for mercy. (So far, *the K-PAX trilogy* has had astonishingly little effect on government policy.)

Because I had an Aunt Mae, however, I have enormous faith in human nature. I sincerely believe we will come to our senses before it's too late. I believe that some day we will say to our governments, "No! Enough is enough: I won't co-operate in the further destruction of the Earth and everything on it, *even if it costs me my job!*" I believe there will come a time when an animal rights activist and/or environmentalist will win the Nobel peace prize (Jane Goodall comes immediately to mind). Only then will it be clear that we are finally getting it, that we have turned the corner and looked the future in the eye.

Our retirement home

ADVICE FOR WOULD-BE NOVELISTS

One of the burdens of having a book published is that acquaintances and cousins you didn't know existed contact you and ask for your help in getting their novels in print. Taking on these assignments is a slippery slope leading to a black hole. Nevertheless, I do it from time to time because I know what it was like to be unpublished and hopeful. And also, by grappling with their mistakes, I sometimes learn not to make them myself.

The first thing the would-be novelist should know is that most hopefuls don't really want to write a novel; they want *to have written one*. They have no idea how a novel is constructed, what makes one work, how to create characters, and all the other fundamentals that have to be mastered before anything good is going to come from their pens or word processors. This means you have to read a lot, indeed *to love reading*, so that you become intimately familiar with what a novel is. Read bestsellers if you like, but also read the classics. You can learn a lot from Dickens. Read Hemingway. Read Dostoyevsky. Unless you want to write crappy sitcoms, kick a hole in the television screen and *read*.

Second: even if you write a beautiful, deep, meaningful book, the chance of getting it into print is close to nil. Editors are looking for bestsellers, and *only* bestsellers, preferably by known writers. New York is Hollywood in print. Take a look at the bestseller lists. Ninety percent of the novelists there are already well-known and predictable writers. So you have to write something extraordinary in order to elbow your way into this group.

Third, when you start a novel (no matter what genre), ask yourself, as you go along, "What if—" When you find yourself writing about some pedestrian event or conversation, ask, "What if this (or that) happened instead?" It can be logical or bizarre, but you have to lift the story out of the ordinary.

Finally, you have to enjoy being alone. There is no other way to write. And you need a certain amount of time (whatever you have) and a place to write every day. Every day.

Here is a myth you've heard many times: Everyone has a story to tell. True, but it's probably interesting only to the teller. Great novels come not from life, but from the imagination. I don't know how many people have said to me, after relating a story about Uncle Charlie's relationship with his ex-wife: "You should write a novel about that!" No, *you* write it. Then put it in a drawer.

Here's another: Write about what you know. Ho hum. Instead, write about what fascinates and excites you, even if you know nothing about it. I'm not a psychiatrist, or even an M.D. I went to the library, read a few books on mental illness, and wrote *K-PAX*.

At writers' conferences, someone invariably asks the question, "Do you write with a pen or on a computer?" "Do you write in the morning or afternoon?" "Do you write 1,000 words a day with great care, or do you produce 10,000 words and then cut out 9,000 of them later?" "Do you know how a novel (or story) is going to turn out when you start?" The answers to all of these questions is: it's irrelevant. The only thing that will work for you is what works for you. If you don't know what works for you, experiment.

Beyond these larger considerations, I offer you a dozen simple rules.

1. STUDY GRAMMAR. Nothing is more maddening to an editor than misplaced commas, misused hyphens, misspellings. If you "just don't understand all the rules," get an English teacher to read your manuscript. Better yet, get two. Even better, start learning the language. You might begin with: lie, lay, lain; lay, laid, laid.

    Here are a few common problems to watch out for:

    Only DNA *replicates* (makes a copy of itself using itself as a template). Everything else duplicates (or is duplicated). You can't replicate an experience, for example.

    Words like "data" and "phenomena" are plurals. The singulars are "datum" and "phenomenon." If you read "The data shows that . . ." or "That's an interesting phenomena," you should feel uncomfortable. Same for criterion/criteria, and many others.

    Periods and commas *always* go inside quotation marks. Exclamation and question marks do with conversation, otherwise no.

    Use care with antecedents. What's wrong with this sentence: *I loaned my pen to someone, and they ran off with it.*

    "Hopefully" means full of hope. If you can't substitute the phrase for the word, you're using it incorrectly, and probably with the wrong antecedent.

    You don't send "an e-mail," you send an e-note or an e-letter by e-mail.

    A light-year is a measure of distance, not of time.

    One visits the Parkers, not the Parker's.

    Two people help each other; three or more help one another.

    Don't change a character's life "forever." That's redundant. Her life will never be exactly the way it was before it changed.

    Somewhat (an adverb), yes. Somewhat of, no. And you're different *from* others, not different *than*.

    Always be clear about what you mean. For instance: *They spoke to the Chinese Ambassador yesterday.* Is the ambassador Chinese? Or is he the ambassador to China?

    Pay attention to usage and meaning: a liquid that has no color is "colorless," not "clear," which means you can see through it.

Worst of all: "healthy" food does not mean it's good for you. "Healthy" means it has no diseases, is not rotten. If it's good for you, it's "healthful." Similarly, you don't eat a diet, you follow it. When someone advises you to "eat a healthy diet," it should 'bout make you puke.

2. AVOID CLICHÉS. If you write a phrase that sounds familiar, or you've heard it before, change it. Nothing turns off an editor more than a worn-out formulation. Set your story in a metropolis that isn't "bustling," or a little town that's not "sleepy." Don't *ever* pen "historic Runnymede" or use "building blocks" to describe the fundamental parts of a structure. And so on.

3. START OUT FAST. There has to be a hook, something to grab an editor by page twenty. He/she must know by then whether he is interested in the story. Don't start at the beginning of your story, start in the middle and fill in any *required* details as needed.

4. OMIT PROSAIC INFORMATION. Unless it's germane, the reader doesn't care whether your characters have kinky brown hair or aquiline noses with a mole on the left nostril. Some description is necessary, but don't overdo it. Give your readers the opportunity to paint part of the picture. The real questions are, what are your characters thinking about, and why? Similarly, don't parade everything you know about a given subject unless it's relevant to the story. The reader will know you're just showing off, trying to impress him.

5. NEVER USE THE SAME WORD (except "a," "the," etc.) TWICE IN THE SAME PARAGRAPH. Or even on the same page, if possible. Similarly, DON'T BEGIN TWO SUCCESSIVE SENTENCES WITH THE SAME WORD. If you find that you've done this, change one of the words, or insert another sentence between the two. Some movement, or a little description, maybe. As with most rules, of course, there are exceptions—for the sake of rhythm, emphasis, poetic license.

6. DON'T BASE YOUR CHARACTERS ON PEOPLE YOU KNOW. Make them unusual, off-beat, crazy—whatever it takes to make them interesting, believable, and sympathetic—but *create* them. Study people, learn what makes them tick, how their mouths react to one or another emotion, but don't copy them. Writing is like acting: you have to get inside your characters and be able to imagine what it's like to be there.

7. AVOID REDUNDANCY. There is no need for a summary sentence (e.g., "It was quite a night!") at the end of a paragraph or section. The reader should already know it was quite a night. If he doesn't, he won't care anyway.

8. PLAY WITH YOUR SENTENCES. Rearrange the words. Does it sound better this way, or that way? Rearrange them again.

9. USE A THESAURUS. This doesn't mean you need to find the fanciest word to describe your intentions. It means there is only one *best* word for a given situation. As you write more and learn more, you'll need the thesaurus less. AND A

DICTIONARY. If you have the slightest doubt about the spelling of a word (spell-checkers notwithstanding), or whether it should be hyphenated or capitalized, look it up.

10. ELIMINATE INANITIES. There is no need to write, for instance, "Needless to say . . ." If it's needless, don't say it. And don't give the plot away with such teasers as "Little did she know that . . ."

11. METAPHORS ARE GOOD, but don't overuse them. I've seen stories where almost every item or action is "like" something else. And when you do use them, make them appropriate, not just something that sounds clever.

12. AVOID WEAK ACTION VERBS. A character can walk anywhere. But the *way* he walks paints a clearer picture of him and the action. Does he ever saunter, tramp, or plod? This doesn't mean he should *never* just "walk." Only that he would probably do something more colorful on some occasions. Other examples are "go," "do," "say." There are many others.

Now that you've written your compellingly original novel, with wonderful characters, beautiful descriptive passages, a strong plot, and no spelling or grammatical or syntactical errors—what do you do with it? You're probably better off getting an agent, if you can find a good one. However, these can be more difficult to find than a sympathetic editor, many of whom won't read anything unless it's submitted by an agent. Another catch-something-or-other.

You *never* send your manuscript, even a partial, to a prospective agent unless he/she asks for it. You send a query letter describing your novel, why you think it will sell, and a bit about yourself, particularly if you already have something in print. If he's interested, he'll ask you to send at least a sample. On the other hand, you can send query letters (or partials, if asked) simultaneously to fifty agents at a time, if you want. Don't worry about more than one of them requesting your complete manuscript. Send it to the one who asks first.

Okay, you've tried fifty agents and no one wants to see your magnum opus. Your other resort is to send a query, along with thirty pages of your novel, to editors at whichever houses (as many as you want to try) publish the kind of book you've written. Your chances of getting some kind of reply are good, a positive one exceedingly slim. If your sourcebook says they don't consider unagented manuscripts, forget it. If any of your editors request a look at the entire manuscript, send it (priority mail with tracking is fine). But if you ship it to more than one editor, tell them it's a multiple submission.

The advantage to having an agent is that your manuscript will be read by whomever he/she submits it to. The disadvantage is that she will only send your work to one editor at a time. The choice is yours.

Whether you choose to try an agent or an editor, probably the best sourcebook for both is the latest edition of *Jeff Herman's Guide to Book Publishers, Editors, &*

Literary Agents (The Writer Books). Many libraries have it. There are also dozens of good books describing the writing experience. The best one I've found is *If You Want to Write*, by Brenda Ueland (Graywolf Press, 10th Edn., 1997).

Whatever your strategy or level of success, be prepared to suffer. You'll need the skin of a rhinoceros and the patience of a saint. Not to mention talent, luck, and, above all, perseverance.

Some final advice

If any of my anxiety symptoms sound familiar to you, please take my advice and talk to a doctor about them. Even if there is a genuine affliction, it's far better to find out early than late, when it might be too late to do anything about it. But the chances are that it's something minor, or merely the persistent symptoms of anxiety. If you're afraid to do this, send me a note. I'll try to talk you through it. Don't waste a half-century of your life wallowing in mind-bending anguish, like I did.

AFTERWORD

Lest the reader think I have written this memoir merely to get even with Jason Laskay, I will say here that I sincerely harbor him no ill will. It must be tough, even devastating, to find that a film similar to your own vision is being made, and tempting to lash out, in hurt and anger, at whomever you think might have wronged you. It's only human nature. For his pain and suffering I am truly sorry.

Nor do I harbor any grudges against my parents. They did the best they could with what they had, and I'm quite happy with the way I turned out. If my parents had been otherwise, I would be someone else. Indeed, I know exactly what Lou Gehrig meant when he said, "Today, I consider myself the luckiest man on the face of the Earth." Despite the bumps and potholes in the road, and some nasty crashes, I have had a terrific life, a loving and supportive marriage partner, and I won't die a total failure. For me, that's plenty. It's been quite a ride, and it's not over yet!

It has not escaped my attention also that if my brain had been allotted more serotonin (or its receptors), everything might have been vastly different. I might still be a scientist, for example. Career aside, my anxiety disorder may have made me far more politically liberal than I might otherwise have been. My fears for my own well-being might very well have made me more aware of the pain and suffering of others, including, of course, that of the non-human animals with whom we share this vastly overcrowded world. Perhaps it made me more observant as well, which didn't do my novels and stories any harm.

In any case, the godawful disorder is finally under control, though I have no illusions that it wouldn't return if I stopped taking Zoloft (or a similar drug). There's an impaired biochemical process in my brain which anti-depressants replace or make up for, if only temporarily and sometimes with side effects. I'm glad I lived long enough to experience that. And having done so, I'm no longer afraid to die.

In fact, I'm kind of curious to know what it's like.

ACKNOWLEDGMENTS

I thank everyone mentioned in these pages; even the orifices I have encountered have made my life more interesting. But I am especially grateful to my wife Karen, who made it possible to write *K-PAX*, and to Ida Giragossian, who found a publisher for it.

PUBLICATIONS

Brewer, E.N., Kuraishi, S., Garver, J.C., and Strong, F.M., "Mass Culture of a Slime Mold, *Physarum polycephalum*," *Appl. Microbiol.*, *12*, 161 (1964).

Brewer, E.N. and Rusch, H.P., "DNA Synthesis by Isolated Nuclei of *Physarum polycephalum*, *Biochem. Biophys. Res. Commun.*, *21*, 235 (1965).

Cummins, J.E., Brewer, E.N., and Rusch, H.P., "The Effect of Actidione on Mitosis in the Slime Mold *Physarum polycephalum*," *J. Cell Biol.*, *27*, 337 (1965).

Brewer, E.N. and Rusch, H.P., "Nucleic Acid Synthesis by Isolated Nuclei in the Mitotic Cycle of *Physarum polycephalum*," *Fed. Proc.*, *25*, 233 (1966).

Brewer, E.N. and Rusch, H.P., "Control of DNA Replication: Effect of Spermine on DNA Polymerase Activity in Isolated Nuclei of *Physarum polycephalum*," *Biochem. Biophys. Res. Commun.*, *25*, 579 (1966).

Brewer, E.N., "Effect of Methylglyoxal on Growth, Nuclear Division, and Synthesis of Macromolecules in *Physarum polycephalum*," *J. Cell Biol.*, *31*, 15A (1966).

Rusch, H.P. and Brewer, E.N., "Effect of Interphase Temperature Shocks on the Timing of Mitosis in *Physarum polycephalum*," *Fed. Proc.*, *26*, 514 (1967).

Brewer, E.N., DeVries, A, and Rusch, H.P., "DNA Synthesis by Isolated Mitochondria of *Physarum polycephalum*," *Biochim. Biophys. Acta*, *145*, 686 (1967).

Brewer, E.N. and Rusch, H.P., "Effects of Elevated Temperature Shocks on Mitosis and on the Initiation of DNA Replication in *Physarum polycephalum*," *Exptl. Cell Res.*, *49*, 79 (1968).

Brewer, E.N., Foster, L.B., and Sells, B.H., "A Possible Role for Ribonuclease in the Regulation of Protein Synthesis in Normal and Hypophysectomized Rats," *J. Biol. Chem.*, *244*, 1389 (1969).

Brewer, E.N., "Isolation of a Mitosis-stimulating Factor from the Slime Mold *Physarum polycephalum*," *Fed. Proc.*, *26*, 514 (1969).

Brewer, E.N., "Regulation of Protein Synthesis through the Mitotic Cycle in *Physarum polycephalum*," *J. Cell Biol.*, *43*, 15A (1969).

Brewer, E.N., "Structure of Replicating and Non-replicating Chromosomal DNA in *Physarum polycephalum*," *Fed. Proc.*, *30*, 1149 (1971).

Brewer, E.N., "Inhibition of Alkaline Ribonuclease Activity by Polyamines," *Exptl. Cell Res.*, *72*, 586 (1972).

Brewer, E.N., "DNA Replication in *Physarum polycephalum*," *J. Mol. Biol.*, 68, 401 (1972).

Brewer, E.N., "Polysome Profiles, Amino Acid Incorporation in vitro, and Polysome Reaggregation Following Disaggregation by Heat Shock Through the Mitotic Cycle in *Physarum polycephalum*," *Biochim. Biophys. Acta*, *277*, 639 (1972).

Brewer, E.N. and Nygaard, O.F., "Correlation Between Unrepaired Radiation-induced DNA Strand Breaks and Mitotic Cycle Delay in *Physarum polycephalum*," *Nature New Biol.*, *239*, 108 (1972).

Brewer, E.N., "Isolation of a DNA Replicase from *Physarum polycephalum*," *Fed. Proc.*, *32*, 452 Abs (1973).

Nygaard, O.F., Brewer, E.N., Evans, T.E., and Wolpaw, J.R., "Correlation between Sensitivity to Ionizing Radiation and DNA Replication in *Physarum polycephalum*," in *Advances in Radiation Research*, vol. 2, BIOLOGY AND MEDICINE, T.E. Duplan and A. Chapiro, eds., Gordon and Breach, London, 989 (1973).

Brewer, E.N., Evans, T.E., and Evans, H.H., "Studies on the Mechanism and Control of DNA Replication in *Physarum polycephalum*," *J. Cell Biol.*, *59*, 22A (1973).

Brewer, E.N., Evans, T.E., and Evans, H.H., "Studies on the Mechanism of DNA Replication in *Physarum polycephalum*," *J. Mol. Biol.*, *90*, 335 (1974).

Rustad, R.C., Brewer, E.N., and Oleinick, N.L., "Synthesis of Mitotic Proteins During G2 in *Physarum polycephalum*," *J. Cell Biol.*, *63*, 293A (1974).

Brewer, E.N., Oleinick, N.L., and Rustad, R.C., "A Radiation-induced Cell Cycle Marker for Cycloheximide Sensitivity," *Radiat. Res.*, *62*, 536 (1975).

Brewer, E.N. and Ting, P., "DNA Replication in Homogenates of *Physarum polycephalum*," *J. Cell Physiol.*, *86*, 459 (1975).

Evans, H.H., Evans, T.E., and Brewer, E.N., "The Inhibition of DNA Strand Elongation by Cycloheximide in *Physarum polycephalum*," in *ICN-UCLA Symposia on Molecular and Cellular Biology*, vol. 3, DNA SYNTHESIS AND ITS REGULATION, M. Goulian and P. Hanawalt, eds., W.A. Benjamin, Menlo Park, CA, 713 (1975).

Brewer, E.N., "DNA Replication by a Possible Continuous-Discontinuous Mechanism in Homogenates of *Physarum polycephalum* Containing Dextran," *Biochim. Biophys. Acta*, *402*, 363 (1975).

Rustad, R.C., Oleinick, N.L., and Brewer, E.N., "A New Mitotic Cycle Marker," *Exptl. Cell Res.*, 93, 477 (1975).

Brewer, E.N., "Joining of DNA Replication Intermediates in Isolated Nuclei of *Physarum polycephalum*," *Fed. Proc.*, *35*, 1418 (1976).

Evans, H.H., Littman, S.R., Evans, T.E., and Brewer, E.N., "Effects of Cycloheximide on Thymidine Metabolism and on DNA Strand Elongation in *Physarum polycephalum*," *J. Mol. Biol.*, *101*, 169 (1976).

Oleinick, N.L., Brewer, E.N., and Rustad, R.C., "Caffeine-Radiation Interactions and Mitotic Delay," *J. Cell Biol.*, *75*, 10A (1977).

Oleinick, N.L., Brewer, E.N., and Rustad, R.C., "The Reduction of Radiation-induced Mitotic Delay by Caffeine: a Test of the CyclicAMP Hypothesis," *Int. J. Radiat. Biol.*, *33*, 69 (1978).

Brewer, E.N., "Isolation of a Stimulatory Factor for Nuclear DNA Replication," *Biochim. Biophys. Acta*, *564*, 154 (1979).

Brewer, E.N., "Repair of Radiation-induced DNA Double-strand Breaks in Nuclei of *Physarum polycephalum*," *Radiat. Res.*, *79*, 368 (1979).

Brewer, E.N. and Busacca, P.A., "DNA Synthesis in a Sub-nuclear Preparation Isolated from *Physarum polycephalum*," *Biochem. Biophys. Res. Commun.*, *91*, 1352 (1979).

Brewer, E.N. and Oleinick, N.L., "Histone Phosphorylation during Radiation-induced Mitotic Delay in Synchronous Plasmodia of *Physarum polycephalum*," *Int. J. Radiat. Biol.*, *38*, 697 (1980).

Daniel, J.W., Oleinick, N.L., and Brewer, E.N., "Progression of the *Physarum* Cell Cycle Is Not Correlated with Fluctuations in Cyclic Nucleotide Levels," *J. Cell Biol.*, *87*, 7A (1980).

Oleinick, N.L., Daniel, J.W., and Brewer, E.N., "Absence of a Correlation between Cyclic Nucleotide Fluctuations and Cell Cycle Progression," *Exptl. Cell Res.*, *131*, 373 (1981).

Brewer, Gene, *K-PAX*, St. Martin's Press, New York, 1995.

Brewer, Gene, *On a Beam of Light* (*K-PAX II*), St. Martin's Press, New York, 2001.

Brewer, Gene, *K-PAX III* (*The Worlds of Prot*), Bloomsbury, London, 2002.

Brewer, Gene, *K-PAX, the Trilogy, featuring Prot's Report*, Bloomsbury, London, 2003.

Brewer, Gene, *K-PAX* (stage play), premiered by Act Provocateur, Ltd., London, February, 2004.

Brewer, Gene, *Creating K-PAX*, Xlibris, Philadelphia, 2005.

Brewer, Gene, "Alejandro," in *Twice Told*, Dutton, New York, 2006.

UNPUBLISHED NOVELS, STORIES, AND SCREENPLAYS

Ralphy, 1981.

Breakthrough, 1983.

2020, 1985.

"The Boy Who Spoke with God," 1985.

Watson's God, 1988.

The American Way, 1991.

Freeland (partial), 1992.

"Branty," 1992.

"Lattie," 1992.

Ben and I, 1994.

Yonderland, 1995.

Murder on Spruce Island, 1997.

Wrongful Death, 2001.

K-PAX II: The Return of Prot (screenplay), 2002.

fled: Part IV of the K-PAX saga (in progress).

visit the author at *www.genebrewer.com*

Lightning Source UK Ltd.
Milton Keynes UK
15 March 2010

151424UK00001B/260/A